Heart of a MARINE

BOOK ONE WOUNDED WARRIOR SERIES

Patty Campbell

HEART OF A MARINE
Copyright © 2021 by Patty Campbell

ISBN: 978-1-953735-58-4

Published by Satin Romance
An Imprint of Melange Books, LLC
White Bear Lake, MN 55110
www.satinromance.com

Published in the United States of America.

Cover Design by Ashley Redbird Designs

Acclaim for Patty Campbell

———

For *Heart of a Marine*

"A hero to fall in love with."

—Author Keira Montclair

For *Jelly's Big Night Out*

"This is a wonderful real-life down-to-earth story of an outstanding sister who gives up her freedom to raise her sister. Yes, there are tears. And yes, there is a happy-ever-after!"

—Author Haven Raines

"A great read with characters you will really enjoy."

—Ms. Goodreads.

For *Once a Marine*

"The storyline was entertaining with high drama near the end."

—Cocktails and Books Review

"I loved this story by Patty Campbell. The story was riveting, and I didn't want to put this book down."

—Author Molly Jebber

This first Wounded Warrior book is dedicated to the Wounded Veteran's Relief Fund. All author royalties for the sale of the series will be donated to WVRF to further their mission. Please check them out at www.wvrf.org.

Chapter One

BIG-BONED, BIG GIRL, FULL-FIGURED—HOW MARLA HATED those stupid metaphors. At five-foot-six, she weighed one hundred sixty pounds. Size twelve, just like Marilyn Monroe, but unfortunately due to the nubile teenage models marketed by Victoria's Secret, Marilyn's charms were no longer fashionable.

Her fraternal twin sister Charlene, on the other hand, was the same height, with one hundred twenty pounds of lingerie-model curves. Charlene wore her thick, golden blond hair like a privileged princess. Rusty brown eye color was the only thing they had in common. Victoria's Secret, eat your heart out.

Marla got the brains. She dearly loved Charlene, but she sometimes wondered what was going on upstairs, except for her insatiable appetite for men. To give Charlene credit, she was very successful in her quest.

Now what was Char doing walking toward her at the construction site today? She shaded her eyes from the bright sun and gazed across the cluttered lot.

"Oh, lordy lord, Marla," her sister said. "How can you stand it? Is he here every day? That man makes my mouth water and my knees quake."

"Give me a clue, Char. Is it the leer or the tool belt?"

"Are you kidding me? You must be blind. He's nothing but

rippling muscles and he's got the sexiest little hitch in his walk. Yum. He's the spittin' image of Gerard Butler. This guy is hot. Have you noticed how he looks at you? I'm jealous. You should talk to him."

Marla rolled her eyes and blew out a long sigh. "I *do* talk to him, much more than I care to. Dwayne Dempsey is a royal pain. It's a new argument from him every day. Just because he's the contractor he thinks he knows more about this project than I do."

Charlene had that moony-eyed grin on her face. "Well, he *is* the contractor."

"Oh, for the love of goats, Charlene!" What was the use? "I own this building. He's supposed to follow my design, my blueprints, not argue about every little detail." She wasn't sure Charlene recognized the difference between employer and employee.

Marla wouldn't admit it, but she did have eyes, and she considered Dwayne Dempsey quite good-looking. Mouth-watering actually. She also knew how much he enjoyed flirting with *the fat girl*.

Dwayne looked up from his cell phone, hitched up his jeans, and winked at Charlene. He turned and waved when a man in the construction trailer yelled, "Yo, Gunny, over here!"

"Oh, lordy. I want him."

"Take him, please. You're welcome to him."

Charlene scrunched her eyebrows. "Who's Gunny?"

"Dwayne. He's a retired marine. His men call him that. Now, what are you doing here?"

Charlene dragged her gaze from Dwayne's back and shoulders as he walked away. Hand on her heart, she sighed. "Look at his perfect butt in those beat-up jeans. I don't know how you stand it."

Marla took the roll of blueprints and tapped her twin on the head. "You didn't answer my question."

"What question?"

Marla rolled her eyes. "What are you doing here?"

"Oh. I thought we'd go for lunch. We have to strategize for the singles dinner thingy. Remember? You promised you'd go with me. It's tomorrow night."

Darn it! She'd forgotten all about her promise to Charlene and her brothers. Charlene had wheedled her about it to the point where she was ready to agree to anything just to get her to stop. It must have been the fact she was exhausted and so worried about the financials for this apartment house condo conversion. She'd better find a buyer for that great new listing she got before she had to start pinching pennies on this project.

Marla blew an annoyed sigh and thumbed across the screen of her iPhone. She had every minute of the day accounted for. "Why didn't you call me last night and give me a heads-up? I'm swamped today."

"I just found out an hour ago that Harry and Barry could meet us for lunch. You know how hard it is to get them to sit for an hour. It was today or never."

Grrr, this meant she had to talk to Dwayne, to let him know she'd be away from the site for a couple of hours. She straightened her shoulders. Might as well get it over with.

Marla waved the roll of blueprints. "Dwayne! Hold up. I want to talk to you."

Delectable Dwayne stopped and turned. He waggled his eyebrows and grinned. "I thought you'd never ask, gorgeous."

Her face and neck blazed. He was the only man on earth who could make her blush. She hated him for doing it and herself for allowing it.

"In case you hadn't noticed, Dempsey, I'm your employer. Don't you think it's a tiny bit improper for you to call me gorgeous?" She gave him her sternest scowl and slammed her hands onto her hips.

The devil grinned. "I believe in honesty, boss. Goes with being a Marine."

Resisting the urge to scream, she told him in a matter-of-fact tone, "I'll be offsite for about two hours." She pointed to a truck that pulled onto the premises. "You'll have to sign for that load of drywall. Check it closely. Make sure they don't try to pawn off some of that cheap Chinese stuff on us, like last week. If you need me, you have my cell number."

"I need you all right." His grin was enough to stop her heart. "But I'd rather have your unlisted home number."

The last thing she wanted complicating her life was an unrepentant bad boy. Marla had her life planned. She knew where she was going, and she was going alone.

He winked.

She silently swore by all that was holy that the big lout changed his posture, tilted his pelvis forward slightly, then grinned like a cat about to pounce on a mouse.

"One of these days, Dempsey."

"It's what I live for, Red."

He referred to her mass of strawberry blond hair, which at the moment was growing larger in the damp breeze. How she hated her hair, especially when he teased her. She whirled around and flounced away before she said something she'd regret.

"Mmm, mmm, mmm," he hummed. "Hey, Red. Wait! I'll need a copy of the invoice."

She stopped, dug through her briefcase with a vengeance, found the invoice and thrust it toward him, noticing again the two missing fingers on his left hand. Maybe he wasn't as good with power tools as he seemed to think.

"Here, take it, Dempsey." She held the paper at arm's length to avoid getting any closer.

Why, she asked herself, did she put up with him? Two reasons—he was the best in the business, and his father and her father had been best buddies for over fifty years. The two old friends were known by their pals as *The Double D's*—Dempsey and Danaher.

She wouldn't fire Dwayne as long as he was doing his job, but she could plan his murder. Maybe she'd ask Char to shag him to death. No, maybe she'd do it herself. Have a little fun while getting rid of him. He'd learn not to mess with her.

Cheeks on fire over her thoughts, she rejoined Charlene. "Let's go before I commit a felony."

Char's beautiful face scrunched with confusion. "Is he related to that old cutie pie, Johnny Dempsey? He looks like him, don't you think?"

"Yes, he's John's middle son. The one we seldom saw when we were kids because he left to live in Wyoming with his mother."

Light dawned like the sunrise in Charlene's eyes. "Oh, yes, now I remember. Barry or Harry said Dwayne hated the wicked stepmother."

Harry and Barry, their twin brothers. Identical twins, not fraternal like Charlene and Marla. Twins ran in the Danaher family. Two Danaher's for the price of one. Or, as they privately joked behind Dadley's back—he only got two cracks at it. Maybe that's all Bradley wanted with their ditzy mother, Silvia. What a family. If it wasn't for Marla, they'd fall apart. When her mother had complications after the birth of the boys, Marla spent a lot of time taking care of them. Gradually, with Silvia's free and easy compliance, she took over more and more of their care. Taking charge came natural to her.

Fortunately for Marla's busy schedule, the restaurant was only a short ten minutes away from the jobsite.

Barry and Harry sat waiting for them in the deli. College boys, they looked the part, like they'd come straight from Central Casting. At seven years younger than Marla and Charlene, few people, including their immediate family, could tell the two twenty-year-olds apart. The boys often finished each other's sentences, and their gestures were like mirror images. It was beyond fascinating to watch them. She had a hunch their professors had long ago given up accusing them of cheating when their test results were nearly as identical as they were.

Electrical engineering geniuses, her boys would someday be filthy rich, live in ocean front mansions in Malibu, drive matching silver Jaguars, have gorgeous trophy wives, and two perfect sets of identical twin children. But for now they were still her baby brothers, and they understood they darn well better not cross her.

Charlene smiled as they made their way through the deli crowd. "There they are. Let's go sit with the best-looking men in the room." She sashayed the rest of the way to their table. "Hey there, sailors," she vamped, "want a date?"

The boys laughed, stood up like proper gentlemen, and held chairs out for them. They'd already ordered iced tea all around.

Marla's baby brothers always evoked a feeling of gooey warmth and love in her chest. She took credit for everything they did right, and blamed Charlene when they'd misbehaved or cursed. Insisting Charlene quit teaching them profanity, Lord and lordy lord became a permanent part of her sister's vocabulary.

Barry, or Harry, leaned over and kissed her on the cheek. "How's it going, BS?"

BS was short for Big Sis, a term of endearment the boys used for both her and Charlene. Being word misers, they spoke with as few words as possible. Why, she didn't know. Charlene used enough for all of them, so it balanced out.

She noticed the little fleck of gold in Barry's left iris. "I'm fine Honey Barry. Have you two visited Miss Emmaline lately?" She raised an eyebrow. "She's very fond of you boys."

"Tomorrow."

"Good. She asked when you'd be home from Cal Tech for spring break." She looked across the table. "Harry, did you go to the nursery to pick up that potted hydrangea for her balcony?"

"In the car."

Charlene asked, "Why is she living in the middle of a big construction project? It must be a pain for the crew to work around her."

Marla's thoughts exactly. "It was a condition of the construction contract when Dempsey accepted the job. He didn't want to displace her while they worked on the building. He insisted they could complete the project with her there with very little extra time."

"Oh." Charlene nodded. "Did you boys order lunch for us?"

"Cheeseburger for you and—"

"—chef salad for Marla."

That's what she meant about finishing sentences.

"Just what I wanted." Marla was sick of chef salads, but the boys were so smug about being able to read her mind, she didn't want to burst their bubble.

"We know," they said.

She barely had time to take a sip of the tea when the waitress brought their plates. Harry, Barry, and Charlene had humongous cheeseburgers and mountains of heavenly smelling fries. Marla swore the waitress twisted her lips when she handed over the salad as if to say, "Diet isn't working, chubby." Wait until the skinny little snot saw the tip she'd get for that look.

Charlene produced a to-do list from her large shoulder bag, purse, overnight-emergency—whatever that she always lugged. Prepared for any eventuality, her Charlene was. God bless her fun-loving little heart. She listened as Char droned on about the singles meet-up. Marla ate about half her salad and pushed the plate away. Half an hour later, she checked her watch and yawned.

Charlene rolled her eyes. "Okay, Marla, I get it. You're on a tight schedule." Char eyed the boys. "Remember, do your dazzle-the-girls-thing and don't mess up my perfect plans. You're there in case Marla or I get stuck with a creep."

The boys bobbed their heads. "Gotcha."

Char took a dainty sip of tea to wash down a big mouthful of fries. "Oh, I almost forgot. Did you boys know Dwayne Dempsey was working on the condo project with Marla?"

"Nope," they said.

"You probably don't remember him, but he's Johnny Dempsey's

middle son. He's, oh, lordy lord, the most gorgeous bundle of testosterone on two feet, if you ask me."

"We didn't." They snickered.

Marla interrupted. "First of all, Charlene, he's working *for* me, not *with* me. I own the building. It's my project, my design, and my money."

Char rolled her big, expressive eyes. "So sorry. A minor detail."

"Hardly. I pay his wages."

Char flashed a dismissive finger wave. "Whatever. You have to admit he's the best-looking man in town." She smiled at the boys. "Other than you two, of course, and guess what?" She winked. "He wants to get in Marla's pants."

That was enough. Marla smacked her hands on the table. "What a pile of horse feathers! You believe all men think about twenty-four-seven is sex?"

The three of them turned to her with identical smirks and bobbing heads. "Um hum."

———

Dwayne served Amber a plate of macaroni and cheese with Vienna sausages then sat across from her at the kitchen table. "Now, that wasn't such a lot of homework was it? I told you we'd get through it in no time."

She grinned, her cheeks puffed with food like a hungry squirrel. "Daddy?"

"Don't talk with your mouth full, sweetheart. I'm not going anywhere. Take your time."

She nodded and swallowed. "Daddy?"

"Yes?"

"How come I don't have a mommy? All my friends have mommies." Her big golden eyes could always melt his heart.

"You had a mommy. She couldn't stay with us. You already know this, hon."

Amber propped her cheeks in her hands. "I don't remember her, but I smile at her picture in my room every night before I go to sleep."

He touched her nose and smiled. "Your mom loved you very much." The lie sat bitter on his tongue. Francine wouldn't have left if she cared a damn about either one of them.

"I know, Daddy, but couldn't you get me another one?" She took on a practical tone. "If you got us another mama you wouldn't have to do everything around here, you'd have a grownup lady to hug and kiss, and I'd have somebody to show me how to make a French braid."

Dwayne chuckled. "Yeah, I kind of botched that up, didn't I?" He marveled at the workings of her six-year-old mind. Where had that grownup hugging and kissing idea come from?

She wrinkled her nose when he put green beans on her plate.

"Just a few. They're so good for you. If you had a mom, she'd make sure you always ate your veggies."

"Daddy, they're yucky." She pulled a face. "They're green."

"That's why they're called green beans."

They chewed in silence for a few minutes. Amber grudgingly ate her beans, acting all the while like they were poison. She took a big swallow of milk. "Daddy?"

"What, honey?"

"Are you too old to get me a new mommy? Grampa Johnny says you're a bratcherler. What's that?"

He laughed. "First of all, I'm not too old, and I'm not a bachelor. Uncle Cluny is a bachelor. A bachelor is a man who never married. Grandpa's wrong, but don't tell him I said so. We wouldn't want to hurt his feelings, would we?"

She grinned. "No, we'll make it a secret from him."

"Good girl." He stood. "Now, Marine, hop to and march your plate to the sink, and then go fill the bathtub. I'll do the dishes and put the movie on when you're ready."

Dwayne wasn't sure how many more times he'd be able to sit through Cinderella. He'd coax Amber to consider a new movie next week, but tonight he was too tired to argue about it.

Yes, he wanted to marry again, to get her "a new mommy." He didn't know the first thing about mothering a little girl. He was raised in a family of boys. A broken one at that. Amber could use a feminine influence, and he needed a "grownup lady" in his life. Boy, did he ever.

He envied his buddy, Cluny. Cluny flitted from woman to woman like a bee pollinating a rose garden. When he left one rose for the other, they parted the best of friends. How did he do it?

Dwayne would love to break his long, very long dry spell, but he had no interest in adopting Cluny's lifestyle. He wanted permanence, a partner in every way. A steady woman he could make love with, laugh with, argue with. A smart, challenging, and uncomplicated woman who chose to be there every day for him and Amber.

Cluny had set him up on a couple of blind dates that weren't worth the price of a babysitter. It was a problem. At thirty-one, with a kid, his prospects were skinny. Desperate single moms scared him more than an Iraqi soldier aiming an RPG at his head, and the thought of Amber ending up with the kind of stepmother he and his brothers got kept him awake nights.

He loved women and he loved to flirt, but the only woman who piqued his interest was Marla Danaher. She had it all in his book. Smart, sassy, opinionated, never married, a magnificent head of strawberry hair, a great rack, and lush hips he itched to get his hands on. The problem—she thought he was a jerk. Ah, well, he could dream.

Every time he pictured gorgeous Marla he got a throbbing ache. He glanced down at his work boots. What would she think if she knew only one boot held a foot? Was Marla the kind of woman who would see beyond his reminder of Iraq and realize he didn't need two legs to be the man for her? One of these days he'd convince her he was sincere, but for now all he seemed to do was annoy the woman. It was probably best if he'd back off and tone it down.

Amber was his number one priority.

Later, after her bath, Amber stood next to him and buttoned her feet-in bunny pajamas. She tugged his pant leg. "Daddy?"

"What, sweetheart?"

"I don't want to watch Cinderella again. I want you to read me a story."

What a relief! Dwayne tossed the dishtowel on the counter and swept her over his shoulder. He smacked her little bottom then planted loud kisses on her cheeks and chewed at her neck, laughing when she squirmed and giggled.

"Daddy, put me down!"

"Do I have to? You're so warm and cuddly, and you smell so good. I want to eat you up, my pretty." He proceeded to growl at the other side of her neck.

Kicking and squealing, she barely choked out, "Daddy, stop!"

He reluctantly set her on her feet. "Okay. What story do you want me to read?"

"Cinderella."

———

Marla ate peanut butter and chocolate ice cream out of the pint container she'd picked up at Baskin and Robbins on her way home from work. Why put it in a bowl? She lived alone, seldom had guests except for family, and didn't allow Skipper to have ice cream even though he begged without letup with his bulgy brown eyes. He'd mastered the *have pity* expression.

She patted the adorably fat Chihuahua. "Chocolate is poison for doggies, Skip. I'll give you a peanut butter treat later. Don't pout. I shouldn't be eating this either, but at least it won't kill me." *Although death by chocolate would be a great way to go.*

The phone rang. "Hi, Char. What, no date tonight?"

"How'd you know it was me?"

"Caller I.D. Ever heard of it?"

"Don't be such a snarky pants. I'm working on Dadley's birthday party next month. Do you think we should go all Mexican on the appetizers or mix it up?"

Every year Charlene went to great lengths to plan a *surprise* party for their father. He hated surprise parties, so Marla always told him the date in advance. That way he could look surprised and happy *and* actually enjoy the party.

"He loves anything Mexican. How can you go wrong unless you were considering a piñata? That would be over-the-top."

"Forget that. Mom would kill me if a single scrap of cellophane ended up on her precious lawn."

"We should have the party at the country club."

"Costs too much."

"I offered to pay, don't forget."

"I can't show my face around there for a while. The golf pro's wife nearly shot us when she caught him feeling me up in the cart shed."

Marla dropped her head on the back of the couch. "Have you ever given serious thought to dating single guys? What's with you and married men?"

"Hey! I date single men. I don't know what you're talking about. Why don't *you* go on a real date? That's why I talked you into the singles thing tomorrow night."

"If by 'real date' you mean jumping in the sack with a man I barely know…"

"It'd make you smile for a change. Date somebody other than Edwin Plimpton. I don't understand what you see in him. You probably need a magnifying glass to find his willie. How about that Dwayne guy? I bet he'd love to show you what a real man can do. I'd jump at the chance."

Marla shook her head and sighed. The sad fact was Edwin had shown no interest in sex since they'd started going out three months ago. Their relationship, such as it was, was purely platonic.

"Forget I said anything. Go all Mexican, the more guacamole, the better. Have it catered. I'm not doing any of the cooking this year. I'll take Sil shoe shopping at Cesare's China Doll. That'll keep her out of your hair while you and the boys get everything setup. I'm sure she can squeeze a couple more pair into her closet."

Charlene's snort came through loud and clear. "Yeah, for sure, Mom's down to fifty or sixty pair by now, poor dear."

"What are you complaining about? She and you wear the same size. You haven't had to buy a pair of shoes for the past five years."

"Oh. Yes. There is that."

"Anything else? Skipper is giving me dirty looks. I promised him a treat." She rubbed the dog's round belly while he rolled on the couch in ecstasy.

"You and that fat pooch. Give Edwin the heave ho. Get a man!"

"Bye, Char. Call me again when you want to share your wisdom." She clicked off and smiled at Skipper. "I don't need another man as long as I have you, my sweetie-weetie. C'mon let's find that peanut butter treat. Then I have to call Dadley to give him a heads-up about his traditional, annual surprise party."

Yes, she loved her dog, and she was pretty sure she could love Edwin, but as she reached in the cupboard for the box of dog cookies, she wondered what it would feel like to have Dwayne Dempsey wrap his big arms around her. To have his...*don't go there, Marla.* Still, what would it be like to know that when he called her *beautiful* or *gorgeous,* he really meant it?

Chapter Two

MARLA'S STOMACH FLOPPED AND PERSPIRATION FORMED AT THE base of her throat. The closer they got to the restaurant for the singles gathering, the more she was sure she did not want to walk through that door. How had she let Char talk her into taking part in this misadventure?

"Char. I don't feel well. I think I'd better head on home."

Charlene grabbed her arm and yanked her toward the entrance. "Oh, no you don't. You promised you'd come. Lordy, you are the biggest coward. What's the worst thing that could happen?"

"For one thing, I look ridiculous in this dress."

"No you don't. You look gorgeous. I don't know why you always wear those dull, unflattering pantsuits."

"They're very practical for business. I'm in and out of the car all day." Her eyes darted to the entrance. "I don't think there's an upside to this fiasco."

"They're just single men. They're not monsters. At least they shouldn't be, because the organizer checks everyone for a past criminal record."

"Oh, for the love of goats! You're making it sound better every minute." Marla pulled her arm from Char's hand and stopped. "Wait. Wait for just a minute. How is this going to work again?" She knew she couldn't stall much longer. The door of Villa Sorrento beckoned with its twinkling lights and delicious aromas.

"I told you already. They draw names based on compatible characteristics from the personality profile. Nobody knows until they start the pairings who they're going to have dinner with."

"How many people are going to be here?"

"You never listen to me. I told you that too." Char threw her arms in the air and pretended to pull out her hair.

"Tell me again."

"Twelve. Six women and six men." She took Marla's cold, sweaty hand. "It's just dinner, sis. Look at it this way—you'll have dinner with a man who's probably more nervous than you are. There won't be any awkward moments about the check because it's already taken care of with the registration fee."

Still resisting the pull of her sister's hand, Marla worked to push back rising panic. "How long do I have to stay?"

"Take a breath and relax. I can't believe you're working yourself into a meltdown over this."

"How long?"

Charlene gripped Marla's shoulders and glared. "The organizers told me they wrap up the evening at eight-thirty." Char squeezed her shoulders tighter. "That's only two hours. Not a freaking lifetime."

Two hours? How was she going to maintain intelligent conversation with a total stranger for two hours? This would be the evening from hell.

Charlene opened the door and nudged her into the foyer. Their mellow lighting and dark wood paneling usually comforted Marla, but not tonight. She moved as if she had a date with the gas chamber.

"Smile," Charlene said through gritted teeth, then let loose a dazzling smile of her own.

Marla took a slow breath and pasted on a small, closed-lips smile. She imagined herself looking like the Mona Lisa. Enigmatic. Mysterious. Amused. Or just plain defeated.

Charlene pulled her toward the podium. She gave their names to the tuxedoed host, received their tickets, and was directed to an informal seating area in the lounge.

Marla took the flimsy stick-on badge and smacked it to her lapel. As they stepped away, a man approached the host, and Charlene's eyes widened with appreciation while Marla only smirked at her sister's reaction. She left her sister's side and walked directly to the darkest corner. Slumping down, she turned her shoulders away from the entrance.

Charlene walked over to her. "Lordy, lord, Marla. You look like you're hiding from the cops." Charlene fluffed her hair, glanced around the room, and sighed. "It'll all be over in two hours. Can you please, please relax and smile. Look." She pointed across the restaurant. "Harry and Barry just got here. They can't sit with us though. They're so cute."

Marla tossed a handful of nuts in her mouth. She watched their brothers from the corner of her eye, noticing that the twins hadn't dressed alike for a change. "Why can't they sit with us while we're waiting?"

"I don't want anyone to know we're related to them."

"Why in the world not?"

"I don't remember now, but I had a real good reason when I arranged for all of us to be here. Anyway, they're seating the men in another section till dinner."

Marla swallowed hard to prevent choking on the peanuts, smiled and gave the boys a finger wave. "I'll never understand you, Char. Your mind works in ways I can only wonder about."

Charlene signaled the waitress. "You'll never admit it, but you're lucky to have me for your sister. I'll grab you a glass of pinot. Knock it back fast. Try and relax."

"In case you forgot, I'm the designated driver."

With a long-suffering sigh, Char looked at Marla as if she were a hopeless case. "The point is, in case you haven't been paying attention as usual, you won't be driving after dinner. The mystery date will be happy to take you home."

"What! I'm not letting some bozo I've never met before find out where I live, and I'm not planning to go where the mystery man lives." She dug in her jacket pocket for some clear lip gloss and applied it without the help of a mirror. "My mouth is so dry I feel like Judah Ben Hur on his death march across the desert."

"All the more reason to have a glass of wine." Char reached for two glasses of wine as the server lowered the tray before her. "Here, just sip it then. One glass won't guarantee a major crash and grisly death on the highway."

"It could."

"Oh, lord. You won't be leaving for over two hours, and you'll have dinner. Look at it this way, maybe the man you meet will be more boring and colorless than Edwin, and you can swap him out for the new guy."

There was no point in arguing with Charlene when she started ragging on her about Edwin. Marla's opinion of him wasn't far off from her sister's. She brought the glass to her lips, took a single sip, and set it down.

A tall, silver-haired man entered the lounge. "Ladies, may I have your attention? Those of you who're participants in the SDO group please follow me to the dining room."

"SDO?" Marla asked when Charlene stood. "Is that us?"

"Yes. Singles Dinner Only. I already told you that, but as I've pointed out several times already. You never listen to me."

Marla stood, straightened her jacket, and huffed. "If only."

Clearly annoyed, Charlene rounded on her. "Can't you just for once in your life do something I say? I am the oldest you know."

Marla snorted. "By ten minutes!"

"I may not be a Nobel Prize winner all wise and powerful *sister*, but ten minutes makes me older."

"Okay. Let's call a truce. You're older." She picked up the suede shoulder bag matching her too-high stilettos and followed Char's swaying hips to the dining room.

When they reached the entrance, the handsome older man said, "Our group will meet in the far end of the dining room to the left. We selected it for its quiet intimacy and conduciveness for private conversation." He smiled warmly. "The gentlemen are seated, and the tables clearly numbered. Plants and screens have been discreetly arranged around the room for added privacy. Check the number on your ticket," he held one aloft, "and find your match for the evening. *Bon Appétit, Mesdames.*"

Panic gripped Marla's chest and throat. She took a deep breath. Two hours, she could do this. Then she'd refuse any of Char's future matchmaker schemes.

She grabbed her sister's arm. "Wait. Char. Where shall we meet? In the bar? I have the car keys."

"Don't you worry about me. I'll find my way home in my own good time." She flipped long silky blonde tresses over her shoulder and started across the room like a thoroughbred out of the starting gate.

Clutching at her throat, Marla dragged through the room. This felt like a date with the guillotine. *I can do this. I can do this.*

Table six was located in the far corner of the dining alcove. A broad-shouldered man wearing a black leather jacket with an American flag patch on the right shoulder sat with his back to her. Close trimmed hair emphasized a strong neck.

Why does he look familiar?

The guy reached back to rub his neck. Two fingers were missing from his hand.

"Oh, for the love of..." she groaned. "Dwayne Dempsey."

He turned. Those piercing blue-green eyes penetrated her gaze like shards of ice. "Well, well, well. Look who's here." He stood and held out the chair for her.

Marla slapped her ticket on the table and dropped into the chair with the grace of a hundred-sixty pound bag of cement. "I don't believe this."

"*You* don't believe this? I didn't know you were on the hunt, Red."

In a thousand years she couldn't have dreamed up a more absurd development for Charlene's scheme. Leaning forward on her elbows, she nailed him with her own penetrating stare.

"Let me make this clear, Dempsey. I'm here under protest. I have no interest in a blind date with any man, least of all you."

He cocked his head and grinned. "Wow. I didn't know we had so much in common, beautiful."

"We have nothing in common." She tugged her short skirt and gulped a swallow of ice water. "So much for the so-called matching they did."

"For your information, I'm here under protest too." He unrolled the napkin around his silver, snapped it open, and dropped it in his lap. "I'd rather be almost anywhere else."

That stopped her. Maybe they did have something in common, other than work on the condo project. "Oh."

"Yeah. Oh." He signaled the waiter. "Shall we order dinner and see if we can get through the next two hours? I don't know about you, but I'm hungry. Might as well get Cluny's money's worth."

"Cluny? The plumbing contractor?"

"Yeah, the guy over there with the blonde." He tilted his head.

Marla turned. "Oh, good grapes, he's with my sister Charlene."

"Lucky him."

"What's that supposed to mean?"

"It means he's a lucky guy. She's beautiful, she's hot, and look, she's actually smiling at him like she's happy to be here."

"Unlike you getting stuck with me you mean."

"I…" Dwayne shut his mouth when the waiter approached to ask what drinks they'd like to order. He deferred to Marla.

"I'll have a glass of pinot grigio, please."

"And for you, sir?"

"Diet Dr. Pepper."

"Very good. I'll just be a moment."

Marla's nose had wrinkled with distaste when he ordered the Dr. Pepper.

"I don't drink alcohol, and I happen to like Dr. Pepper," he said. "Is that okay with you, boss?"

"Yes, of course. I'm sorry I'm acting like such a witch. Charlene's been driving me crazy with this singles thing, and it was a long stressful day at the project."

"I was there all day. Remember, gorgeous?"

No time like the present to tell him how she felt. "I wish you wouldn't do that."

"Do what?"

She pressed her lips together and sniffed. "Call me beautiful and gorgeous when you mean the opposite. The teasing about my weight has gone on long enough." She stared at her plate, hands fisted on the table.

He didn't say anything for what seemed like hours. Finally he reached across the table and ran his index finger over her clenched fist. "I'm a jackass."

"Yes." She snatched her hand away. "So, don't do it anymore."

Dwayne blew out a breath and chuckled. "That'll be easier said than done."

Her eyes met his. Was that remorse hovering in the gaze behind his smile? "Why? It's a bad habit and bad manners. Can't you manage to restrain yourself between eight and four?"

He leaned back and crossed his arms over his broad chest. The leather jacket made a slight chirp when he shifted. "There's a big problem."

"What? You're unable to control your mouth?"

"No. It's a problem because it's true."

"I think I've lost track of this conversation. What's true?"

"You *are* beautiful and gorgeous."

"Oh, come on, Dempsey." Marla tilted her head in the direction of her sister and Cluny McPherson. "Charlene is the definition of 'beautiful and gorgeous.'"

"Hey, I'm not blind. I can see that, but women with her looks are a dime a dozen, Red. She can't hold a candle to you."

Marla knocked her fists on the table. "Oh, for…"

Dwayne raised his big hands. "Okay, okay. We're not getting anywhere. Let's order dinner and pretend we like each other. I have to retreat at eight sharp so I can pick up my kid." He held up the menu and raised his eyebrows.

His kid? Marla opened her menu. *His kid?* Her shock at his comment was profound. She didn't know anything about this man. Their families had been close all her life. How was it possible she didn't know he had a child? She didn't know much about his two brothers either.

John Dempsey, Dwayne's father, and her dad had been boyhood friends, and as far back as she could remember John came and went like a family member. Even though the two men remained friends to this day, Silvia had taken such a dislike to John's second wife that she refused to accept them as a couple. John's infidelity had soured her on him. As a result, Marla had seen little of John's three sons after the messy Dempsey divorce. The oldest and youngest of John's boys chose to stay with their dad, but Dwayne had moved to Wyoming with his mother and remained there until he'd joined the Marines. Marla thought Dwayne's younger brother was in the military but wasn't sure. His elder brother owned the only furniture manufacturing business in Spring Grove.

She cleared her throat. "I'll order for myself, if you don't mind."

"Why would I mind? Are you ready?" When she nodded, he signaled the waiter.

A few minutes of awkward silence followed after the waiter departed. She was aware of his gaze as she glanced around the room to avoid meeting his eyes.

A sudden burst of laughter she recognized as Charlene's drew her attention. "They seem to be enjoying themselves."

Dwayne's gaze followed hers across the room. "Cluny's a funny guy. Your sister's enjoying him."

Marla's eyes searched the room for either of her brothers. As if sensing her thoughts, Dwayne said, "I saw those two blonde guys when they ushered the men into the dining room. They've been on the jobsite a couple of times visiting Miss Emmaline. Do you know who they are?"

"Yes, they're my twin brothers, Harry and Barry. They met Miss Emmaline during Christmas break. She took a shine to them, and it was mutual. How is it you know her? She was living in the building when I bought it. She must be what? Eighty?"

Dwayne's grin caused a fluttering sensation in Marla's chest. He chuckled.

"I think she's at least that. When I was about ten I asked her how old she was, and she wagged her finger in my face and said, 'A lady who tells her age will tell anything.' She used to be our nanny."

Marla's chin bobbed with surprise. "Your nanny?"

"Yep. Our mom hired Miss Emmaline when she decided to manage Dad's office in his construction company. I think I was five at the time. Dylan must have been seven and Donovan about three."

"I never knew that. I suspected there had to be a good reason why you wouldn't agree to relocating her during the condo conversion."

Dwayne grinned and leaned forward on his elbows. "Yes, the old gal moved out during our adolescent years. She's like a grandmother to us."

Marla's heart flopped in reaction to his grin. *Down girl!*

Obviously, she could have asked Dwayne about the elderly woman when they worked out the contract for the renovation project. Why hadn't she? Well, because she got so fluttery when they were in close contact her brain went mushy, that's why. She'd been determined to keep their relationship strictly business.

Without realizing it, she'd come to adore Miss Emmaline herself.

———

Dwayne gazed at Marla and speculated on how she processed the information he'd just given her. He enjoyed the rare intimacy of their conversation. Her face relaxed, the double tension lines between her eyebrows nearly invisible.

He knew from the way she studied every construction detail and examined every invoice with a fine-tooth comb that she worried about financing for the project. She worked like a son-of-a-gun selling real estate every time she left the jobsite.

They'd finish on time and under budget. His small crew of former Marines were sober, hard-working men and excellent craftsmen. Dwayne ran a tight ship and took pride in the quality and reputation of his company.

Dinner arrived and they continued their relaxed conversation, keeping mostly to the subject of the renovation. Her frequent smiles and animated features contrasted with her usual all-business demeanor. She knew every aspect of the job down to smallest details.

Forcing himself to turn his eyes from her beautiful face, he glanced at his watch. "It's almost eight. I gotta go." He extended his hand. "I had a good time."

Marla grasped his hand. "Me too. I'm sorry I was such a witch when I first sat down."

He allowed himself to hold her hand for a beat longer than necessary. "No problem, Red. I was nervous as hell myself. Can I offer you a ride home?"

Avoiding his eyes, she slid her hand from his and swiped at a curl falling on her cheek. "No, thanks. I have my car."

He stood and helped her with her chair, then draped her jacket over her shoulders. "I'll see you through the parking lot." He wouldn't think of letting a woman walk alone to her car after sharing dinner.

Marla stopped just short of the steps leading to the parking lot. "Holy goats. It's dark. They really should have more lights here."

"Yeah, they're leaving themselves wide open for a lawsuit." He picked up her hand and placed it in the crook of his arm. "Hang on to me. I have good night vision. Miss Emmaline used to claim I was part cat."

Instead of protesting, she gripped his arm and stepped off the apron with him. The warmth of her touch shot straight to his bone marrow. The thought of putting her behind the wheel of her car and making sure she'd locked the door took a toll on his libido.

They reached her car. Their hands bumped as they both grasped the door handle. He tugged.

"Oh, sorry, I didn't unlock it."

She dug to the bottom of her small purse and clicked the button on the key tag. The car chirped and the lights blinked.

Dwayne opened her door, and she slid behind the steering wheel.

He thought of kissing her on the cheek but stopped himself before she shut the door.

He tapped on the window. When she lowered it, he leaned in, "Start 'er up and turn on the lights."

"Why?"

"I want to make sure you're okay before I take off."

She turned the key in the ignition and the engine roared to life. The lights went on automatically. "Okay?"

He grinned and slapped the hood of the car. "You're good to go, beau...uh, Marla."

He nodded and headed for his truck before she had a chance to nail him with a glare.

What a babe.

———

Marla stared as he walked across the lot, the curious hitch in his stride more pronounced tonight than usual. Perhaps he had a hip problem or a bum knee. It didn't seem to affect his ability to put in a good day's work on the job. He personally supervised every aspect of the renovation.

He appeared so different tonight, dressed in a nice pair of slacks with an open-neck dress shirt beneath his bomber jacket. Every other time she'd seen him he'd been wearing worn jeans, a faded work shirt with the sleeves rolled up, a tattered baseball cap, and heavy boots.

Marla smiled and shook her head. She had to admit Dwayne Dempsey made one sexy male package. No matter how he was dressed. And she stopped right there. No way would she allow her imagination to wander in the direction of how he'd look undressed. But, did he have hair on his chest? What about tattoos?

Stop it, Marla. What are you doing?

Dwayne hauled himself up into the driver's seat of his well-used, black pickup truck. He touched his forehead and grinned in her direction before he closed the door. Great goats! Had he read her mind?

He pulled out of the lot and turned right. She backed out and stopped at the exit to the parking lot. As she checked traffic to her left, the lights from the commercial section gave the night sky a soft glow in contrast to the near darkness of the residential area where they both lived.

She tapped her brakes when his truck bounced into the lot of the condos. What was he doing? The place was dark except for a few security lights to discourage after-hour intruders. He stopped in front of the chain link fence, spoke to the guard dog, Hercules, then let himself inside. Marla pulled over and turned off her lights. She glanced at the building and made out the faint glow of lights from Miss Emmaline's apartment. He must be checking on her.

After a few minutes, Dwayne stepped out the front entrance carrying a sleeping child. The girl stirred and Dwayne's big hand stroked the kid's back, and he brushed a kiss on her hair. He spoke to the big malamute again, closed the gate, and snapped the padlock. Holding the child securely, he opened the passenger door and with gentle care lowered the sleepyhead onto the car seat. He fastened the seat belt, and Marla saw the little girl smile. He kissed her and rounded the car to the driver's side. Her heart clenched at the adoring look the little girl bestowed on her daddy.

Marla waited several minutes after he left before she started her car. She didn't want him to think she'd been spying. She wasn't really spying was she? She'd just stopped to see why he had returned to the jobsite after hours. It made sense now. Miss Emmaline had been taking care of his little girl while they were at dinner.

She'd find an excuse to talk to Miss Emmaline. See if she could learn something about him. Why was he a single father? Where was his wife?

Chapter Three

THE NEXT MORNING, MARLA HAD APPOINTMENTS TO SHOW A couple of houses that promised to be good prospects for the buyers she'd been working with. The heavenly aroma of fresh-brewed coffee surrounded her when she stepped inside the local Starbucks. She'd allowed enough time to order her café macchiato and find a nice table with room to spread the property photos and the pertinent information about the school districts.

Her clients, Pete and Rosalie Wyland, arrived shortly after she sat. "I have a couple of very nice properties to show you this morning." Marla indicated the photos.

She explained the pros and cons of both properties, the proximity to schools and the zoning.

"It sounds like there's a lot to like about both places. Shall we get started?" Rosalie stood and settled the strap of her large purse on her shoulder.

Hours later, Marla dropped Pete and Rosalie off at Starbucks where they'd left their car. "See you in the morning?" she asked.

"We'll go over all the details this evening." Pete nodded. "We're prepared to make an offer once we decide."

Marla flashed a bright, confident smile. "If you need any other information or have questions, please feel free to call me at any hour. You have my cell number and it's always on."

The couple nodded and waved when they reached their car.

Marla's cell phone vibrated in her jacket pocket. *Mother,* blinked the caller ID. "Hi, Sil. How's tricks?"

"What am I going to do with your father, Marla? The man is impossible. I can't take it anymore."

Marla had heard these words often for the last quarter century. Somehow her mother had managed to "take it," whatever the crisis de jour happened to be.

"What's he done now, Mom?"

"I don't want to talk about it. I'm just about to explode this time."

"Shall I hang up then?"

"No! I need your help. Why would you hang up on me?"

"Sil, you just told me you didn't want to talk about it."

"Never mind what I said. You're as bad as Bradley. I don't know why you didn't take after my side of the family."

Thank the angels for that.

"Are you going to tell me what Dadley's done that's so impossible? Or are we going to go around in circles, Mom?" Marla immediately regretted her words when she heard what sounded like a sob on the other end of the line. "Mom? Talk to me."

"Charlene just got here. Can you come over?"

"Char's there? Why?"

"I called her."

"Isn't she supposed to be at work?"

"She doesn't work on Saturday, Marla. Do you think I'd call her from work?"

As you've done so many times in the past? It was a wonder Charlene could hold onto a job, as often as Silvia called her with some kind of trivial crisis. "I'm on my way. The sun's over the yardarm so have an early cocktail and relax. I'll be about ten minutes."

The minute she pulled in the driveway, Charlene stormed out the front door of their parents' house, her scowl black as the clouds of a pending thunderstorm.

Marla set the brake and stepped out of her car. "What's the matter?" Maybe it *was* something serious this time. Her neck prickled.

"I am so mad at you I could spit! This time you've gone too far, Marla. You've ruined everything."

Marla took a step back. She'd never seen Char so angry. "What have I ruined? What have I done? You're scaring me."

"You told Dadley about the surprise party the boys and I are planning for his birthday, that's what. Now Silvia is a basket case because he told her he wouldn't show up unless Johnny and his wife were both invited."

A sigh of relief preceded Marla's response. "Great Caesar's goat, is that all?"

Slamming her hands on her hips, Charlene stared, eyes agog. "Is that all? You've ruined the surprise."

"In case you don't remember, our father hates surprise parties and John Dempsey is his best friend."

"He always has a great time. What are you talking about?"

"That's because I tell him in advance about the *surprise* party so he won't be surprised. You are clueless, Charlene. You and Sil both. You scared the daylights out of me. I thought there was a real emergency."

Her phone vibrated in her pocket. "I have to take this. It's an important client."

"More important than your family?"

"In this case that would be a big yes." Marla turned and placed the phone to her ear. "Marla Danaher. Yes. That's great, Mr. Wyland! I'll be right over. Thanks for calling." She switched off the phone. "I have to go close a big deal. I'll come over later and we can sort through this. In the meantime pour a few martinis down Mom's throat."

Charlene sputtered and waved her hands as Marla backed out and headed for the motel to meet her clients. She did a quick mental check of her portfolio. The offer forms were there. She remembered being afraid she might jinx the sale if she put them in with the other papers before she met with the couple this morning. A smile grew on her face with every mile she drove. She could see that big fat commission check now.

Poor Skipper. I'm so late tonight.

Turning into the parking lot of the Grove Motel, Marla spotted a pickup truck that looked familiar. As she got closer, the sign on the side, Big D Construction confirmed it. What in the world would Dwayne be doing here?

Portfolio in hand, she found Room 14 and tapped on the door. It immediately swung open to reveal Dwayne with a big grin on his face.

"Hey, Red, come on in." He made a sweeping gesture toward the small sitting area. Pete and Rosalie Wyland were seated at the table. An ice bucket with a bottle of champagne and five glasses sat in the center.

Marla recognized Dwayne's little girl who sat crossed-legged on the bed fully absorbed by a Cinderella DVD.

Feeling like she'd entered another dimension, totally confused, Marla sputtered, "What…you…why are you here?"

His big hand on her back, he directed her to the table. "Rosie is my cousin. They're relocating here so she can take over the interior design department at Dylan's furniture business. The name change to Spring Grove Furniture and Design will be announced any day."

Pete stood and pulled out a chair. "Dwayne came over to help us decide. Let's get to the paperwork and have a glass of champagne."

Dwayne's daughter glanced at the table and asked, "Do I get some champagne, Daddy?"

"Got ours right here, Amber." He tapped a can of soda. "Soon as we're done with business." He patted her head and took the empty chair between Marla and Rosalie.

Not sure whether to be miffed, Marla said, "Why didn't you tell me the Wylands were your cousins, Dempsey?"

"I dunno, I suppose I thought it would be better if you considered them as any other clients and not my relatives." He winked. "Don't get your hackles up. I was doing them a favor."

"Hmm, I can see your point," Marla admitted. She favored him with a smile, and his reaction pleased her.

Rosalie said, "We've decided on the first house. There's so much to like about it, and when we found out Dwayne built it, it was a no-brainer."

Astonished, Marla gawped at Dwayne. "You built that house?"

"Yup, it was the first project I handled after taking over Dad's construction company when Amber and I moved to Spring Grove. I'm proud of that house. Almost moved into it myself."

Lips pressed, Marla shook her head. One more fact about Dempsey to add to her list of ignorance.

Marla explained the paperwork and slid each sheet across the table for them to sign. The Wylands made a decent, realistic offer. Because she was a dual agent representing both the buyer and the seller, she was sure the offer would be accepted without endless back and forth. She placed the document in her portfolio and smiled.

"I think you just bought yourself a house. The sellers are out of town until tomorrow. I'll contact you right after I meet with them."

Pete lifted the champagne from the ice bucket. "Time to celebrate." The cork made a gentle sigh as he removed it. The man knew the proper way to open a bottle of sparkling wine.

"Amber." Dwayne patted his lap. "Come sit with us while we celebrate with Uncle Pete and Aunt Rosie."

The girl hopped into her daddy's lap. She held the glass Dwayne placed in front of her while he poured the clear soda. "Before we toast, I'd like you to meet Ms. Danaher. Marla, this is my daughter, Amber."

Marla took the small hand in hers. "Very nice to meet you, Amber Dempsey."

The child grinned. "Uh huh." Then she turned to her father. "She's pretty, Daddy. Do you like her?"

"Yes, I do, honey."

The unexpected warm flush crawling from Marla's chest to her cheeks sent her stomach jittering. That small exchange between father and daughter sent her heart racing. Of course he'd answer that way. What else could he have said? It would have been rude for him to say anything else. She told herself it meant nothing. The big lummox worked for her.

Dwayne gazed into her eyes when he handed her the glass of wine, his expression unreadable. No hint of a smirk or a smile. Seeing into another person's soul through their eyes seemed romantic bunk to Marla. The stuff of romance novels. She didn't have a hint of what he may be thinking.

"Boss? Champagne?"

She jerked out of her reverie and took the glass. His big, callused fingers brushed against her hand, sending her pulse into overdrive. She needed to empty her glass and leave as soon as politeness permitted.

"Ms. Marla? Could you come home with us? Daddy made my favorite for dinner. We have lots and lots."

Marla choked, champagne backing up into her nose. Dwayne's cousins burst into laughter.

With a gasp, Marla patted her chest. "I don't—"

"She's right, boss. I made enough for everybody. Why don't you join us?" He waved his hand around the table.

Rosalie shook her head. "Oh, Dwayne, I forgot to tell you. Pete and I are having dinner at Uncle Johnny's tonight. Sorry. After the house hunting we came back here and called the kids."

Marla was beginning to recover her aplomb. "Thank you, Amber, but my little dog…"

Amber wriggled with excitement. "You got a dog?"

"Yes, I do. He's…"

The child tugged on Dwayne's sleeve. "She can bring her dog, can't she? Please, Daddy, please?" Her eyes round, she gazed into Dwayne's face with the same expression Skipper used when he wanted ice cream.

Marla suppressed a smile. Amber had put Dwayne on the spot. He clearly struggled with what to do about it. She enjoyed his dismay.

"Well, Amber, if your daddy says I can bring my dog, I'd love to share your favorite dinner with you." Take that Dwayne Dempsey!

Rosalie seemingly enjoyed her cousin's discomfort as much as Marla. "Dwayne loves dogs. Don't you, Dwayne?" She poked his shoulder. "You said you were going to get Amber a dog after you got settled in California. It's been three years. What's the problem?"

Dwayne raised his hands in surrender. "Look, I know when I'm being ganged-up on by females." Facing Marla, he added, "Ms. Danaher, would you and your dog care to join us for macaroni and cheese?"

A wide grin on her face, Marla nodded. "How serendipitous. That's Skipper's favorite too." She stood. "I'll take the paperwork home, pick up my baby, and join you at your house. Half an hour?"

Amber slid off Dwayne's lap. "Daddy, may I go with her? May I?" She grabbed Marla's hand. "Can I come with you? I'm very well behaved."

Chuckling, Marla squeezed her fingers. "If it's okay with your daddy, you can come with me to get Skipper." She gave Dwayne a sidewise glance. "I'm a very good driver, and Skipper is a very well-behaved dog."

Dwayne rolled his eyes. "Okay, I know when I'm staring defeat in the face." He picked up her booster seat, handed it to Marla, and smacked Amber on the butt. "You behave yourself, you hear?"

Amber bounced on her toes with excitement. "Okay, Daddy."

The little girl chattered with excitement during the short ten-minute drive to Marla's house. She'd probably reveal any of Dwayne's secrets if Marla was inclined to use a child for information, which she wasn't. The Wylands weren't joining them for dinner, so this misadventure was probably a bad idea.

As they passed the condo construction site, Marla noticed a couple of workmen loading equipment into the back of a pickup. She'd ask Dwayne about that because as a rule nobody worked on Saturday afternoons.

At the door of Marla's small house, Skipper's greeting bark echoed from the entry the instant her key went in the lock. "I'm home, Skippy."

Skipper was so surprised to see Amber with his mistress that he applied the brakes to his forward momentum only to skid across the slick entry floor and collide headlong into Marla's shins.

Amber bounced on her toes and squealed her excitement at the tiny mutt. She bent forward with her arm extended.

"No!" Marla grabbed her hand. "Let me show you the way to approach a strange dog." She formed her hand into a fist and instructed Amber to do the same. "Now, slowly reach out and let him sniff your hand. Skip's not a biter, but when dogs get startled or scared they sometimes nip. See? Once he checks you out, you can open your hand. Okay? Now you can pet him."

Grinning, Amber knelt, and Skipper went on his hind legs to lavish her laughing face with dog kisses. Marla wasn't sure which one of them was more excited. She reached for the dog's leash hanging on the coat rack.

"Let's take him for a stroll in the backyard. He has to pee by now."

"Doesn't he have a doggy door?"

"I locked it after a starving stray kitten came in here and couldn't find its way out. Hungry skunks and raccoons can smell Skipper's kibble too."

Amber's bottom lip pushed out in a sad pout. "Ohhh, the poor kitty."

Marla patted her head. "Not to worry. She got a good home. I wrapped her in a towel and took her to Miss Emmaline."

Wide-eyed, Amber sucked in a breath. "Princess Elizabeth? Is that Elizabeth?"

"Yep." Marla chuckled. "That's her."

"I love Elizabeth. She cuddles with me when Miss Emmaline babysits me. She tickles my nose with her rilly fluffy tail."

Marla led the way through the cozy entry, across the living room, through the kitchen and out the back door.

Amber didn't miss a single detail. "Oh, your house is pretty. It smells good too. Ours is nice, but it's kinda plain. Daddy doesn't have flowers and perfume and stuff."

Knowing she'd soon find out for herself, Marla didn't comment. A sweet, innocent child, Amber didn't seem to have a contrary bone in her body.

Marla left them in her small, fenced back yard and went inside to change into a pair of jeans and a sweatshirt. This evening wasn't a date. She had no intention of glamming up for Dwayne. Macaroni and cheese with a man and his little girl. That's all it was.

Chapter Four

DWAYNE PULLED THE BUBBLING MACARONI AND CHEESE OUT OF his oven and set it on a wooden cutting board to cool. Slamming car doors alerted him to Marla's arrival with Amber. After a quick glance around the kitchen to make sure all was in order, he yanked the dishtowel from his waist and made his way to the front entry.

Amber bounded through the door, a happy fat pooch clutched in her thin arms. His heart squeezed painfully at her look of sheer joy.

"What have you got there?" He bent forward to scratch the dog's chin.

Amber whirled out of his reach. "No, Daddy! I'll show you how." She held Skip's leash, set him on his feet, and said, "Make a fist like this, then put it by his nose rilly rilly slow."

He glanced at Marla and smiled when she stepped inside and heard Amber give him his marching orders. She raised her eyebrows, pursed her lips, and watched him follow his daughter's precise instructions.

"What's this bruiser's name?"

"His rill name is Skipper, but Marla calls him Skippy Wippy. Isn't that silly?"

"Yeah. He'd probably prefer a name like Genghis or Killer. What do you think?"

Amber released a tortured sigh. "Daaad! You're even more sillier than Marla." She tugged the leash. "I'm taking him out back to pee." The dog willingly followed her in a fast trot down the hall. The back screen door banged.

Arms akimbo, Dwayne smirked. "Where's that mouse sleep? In a jewelry box?"

Mimicking his stance, Marla stuck out her chin. "No, in a demitasse cup."

"I thought so." Dwayne pointed toward the back of the house. "We'd better keep an eye on those two. Come on."

They made their way through the kitchen. Marla sniffed appreciatively. "That smells heavenly. It looks yummy too. When do we eat? I'm starving."

Not only was she hot and vah-voom, she wasn't afraid to reveal her healthy appetite. One more point for her. At this rate she'd surpass the perfect ten rating he'd secretly bestowed. But he was no fool. He'd keep that information to himself.

They stood inside the laundry room door and watched while Skipper explored the backyard and found several places to squeeze out a few drops. Amber followed, her mouth moving as she spoke to him.

Finally she raised her arm and called out, "Skipper's hungry, Daddy. I hope you made enough."

"No problem there, squirt. Come on in and get those hands washed." He held the door open for them. "Dinner is ready, and Marla is starving."

Marla asked, "Is it okay to take him off the leash?"

"Sure. Follow me. I brought the rest of the champagne home so you could have a celebratory glass. Sound good?"

Her footsteps echoed behind his as they returned to the kitchen. "Did you send your cousin my way?"

"Yep. She asked for a referral. I knew you'd take good care of them."

"You have no idea how relieved I am to close that deal, Dempsey. It's been lean pickings the past few months. Your cousin is getting a great house and the price is right."

He reached in the refrigerator and retrieved the ice-green bottle. "That's what I told them. Rosie likes it that I built the house. I think that's what sealed the deal for them."

Marla reached for the juice glass he held. "I owe you one."

He speculated on various ways he'd enjoy collecting his debt. None of which he could say out loud because there was a child in the house. But that didn't stop him from imagining how Marla would look if he ever managed to get her naked. He cleared his throat and turned toward the sink. "Have a seat. I'll grab the salad and get the bread from the warming oven."

"Isn't this the old Crocker house? I vaguely remember attending a Fourth of July party here one summer when I was a kid."

"Yes. I swapped it for a vacation cabin I built in Montana. Old man Crocker decided he wanted to go fishing as much as possible after he retired. They have a small condo in San Diego to escape the winters. I palled around with their son, Ryan. Do you remember him?"

"Ryan! Oh, my gosh, yes. We were in the same class at Spring Grove High. He got married last year. I think he manages the Ace Hardware store Simi Valley."

"He owns it. I give him a lot of business."

Dwayne set a bowl of salad in the center of the table and put three different bottles of dressing next to it. Amber skipped into the kitchen with Marla's mouse in her wake.

"Sit down, sweetheart. Do you want milk or lemonade?"

"Milk." She turned her gaze to Marla. "Can Skipper have some?"

"Afraid not, honey. I'll give him his regular food and put a spoonful of macaroni on top. That way he'll think he's getting the same thing we are. Dwayne, do you have a small bowl or saucer I can put some kibble in?"

He took a sauce dish from the cupboard. "Here you go."

Marla dumped the contents of a plastic snack bag in the bowl. When Dwayne set the steaming casserole on the table he dropped a spoonful on top the kibble.

"Better let it cool a minute."

Marla took a deep, appreciative sniff of the macaroni. "No kidding. It smells so good he'd wolf it right down the minute I set it on the floor."

The minute he sat, Amber said, "I get to say grace."

"Hey, it's my turn."

"You can have two turns in a row."

"Promise?"

She clasped her hands and bowed her head. "Thank you for

Daddy's good macaroni and cheese, God, and please tell him to get me a new mom and especially a dog. Amen."

Dwayne and Marla eyed each other and smiled. He winked and ruffled Amber's hair. "You'll have a dog one of these days. I promise. Soon as you're old enough to take responsibility."

Amber dropped her cheeks to her fists. "You always say that."

"Elbows off the table, miss." Dwayne dished up a portion of the macaroni for her and added a spoonful of salad. "Eat all your salad and I'll let you have ice cream for dessert."

She pulled a long face and stuck out her tongue. "Yucky. It's green."

He turned to Marla. "As you may have guessed, Amber has taken a dislike to anything green."

"Charlene's the same way. Except for greenbacks."

He loved her quick retorts. She laced her comments with a tinge of sarcasm, but they never smacked of meanness. Maybe one of these days they could have a real conversation. She just needed to relax.

He'd ease off on the teasing. He hadn't understood before Friday night how she had misinterpreted his remarks. While he'd been clumsy but sincere, she'd thought he was poking fun at her. That would stop as of now.

He extended a warning hand. "Amber, that's hot. You'd better blow on it first." Dwayne blew on his macaroni.

Marla blew on hers. Then she blew on the dog's dish and tested the noodles with her finger. "Oh boy, Skip. You're in for a treat." She set the dish on the floor between her and Amber. "Watch how fast this disappears."

Amber giggled when the treat was gone the instant Marla set it down. "He's a little pig, isn't he?"

"True. If he could get to his food without my help, I don't think he'd stop eating until his little pot belly dragged the floor."

She looked at Dwayne. "Oh, I almost forgot to ask you. Who are the men you have working today?"

"What?"

"The two men loading a truck. I saw them when we were on our way to my house and back here, but I didn't recognize them."

He leaped from the table so fast the dishes rattled, and his chair teetered. He grabbed his cell phone off the counter and punched a couple of keys. "Pick up, pick up! Cluny? Dwayne. Get your ass over to the jobsite. Sure, bring them. Yes, double time. I'll meet you there."

Marla had a hand on her chest. "What's the...?"

Snatching his wallet and keys, he headed for the front door.

"Dempsey!"

"Stay here!"

She jumped to her feet. "If you think I..."

"I said stay here, dammit!" He slammed out the door.

———

Stunned, Marla slumped back in her chair with a thump. Her heart clenched. Something was very wrong at the jobsite. Who did he think he was yelling and ordering her around? When Skipper leaped into her lap, she gasped and realized she'd been holding her breath.

A shaky voice interrupted her fury. "Daddy said bad words."

The child stood by her chair, knees wobbling, face twisted with worry. Golden brown eyes swam with unshed tears.

Marla's stomach clenched for the poor kid. She shooed Skipper away and lifted Amber onto her lap. "It's okay, honey. Don't worry about your daddy. I'll be here until he gets back."

"Daddy never says bad words unless it's rilly rilly serious."

Expressing confidence she didn't feel, Marla rubbed Amber's back and smiled. "I'm sure he'll call soon." She set Amber on her feet. "Let's put your daddy's plate in the oven so his dinner won't get cold. We'll finish ours, then sit with him and keep him company when he gets back. Okay?"

On a big sigh, Amber took her seat. She pointed to the dog. "Skipper's worried too."

Marla chuckled. "Chihuahuas always look worried. It's those too-big brown eyes. He's fine. That's his feed-me stare."

"Can he have some more?"

"I suppose it won't hurt this time. He'll be thrilled if you take a small spoonful from your plate and drop it on his."

Amber giggled with delight at Skip's excited reaction. His entire body from neck to tail wagged when he realized he would get more of the cheesy noodles.

Marla's mind wandered for the next few minutes while they finished eating. Dwayne's abrupt departure had sent a stab of fear through her chest along with anger at his command. From his instant reaction, she figured he hadn't authorized any of his men to be on the job today.

She glanced across the table. Amber had asked her something. "I'm sorry, sweetie. My mind wandered. What did you say?"

"Would you tell Daddy I ate all my salad?"

"Absolutely. If you eat all of it."

A dramatic sigh and big pout preceded Amber's reply. "I didn't think you would." She jabbed a fork in a piece of tomato. "This is the only part that's not yucky."

"You know what? I didn't like salad when I was your age either."

Eyes wide, Amber said, "You didn't?"

"Nope. Then I realized that lettuce didn't taste like anything. All I had to do was chew it and swallow. Besides, I wanted to set a good example for my little brothers."

"You got little brothers?"

"They're not so little anymore. All grown up, handsome, twenty-year-old twins."

"I wish I had a brother."

Marla laughed. "Careful what you wish for."

Head cocked like a curious puppy, Amber asked, "Why?"

The comment had gone right past the little girl's head. Not used to talking to children, Marla realized she'd have to pay more attention to her words. "Nothing, I'm just teasing. Now finish up and we'll clear the table."

Another tortured sigh. "Ooookay."

Marla rinsed dishes and placed them in the bright new LG dishwasher. Dwayne had updated the old Crocker house. She admired the top-of-the-line Jenn-Air stove. The cupboard hardware looked modern, and the faux-wood floor was definitely a new addition.

Amber handed over her empty plate and Skipper's empty dish.

Marla smiled and took it from her. "See, that wasn't so bad, was it?"

"No, but I still don't like green stuff. Do you like Cinderella?"

"I love Cinderella! Why?"

"Daddy borrowed me a new DVD from the liberry, Barbie Cinderella. Wanna watch it?"

"I can't think of anything Skippy would rather do than cuddle in your lap and watch Cinderella." Marla hung the damp dishtowel on the oven door bar.

———

Dwayne's truck peeled onto the gravel jobsite lot just as two men jumped into a truck loaded with tools and equipment. He slammed on his brakes, activated his car alarm, grabbed his Louisville Slugger, threw open his door, and ran toward them.

The red-bearded driver got the truck started just as Dwayne smashed the windshield and driver's side window. The man threw open his door and knocked Dwayne off his feet. Then he jumped out and made a grab for his throat. Dwayne blocked him with a stiff-arm to the chin. The guy went down on his butt with a thump and raised a cloud of dust.

Exchanging punches, the two men struggled. Dwayne had gained the upper hand when the other guy jumped on his back and knocked him down again. A hard elbow to the jerk's neck had him clutching his throat, gasping to breathe.

"Nobody messes with my boys!"

From the corner of his eye he saw Miss Emmaline charge from the door of the building wielding a broom like a weapon. "Get back inside!" he yelled.

She didn't slow down. "Don't you tell me what to do, young man," she snarled, then walloped one of the men on the head with her broom. She landed another whack on side of the guy's shoulder, then pointed the bristles at his face and jabbed.

He fell back howling and raised his arms to protect his eyes. "Stop it, you crazy old bitch!"

"That does it!" Dwayne's jaw tightened. He struggled to his feet and slammed his elbow hard against the man's nose. Bone cracked. Blood spurted as the bastard fell to his knees.

"Where do you think you're going?" Emmaline growled at the driver trying to get back in the vehicle.

The creep scooped a handful of gravel and flung it at her. Her glasses went flying and she staggered back.

"Why, you cretin, you scoundrel." She raised the broom again. Dwayne moved to shield her.

Cluny's big green muscle car slid to a skidding halt a few feet from them. Doors flew open. Cluny, Slim, and Jack leaped out, all carrying baseball bats. Cluny ran to the man standing by the open truck door and slammed the bat hard into the guy's solar plexus, doubling him over.

"Better think twice before you mess with a bunch of Marines, pal!" He shoved him to the ground.

Slim and Jack used their bats to break the headlights and the rest of the windows in the truck.

Dwayne shook his head at the ringing in his ears. "At ease, men."

It was over as quick as it started. Sirens howled in the distance. A beat-up blue car that had been parked at the curb, engine idling, tore off like a rocket and disappeared around the corner. Dwayne was sure he'd seen the driver before but couldn't place the bastard. Was he part of this crew or just a curious onlooker?

Dwayne retrieved Miss Emmaline's glasses from the ground and put his arm around her bony shoulders. "What did you think you were doing, old woman?"

"Don't you 'old woman' me, youngster. I can give as good as I get. Always could." She straightened her spine and in a universal womanly gesture, smoothed her hair. "That'll teach them."

Dwayne laughed and swept her off her feet. Against her struggles, he whirled her around and gave her a crushing hug.

"What am I gonna do with you?"

She pounded his big shoulders. "You should be more concerned about what I'm going to do with you once you put me down, you good-for-nothing." She kissed his cheek.

Chapter Five

DEMPSEY HAD BEEN GONE FOR THREE HOURS. THE TENSION IN Marla's neck got worse by the minute. She tried his cell number only to hear it ringing on the floor by the front door. He'd been in such an all-fired hurry to leave he hadn't noticed he'd dropped it. Amber slept against the cushions at the corner of the sofa while Skipper snored on the child's chest, his nose buried under her chin.

At the sound of Dwayne's truck engine, Marla jumped to her feet. Skipper's ears perked up and he raised his head. "Good boy, Skippy, go back to sleep." He buried his nose in Amber's neck, and Marla tiptoed to the entry.

She extended a warning hand and put a finger to her lips before Dwayne had a chance to speak and pointed to the kitchen.

"In there."

When they stepped through the door, she whirled on him and whispered, "Amber's asleep. Where in heck have you been all this time? I'm ready for a big dose of Prozac!" She raised an accusing finger. "You charge out of here shouting orders like I was one of your workmen," another finger up, "leave me in charge of your child," a third finger, "you don't call," fourth finger shook in his face, "because you left your phone here, you...oh, holy goats! You're bleeding, Dempsey. Are you all right?" She touched his cheek.

"Yeah." He blew out a breath and nodded. "Sorry. I need to sit down and get off my leg."

Without waiting for her reply, he brushed past her. Marla pressed a hand against the back of her neck and dogged his limping steps. More than his face had been hurt. Something happened to his leg.

She hurried to the sink, wet the dishtowel in cold water, wrung it out, and pressed it against his cheek. "Were you in an accident?"

"No, a battle. We caught some losers red-handed, stealing our tools and equipment."

"We?" Marla lifted the wet towel to look at the cut on his cheekbone. She sucked in a sharp breath between clenched teeth. "Who's we?"

"Me, Cluny, Slim, and Jack. We got there just ahead of the cops." He chuckled, and that brought on a wince of pain. "Miss Emmaline called them when she heard my car alarm, then she jumped into the middle of the fight and gave one of those bastards a good beat-down with a broom."

"She did?" Her eyes grew wide with surprise. "Were those the men I saw? How'd they get in? Where was Hercules?"

"His handler brings him over just before dark. He works the night shift. We never thought anybody'd try to rip us off in broad daylight." He grasped his left leg just below the knee. "Dammit! Will you do me a favor and grab those crutches by the front door?"

Marla pressed the towel against his cheek. "This town is going down the tubes. Did those thieves get arrested?"

"Youch! Take it easy." He leaned back to ease up the pressure. "The cops took them in. All but a guy in a blue car who was probably their lookout. He hauled ass right after the fight started."

"Sorry, you probably need a couple of stitches. Shall I take you to the ER?"

"No, it's only a scratch. Just bring the crutches, please. I need to get my weight off this leg and take my pants off so I can have a look at it."

"Keep the towel pressed there while I get them."

When she retrieved the crutches and handed them over, he dropped the towel and struggled to his feet. She sighed with relief that the bleeding on his face had stopped.

Dwayne thumped down the hallway in the direction of his bedroom. She followed.

"I'm gonna drop my pants, Danaher. You might want to stay out."

She huffed and stepped in front of him to open the bedroom door. "I've seen men's underwear before, Dempsey. I have two brothers I practically raised on my own."

"In case you haven't been paying attention, I'm not your brother."

"Shut up. I couldn't care less about how you look in your underpants. I want to make sure I don't need to get you medical help."

"Your call."

Leaning his crutches against the bed, his back to her, Dwayne unbuttoned his jeans and pushed them below his briefs.

Marla swallowed, Oh, my. Then she brushed off her reaction to step in for a closer look. Right the first time, he isn't my brother.

He twisted around, sat on the bedspread, and pushed his jeans below his knees.

Sharp shock took her breath away when she gaped at the prosthesis attached to his left leg. "Dwayne…what hap—?"

"Daddy?"

Marla spun around to see Amber standing in the doorway, rubbing sleep from her eyes. Skipper's toenails tapped on the floor as he trailed behind.

"I'm here, squirt. Come on in." He pointed to his pants. "Help me pull these pants off, Okay?"

"Are your toes itching again?" Amber knelt on the floor in front of him and scratched the toe of his empty boot. "I'll scratch 'em for you."

Marla's head swam, her breathing rapid and shallow. Dwayne had part of his leg missing! When had that happened? How had she not known it before now?

"They don't itch tonight, sweet pea. I just need you to help me get this contraption off."

"What happened, Daddy?"

"I took a spill and it's sore. I gotta get the pressure off, that's all."

Without realizing she'd moved, Marla knelt beside Amber and untied the leather thongs on his right work boot. "Do you have something to put on that?"

Amber jumped to her feet. "I know where Daddy's feel-good goop is. I'll get it." She ran to the bathroom. Marla heard the opening and closing of cupboard doors. She returned holding a large jar. "Here it is."

"Thanks, honey. I'll unhitch my gear and you can help Marla pull

Daddy's jeans off." He undid the fasteners on the prosthesis, then leaned back on his elbows and held out his leg so Marla could haul his right boot off.

Amber tugged the prosthesis free from his left pant leg, and then together they pulled on the hem of his jeans.

Dwayne exhaled. "Jeez, what a relief. This thing hurts like a son-of-a-gun." He sat straight, hooked his hand under his right knee, twisted sideways, and lifted it so both of his legs rested on the bed. He tugged off the gel-sock covering the stump. It flamed red with an angry bruise slashed across the area above and below his knee where the brace had been attached.

He reached for the jar, but Amber held out of his reach. "I can do it."

Marla's heart banged against her ribs. She stared at this little girl who had taken over the care of her father. Her little fingers dipped in the jar and plucked out a blob of clear gel. She massaged it on Dempsey's damaged limb.

The medication was odorless, but Marla got a whiff of Dwayne. Even though sweaty and disheveled, his seductive male scent got her heart tripping.

He sighed and fell back against the pillows. "Thank you, squirt. You're the best nurse I ever had."

Marla blinked when Dwayne pointed to the chair next to the bed. "Sit down before you fall down, Red."

Desperately working to organize her thoughts before she spoke, Marla sat and stared. Skip hopped onto the bed to investigate Amber's progress. He sniffed around then walked up Dempsey's body to his chest where he flopped on his belly as if to hold Dwayne prisoner while Amber worked.

"Skipper! Get down from there."

Before she could move, he placed his hand on the dog's back and grinned at the mutt's bulgy-eyed stare. "He's okay. You're fine, aren't you, soldier?"

Skipper's tail thumped a steady rhythm against the man's flat belly.

Dwayne faced Marla. "You better start breathing soon, Red, or my nurse will have two patients on her hands."

Marla closed her mouth and wondered how long it had been hanging open. A hot flush burned her cheeks. "I'm...I...wow. How long have you had...what happened?"

"Operation Iraqi Freedom, March '03. Nearly got my ass blown off over there."

Amber aimed a disapproving face at him. "You're saying a lot of bad words today, Daddy. No ice cream for you."

"Yeah, sorry. I'll clean up my act." He tugged a lock of her hair. "You keep me in line."

Marla marveled at the easy interplay between father and daughter. Even though six-year-old Amber had innocently prayed for Dempsey to get her a new mom, heaven help the woman who ever tried to get between those two.

"Does everybody know about your...your uh...foot, except me, Dempsey?"

"I don't advertise it. My family knows. And that includes Miss Emmaline. The men on the job know. They're all Iraq vets."

Hoping she wasn't being obnoxiously nosy, Marla asked, "Are any of the other men...wounded?"

"Cluny got hit in the same battle." He threw his forearm over his eyes. "But nothing you can see."

She twisted her hands. "Shall I get you something? Tylenol? Aspirin? I can see how uncomfortable you are."

Dwayne lowered his arm. "Thanks, Danaher, but no. You and your mouse have had enough excitement for one day. It's late. Tomorrow's Sunday. I've got a great nurse, and I'll be ship-shape by Monday morning. Why don't you take off? You have some work to do tomorrow to wrap up the sale on the house for Pete and Rosie."

With a sigh, Marla stood. "Are you sure? If you need me to pick up something, or do anything before I leave, tell me now." When Dwayne rolled his head on the pillow, she lifted Skip off his chest. "I kept your dinner in the oven. It's probably pretty dried out by now."

"No sweat, Danaher. It'll be a helluva lot better than an MRE." They glimpsed Amber's expression when she grumbled. "Sorry, nurse, I'll get to work cleaning up my language."

"You better, or you'll never ever get to eat ice cream again, Daddy. Rilly."

Marla chuckled and hugged Skipper against her sweat-shirted bosom. "Okay then. I'll see you Monday. I had a good time visiting with you, Amber. So did Skip."

"Me too, Marla. I love him."

"You take good care of your daddy. I'll find my way out."

———

So now Marla knew.

He'd have had to reveal it at some point, so tonight was as good a time as any. She was shocked, but to give Red credit, he hadn't detected any pity in her reaction. She'd been as bossy as ever, ready to take charge. No phony blushing when he'd dropped his pants, she'd done what needed to be done.

Dwayne couldn't stomach pity. He was lucky to be alive and had no regrets about his tour of duty. He'd volunteered to go and would go again if they'd have him.

One thing he did know—an Iraqi dad loved his kids just as much as Dwayne loved Amber. Nobody deserved to live under the heel of a murdering tyrant. Some of the things he'd seen over there would always haunt him. Whatever it took, he'd defend his home, his daughter, his town against any evil bastard intent on doing harm.

Amber sat back on her heels and screwed the top on the jar of salve. "Is that better, Daddy?"

"I'm good as new thanks to you." He dragged his pajama bottoms from under his pillow and pulled them on. "I'm starved. What say we see what's left of my supper?"

"Wait, I'll get a Band-Aid." Amber hopped down and held his crutches in front of him. "Sit on the side of the bed."

"Yes, ma'am." He pulled on a sock and waited patiently while she dabbed his cut with antibiotic ointment and stuck the bandage on his cheek.

"Will I live?"

"Probly."

"That's a relief." He stood and put the pads of the crutches under his arms and headed down the hall.

Amber darted ahead of him. "I'll get your soda. Marla put it back in 'frigerator when you left. I rilly like her. She's not married and her boyfriend is rilly boring. She told me. Did you know she had a twin sister who doesn't look anything like her and twin brothers who nobody can tell apart but her? Her dad is best friends with Grampa Johnny, and her mother's name is Silvia, but they call her Silly Silvia when she isn't listening. They make a surprise party every year for their dad's birthday, but Marla always tells him before because she says he doesn't like surprises. I like surprises."

Dwayne laughed as he followed her running dialogue to the kitchen. "I'm calling the FBI Monday morning to see if they'll give you a job interview. You wormed more information out of Marla Danaher in one evening than I have in the last six months."

"She said we could be girlfriends and tell each other everything. She wondered where my mom was, and I told her you revorced her last year because she had to leave and wasn't ever coming back and she wanted to know if you had a girlfriend and I told her no." Amber opened the fridge and set his Dr. Pepper on the table.

"Whoa. I changed my mind about the FBI. You must already be moonlighting as an agent for the CIA."

He propped one of his crutches against the counter and opened the door of the barely warm oven. Holding a dishtowel, he lifted his plate off the rack. "Mmm, mmm, mmm, just the way I like it. When it's brown it's cookin' and when it's black it's done."

Amber set the salad bowl on the table and removed the plastic wrap. "Marla made me eat all my salad."

"How'd she manage that miraculous feat?"

Amber wrinkled her nose. "She's rilly bossy."

He laughed. Yes, Marla was "rilly bossy." Definitely a take-charge woman. A woman he liked more every day, and who apparently had some interest in him, or why had she wormed so much information out of his daughter?

He shook his head when he thought of the monumental paperwork battle required to finally get his divorce from Francine. She'd deserted them, and he hadn't seen or heard a peep from her in nearly six years. He'd spent a fortune on all the legal advertising and hoops he'd had to jump through. For all he knew, she was dead by now.

The way Francine liked to live in the fast lane, he wouldn't be surprised. He'd been totally seduced by her wild child ways in those days. Their first explosive sexual encounter had been her idea, and he'd enjoyed every down-and-dirty minute of it. What a dumb kid he'd been back then.

"If I eat all my salad will you let me have some ice cream, nurse? I promise to clean up my act."

Amber pursed her lips with skepticism. "You always promise." She scowled across the table, arms crossed in front of her. "Okay, but this is the last time. I rilly mean it, Daddy."

Chapter Six

"Dang it!" Marla was halfway home when she remembered she'd forgotten her promise to Charlene to return to their parent's house after she met with the Wylands. She'd left her cell phone in the car while at Dwayne's. Her mother and sister had probably left a gazillion hysterical voicemails by now. She looked at the screen and groaned.

"What am I going to do, Skippy?" She sighed and made an abrupt U-turn in the middle of the block to retrace her route. Might as well face the music.

Her parent's house appeared quiet when she pulled in the driveway. Charlene's car wasn't there. Gritting her teeth against the expected meltdown, she picked up Skipper, went to the front door, and pushed the bell.

Her dad opened the door. "Hi, honey. Come on in." He stepped aside and held the door open.

"Hi, Dadley. Is Mom here? She's probably ready to kill me."

"No, and I doubt it." He took Skipper from her and let the dog lap his face. "Why would you think that?"

"She called me in a fury over your birthday party. I got the impression you'd soon be divorced or she'd be a widow. She said you told her you wouldn't come to your own party if John Dempsey couldn't bring his wife. What a mess."

Bradley Danaher pointed to a chair next to his recliner. "Take a load off." He took a seat and set Skip in his lap, held up a glass of Irish whiskey and raised his eyebrows.

"No, thanks. Where is Mom? Where's Char? I want to get it over with."

"They were smiling and yapping when they went out shopping this afternoon, then they called and said they were adding dinner and a movie. Your mother seemed reconciled to my ultimatum. I think it took her all of five minutes to get over it."

"You gave her an ultimatum?" Dadley never gave ultimatums. "Wow! I almost got an ulcer on the way over here." Marla stuck her legs straight out in front of her, slid down in the chair, and dropped her head back. "I'll have a wee dram after all, Dad. Those two are making me old before my time."

Bradley chuckled and poured Jameson's into a heavy crystal glass and handed it to her. "You were born grown up, my darling girl. You're an old soul." He tipped his glass at her. "Slainte!"

Marla smiled at her dad and took a sip. "Good health to you too, Dadley."

They sat in companionable silence. Marla gazed around the room. Sil, a gifted decorator, made their home elegant and inviting. A fragrance of lemon lingered in the air, and a wave of nostalgia for her childhood engulfed Marla's chest. What childhood? Like Dadley said, she was born grown up. She must have popped out of the womb wearing a suit, carrying a briefcase, and with a schedule for managing her parents and siblings. Somebody had to do it.

"Dad? How long have you known John Dempsey?"

"About forty-five years. Since we were in high school. I thought you knew that."

Marla nodded. "I did. I guess my question is…why were you and Johnny friends in the first place? You're really not very much alike."

Bradley chuckled and set down his now-empty glass. "Our differences attracted us to each other I suppose, but we started out as rivals for your mother's affections. Both of us panted after her as only two sixteen-year-olds could."

Marla stared at her father. "What! You and John both wanted to date Mom?" John Dempsey chasing her mother? That was the last thing she expected to hear.

He poured himself another tot of whiskey and held up the bottle.

She shook her head, so he put the stopper back in, took a sip, and continued. "Date is the polite way to say what we wanted."

Heat crept from her chest, to her neck, and her scalp blazed. "I never knew that. I can't imagine Sil going out with Uncle John."

"They did more than 'go out.'" Her dad waggled his eyebrows. "They were a hot item for almost two years. You couldn't separate them with a crowbar." He toasted the past and took a sip of the whiskey.

"Dad! I can't believe this. How could you and John have remained friends?" Anger against her mother burned her stomach. The idea of Silvia choosing Johnny Dempsey over her perfect, wonderful father back then—beyond belief.

"We remained friends because I loved both of them. It's hard to explain."

She held out her empty glass. "Give me a refill and try. I feel like I entered the Twilight Zone."

"Here's the thing." Bradley sighed and poured a finger of the Irish into her glass. "I knew Johnny had a wandering eye, and I held out hope Silvia would get fed up with him and give me a second look. It's as simple as that."

Marla puckered her lips and thought about that. "Are you sure you're remembering correctly?"

"You think I'm ready for the funny farm?" His voice was tinged with annoyance. "Of course I remember. Need I remind you that you don't always know everything?"

Contrition descended. "Sorry, Dad. It's just...wow...Mom and Johnny. Who woulda thunk it? Not me. I can't get my mind around it. Wow." Sipping the whiskey, Marla eyed her father. His face wore a wistful smile. He looked old. When did her dad get old?

"That's okay. And quit looking at me like I've got a foot in the grave. You're not getting any younger yourself. When are you going to start living your own life and stop thinking the rest of us can't take care of ourselves? Get a husband, I want some grandkids."

Dadley had never spoken so plainly. Both her parents hinted that the time had come for her and Charlene to find husbands and settle into *normal* lives. At twenty-seven, they still had plenty of time. She had no interest in saddling herself with a husband and kids, and Char was too busy sampling every unmarried man within the city limits and beyond.

"I don't want a husband and kids. I have other plans. Anyway, I want to know what happened between Silvia and John."

Bradley stroked Skipper's back and wrinkled his nose at her little dog. "Peeyew, Skipper farted. What have you been feeding him?"

"He had macaroni and cheese earlier and quit trying to change the subject."

He picked up a magazine and fanned the air around Skipper. "John met Kathleen, fell flat on his ass in love, and showed Silvia the door."

"Kathleen? Dwayne's mother?"

"Mother to all three boys. Dylan, Dwayne, and Donovan."

"John threw Mom over?" Her father's story stunned her. *Welcome to bizarro world, Marla.*

"Yep, and I caught her. The rest is history."

"Well, I suppose the good news is—she got over it."

"She never got over it. She hated Kathleen, she hated every woman John dated after Kathleen left him, and she hates his current wife, Irene. But she never stopped loving Johnny."

"Dad! What are you saying?"

"It is what it is, honey. I've always loved your mother and I always will. We've made a good life together, but today I finally laid down the law about her excluding them from our social life. John and Irene are my friends."

How could this be? Her mother loved John Dempsey? "But, Dad, Mom loves you, I know she does." Her tall, blond father had always been a Nordic prince in her mind. Harry and Barry got their coloring and handsomeness from Dad. John Dempsey came up short in the looks department with his muscular bulk and black curly hair. He couldn't compare to Bradley Danaher's male beauty.

"Yes, Silvia does love me. I waited for her. I never felt like I got the leftovers. We have a good life, a nice home, and four great children we're both proud of." He eyed her and pointed a finger in her face. "Don't look at me like that. Since when do you believe in fairytales?"

"I watched Barbie Cinderella tonight with Amber, Dwayne's little girl." She sighed. "Was I ever a little girl, Dad?"

"Not for long, honey. You've been trying to manage this family since you were Amber's age. There was nothing we could do to stop you. Still isn't."

"Am I that awful?" She wondered why she had such a driving need to manage everybody's life. They were all capable of taking care of themselves.

"No. And quit feeling sorry for yourself. That's not like you. We just wish you'd pay more attention to your own happiness."

"I..."

"How's things between you and Edwin?"

Marla rolled her head against the back of the chair and sighed. "Edwin." She sighed again. "Poor Edwin. He died a while back and hasn't realized it yet. I don't know why I don't stop seeing him. He's more boring that watching glaciers melt."

Bradley's bark of laughter startled Skipper and he jumped off his lap.

"Your baby is glaring at me. He looks insulted." He slapped his knee. "Come on, boy. Come on."

Skipper sat and stared, then hopped on Marla's lap. "What's the matter, Skippy? Did that big bad man scare you?" She hugged and cuddled him, murmuring silly baby talk.

"My god, daughter. Why are you wasting all that gooey affection on a mutt? You need to find yourself a man. Somebody who'd treasure the woman you are."

She waved a hand in dismissal. "Dad, did you know Dwayne Dempsey lost part of his left leg in Iraq?" Now why had she asked that out of the blue? She wasn't interested in Dwayne Dempsey. No, she didn't have a single ounce of interest in him! Not even half an ounce.

As if he'd read her mind, Bradley asked, "Are you interested in him? Now, there's a man's man, if you want my opinion. He's somebody who'd appreciate a hardheaded woman like you. Why don't you give Edwin the heave ho? Dwayne is a much better prospect."

"Dad! What brought that on? I'm not the least bit interested in him in that way. I just wondered if you knew about his wound." Dump Edwin? She wasn't being fair to him, but she wasn't ready to go it alone either. Edwin was safe, stable, reliable.

"Of course I knew. John's my best friend. I've known about it from the day he got notified by the Navy Department. Why? Is that a problem for you? I doubt it has any effect on him in the manhood department, if you get my meaning."

"Good grapes! The man works for me. What could be more inappropriate? Anyway, he's the last man in this town I'd ever be interested in." *Liar, liar, liar.*

Skipper's ears perked up. He jumped off Marla's lap and ran to the entry hall barking his little head off.

Bradley stood. "Ah, the two dragon ladies are home. I wonder how much of my money they spent this time."

"Skippy!" Charlene's squeal echoed down the hall. "Marla's here." She struggled in with several shopping bags and dumped them on the floor.

Silvia followed, also burdened with boxes and bags. "We hit a fabulous sale at Nordstrom. Wait till you see the cute shoes I bought." She crossed the room and kissed Bradley on the cheek. "I see you had company while we were gone." Hugging Marla, she said, "I'm sorry you didn't get back earlier, sweetheart. You could have gone with us. Where were you all day?"

"Well, I closed the sale on..."

Silvia opened a shoe box and showed her a pair of glittery red pumps that could give Dorothy some competition in Oz.

"...the house for the Wylands. You drove all the way to Northridge?"

Bradley rolled his eyes at the shoes. "They're great, hon." He looked at Marla. "Rosalie Wyland? Dwayne's cousin from Wyoming?"

"Am I the only person in this town who didn't know that?"

"Oh, Lordy lord, Marla. Will you look at this blouse? Isn't it to die for? Mom bought it for me. It's the perfect color for my eyes. I can't wait to wear it."

Brad cocked his head. "I thought you took them to see that house because Dwayne built it. You mean you didn't know they were related?"

"Not until I got to their motel today. He was there. He never said anything to me."

"Sis, wait till you see this." Charlene proceeded to peel off her blouse, revealing perfect rosy breasts barely covered with pale peach lace.

"Char! You're undressing in front of Dad!"

"Lord, Marla. He's our father."

"He's a man." She huffed and rolled her eyes at her twin's cluelessness.

Dadley squeezed his eyes shut. "I'll close my eyes."

"Turn your head, darling." Silvia put her hands on Bradley's shoulders and turned him away.

Marla glared at Charlene. "See? You can't just take your clothes off whenever the urge strikes. What are you doing?"

Instead of answering, Char slipped the blouse from the hanger and dropped it over her head. The heavy peach silk drifted down and settled on her breasts.

Marla sucked in a breath and pressed her hand against her chest. "Char, it was made for you."

"Isn't it perfect? Sil spotted it from clear across the sales floor."

Bradley twisted his head. "Can I look now?"

Silvia tugged his elbow and grinned. "Isn't she stunning, darling?"

Clutching his heart with thespian passion, he said, "You're the vision of a fairy princess, Charlene. I can barely breathe." He put a finger on her shoulder. "Turn. I want the full effect." She made a slow, complete circle. He spotted the price tag. "You paid a hundred-forty dollars for this?" His voice had risen a full octave.

Echoing Dadley's words, Marla said, "You paid a hundred-forty dollars for that?"

"Yes. It's a Vera Wang. We got it for half price." Hands to her cheeks, Char's feet thumped up and down running-in-place. "I'm so excited. I've never owned a Vera Wang."

Marla crossed her arms. "I can understand why, sis. I can't imagine paying that kind of money for a blouse."

Silvia lifted a Nordstrom bag from the floor and ruffled through a mountain of tissue. "Ta da! We got one for you too." The paper fluttered to the floor, and Mom held aloft the same style blouse in a deep shimmery aquamarine. "This will look beyond fabulous on you, Marla."

"Don't take off your sweatshirt in front of me, please. I'll have to close my eyes again." Dadley winked.

"Bradley, leave the room this minute!" Silvia smacked his shoulder and shoved him in the direction of the hall.

He grumbled. "I paid for it. Shouldn't I be allowed to get my money's worth?"

"You got more than your money's worth the day these girls were born. Now leave the room. I'll call you back in when she puts on the full outfit."

Marla touched the blouse, the silk cool and slick on her hand. "There's more?"

"Lordy, I can't wait. Get those ugly jeans and sweatshirt off. Mom bought the skirt they had on display with it. Both were in size twelve. It was like they knew we were coming."

They knew you were coming all right. I'm willing to bet the head of the women's department knows both of you by your first names. "Char. Mom. I can't wear this kind of expensive stuff. I never go anywhere. Anyway, I can't afford it."

"Don't worry, dear. Your father paid for it. We'll call it an early birthday present." She held up a beautiful ivory colored jacquard skirt, flat pleats all around with a back zipper. Marla nearly swooned. She'd never owned anything so beautiful.

"Our birthday isn't for five months! And it probably won't fit. I'll pass."

"Oh, no you don't." Charlene grabbed the bottom of her sweatshirt and pulled up. "Lift your arms."

"You're ganging up on me!" They paid no attention. While Charlene tugged the sweatshirt over her head, Silvia unbuttoned her jeans and pushed them down to her ankles.

"Kick off your shoes, dear, and step out of these."

I might as well accept defeat. Soon, Marla stood in the middle of her parent's living room barefooted, in her underwear. Her plain white, practical underwear.

"Lordy, we've got to get you some better lingerie."

"Char, I like my lingerie just fine."

"Maybe you do, but those things do not qualify as lingerie. You've got the body of an Italian movie actress. You should show it off with panache."

"Panache. I've been running short on that lately."

Silvia put a hand on her chin. "I'd forgotten what lovely curves you have. Charlene's right. You're not showing yourself to your best advantage."

"Who am I going to show myself to for the love of Pete!"

Charlene pursed her pretty mouth and pointed her finger at Marla's nose. "I plan to take care of that. I booked another single's dinner for next week."

"Charlene!"

Dad's voice echoed from the hall, "Can I see what my money bought?"

"No!" the three of them shouted.

Chapter Seven

What's with the boss lady today?" Cluny asked when he entered the door of the construction trailer. "She actually smiled at me just now."

Ignoring the question, Dwayne looked up from the scribbled note. "Did you take this phone call?"

"Huh? What phone call?"

Dwayne held up a piece of paper. "This note was beside the phone when I got here. It's dated today."

"What's it say?"

"I'm in town. I want to see the kid."

Cluny had his jacket off and was reaching for the coat peg when he stopped. For a second he stood like a department store mannequin. "Are you shittin' me? It's from Francine?"

He shrugged and furrowed his brow. "Doesn't say." Head swimming, he slumped in the squeaky desk chair. It couldn't be Francine, could it? He hadn't heard a peep from her since Amber was an infant. He'd hired private investigators to search for her and lawyers to handle the mountain of paperwork to get his divorce from her. She'd vanished as if she'd never existed. "I don't know who took the message."

Cluny stuck out his hand. "Give it to me." He held the bright pink "While You Were Out" note and squinted. "This is Slim's pathetic scrawl."

"Get him in here."

"He just left for the warehouse to get some pipe fittings. I told him to check with me when he got back." Cluny stared at the note and paced. "Crap. What if it is Francine? What are you going to do?"

Dwayne rubbed his temples. His neck and head pounded like they were in an enemy bombardment. "I don't know. I don't want her to see Amber."

"You got sole custody of Amber in the divorce. She has no parental rights." Cluny handed him the Styrofoam cup he'd just bought off the Gaggin' Wagon. "Here, you need some coffee."

"Thanks, bud." Dwayne blew on the cup and took a tentative sip. His stomach clenched when the hot coffee hit, but he took another swallow. "This'll help."

"I'm goin' back out to get myself another cup before Luis leaves to poison the next construction crew down the road." He put his jacket on and opened the door. "Be right back."

"Get a couple of those greasy doughnuts," Dwayne called before the door closed.

Worrisome thoughts bounced through his mind. What if it was Francine? Cluny nailed it—she had no legal right to see Amber, but did he have the moral right to deny his daughter the chance to meet her mother? Scalp tingling, he set the cup on the desk and raked his fingers through his hair. Scrubbing hands over his unshaven chin, he studied the note again. Slim hadn't written down a callback number.

Francine, she wanted something. Francine always wanted something. A relentless user, he remembered how she manipulated everyone around her into doing her bidding, including him.

He swiveled the chair around and pulled out a drawer in the file cabinet behind his desk. This is where he kept all the legal stuff. He didn't leave any of it at home where Amber might come across it.

The door opened and he stayed hunched over the drawer looking for the file. A gust of cold wind hit him in the back. "Did he have any doughnuts left?"

"What?"

He slammed the drawer shut and swung around, wincing when he twisted his left knee.

Marla dropped a pile of mail on his desk. He saw right away that she looked at his hand where he rubbed his leg.

"Nothing, I thought you were Cluny." He looked through the

stack. "Where'd all this come from?" If she got any more beautiful he'd have to join a seminary and take a vow of celibacy. Her glorious hair tumbled around her shoulders in windblown waves. *Please, God, I want a handful of that.*

"I stopped in to see Miss Emmaline. She asked me to bring this to you. It's probably junk. It's addressed to Big D Construction here, not your company address."

Dressed for business, there was still no way she could hide her fabulous rack and lush hips. He clenched his hands into fists to stop the itching in his palms. *Quit it, you idiot. Get your mind around what you're going to do if Francine is back in the picture!*

He cleared his throat. "You going someplace special?"

She followed his gaze and glanced down at her blouse. Her cheeks turned a delightful shade of pink. "Um, yes, I'm meeting Pete and Rosie at the escrow office. The seller accepted the offer and we're signing the papers on the house. I, uh, just wanted you to know I won't be around today."

"I'll try to survive without you breathing down my neck."

"Like you said at that fiasco called Singles Dinner Only, 'you're a jackass.'"

He grinned. "I need to work on that."

"No kidding."

She turned toward the door and gave him a good view of her curvy behind in clingy black slacks. He needed a bite of that.

"Shit!" Cluny bobbled the coffee and doughnuts when Marla flung the door open and nearly knocked him off the steps.

She stomped down the stairs. "Watch where you're going, McPherson. You nearly knocked me over."

"I nearly—?" He backed up, huffed, watched her leave, and stepped inside. "You must've said the right thing, Gunny. Her smile is gone."

"Yeah, I seem to have a knack for it." Dwayne reached for the paper-wrapped doughnuts. "What's taking Slim so long?"

"That's his truck pulling in now."

"Give him a shout. I need him to translate this note."

———

If there was a single individual in the entire universe who irritated her more than Dwayne Dempsey, she didn't know who it could be. Well, maybe Charlene sometimes, and definitely her mother, but Dwayne? He was the champion irritator of all time.

And why was everybody picking on her lately? First Dadley telling her to quit managing the family, Sil and Charlene insisting on *improving* her wardrobe, and the topper—Dempsey by a mile.

If he didn't quit staring at her boobs, she'd sock him in the nose one of these days. And his snarky remarks about trying to manage without her? It was *her* building he was renovating, not his. The man drove her nuts.

Sure, he was tall, dark, single and sexy, and he had a sweet child, but he worked for her, darn it! Swaggering around the construction lot like he was God's gift, giving orders to everybody, including her.

Well, okay, he could give orders to them, but not to her. He worked for her!

She gripped the steering wheel and ignored the prickles invading every muscle in her body, especially the ones she sat on, and told herself to calm down. Maybe Dadley had a point. Maybe she did try to control everything and everyone. It wasn't like she thought the world would stop if she got off. It *would* stop for her but keep right on turning without her.

What a horrible thought. True, though.

She clenched her jaw and nodded. "Okay, Marla, here's the plan. You'll put on those obscenely expensive Vera Wang's, buy a pair of super sexy shoes, glam yourself up with Charlene's expert help, and go to the singles dinner. Then show Edwin, the zombie, the door." For emphasis she gave herself a schoolmistress scowl in the rearview mirror.

Charlene's voice answered through the phone speaker. "It's about time." Marla nearly lost control of the car.

"Char, you scared me half to death! Why are you calling?"

"You called me!"

"No, I...oh, for the love of...I accidentally pushed the phone button on the steering wheel." What idiot of an engineer thought of putting it there in the first place? It was a wonder she hadn't run right off the road.

"Serendipity. I was about to call you to make sure you were on for the singles dinner."

"Look, I've got an appointment. I'll discuss the dinner with you tonight."

"Okay, I'll see you and the boys later."

Two hours later she handed Rosalie Wyland the keys to the house that Dempsey built. The woman's excitement gave Marla a warm feeling of satisfaction. As she turned to leave, a van pulled into the driveway.

"Oh, wait, Marla. Here's Dylan. Stay and say hello."

Marla smiled and waved as Dwayne's big brother stepped out of the shiny black van with *Spring Grove Furniture and Design* painted in fancy gold script on the side.

Rosie ran down the walk and jumped into Dylan's open arms. "You already changed the name? I love it. Marla, look, Dylan already changed the name on the van."

Marla smiled. "Hi, Dylan, great to see you." Since when had he matured into such a good-looking man? He strongly resembled Dwayne, only taller and more slender. Those Dempsey boys got some of their looks from John, but their mother, Kathleen, must have been tall with blue-green eyes like Kate Middleton. Marla couldn't remember Kathleen that clearly. She'd left Spring Grove when they were all pretty young, and Dwayne had gone with her.

"It's been a while since the two of you have seen each other, I'll bet."

"It's been too long," Dylan said, and leaned in to kiss Marla's cheek. "How have you been, babe? I haven't seen you in a long time. I forgot how gorgeous you are."

Marla felt her blush rising. She'd had a crush on Dylan Dempsey when they were in school. "I'm still waiting for you to ask me to the senior prom, Dyl. You broke my heart. I cry myself to sleep every night thinking about it."

Dylan threw his head back with a hearty laugh, put an arm around her and Rosalie, and walked them to the front door. "Let's go inside and see what we have to work with here. I haven't seen this place since Big D finished building it."

Marla trailed behind them as Rosalie walked through the house snapping dozens of pictures with her cell phone. A warm glow encompassed Marla. One of the most rewarding aspects of a real estate sale was a happy buyer.

Marla's iPhone vibrated in her pocket. She returned to the entry hall and answered, "Hello, Char."

"Are you still coming for dinner tonight? The boys and I have finalized all the plans for Dadley's no-longer-a-surprise birthday party. We want your seal of approval."

"You don't need my seal of approval, but yes, I'll be there. Six?"

"Make it six-thirty. The boys can't be here before seven. You know how bad the traffic on the 210 freeway is with everybody heading home on a Monday night. You and I can put the final touches on dinner before they show up."

"Okay, sis. See you then." She clicked off the phone and returned it to her pocket. Dylan was staring at her, chin in hand. "What?"

"I was wondering if you could make it over for dinner tonight. Grace would love to see you. It's been too long."

"Thanks, Dyl. I can't make it. Charlene is up to her earlobes in the final tweaking for Dad's birthday party. The twins and I are having dinner tonight at her place."

"That's right, Brad's party is next Saturday evening. Grace and I will be there with our kids. It's been a long time since all the Danahers and Dempseys got together for a high old time. We're hoping Donovan can get away from Camp Pendleton for the weekend to join us."

"Donovan! He's the Dempsey I haven't seen in forever. How's he doing?"

Dylan's face filled with pride when he spoke of his little brother. "Master Sergeant, Donovan Dempsey, made it back in one piece from his third tour in Iraq, thanks be to God. He's up for reenlistment, but he hasn't made a decision on it yet. I haven't seen him myself for almost a year."

Marla pictured the gangly brunette with devilish eyes who always tagged behind Dylan. "Did he ever marry that girl in San Diego?"

"No. She wouldn't play second fiddle to the Marines. Poor old Donovan got a Dear John letter half-way through his second deployment."

"You better warn him in advance that Charlene's on the prowl."

"Still?"

"Always. A single Marine? He'll be added to the endangered species list once he sets foot in Spring Grove."

———

Dwayne held up the phone message. "So who left this, Slim?"

"It was a woman, Gunny. Sorry. I asked her, but she wouldn't leave her name, she said you'd know who it was."

"Six-thirty a.m. That right?" Maybe it wasn't Francine. She never got up before ten in the morning.

"Yeah, the phone was ringing when I opened up this morning. Anything else? Cluny's waiting for me to help with that load of copper pipe."

"Did you ask her to leave a number?"

"Said she was on the move and would call back."

"Okay, bud. Thanks. Get to that pipe before Cluny blows a gasket." He clapped Slim on the shoulder, sat heavily in his chair, and stared at the wrinkled scrap of bright pink paper. His ears had been ringing ever since that last battle in Iraq, but the high-pitched squeal now reached deafening volume.

Francine wanted to see "the kid." No. He'd decided that was not going to happen on his watch. Thanks to his misguided parenting, Amber had a little girl's fairytale notion about the selfish tramp. He'd done it to protect her, had allowed her to nurture whimsy, hoping the day would never come when he'd have to tell her the truth. His gut cramped.

He'd run out of time.

Chapter Eight

Marla smiled when she saw the results of Saturday night preparations for Dad's birthday party. Everything had come together like clockwork.

Charlene, Harry, and Barry, with little direction from her, presented a mouthwatering Mexican buffet feast on the back patio. Pork sizzled on the barbecue, filling the mild spring evening air, and the neighborhood, with delicious aromas.

Since all their old neighbors were among the invited guests, they were not tortured by enticing smells. The feast was for the neighbors as well as other family, friends, and business acquaintances of Brad and Silvia.

Marla answered the front doorbell for the tenth time. Okay, it was time to do something about that. She slapped together a makeshift sign directing arriving guests through the side gate leading to the back-yard. Then she joined Harry at the beverage table.

"Remember all the great birthday parties we had here when we were kids?" Harry asked.

"How about the backyard camp-outs? Char and I loved to terrorize you boys and your friends with ghost stories in your tent on dark nights. I'm still wondering why the cops never got called when the neighbors heard the blood-curdling screams." Marla chuckled at the memories. "Holy goats," she pointed to the latest arrivals. "Do you believe that?"

They watched as Silvia rushed to greet John and Irene Dempsey and threw her arms around Irene like a long-lost friend. John stood by, bemused at her turnabout.

"Beats me." Harry poured a Coke for a young lady who'd sidled up to the table. He rewarded her with a dazzling smile.

Her heart went out to the poor girl. Twenty-year-old Harry was well out of her reach, if she harbored any romantic notions.

Marla touched her shoulder. "Hello, Renee. My, how you've grown. I remember when Charlene and I walked next door to babysit you. What are you now? A junior in high school?"

Crestfallen, Renee sighed and said, "I'll be a senior in September. I'm seventeen and a half." She cast a hopeful, moon-eyed glance at Harry, who'd turned away to serve another guest.

"Well, you have a good time tonight. We've got some fun things planned for the younger crowd."

The baleful glance Renee threw over her shoulder told Marla she didn't consider herself one of the kids interested in games.

Charlene waved Marla over to the food buffet. She sighed and placed a hand on her chest. "Oh, lord. Did you see who came in with Dylan and Grace and their kids?" She pointed to the back corner of the lawn where Donovan Dempsey, sporting a Marine haircut and dressed in jeans and a T-shirt, stood talking to Renee's father. The shirt, snug on his broad chest, emphasized his shoulders to perfection.

"Oh, I see Donovan got leave. Dylan told me he was stationed at Camp Pendleton and would try to get here tonight." She pursed her lips and made a low whistle. "He looks like a real lady-killer, doesn't he?"

"That's Donovan Dempsey?" Charlene gaped. "In that case, I aim to get killed. The last time I saw him, he was skinny and zit-faced. How old is he?" She patted her chest and swooned with drama.

"Hmm, let me think. Dylan is thirty-three and Dwayne is thirty-one, so Donovan must be about twenty-nine. No question, he turned out to be the best looking one of the Dempsey boys."

"Is he married?" Charlene tugged at the hem of her tank top, exposing more cleavage, and fluffed her hair. "He was engaged the last I heard."

"No, Dylan said his girlfriend walked away while Donovan was on deployment."

"She must be nuts. Stay here. I'm going re-introduce myself to him."

Before she could protest, Charlene was halfway across the yard, hips swaying as she pranced in high wedge sandals. Marla had the urge to yell, *Donovan! Incoming! Char has you in her sights!*

"Marla!" Amber ran to her. "Where's Skipper?"

"Hi there, girlfriend. Skipper stayed home tonight. There are too many people here and the gate would be opening and closing all evening. I was afraid he'd get stepped on or get out of the yard."

Amber's face fell, her stricken look almost comical. "I love Skippy. I wanted to see him."

Marla leaned down and lifted her chin. "Tell you what. I'm taking him to the dog park tomorrow. Would you like to go with us?"

Eyes bright, a big smile bloomed on her face. "Can I?"

"Ask your dad. If he says it's okay, I'll pack a lunch and pick you up about eleven—" Before she finished the sentence, Amber streaked away across the patio searching for Dwayne.

"That's one excited little girl." Bradley put his hand on her shoulder. "What did you do, promise her the moon?"

"Hi, Dad. Almost as good. I invited her to come with me and Skip to the dog park tomorrow." She leaned into him and dropped her head on his shoulder. "Happy Birthday."

"Thank you. This is a great party. Did you happen to notice your mother when she greeted Irene and John?"

Marla snorted. "What did you drug her with?"

Brad squeezed her in a one-armed hug. "She'll always be a mystery to me. Looks like she decided to drop the grudge. Maybe she got bored maintaining it." He shook his head and fixed his gaze on his wife. "Look at her. She is more beautiful every year."

"Dad, if I could find a man like you I'd get married tomorrow. You're perfect."

"Don't put me on a pedestal, sweetheart. Take a look around here. There are two strapping, eligible bachelors here tonight. Looks like Charlene isn't wasting any time. Donovan Dempsey won't know what hit him." He chuckled and kissed her cheek. "I'm going to circulate. Have fun tonight, that's an order."

Unexpectedly awash with sadness, Marla watched her dad join

John, Irene, and Silvia. The men exchanged handshakes and drifted off, leaving the women chatting and laughing like best friends. Why the sadness? Her life was going great. She had a great job, her condo renovation investment promised to be profitable, and she'd have the funds to buy more Spring Grove real estate. What more could she want?

Hunger began to drive people to the buffet, and Marla smiled while handing over plates. "Eat up. Charlene and the boys ordered enough food for an invading army."

Rick Sandoval, a Cal Tech schoolmate of Harry and Barry, played Mexican music on his classical guitar on the far corner of the patio. His rich baritone voice filled the coming darkness with romantic love songs beneath the winking lights strung under the awning.

Her heart squeezed in spite of the festive atmosphere and the happy laughter of the large crowd.

What's wrong with me?

———

Dwayne watched Marla from the corner of his eye, wondering why she had such a dejected look on her face. The party couldn't be better. All the planning she and her sister had done seemed to be going off without a hitch.

Her wild strawberry blonde hair reflected the twinkling lights on the patio, seeming to sparkle as strands drifted in the breeze. He'd agreed to let Amber go on the picnic in the dog park tomorrow. Now he wondered if that was such a good idea. He should talk to Marla about it first, and make sure it was her idea and not Amber's.

She probably had better things to do than babysit his kid on a Sunday afternoon. Wasn't that the day women set aside to pamper themselves with facials and manicures? Hand-wash their filmy lingerie, take long bubble baths in candlelight, and listen to romantic music?

Jeez, Dwayne, get a grip. You're talking yourself into a sexual fantasy over the woman.

Charlene's laughter distracted him, and he drifted toward her and Donovan. Dylan got there just ahead of him. "What are you two laughing about?"

Donovan gestured to his brothers. "Come over here. Char and I were just remembering that fiasco during the homecoming football game in your senior year."

Dylan rolled his eyes. "Look, I threw the ball right at Dwayne. It's not my fault he was showboating and tripped over his own big feet, and then landed right on top of Grace at the sidelines."

"Right at me, my foot! I had to jump a yard off the ground to reach the damn thing." He grinned and winked. "It was kind of nice to be on top of Grace in the grass for a few seconds though. Sorry I never got another chance."

Dylan gave him a light punch on the shoulder. "No, and you never will, brother." His head jerked back. "Oh, my god! Is that Francine?" He nodded to the side of the yard by the gate.

Dwayne's heart nearly stopped when he spun around. Francine, the woman he never expected to see again, was making her way toward several kids playing tag. Amber was among them. Heart racing now, he fast-walked to intercept her.

"What the hell are you doing here?" he demanded.

"I came to see my kid." Her nostrils flared with defiance as she came to a stop. "I have a right to see her. Which one is she?"

"You have no rights where she's concerned." He grabbed her arm and turned her in the direction of the gate, ignoring her angry struggles. When he reached the gate, he threw it open and pulled her outside. "You gave up any rights you had when you walked out on us. She was two weeks old. Just two weeks! That fact hardly earns you a mother-of-the-year-award. Get away from here." His face inches from hers, he added, "Now!"

"You get your hands off me." She yanked her arm from his grip and took a step back. "She's my kid and I want to see her."

"Over my dead body, Francine. Now get the hell away from here."

When she glanced over his shoulder, he turned to see his brothers take up positions on either side of him.

"Well, well, well. A wall of Dempsey's against little old me." She glared at them. "I'll be back Dwayne, and next time I'll have the cops with me. She's my kid."

"Good luck with that," he shouted at her retreating back.

She whipped around and sneered. "You're not her father, asshole."

Pain and anger ripped through him. He lunged for her. His brothers held him back.

"What the hell is she talking about?" Donovan mumbled.

"Is she nuts? Where did that come from?" Dylan asked.

Dwayne flexed his fists, jammed his hands in his pockets, and took a couple of steps in Francine's direction. She yanked open the passenger door of a battered blue Mustang and got in. The man in the driver's seat pulled away from the curb and sped down the street. He'd seen that car somewhere.

Dizziness swam in Dwayne's vision. He bent forward and braced his hands on his knees to keep from falling over.

Dylan grabbed one of his arms. "Take it easy, bro. She's always been nothing but hot air."

Donovan took his other arm. "Come over here," he urged. "Sit on the garden bench. We'll hang out here for a while and make sure she doesn't come back."

Head in his hands, Dwayne rocked back and forth on his butt. "Shit. What a nightmare. Why is she here now?"

"Daddy?"

At the sound of Amber's voice, Dwayne's head flew up. She trotted in his direction. His dad, John, tried to catch up with her. "Come back here, honey. Your dad's okay."

"Daddy, who was that lady?"

Dwayne extended his arm and drew her into a hug. "Nobody you need to be concerned about. Everything is fine. Go back to the party with Grampa. I'll be there in a minute." He patted her head and urged her into his dad's arms.

John lifted her. "Time to get dinner. Grampa Brad has a nice picnic table all set up for you kids. Did you see that big birthday cake? No? Well, let's go have a look at it, sugar." They disappeared behind the gate. It clanged shut.

Dylan sat beside Dwayne. Donovan paced back and forth in front of them, eyes on the street.

"What did Francine mean when she said, 'you're not her father'?" Dylan asked.

"God, I don't know. She was raving."

Donovan stopped in front of him. "She was screwing around the whole time you were in Iraq, then when you were in Bethesda. Everybody knew that."

"Yeah, and it was nice of 'everybody' to let me know," Dwayne sneered. "My thanks to all of you."

Dylan grabbed his shoulder. "Knock it off. You know why we kept our mouths shut about it. For one thing, it wasn't our business and for another, you had enough to deal with without that thrown into the mix."

"You'd have been a lot better off if you'd never got mixed up with that witch," Donovan added.

Dwayne sat straight as fury burned in his chest. It wasn't their fault. He knew that. It was his choice to go after Francine and rush into marriage before he deployed. It was no secret that she'd been around the block a few times before she married him.

"That's one way to look at it, but if I hadn't married her I wouldn't have Amber. She's the best thing that ever happened to me."

That shut them up for the moment.

Donovan paced. Dylan joined him. After a moment he walked away from them to the street.

"Where are you going, Dyl?" Dwayne called.

"I'm going to drive around and see if she's still in the neighborhood."

Dwayne stood. "Wait, I'll go with you." He had no idea what he'd do if they spotted her. What could they do?

"No, you stay here and look after your daughter. I won't be long."

"Come on. Let's go back before everybody comes out here to investigate." Donovan nudged Dwayne.

"Yeah. Okay." He stood and they re-entered the Danaher's back yard. "I can't think. I don't know what to do."

"We'll figure something out."

Chapter Nine

Marla detected the flurry of anxiety whiffing through the party crowd when the strange woman came through the back gate, and more so when Dwayne quickly escorted her out.

She left the buffet table and joined Charlene. "Who was that?"

Char took her arm and moved away from the children. Alarm still registered on several of the Dempsey adult faces, but most of the kids remained oblivious to the incident. "Dwayne's ex-wife," she whispered. "She just showed up out of nowhere. His brothers followed them, probably to help get rid of her."

"Why in the name of green grass would she come *here* looking for him? And how could she have known he'd be here? Our parents never had anything to do with her that I know of. She and Dwayne met and married in Wyoming, didn't they?"

"Lordy, how would I know? I've never seen the woman before. The Dempseys seem pretty upset about it though." Charlene's eyes scanned the crowd. "It looks as though most of the other guests didn't take notice."

"Oh, look. There's John. He's got Amber, but the brothers are still out there."

Marla and Charlene jumped when they heard their mother's voice behind them. "Come, girls. Let's gather the children to their table and feed them. It'll be a good distraction. I don't want anything to spoil Brad's party."

"Mom, that was Dwayne's wife, right?"

"Ex-wife. I can't imagine why she turned up here. Johnny said nobody had heard so much as a whisper since she disappeared. That was years before Dwayne moved back to Spring Grove to take over John's business." She led them to the buffet. "You girls make up some plates. I'll get the children seated."

Marla checked her watch. Several minutes passed before Dwayne and his two brothers returned to the party. They went about checking on the kids, then made their way to the buffet table and loaded up on food as if nothing had happened.

"Marla, I need to talk to you," Dwayne said quietly when his plate was full. "Would you sit with me for a minute?" His serious gaze lingered on hers for a beat.

"Uh, sure. I'll get my dinner and be right there."

"Thanks." He nodded and carried his plate away.

Char's eyes swam with curiosity, and she wasted no time stepping close to Marla. "What did he want? Did he tell you anything? About his wife? Where did she come from?"

"For heaven's sake, Charlene. He said he needed to talk to me. That's all. Now, move over and hand me a plate. I'll tell you later."

"You'd better. Word for word." She fluffed her hair. "I'll go sit with Donovan. Maybe he'll tell me something." She tottered across the lawn and sat on the grass next to the good-looking Marine. Marla suspected she was angling for more than information.

Although she was as curious as her sister, maybe more, Dwayne's expression had alarmed her. She'd spent enough time in his company to know when he was deeply upset. The strange woman had him in a tailspin.

She joined him at a small wire bistro table with two chairs under a large eucalyptus. "What's going on, Dempsey?"

He took a long swallow of soda before answering. "It's complicated."

"I got that much on my own." She hated beating around the bush. "Was she your wife?"

"*Ex*-wife."

"What did she want? Why was she here? Did somebody in your

family invite her?" As bizarre as it sounded, the thought had entered her mind.

"Not unless they had an early death wish." He set the bottle down and leaned back. "I got a phone message last Monday. All it said was, 'I want to see the kid.'" He sighed and shook his head. "Then nothing until she showed up here out of the blue."

"What are you going to do?"

"Jeez, Red, I hate getting you involved in this."

"Hey, you work for me, so I'm already involved. I'm crazy about Amber, about all your family with the exception of you." She grinned when he flashed a glare.

"You are a piece of work, Danaher." A hint of smile tipped the corner of his lips.

"I'm kidding. What are your plans? What do you want me to do?"

"I need some time off. School's out for the summer on Wednesday. I'm going to take Amber to stay with my mom at her ranch in Wyoming."

"You're going to be gone all summer? But what about—?"

Her stomach lurched at the thought of him abandoning her project. At the same time, she cursed herself for thinking of her interests when Dwayne had a family emergency to deal with.

"No." He waved his hands. "I'll take a few days to get her settled then come back. I want to leave her there until I find out what Francine is up to."

He stopped talking when one of her twin brothers approached them with a large bowl of tortilla chips.

"Uh, thanks, uh…" Dwayne took a handful of chips and put them on his plate.

Marla smiled, knowing he had no idea whether it was Harry or Barry.

"Name's Barry." He glanced at her. "Want some, BS? Going fast."

"No thanks, sweetie. We're good."

Barry strolled away, offering chips as he went from table to table.

"How the heck can you tell them apart?" He stared at Barry's back, then over to Harry who still manned the bar while eating between pouring drinks. "Why did he call you BS?"

Marla smiled. "Stands for Big Sister. The boys like to ration words. As for telling them apart, even our parents have a hard time with it."

She smiled while thinking how mean she was not to tell Mom and Dad her secret way to identify them. A tiny fleck in Barry's iris. She noticed it the day they came home from the hospital and had kept it to herself for twenty years.

"Let's get back on the subject, Dempsey. When are you leaving, and who will take over while you're gone?"

"Not you? I thought you'd jump at the chance to run the whole operation."

"Jerk."

"Yeah, I am, especially today."

"Every day." Which made it difficult for her to understand why she was increasingly attracted to him. Maybe because he wouldn't jump to her tune.

"Cluny will take over. He's a subcontractor, but I'll have him sign a waiver if that'll make you feel more comfortable. He'll have to leave now and then to attend to his own business."

"A waiver's not necessary. But aren't you about to tackle the finishing work inside? That's going to make it difficult to work around Miss Emmaline." Grateful for not having to relocate, the old woman had not uttered a single complaint about living in the middle of a construction zone.

"I'll take her with us. She'll have a little vacation on the ranch while we do the work in her apartment."

"What a good idea. I've lost sleep over how you were going to accomplish your final bit without disturbing her." His concern for their old nanny touched her. He had a big soft spot for the woman. "Do you think she'll mind?"

"Nah. She always liked my mother but wasn't happy when I left here at sixteen to move up there. I'm sure they'll have a good time catching up and badmouthing Dad. Mom has tons of room in the old ramshackle house she grew up in."

"How long has she owned the ranch?"

He hesitated. "In reality, I'm the legal owner. Grandad left it to me in his will with the caveat that Mom could live there for the rest of her life if she chose."

"You own the ranch in Wyoming? How do Dylan and Donovan feel about that?"

"Except for having it available to them for family vacations, they have no interest in owning three thousand acres of Wyoming ranchland."

Three thousand acres!

Her real estate broker's brain went into high gear. "Three thousand acres? It must be worth millions. What do you plan to do with it?"

He shrugged. "Go back someday, I suppose. Mom has a good crew but someday she'll get tired running all those cattle and bison."

"Why bison?" Weren't all the bison in Yellowstone Park?

He grinned. "They're good to eat, Danaher. What do you think the Plains Indian tribes lived off for hundreds of years? They weren't growing wheat."

"Don't be a smart aleck. How would I know? The closest I ever got to a wilderness is Sequoia and Yosemite parks."

He snorted. "Compared to Montana and Wyoming, those parks are like downtown Denver. You really are a pampered city girl, aren't you?"

"And you're really a jackass, aren't you?"

Face relaxed, Dwayne laughed. "You're good for my black mood, Red."

She failed to keep the smile from growing on her face and shook her head in defeat.

They ate the fast-cooling food in comfortable silence for a few minutes, then Marla said, "What about taking Amber to the dog park tomorrow? Do you think I should cancel it?"

"I hate to disappoint her. So, if it's okay with you I'll come along too. I need to keep an eye on her in case Francine shows up."

"Oh. Uh, okay, sure."

Squealing children drew their eyes to the patio. Bradley's cake had been lighted and flamed like a small forest fire. A raucous version of *Happy Birthday* began. "Come on, Red. Let's help with the chorus. I want a big slab of cake before it disappears." He reached for her hand, and without analyzing her action, she grasped his. A melting sensation filled her middle and grew warmer when he tightened his grip and tugged her toward the crowd.

Dwayne got his big slab of cake and there still remained enough for another party. Marla gave Charlene credit for innovative thinking because she'd brought a couple dozen small cake boxes for guests to take the leftovers. Char and Donovan got busy cutting and boxing cake and stacking the boxes high on the table.

Amber whispered in Marla's ear, "Uncle Donovan has a new girl-friend." She pointed to him and Charlene packaging the cake. "I heard him ask her out on a rill date."

"No kidding?" Why was she not surprised? "Where are they going?"

"They're having a picnic in the dog park with us tomorrow, right Daddy?"

Marla blinked and stared at Dwayne.

"Oh, did I forget to mention that?" He stared back with childlike innocence.

"Duh. Why don't I stay up all night making sandwiches? How many more did you invite, Dempsey?"

"None, and they're bringing their own sandwiches, Red, so relax. Anyway, I think they need chaperoning, don't you?"

"Donovan looks like he can take care of himself."

"I don't want Charlene taking advantage of my little brother's broken heart."

"What! You told me it was broken years ago."

"Yeah, but you never know. He has PRSD."

She scrunched her face in confusion. "Do you mean PTSD?"

"No. PRSD: Past Romance Stinks Disorder."

Marla crossed her eyes and mouthed, *Jackass.*

"Uncle Donovan and his new girlfriend will be happy playing in the park with Skipper, Daddy."

"We'll all have fun chasing Marla's mouse till he drops, right?"

Amber grinned and ran off to join Dylan's kids.

"Look, the real reason I'd like Donovan along is in case Francine shows up. I could use an extra set of eyes."

Dwayne reached to tuck an errant curl behind her ear. Heart thud-ding, breath caught in her throat, the warmth of his fingers coursed through her cheek and neck. His closeness threatened to unravel her composure. "I know I'm not allowed to say it, Danaher, but you're beautiful."

His words stole her breath. Giggling nervously, she said, "You've had too much beer. Let's get some coffee."

"I don't drink alcohol, remember?"

Did he mean what he'd said when he'd touched her? She didn't want to complicate her well-ordered life, to get hurt. They'd become friendlier, that's all.

Friends? Who was she kidding? The guy had cast some sort of spell on her. Why would she want to get entangled with Dwayne Dempsey any more than she already was? He worked for her, and he had a crazy ex-wife to deal with.

She'd get a grip on her emotions, starting tomorrow.

Chapter Ten

MARLA PLACED THE HAM AND SWISS SANDWICHES FOR HER AND Dwayne and a PB&J for Amber in a cardboard box by her front door. As an afterthought, she dropped a handful of dog cookies on top. She returned to the kitchen for her small beverage cooler and opened it to check if she'd forgotten anything. No, it was all there, iced coffee, milk, bottled water, and two cans of Dr. Pepper.

She'd made a quick run to the store this morning to get the Dr. Pepper because she knew Dwayne preferred it. She had second thoughts about taking it. He knew she didn't drink the vile stuff, so he'd think she'd bought it for him. That didn't mean anything other than she was a thoughtful, considerate person, right? Her hand hovered over the cans for a couple of seconds, then she snapped the top down. He could think whatever he wanted. Why did she care?

Skipper barked at the sound of Amber's voice calling his name. He made a skittering beeline for the front door and yipped impatiently for her to open it. Marla failed to grab Skip before he bounded out the door into Amber's arms.

Dwayne strolled up the front walk behind Amber and grinned. "Hey, Red."

"Hey, Dempsey." She handed him the box with sandwiches. "I'll get the cooler and Skipper's harness."

He stepped inside. "We're a little early. I'd like Amber to use your bathroom before we leave. She was so excited to see that little rat dog of yours, I couldn't get her to go before we left home."

"Oh, sure. Set the box down there." She called her dog in a sing-song voice, "Skipper wipper, come to Mama. I've got a treat for you." The fickle mutt immediately lost interest in Amber and bounded into the house, eyes bugging with anticipation.

Dwayne placed his hand on his daughter's head. "Let Marla show you where her bathroom is, squirt. You need to make a latrine call before we head to the park, okay?"

Amber sighed with reluctance. "Oookay."

She took Marla's extended hand and followed her to the guest bathroom. Marla lingered outside the door in case the child needed anything, but in reality she needed a moment to get her wits back to normal.

"Everything okay?"

She nearly jumped out of her shoes at Dwayne's rumbling voice right behind her.

"Cripes, Dwayne, you nearly scared me to death sneaking up on me like that!" She smacked his shoulder. "Darn it!"

He laughed and rubbed his arm. "At ease, soldier. You need your hearing checked. I wasn't sneaking, sorry."

She closed her eyes, pressed overlapping hands on her breastbone, and willed her breathing to slow. He trailed a finger down her arm. Her eyes flew open. "What are you doing?"

"Touching you."

"Don't." She leaned back against the door. Amber opened it, and Marla nearly fell on her bottom before Dwayne grabbed her and pulled her to his chest.

"Whoa there." He stepped back. "Okay?"

She nodded, mute.

"What's wrong, Daddy?"

"Nothing, squirt. Marla stumbled. I caught her."

"Can we go now? I want to play ball with Skippy."

———

Dwayne carried the box and cooler to his truck. He lifted Amber then Skip to the backseat while Marla returned to unlock the house and retrieve a picnic blanket she'd forgotten. Was it any wonder? The shock wave that rolled over them when he'd pressed her to his chest still vibrated every muscle in his body. She'd felt it too. She could deny it all she wanted, but her face said it all.

"Got everything?" he asked when she reached the truck. He held the door open for her.

Her voice breathy, she replied, "Yes," and stepped inside. He was rewarded with a great close-up of her butt in tight denim Capri's. "Jesus," he groaned.

"Did you say something?" Her suspicious brown eyes inquired from her flushed face.

"Nope." Dwayne closed the door and rounded the front of the truck to the driver's side. He started the engine and backed from her drive.

Marla looked over her shoulder. "Hold Skipper on your lap, honey, so he doesn't fall if your dad has to stop fast."

Dwayne shook his head and cast a sour look at her. "I know how to drive." He slammed the brakes to avoid hitting a compact car that seemed to appear out of nowhere.

"I can see that." Marla clutched the handle above the passenger window. She giggled. "Good job."

Could this eight-minute drive to Lemon Tree Dog Park get any more awkward? At least Amber's steady chatter to Skipper filled the truck with happy noise and gave him a chance to regain his equilibrium. It was a good thing Charlene and Donovan would also be there.

Marla pointed. "That's Char's car. I don't see them, do you?" She leaned forward and craned her neck.

"They're at the picnic table at the edge of the old lemon grove." He tilted his head. "Over there."

"Oh, good, they're in the shade."

He suspected the relief in her voice had more to do with the fact her sister and his brother were already here and less to do with the shade. "I'm going to park at the end. It's a bit of a walk, but by the time we leave, this part of the lot will be in the direct sun. The seats will get hotter than a griddle."

"Ah, good thinking."

He parked and lifted Amber out of the backseat, then handed the sandwich box to Marla. "Hold on to that critter, squirt. He's itchin' to join those other dogs behind the fence." Carrying the cooler in the direction of the tables, he reached for Amber's hand and led the way.

"Wait, Dwayne."

He stopped and looked over his shoulder. "What? Did we forget something?"

"No. I'm going to let Amber take Skip inside. I need to show her how to work the gate." She motioned for Amber to join her at the fence.

Marla pointed. "See this thing? It's the dog park tag scanner. You need to hold Skip still in front of it for a second and the gate will unlock. See? When you go in and out you must be very careful that no other dog gets out. As soon as you're inside, make sure it latches, then let Skipper off the leash. He'll run and join the other dogs, but soon as he works off some of his excitement, he'll come back to play with you. Okay?"

Dwayne watched Amber nod her understanding of Marla's instructions. His kid was smart and eager to please. He didn't doubt she'd follow them to the letter. He couldn't look at her without a big swell of love in his heart. God, she was beautiful, and she was his daughter.

"Have fun," he said, "and come to the table when you get hungry."

"Okay, Daddy." She shut the gate tight and let the dog go.

Marla joined him. "You have a very special little girl." She bit her cheek to suppress her smile. "Hard to believe you're her father."

He grabbed his chest. "That hurts."

"Uh, oh," Marla said. "Do you see what I see?"

"If you're referring to the unmistakable afterglow of great sex on both their faces, then yes, I see it."

"I was afraid that would happen. Charlene is relentless when she sets her sights on a good-looking man. Poor Donovan."

"Why poor Donovan? He looks like a satisfied and happy man to me. Why not poor Charlene?"

Marla sighed. "She tends to love 'em and leave 'em. I'd feel bad if Donovan expected her to stick."

"Give it a rest, willya? He's a twenty-nine-year-old Marine combat veteran. She's the one you should worry about, if that's something you feel you need to do. Why not just smile and be happy they had a great time in the sack, which it's obvious they did?"

"Go to hell, Dempsey." She bumped his shoulder and stormed ahead of him.

"Most likely." He shook his head. He'd managed to get her Irish up again. He couldn't say anything without making her mad, but he was right, damn it. She should mind her own business. As adults, Charlene and Donovan were fully capable of making their own decisions.

They reached the table to the smiles and waves of Marla's sister and his little brother. Dwayne set down the cooler and fist-bumped Donovan. "I'm hungry, how about you guys?"

His eyes bored into Donovan's. Dwayne tilted his head and raised his eyebrows. His brother answered the unspoken question with a barely perceptible head-shake. No sign of Francine.

Charlene grinned from ear to ear and leaned into Donovan's shoulder. "I'm starved. We thought you'd never get here, huh, Donnie?" She gazed into his eyes and without a hint of shyness. Donovan bent to kiss her.

"Yeah," he said when he came up for air, "we're starved." He gave her a squeeze and grinned at Dwayne and Marla.

Dwayne got the full meaning of his brother's grin. *Look what I bagged, bro.* He took the sandwich box from Marla, set it on the table, and whispered in her ear, "If anyone other than your sister called him Donnie, they'd get knocked on their ass." Then is a normal voice, he said, "Let's eat, Red. What have you got to drink?"

He popped open the lid of the cooler. Two cans of Dr. Pepper. She cared enough to go out and buy them especially for him. Promising.

He lifted one of the cans. "Thanks, Red, very thoughtful." Under the table he put his hand on her thigh and squeezed, then silently laughed at the blush blooming on her cheeks.

"Y-you're welcome," she stuttered. "I had some in the refrigerator."

Like hell you did, gorgeous.

He left his palm on her leg. She shoved it away. He put it back.

She stood and said, "I have to check on Skipper."

Charlene grinned at Dwayne when her sister walked away. "Don't ever find yourself drowning alongside that dog, because you'd be second in line for Marla to save."

"I get the picture."

———

Grateful for Charlene's endless chatter, Marla worked to relax, if that was even possible with Dempsey's big warm hand on her leg. She reached under the table again and lifted it away. He squeezed her fingers and let go. She couldn't look at him, so she nodded wide-eyed at Charlene, pretending to be interested in what she had to say.

"Then when we got to my apartment, I couldn't find my keys. It's not possible to lose keys between turning off the ignition of my car and walking to my front door, which can't be more than fifteen feet from the curb, but that's exactly what I did. You should have seen us crawling around the grass in the dark looking for them." She giggled and gazed into Donovan's eyes. "Right, Donnie?"

"Right, sugar." He kissed her again.

Marla cleared her throat. "Should Dwayne and I move to another table? I get the feeling we're intruding on a very intimate moment here."

"Oh, lord, Marla. Don't be a sourpuss."

She was about to respond to her sister's insult when Dwayne put his hand back on her leg. The retort got firmly stuck in her throat.

"Hey, why don't we change the subject?" Dwayne suggested. "Donovan, I'm taking Amber and Miss Emmaline up to Wyoming to spend the summer at Mom's place. I was thinking you might want to drive up with us if you have enough leave time. I know she'd love to see you."

"It takes two days to drive each way, so I'll have to pass. I only have three more days leave. I'll visit the ranch this summer though. I've already talked to Mom about it. It'll be great with Miss Emmaline and Amber there too. How long are you planning to stay?"

The look of relief on Char's face when she heard him say he wouldn't be leaving Spring Grove surprised Marla. Was it possible she cared about Donovan that much? The next few days promised to be interesting.

"That's good you're planning to visit this summer. It's about time you got back on a horse. I'm only staying a couple of days myself. I'll spend more time at the end of summer when Marla's construction job is put to bed."

She swallowed and tried to will the heat of a blush away at the word "bed." Again, she reached under the table and pushed Dwayne's hand off her leg and scooted a few inches away from him. "Uh, you're leaving right away?"

"Tomorrow afternoon, soon as school's out." The wry twist on his lips infuriated and unsettled her.

She knew he'd put her on edge deliberately, and there didn't seem to be anything she could do about it. She threw her leg over the bench and stood. "I'm going to check on Amber and Skip."

Dwayne got up. "I'll go with you."

She walked fast in hopes he'd have trouble keeping up with her. He caught up, darn him. "What did you think you were doing back there, Dempsey?"

"Feeling up your leg, Danaher." He chuckled. "Felt good too, all that feminine softness and heat."

She stopped and slammed her hands on her hips. "I asked you not to do that. Did your hearing get damaged in the war too?"

"Yes, as a matter of fact it did, but there's nothing wrong with my instincts, and I know you enjoyed it."

"You're a bonehead. How and why would I enjoy being touched by somebody who's always teasing me about my weight?"

"I have never once teased you about your weight." He rolled his eyes and shook his head. "Let me make myself clear. You're. Not. Fat. Your weight is perfect. In fact, I'd love to get my hands on every single sexy ounce of you, Marla Danaher." He threw up his arms and stalked away.

Charlene called, "Marla, Donovan and I are leaving."

She returned to the table. "We just got here twenty minutes ago. What's your hurry?"

"You and Dwayne are at each other's throats. You're putting a damper on our good mood, so we're going to go back to my place and work on improving it." She picked up their blanket and handed it to Donovan. "We'll see you later at Mt. Fuji."

"What? Mt. Fuji? What are you talking about, Charlene?"

"Did you already forget that we're meeting Sil and Dadley there for dinner tonight?" She shook her head and sighed. "Yes, I can see you forgot. Be there by seven." She took Donovan's hand. "Come on, honey. Let's see if we can work up an appetite for dinner."

He grinned and definitely would have panted if he'd been a dog. "Oohrah. You don't have to ask me twice, sweet thing."

Marla's face burned with embarrassment at her sister's blatant innuendos. They wasted no time getting to Char's car.

Great, just great! Now she was stuck here with Dwayne. He was her ride home. Five miles was too far to walk in this heat, poor Skip would expire. Face it, Marla, she told herself. Be the grownup in the room. Forget what he said and what he did. Pretend it never happened.

But he said he liked her body. He thought she was sexy.

————

Dwayne clasped his hands and leaned on the top rail of the fence. He watched Amber and a few other kids gamboling around the large grassy area, playing with dogs of various sizes and breeds. He gritted his teeth and dragged a hand through his hair. He shouldn't push Marla for more than friendship yet. He had a potentially serious problem to ward off with Francine. The timing with Marla was all wrong.

Amber ran to him and gripped the fence. "Hi, Daddy. Want to come in and play with us?"

He put his arm over the top and ruffled her hair. "Not now. Why don't you come out for a few minutes and chow down on the great-looking sandwich Marla packed for you. She also put ice-cold milk in the cooler. Just the way you like it."

"Okay. I'm rill pooped anyhow. Should I get Skipper?"

"Nah. He's having fun. Come on, I'll unlatch the gate for you." He was about to walk to the gate when she ran off.

"I can do it." Of course she could. She was growing up way too fast.

In seconds she joined him. He threw her in the air and caught her while she squealed and laughed, then he set her on his shoulders and returned to the picnic bench.

Marla strolled between the rows of lemon trees beyond the table. She looked up and smiled at Amber.

"Here you go." Dwayne put the bagged sandwich in front of Amber, opened the milk, and poured some into a paper cup. "Wipe your hands with one of these things." He tugged a hand wipe from the plastic container Marla had put in with the sandwiches.

He glanced quickly around the park for any sign of Francine. "You eat all of it now. I need to go talk to Marla for a minute, okay?"

"Mmm hmm," she mumbled through a big bite of peanut butter and jelly on thick, squishy white bread.

"That's my girl."

He ambled to the lemon trees. They'd been planted in Spring

Grove generations ago, and hadn't been harvested since the big Sunkist co-op had closed in the 70's. He, his brothers, and other boys had played in the abandoned processing plant often, crawling over and under the rusted equipment, playing war, playing power rangers or having a light-saber fight with Darth Vader. Good memories.

He stopped in front of Marla. "Hey, Danaher."

"Hey, Dempsey."

"Truce?"

He held out his hand. She was unpredictable. Would she take it? She took it.

Chapter Eleven

Marla groaned and shook her head at Dwayne's haphazard filing. It had been two days since he'd left. It seemed longer. She dug through the stack of invoices. When she couldn't find the one she wanted, she shuffled them and began to categorize them by material, price, order date, and delivery date.

The door banged open hard enough to shake the trailer, and a woman marched straight to the table. She slapped a paper on the surface. "Where is he?"

Marla bolted back in Dwayne's chair and took a breath to calm her shattered nerves. "Excuse me?"

"I said where is he?"

She stared at the woman, took another breath, and laid the invoices down. "Where is who?"

"Don't play games with me."

Cluny McPherson tromped up the steps and through the open door. "What do you want, Francine?"

Oh! Now she recognized the petite woman. Dwayne's ex-wife. Amber's mother.

Francine's face twisted in an ugly scowl as she whirled on Cluny. "Mind your own business, Cluny!"

"This jobsite is my business. I'm acting supervisor. What do you want here?" He crossed his arms and widened his stance.

"I'm serving a summons on that sneaky bastard, Dwayne Dempsey."

He snorted. "You're out of luck. He's not here."

"Where is he?"

Marla's heart pounded. Glued to her chair with trepidation, she watched their exchange. Cluny knew Dwayne's ex-wife. He also had a hair-trigger temper, and Marla crossed her fingers in her lap, hoping their confrontation wouldn't get ugly. She had no idea what to do.

Cluny scowled. "He's out of town. He took his daughter to Florida for a Disney Cruise vacation. He won't be back here for a couple of weeks, so take your summons and clear out."

"You mean *my* daughter." Francine crossed her arms and looked daggers at Cluny. The woman wasn't going anywhere.

He shook his head and sneered. "Your daughter? That's a laugh. Where do you get the nerve to show up after all these years and demand access to '*the kid*' you deserted six years ago? You always were a nasty piece of work." His deep disgust hung in the air like a thick fog.

"Dempsey's not her father. My husband and I are suing for custody." She grabbed the summons and shook it under his nose.

"Your husband?" Cluny rolled his eyes. "He must be a real prize."

"Don't give me any lip, you raggedy-ass Irishman. I married Luke Henry, the girl's biological father. He's in the car waiting for me."

Cluny snorted. "You married that skinny snot jailbird? It figures."

"Luke served his time. And for your information, he was framed. I've been waiting for him to get out of Montana State Prison so we could come and claim our kid."

Marla's head buzzed. How could this appalling woman be Amber's mother? She'd come, with no thought for the child, armed with legal documents, threatening to take Amber away from the only loving parent she'd ever known. Cluny's quick-thinking lie, that they were on a cruise, should buy them time. If only he could get her to leave.

To Marla's horror, Cluny gave Francine a little shove. "*Your* kid? What kind of mother are you? You don't even know her name." Cluny huffed his disgust and pointed to the door. "You need to get out. This is private property, and the person you're looking for is not here."

"You're a goddamn liar, Cluny!" Francine jammed the summons into her purse. "When I come back I'll have the U.S. Marshall with me."

Marla's alarm increased at Cluny's clenched fists and the growing redness in his face. Afraid he would lose it she stood and cleared her throat. "Um, he's telling the truth. Mr. Dempsey isn't here. He's out of the state."

"Look, Miss Secretary, or whoever the hell you are, sit down and shut up. This doesn't concern you."

Shocked at the woman's crudeness, Marla shouted, "No, lady, you look here!" She startled herself with her angry reaction. "I'm no secretary. I own this property, and you are trespassing. I suggest you leave now before I call the county sheriff and press charges against you."

Francine shoved Cluny in the chest to clear a path to the door. He staggered back and raised his arm.

"Cluny!" Marla grabbed the back of his shirt. "Don't give this disgusting person any reason to come back here." To her grateful surprise, he lowered his arm and gulped a big breath. Francine slammed out the door, leaving both of them temporarily mute.

Marla sat in Dwayne's chair before her knees gave out. She hated ugly confrontations. Head spinning, she waved her hand. "Cluny, sit down. What should we do? We have to do something."

He reached in his pocket and removed his phone.

"Who are you calling?"

"I'd call Gunny, but cell phones don't work worth a crap in Wyoming. I'll call Kathleen Burwell, his mom. He should be there later today." He waited. "Kate? This is Cluny McPherson. I'm fine, ma'am, and you?" He nodded and ran a hand across the back of his neck. "Look, ma'am, I need to give Dwayne a heads-up about a situation here. No, no accidents. Everybody's good. It's a legal matter. Okay, have him call me on my cell no matter what time he gets there. Thanks." He clicked off, set the phone and his elbows on the table, and lowered his head in his hands.

"You okay?" She thought she should pat his shoulder or something, but she didn't know the man that well, didn't know how he'd take it.

"Yeah, thanks to you." He raised his head and held up a fist, his thumb and forefinger a fraction apart. "I was this close to picking her up by her scrawny neck and tossing her boney ass out the door." He blew a breath between tight lips. "Close, too close."

She didn't disagree. "How did he ever get mixed up with that hard-looking psycho shrew?" It wasn't really any of her business, but she knew Dwayne better now. He was a steady man and good father. She couldn't imagine him ever being attracted to a hellcat like Francine Henry.

"Time hasn't done her any favors. She's changed a lot, used to be a cute and sassy party-hearty cowgirl. Dwayne met her when we were home in Wyoming, on leave from our first tour of duty in Iraq. He fell like a lead weight, and she got her hooks into a big tough Marine. They ran off to City Hall in Sheridan and got married. I tried to talk him out of it, told him he could get her in the sack without a wedding ring, but he wouldn't listen to me, to his mom, to anyone."

Marla reached for the water thermos, poured a cup, and handed it to Cluny.

"Thanks." He took it with trembling fingers.

She poured a cup for herself then sat in the swivel chair to face the door again. "This entire episode is upsetting. Why do you suppose she showed up after all these years?"

Cluny shrugged. "She's up to something."

"You think she wants money?"

"She's out of her freakin' mind if that's what she's after. Gunny doesn't have any money. Anything he has is tied up in Big D Construction."

This was a revelation. Cluny apparently didn't know Dwayne owned all that prime ranch land. Why would he have told her and not Cluny, his closest friend? She had a sneaking suspicion Francine somehow knew.

Marla had to talk to Dwayne.

"I don't know anything about his finances, Cluny. I'm grasping at straws. Wondering what she's all about. If he calls before we close shop today, would you tell him I need to talk to him?" She tapped her fingers on the invoices. Cluny didn't need to know the real reason she wanted to speak to Dwayne.

He gave her a Dwayne's-got-more-important-problems frown. "Yeah, sure. I gotta get back to work."

———

Dwayne slowed to a crawl to keep the truck from shaking apart on the last mile to the ranch after they passed through the arches sporting the rustic sign, Big D Cattle-Horses-Dogs. He'd see to getting some of these potholes filled with fresh gravel before he left.

"Are we there yet?"

"Almost." Dwayne grinned and ruffled Amber's hair. "See that big line of cottonwoods up ahead?"

She sat as far forward as she could, straining against the seat belt, and pointed. "There?"

"Yep. Soon as we get past those tall trees, you'll be able to see over the rise to the ranch house."

"Cows!" Amber bounced with excitement and pointed out the side window. "Look Miss Emmaline, cows!"

Dwayne and Emmaline laughed at the child's excitement. The fatigue of the tedious drive from California faded the closer he got to his teenage home.

"Daddy? Do you think Grammakat will remember me?"

"Of course, squirt. It's only been a year since you were here. She can't wait to see you." He glanced to the backseat. "How you doin' back there, Miss Emmaline?"

"Don't you worry about me, youngster. The closer we get to that ranch house the younger I feel. The air here is bracing."

"Yes, it's still early enough in the year so it cools off fast when the sun goes down." He pointed ahead. "There's still snow on the Bighorn Mountains."

"There's always snow up there," Amber said.

"You're right. Some of what looks like snow is glaciers. They never melt." He grinned. "There's the house." He leaned on the horn to alert his mother. He took the circular drive to the front of the weathered ranch building.

The screen door flew open and Kathleen, followed by an ambling, old golden Lab, stepped onto the long, covered wooden porch.

"Jarhead!" Amber bounced and pointed. "Look, it's Jarhead. He remembers me."

Dwayne doubted Jarhead, a boyhood pet, remembered much of anything and was half blind to boot, but why spoil her childish fantasy? "Of course he remembers you. Go give Grammakat a big hug. She's waited a whole year to see you."

Amber opened the door, jumped down from the truck, then ran pell-mell to throw herself into the welcoming arms of his mother. He opened the back door to lift Miss Emmaline down, in spite of her grumbling protests.

"I can get out of this vehicle without your assistance, I'll have you know." She thrust the cat carrier into his hands. "Here, if you want to do something helpful, take Princess Elizabeth. I'll manage on my own."

Dwayne took the cat and stepped back to give the stubborn old woman room to maneuver herself out of the truck.

Kathleen approached them. "Emma! I'm so glad to see you. Come in everybody. Leave your things. I'll have Arturo fetch the bags when he gets in from the barn. We're just putting dinner on the table."

Amber knelt on the porch and let Jarhead cover her with sloppy dog kisses, his tail whipping at warp speed. His old dog's tongue was as big as Marla's mutt. *Looks like the ancient Lab remembers her after all.*

Dwayne gave his mother a crushing hug. "Mom, you get more beautiful every year. How do you do it?"

"Working from sunrise to sundown, I imagine. It's good to see you, son. How are your brothers?"

"They're great. Dylan and his family are coming up this summer. I saw Donovan this past weekend while he was on leave. He's presently languishing in the arms of a beautiful woman, so he's a happy man, but he did say he would get up to see you when he gets his next leave."

"A woman? Really?" She smiled and cocked her head. "Anyone I know?"

"Do you remember Brad Danaher's daughter, Charlene? When you left California she was probably only twelve or thirteen."

"I do remember her and her twin sister, Marla. I always thought Marla would be a stunning woman when she matured."

Dwayne winked and grinned. "You were right, they're both beautiful, but Marla is hot, hot, hot!"

"Is there something you're not telling me?"

"I wish." He hugged her close.

She patted his shoulders and pushed back. "Let's get Emma and Amber some dinner first, then you and I need to speak privately before we turn in tonight." She took his arm. "Come on, Cookie will skin me if she has to wait much longer to see you. She's been cooking all day, everything you like. Go to the kitchen and spend some time with her, but first, use my house phone to call Cluny. He called a couple of hours ago, said it was important."

—————

Dwayne and his mom sat bundled in heavy jackets on the porch after eleven that night. The ranch house sprawled dark and quiet around them like a soft blanket. They sipped hot cocoa and stared at the billions of stars above the Bighorn Mountains.

Dwayne tapped the arm of his chair. "Francine showing up in Spring Grove totally blindsided me. Fortunately there were about eight kids at Brad Danaher's birthday party. She didn't know which one of the girls was Amber. I hustled her out of there before she made a scene. After getting rid of her, I felt the only option was to get Amber as far away from her as possible."

"Did Amber know Francine was there?"

"She saw me escort a woman out, but Dad stepped in and distracted her with birthday cake. Later she asked me who it was, and I sidestepped with a vague answer. She seems to have forgotten in the excitement of coming to the ranch."

"What do you plan to do?"

He sighed and took a moment to answer. "I'm not sure. I'm struggling with whether or not I should allow Francine to see her. Would Amber hate me if she found out years from now that I'd prevented her from meeting the mother she's got some childhood fantasy about being a mysterious fairy princess?" His stomach knotted with indecision.

Kathleen breathed out through tight lips. "There's no way to know until the time comes."

"Francine said something when my brothers and I escorted her off the property and told her to get lost. I can't get my head around it."

"What did she say?"

"'You're not her father.'"

"Dear God, that disgusting tramp! What a thing to say." She placed a reassuring hand on his arm. "That's baloney. You are her father."

"I'm her dad, and she's my daughter, but God's honest truth is, I don't know whether or not I'm her father. Everybody but me knew Francine was screwing around before I got back here."

"Oh, honey, I'm sorry. I know I should have told you, but you were just home from the war, and you'd spent so many agonizing months in the hospital and rehab, I didn't have the heart to say anything. I feel certain Francine wasn't with any other man once you finally got home."

"Maybe, but it seems too much of a coincidence that she got pregnant so fast after we managed sex the first time. As I recall, she was throwing up the next morning."

"It happens, Dwayne. For goodness sake, I got pregnant with Dylan the first night I slept with John. There was no mystery about why we got married in such a hurry."

He cocked his head and grinned. "You never told me that."

"There was never a need to. It wasn't your business, and don't you dare say anything to your brother."

"Dyl can figure it out if he cares to, Mom."

Kathleen sighed. "Yes, I suppose you're right. He weighed almost ten pounds at birth, so it would have been a stretch to claim him premature." She chuckled. "Oh, the things one does when young and in lust."

She poked his shoulder. "Speaking of lust, is there something you'd like to tell me about Marla Danaher?"

"Hell yes. I'd *like* to tell you she's head over heels crazy for me and we're ripping up the sheets every night of the week."

"But?"

He closed his eyes and rested his head on the high back of the old wooden rocker. "But she thinks I'm a jackass, and we do nothing but bicker. She's constantly breathing down my neck on the jobsite, with her nose in every minute detail. I'm tempted to pick her up and toss her out every day." He smiled ruefully and shook his head at how much he wanted Marla, in spite of the constant state of warfare between them.

"Ah. Sounds like love to me." She took his cup and stood. "I don't know about you, but it's getting too cold to sit out here."

The triumphant howl and bark of a lone coyote in the hills broke the vast silence to announce a successful hunt.

Dwayne grinned into the inky darkness. "I forgot how much I loved that sound."

Still, a pervasive uneasiness sent a cold chill arrowing through him.

Chapter Twelve

When will you be back?" Marla demanded over the phone. He'd only been at his ranch a day, and already she was counting the hours until his return. She wasn't sure what she missed the most—the way Dwayne looked at her, or their constant sparring. The construction office was much too quiet.

"Not before next Monday. I'll leave here on Friday. Cluny filled me in on Francine showing up with a summons. Do you have anything to add?"

"Only that she seemed certain you'd be here. She acts confident that she's got standing, and she's obtained legal advice. Do you have a lawyer down here?"

"No. That's something I need to take care of when I get back. The man who handled my divorce and custody settlement lives near the ranch, in Buffalo, but he's retired. I'll talk to him, see if he knows anybody in Ventura County."

"Is that Amber I hear? What's all the excitement?"

"Mom just told her we're taking horses up to the hills to check on the cows that haven't come down. She's excited because she gets to ride her own horse and tag along with us."

He laughed, and the sound buried itself deep in Marla's chest. Shocked she'd missed his laugh after such a short time, she cleared her throat. "Do you have an attorney who handles legal matters for Big D Construction?"

"Yeah, but family law is outside his area."

"I bet he can recommend a good lawyer here. Would you like me to call him?"

"Nah, I already asked Cluny to get on it."

She responded with a weak, "Oh." It wasn't her place, but she wanted to help him.

As if he'd read her mind, he said, "I know you want to help, Red, but I'll be back on the job in a few days. It'll all get resolved."

"I'm not worried about you being back on the job, you big jerk. I'm worried about your daughter and your ex-wife and what she's up to."

"Uh, okay. See you next Monday."

———

Dog tired, Dwayne pulled into his driveway and turned off the ignition. He groaned and dropped his head on the headrest. Every muscle and bone in his body ached. He'd been on the road for over twelve hours. He should have spent more time sleeping in the noisy fleabag motel and not made the grueling drive to get home by Friday night.

But he'd promised Marla he'd be back on her jobsite by Monday. The sooner he finished her project and moved on to the next job the better. He needed to put some breathing room between them. They'd never be a couple, and he didn't see any point prolonging the agony. His first priority had to be Amber. Once she was grown up and on her own, he'd consider a romance. In any case, it wouldn't be Marla Danaher. Her micromanaging drove him nuts.

A light winked on in the neighbor's house. Dwayne saw movement at the window. He waved and the man waved back then closed the blinds and turned off the lights. It was good to have neighbors who looked out for each other.

The house would be quiet, dark, and empty without Amber.

He couldn't remember what he left in the refrigerator and he hadn't stopped for dinner. He pulled open the door and the light came on to reveal a carton of milk and some black bananas. He sniffed the milk, grabbed a banana, and pulled a box of Cheerios from the cupboard.

Other than air-conditioning, the thing he missed most while in Iraq was Cheerios.

He polished off a medium mixing bowl full of cereal, dragged himself down the hall, and flopped on the bed fully clothed. Sleep came fast, and the sunlight of early morning even faster.

Showered, shaved, and wearing heavy, clean work pants and a denim shirt, Dwayne rolled up the sleeves and headed for the grocery store. He needed more Cheerios and milk, the staples of his bachelor diet. Perusing the frozen food section, he threw a half dozen frozen dinners in the basket then added a big can of coffee and a box of Entenmann's doughnuts. It was a good thing he usually had a kid to take care of or he'd either have had a heart attack by now or be over-weight and severely malnourished. He wouldn't survive the summer at this rate.

Oh for the love of...

Marla pushed a shopping basket around the corner of the aisle and banged right into him.

"Oh, I'm sorry I...Dempsey?"

"Are you referring to the nearly departed Dempsey? Where did you learn to drive, Danaher? You're dangerous."

Clearly flustered, Marla huffed. "What are you doing here?"

"Shopping for groceries. My only reason for coming to a grocery store. Are you out sightseeing?" Her heaving chest presented an attractive picture, and he broke out a smile.

"What are you grinning about?"

"Just enjoying the view." He heard a noise coming from her purse. "What have you got in there?"

Marla put a finger to her lips. "Shhh. It's Skipper. He wasn't feeling well, and I didn't want to leave him home alone."

"He's in your purse? Are you planning to suffocate the little rat?"

"You're an idiot. This isn't my purse. It's a dog carrier, and it's well ventilated." She smacked the leather strap resting on her shoulder. "This is my purse. Now be quiet, please. They don't let dogs in the store unless they're service animals."

"You can always slap a vest on him and say he's essential to ease your emotional insecurities, although if that were the case he's falling down on the job." He grinned at her outraged expression.

"Why do you have to be such a jerk?"

"Can't help it."

What was it about this gorgeous woman who brought out the worst in him? "Look, I apologize. If you'll back up, I'll turn my cart around and get out of here."

She sneered at the contents of his basket. "I hope that unhealthy drek is not what you feed Amber."

"Considering she's eleven hundred miles from here, that's unlikely." He watched as she pursed her lips and sniffed. "Do you want me to put it back? I will if you'll cook my dinners, otherwise this is what I eat when I'm on my own. Get over it."

"Come to my house at seven." She glared, backed up her cart, and headed down a different aisle.

Dwayne grinned and turned in the direction of the produce section. On the way he picked up a six-pack of Dr. Pepper and a bottle of red wine. He grabbed a large bouquet of flowers and headed for the checkout lane. *Ooh rah.*

————

Rushing down one aisle after the other, she finally spotted Charlene. "Char! Char," she hissed hoarsely. "Come here quick. I need your help to get me out of something stupid I just did."

Charlene rushed to her side, eyebrows raised with alarm on her usually sunny face. "What happened? Did they catch you with Skipper?"

"No, it's much worse than that. I don't know why I did it."

"Did what? Marla, you're unnerving me. What?"

"I just ran into Dwayne Dempsey. Literally. I ran my cart right in to him." She pressed both hands against her burning cheeks.

Charlene gasped. "Is he hurt?"

"What? No!"

"What's the problem then?"

"I invited him to dinner tonight. I don't want him to come to my place when Amber isn't with him. What should I do?"

"Lordy, is that all? Call him up and un-invite him."

"I can't do that."

"Of course you can. You're always telling everybody what to do and not do. Why does he get special dispensation? Tell him you changed your mind. It's easy. I do it all the time."

"I'm not you, Charlene."

"No kidding."

Marla's stomach did flips. Skipper picked up on her anxiety and emitted tiny moans from inside his carrier. She shushed him and fanned her cheeks with the grocery list.

"If you don't calm down, I'm calling an ambulance. Anyway, I know what to do."

"Oh, thank goodness. What?"

"Simple. I'll come to dinner too. I'm sure he won't think you invited him over for a threesome." She giggled as if she thought it might not be a bad idea.

Marla took a deep breath. "Thank you, Char. You saved my life."

"I doubt it, but you owe me. I was planning to talk on the phone to Donovan all evening. I hope he can get more leave soon. I miss him. I'm mad about him."

"You're mad about every man you sleep with. For a while at least."

"This is different. He's *different*. If he can't get leave I might go down to Camp Pendleton to visit him for a few days."

"How are you going to get time off?"

"I'll tell them I'm quitting if they don't give me a couple of days off. I have a lot of accumulated vacation coming, especially after the tax season we had this year. I put in a lot of overtime before April 15th, and plenty after on returns for people who filed for extensions."

"Okay, we need to figure out dinner. I don't know what to fix. He'll be there at seven."

"I hate to make life too easy for you, but I've got a freezer full of leftovers from Dadley's birthday party. We can do a whole new Mexican dinner. I even have cake left. How's that?"

Marla sighed and hugged her sister. "You're the best, Char. Let's grab a couple of fresh avocados and a bag of grated cheese."

———

Dwayne grinned all the way home. So, what happened to his resolve to forget about her, to get away from her, and put any idea of a love life out of his plans? As a gunnery sergeant, he'd possessed a cool head and the ability to plan strategically when he and his men found themselves in dangerous situations. But with this woman, his mind turned to mush. He shook his head to suppress the looming sexual images of him and Marla in bed together.

Determined not to spend the entire day mooning over her, he threw himself into cleaning the house, mowing the grass, and tackling a full laundry hamper. And—he'd left town right in the middle of rearranging his tool shelves in the garage.

He was halfway done trimming the top of the hedge between his house and the neighbor when the guy called to him.

"Dwayne, I'll do the rest. I was planning on tackling that this weekend anyway." He sauntered over and wagged a bottle of Kona Longboard. "Want one?"

"No, but if you've got anything soft, I'm game."

"Come over. The wife just put a big tray of sandwiches out on the patio. There's enough for a regiment. It's her form of bribery for the afternoon of shopping she's got planned."

Dwayne set down the trimmer and ran his arm over his forehead. "Don't mind if I do. I was about to go inside and rustle something up."

"Great. I've got the Angels game on. They're about to throw out the first pitch. You can play bachelor while your little girl's out of town."

Play bachelor. Yep. That's what he planned on doing tonight if things went the way he hoped.

At nineteen hundred sharp he rang her doorbell and was greeted by her mouse's yips. Rolling his shoulders, he took a breath and waited for her to answer the door, taken off guard by the flutter in his gut.

"Dwayne! Marla said you were coming. Come in, come in." Charlene gestured and reached for the flowers. "For me? You shouldn't have."

"No, they're not for you, and what are you doing here?"

With a stage wink, she said, "Protecting my little sister from the big bad wolf."

"Ha ha."

Any hopeful fantasies he'd been harboring flew right out the window. He held on to the flowers and handed Marla's sister the wine.

"Oh, you are so kind—for such a grumpy bear. How come you're not more like your little brother? He's very sweet, In fact, he's perfect." The wink again.

Ah yes, his lucky little brother. At least one of them was getting laid.

He picked up Skipper, who'd been pawing with excitement at his leg. "How's it going, bruiser?"

"Have a seat, and I'll pour you a glass of this," Charlene said.

"No, I don't drink. Water will be just fine with me."

"Oh, please don't tell me you had plans to break down my sister's defenses with wine. For shame. Here, give me those flowers. I'll put them in water."

He thrust the flowers into her hands and made a face, then strode to the living room, Skipper tucked in the crook of his arm. He plopped down on the end of the sofa and sighed. Staring into the tiny dog's big eyes he whispered, "If I'm not careful your mom will have my balls, just like she got yours, soldier."

Skipper took on a hangdog expression as if he understood exactly what Dwayne had said. He rewarded the little guy with a vigorous belly rub.

———

Marla relaxed and enjoyed the dinner table banter between Dwayne and Char. Her sister tried to wheedle information about Donovan out of him. He wasn't having any of it. Instead he turned the tables on her with questions about her past as if conducting a job interview. "So how many hearts have you broken, Ms. Danaher?"

Charlene turned to Marla with a look of phony outrage on her face. "Do you believe this? Tell him. I'm not in the business of breaking hearts. All my exes love me."

Marla snickered. "Maybe not all, but I have to admit you're very clever when breaking up and making them think it was their idea."

"Speaking of breaking up, have you shown Edwin the door?"

Now why did Charlene say that? It wasn't her business, or Dwayne Dempsey's either. Her arrangement with Edwin was convenient and without unsettling fireworks. A companion for dinner and a movie, with Edwin she never had to worry about the turmoil she drowned in whenever she was with Dwayne.

"Edwin's been in Brussels, at the company headquarters for the past few weeks. He'll call me when he returns."

"I'm sure he calls you every night, right? Because he misses you so much?" She faced Dwayne. "Edwin Plimpton is Marla's boyfriend." She cocked her head. "You didn't know she had a boyfriend?"

"No. Uh, who does he work for?"

Marla's stomach cramped at the defeated look on his face. Why should she care? It wasn't her fault he didn't know she already had a boyfriend and wasn't looking for another.

Before she got a chance to answer, Charlene jumped in. "He's some kind of big executive at BDO. He travels all the time. Wasn't he in Australia last month, Marla?" She pursed her lips. "He's hardly ever around."

"Is that why you dragged her to the single's dinner?" He looked at Charlene then turned his gaze to Marla.

"Time for dessert." Marla stood. "I'll get it." She hurried to the kitchen. If she didn't commit fratricide before the evening was over it would be a small miracle. She gritted her teeth and fussed over the cake plates, heard them laughing, and decided she'd add homicide to the fratricide. If she was going to spend her life on death row, she might as well make it worthwhile.

Chapter Thirteen

MARLA HAD ALL DAY SATURDAY AND SUNDAY TO GET HER HEAD and heart straight. She failed miserably. Not looking forward to facing Dwayne, she nevertheless had to go to the construction office to retrieve her laptop before heading to the real estate office downtown.

She pulled into the lot just as a large flatbed truck with a *We're The Tops* logo finished unloading a shipment of granite countertops. Dwayne signed the manifest and handed the clipboard to the driver. The truck rumbled away as he bent to examine the stone more closely.

Marla parked, stepped from her car, and approached him. She stared at the cut granite countertops. "This isn't what I wanted. Why didn't you send it back?" Chin forward, she glared at him.

Dwayne thrust his hands in the air, and then slammed them on his hips. "I ordered this instead, because it's superior quality for a little more money." He strode to the construction trailer office, flung open the door, and stomped inside.

Marla followed him inside. "It's *my* money, Dempsey! When are you going to start paying attention to what I want?"

He spun on her. "When are you going to stop micromanaging every step of this project, Danaher?"

She clenched her fists. "Grrr! You are the most exasperating person I've ever worked with."

He leaned his face dangerously close to hers, the muscles in his jaw tensing. "You're the most exasperating person I've ever worked *for!*"

"I don't know why I hired you in the first place."

"I don't know why I accepted the damn contract. You're impossible to please, and half the time you don't know what you're asking for. Why don't you leave the contracting up to the contractor?"

Glaring, she crossed her arms and invaded his space. "I have half a mind to fire you!"

"Oh, yeah? I have half a mind to quit!" He took a step closer.

"You have half a mind all right, you..." Marla shut her mouth at the dangerous glint in his eyes. She might have pushed him too far. Hah, as if she could push the stubborn lout an inch in any direction. She dropped her hands to her sides. "I'm..."

He put a finger to her lips, closed his hands on her upper arms, and pulled her to his chest. "Shut up, Red."

Her knees wobbled. She stopped breathing.

Dwayne's mouth covered hers. His arms captured her, the hand at the back of her neck strong and warm. He crushed her against his strong body, tilted his head, and teased her lips open with his tongue. Sliding his free hand down her back, he pressed her hips against his pelvis.

Oh, my. Oh. My.

Twenty-seven years old and she'd never been kissed like this. She should struggle, push him away.

He relaxed his mouth but didn't move his lips from hers. "I want you in my bed, Danaher."

Marla gasped when a hot flush zipped from her hips to her ears then all the way to her toes. "No, Dwayne, we can't."

"Like hell we can't." He slid his hands up her arms, stepped back, and gazed into her eyes. Without another word he grabbed his jacket from the peg on the wall.

"But...where are you going?" Was he quitting? He couldn't quit. She didn't want him to quit.

"I'm gonna knock off early. I've got some personal business to take care of in Simi Valley. Mostly I need to get away from you." He stepped through the door just as Cluny McPherson mounted the first step.

"But, Dwayne, we..."

Instead of answering, he shook his head, held up his arm, and dangled the keys to his truck. "I'm outta here."

The protest died on her tingling lips as she watched him climb inside the truck. The engine roared to life and he backed out, turned, and drove away.

"Everything okay here?" Cluny set a faucet and a couple of chrome fixtures on Dwayne's worktable.

How long had she stood there with her mouth hanging open? The mouth still telegraphing shocks through her body from the pressure of his lips on hers? She took a ragged breath and absently brushed at her blouse. "I don't know."

She reached across the table to her laptop, snapped the cover shut, and shoved it in her bag. Without another word to Cluny, she hurried to her car, started the engine, and drove onto the main road heading for town.

Ten minutes later, she sat in her car, in her office parking lot, hands gripping the steering wheel. She'd turned the engine off, but with the windows raised, the car quickly grew uncomfortably warm. She had no recollection of the drive. Finally, she opened the door, gathered her things and went inside, still dazed.

"Hi Marla." The receptionist smiled and handed her several slips of paper. "You have messages, and Ted wants to talk to you."

An absent, "Thanks," and she continued to the desk in a far corner. She'd asked for that location away from the traffic pattern of the busy office. She spread the messages on the desktop in order of time received. Decided none of them were particularly urgent and sat down to stare out the window.

———

"I doubt she has a leg to stand on, but first, Mr. Dempsey, I need to consult with my clerk. I want him to check Wyoming divorce statutes to make sure there's no loophole your wife can use for leverage."

"*Ex*-wife."

"Yes, of course." The busy lawyer stood. "There's no need to take more of your time this morning. All your paperwork is in order." He tapped the file Dwayne had provided. "I'll call you as soon we've completed a thorough review. If you have any questions or concerns in the meantime, don't hesitate to contact me."

Dwayne shook the man's hand. "Thanks for seeing me on such short notice."

"It was my pleasure to meet with you." He rounded his desk and opened the door. "You may leave your retainer with my secretary."

Dwayne smiled to himself. At least the man hadn't charged him for the initial consultation. He had a good feeling about him, and he'd come highly recommended by his local business attorney.

All he wanted now was to get Francine out of the picture, finish Marla's damn building, and move on to his next project. What the hell had he been thinking when he kissed her? Sure, he'd like to sleep with her, but then what?

He could see no good outcome in pursuing a relationship with her. Now was not the time to start something he couldn't finish. What kind of man would he be to hook up with Marla Danaher without considering how his actions affected her?

That damn woman invaded his thoughts day and night.

———

"Marla? Got a minute?" Ted's voice called from the door of his office.

She mentally slapped herself. *Get back on track, kiddo, you've got a living to earn.* "Sure, I'll be right there."

She took a minute to look at the messages again, arrange her desk, take a deep breath, and straighten her clothing before following him through the door.

"What's up, Ted?"

"Close the door."

Now what? "That sounds ominous."

He laughed. "No, I don't want the staff to hear what I'm talking to you about before I get your take on it." He indicated a chair. "Sit. You know that Cartwright property on the edge of town? I heard through some sources I trust that the old man is finally planning to sell out."

"Wow. That *is* news. His family's owned that property for over a hundred years. There was nobody in this valley except for a few nomadic Indian tribes before the Cartwright's came to run cattle on their original Mexican land grant."

Endless possibilities on how the land could be developed bounced around her brain. "It hasn't been used for anything except movie locations for the past forty years. Most production companies have moved to Canada for their location filming. Are you going after the listing?"

"Not exactly." He tilted his chair back and steepled his fingers. "Think about this. I'm forming a consortium of investors to buy the property and develop it. It's a once in a lifetime opportunity. I want you in the group."

Ted was right, this could be the one she'd been waiting for, her big step to financial security. Marla's heart sank. The timing couldn't be worse.

"Holy goats, there's nothing more I want than to get in on it, but every penny I have is tied up in the condo project."

"Isn't it about finished?"

"We're in the very last stages. The painting contractor is starting on the exterior in a couple of days, then they'll do the inside. My building contractor is putting the final touches on the interiors now. But it's going to take some time for me to get the units rented to create an income stream. I just don't have any money lying around right now." She groaned and shook her head. Timing—wouldn't you know it?

"Listen to yourself. You have to think big. Finish the building and sell it. Think of it as a stepping stone. If we secure the Cartwright property we can develop it into a high-class residential neighborhood and a golf course, maybe even include a resort hotel. Your condos are small potatoes by comparison."

Sell her condos? What of her plans for predictable rental receipts? The building was to be her future income stream. Not only that, she'd promised Miss Emmaline she'd always have a home there. Would a new owner honor her promise? She couldn't take that chance, wouldn't take it. No, Ted's plan was too risky.

"Ted, I don't see how I can do that. I have so much riding on the building, and I've made promises to some of the rental tenants waiting to move back in. One elderly lady has stayed in the building throughout the renovation."

"You need to think big. I'll give you overnight, but we have to act fast. Once Kreisler gets wind of it, we're screwed. I can't keep it under wraps for long."

"Wouldn't Ben Kreisler be a potential partner in the deal?"

"Are you kidding me? That greedy bastard would like nothing better to have it all for himself."

"Where will he get the money in this economy?"

"I don't know, but he's always been able to ace everybody in a cash deal. I'm not taking any chances. He has his own sources, and he'll know what Cartwright's plans are soon enough. We have to move on it. You've got till tomorrow night."

Back at her desk, she stared at her messages and saw a couple more had been added. None of them seemed important enough to answer while she tried to get her mind around Ted's offer.

Feast or famine. It never rains but it pours. If anything can go wrong, it will. And every other dang cliché I can think of.

She froze with indecision.

———

Dwayne rolled his shoulders and surveyed the work he, Slim, and Jack had sweated at like hogs all afternoon, hauling the stone countertops to each unit for installation the next morning. Cluny finished with the new plumbing fixtures after the last of the modular showers was positioned. They looked great. The glass man would arrive in the morning with the new shower doors.

He rubbed his lower back. Kitchens would be the last step before painters began work inside each unit. Dwayne spent the evening hours after the crew knocked off for the day personally masking woodwork and covering Miss Emmaline's furniture and possessions with drop cloths. Carpeting would wait to be installed in individual condos until the epoxy floor coatings dried in the hallways and foyers once the walls got painted.

He estimated they had ten days max to wrap up the project. What a relief! Another contractor would finish the driveways and parking areas before the landscapers got access to the grounds. It was coming together beautifully, a month sooner than he'd promised, and under budget.

Ready to drop, he locked the building and left by the front entry. He'd parked his truck on the street so the security company could drop off Hercules and lock the perimeter fence.

His phone vibrated. "Yeah?"

"Hi, Daddy. I miss you. I want to come home."

"Hey, squirt. You just got there." He missed her too.

"I know."

"Tell you what. Give it a week. If you want to come home then,

I'll come and get you. But I know Grammakat and Miss Emmaline would like you to stay a little longer. Okay?"

She heaved a huge sigh. "Okay. I love you, Daddy."

"Not as much as I love you."

"Do too."

"Do not."

"Bye, Daddy."

"Bye, sweetheart. I'll talk to you later."

Eyes heavy and aching all over, he pulled into his driveway and locked the truck. He shed his clothes, piece by piece, as soon as he got in the house and headed for the shower.

Sitting on a plastic bench, elbows on knees, he let the hot water sluice down on him, his muscles relaxed, and tension in his shoulders and hips eased. He'd often speculated that Iraqi tribesmen who lived in some of the most parched areas of their godforsaken country might not be so enraged and fanatical if they could regularly avail themselves of hot showers.

Food, he needed food.

Cheerios never tasted better. Halfway through his second bowl, the doorbell rang. Who'd be at his doorstep this late? He pulled himself up on his crutches and glanced around for a shirt. He'd worn the one thrown on the back of a chair all day. In nothing but his pajama bottoms, he shrugged and headed for the door. *Please, God, don't let it be Francine leaning on my bell.*

Hand hesitant on the doorknob, he finally turned it and pulled. He swallowed.

Marla stood in the dark holding her dog.

"Dwayne, I know it's late, but can I come in? I need to talk to you."

Chapter Fourteen

DWAYNE TOOK A HOP BACK AND OPENED THE DOOR WIDER. "Sure, come in. I wasn't expecting..."

Marla stepped past him. "I know. I'm sorry, but we need to talk about the situation that came up today." She set Skipper on the floor and started toward the living room.

"No."

She stopped and turned. "No?"

"No." He tilted his head. "I mean...in the kitchen. Let's go in the kitchen. I was eating."

Her cheeks flushed. "This is dumb. I should leave."

"No, come on. We have to talk about it."

"You know why I'm here?"

"Yeah." He lifted a crutch in the direction of the kitchen. "After you." He followed her to the table, wishing he knew when to keep his big mouth shut. Might as well get it aired. "Sit, please." He nodded at a chair, went to the sink and filled a pan with water, then set it on the floor for Skipper. Furtively glancing around the room, he looked for anything else to do to delay facing her.

Her mouse tap-danced across the tile and lapped at the water. Dwayne gave up, went to his chair, and sat across from her. He cleared his throat.

"It's good you came."

"I'm so relieved you feel that way. Please know it wasn't anything I thought of in advance. I was completely surprised." She shifted in the chair and took a breath. "The first thing I thought of this afternoon was that I couldn't think of going to bed without talking it over with you, without discussing every aspect of it."

He raked a hand through his thick dark hair, a nervous tic she'd probably noticed by now. "Believe me I was just as surprised when it happened as you were." Was that his pulse bouncing around, obscuring his vision?

Steady, soldier.

"Well, it did come out of nowhere, didn't it? It's something I've dreamed of for a long time. Then all of a sudden it's here for the taking. I don't know where to start." She fidgeted and reached to pat Skip's head. "Why don't you say how you feel? Don't spare my feelings. Tell me what you really think."

He swallowed the fist-sized lump in his throat. "You've dreamed of it? Since when?"

Marla sighed and relaxed against the back of the chair. "I'm not sure, but I wouldn't jump into something like this without giving it a lot of thought. I need you to help me through it. The decision, I mean." Her eyes took on a look of soft pleading.

"Look, Red, it's your decision. I can't make it for you. I know how I feel. The rest is up to you."

She gazed at him with flaming cheeks. "Would you do me a favor?" Her eyes took aim at the top of the table. She stared at the half-finished bowl of cereal.

"Name it, beautiful." He counted the beats of the pulse in her neck.

"Could you, um, put on a shirt? Your, uh... Good grapes, Dempsey, I can't think clearly with you sitting there half naked."

He slapped his hands on the table and pushed himself to a standing position and grabbed his crutches. "Don't move. Stay right there. I'll be back in a flash." That said, he thumped down the hall as fast as possible. Yanking open a drawer, he pulled out a T-shirt, dragged it over his head, then flopped on the side of the bed to put on his prosthesis and fastened it. His eyes scanned his bedroom. Yes, everything was ship-shape.

Back on two feet, he adjusted the loose pajama bottoms, shook himself, and walked to the kitchen. He wasn't dreaming. Beautiful, bossy, sexy Marla still sat there. He wasn't sure what to do next. It would probably be best to let her take the lead and then play it by ear.

He grinned and gripped the back of his chair. "Want to go to the living room?"

"Heavens no, I interrupted you while you were eating. Go ahead. Finish. I'll just…uh, start first."

"If you're going to start first, we better go to the living room. I'm not hungry anymore." He pointed to the hallway. "Come on. We'll be more…comfortable…talking." She wanted to start first. *Ooh rah.*

"Oh, okay." She scooped up the mouse. "Come on Skippy, Dwayne wants me on the couch."

On the couch, on the bed, on the floor, against the wall, he wasn't picky. Wherever she wanted it. Like a good Marine, he was there to serve. Dwayne followed her gorgeous ass to the next room. His knees threatened to collapse at the view. If he didn't get his hands on her in the next five minutes he might have a coronary.

Marla sat and sent him a welcoming smile. "This is more comfortable. Where do you want me to start?"

Dear God in heaven. Thank you. Thank you. Thank you.

"I'm all yours. Any place you want to start is good for me. I admit I'm surprised. But it's a fine, fine surprise."

"Really?" She pushed some of that glorious strawberry-colored hair over her shoulder and sighed. "You have no idea how relieved I am. I thought for sure you'd give me a hard time when we got right down to it. I've been gnashing me teeth all day about Miss Emmaline."

He snapped to attention. "Say again?"

"Miss Emmaline. I promised her."

"You promised her what?"

Eyebrows up, she said, "That she'd never have to move."

Dwayne raised his hands in front of her like a crossing guard. "Hold it. Stop. Wait. What in hell are we talking about here?"

Her beautiful brown eyes widened, her luscious lips formed a heart-stopping O, and a blush bloomed on her cheeks. "What did you think we were talking about?"

"Getting it on?"

"Getting it…" Her hands flew to her face and she screeched, "Aaargh! I could die. I want to die." Her head tilted up, elbows bobbing, she fell back against the cushions. Bug-eyed, Skipper yipped and bounced. He clawed frantically at her hands. "You must think I'm...oh, I could just die."

A chuckle took shape deep in his chest, and he swallowed it back. "Marla, sweetheart, it's cool." He drew her into his arms. "Honey, I'm sorry." God help him, he couldn't hold the laugh back any longer. His chest bounced with an explosive guffaw.

Skip yipped as he got mashed between them, and he finally scrambled away onto the floor. A tiny growl curled his lip.

He stood his ground until convinced Dwayne wasn't harming her. Marla shoved against his chest. "Let me go. Stop laughing." But, with a fistful of his shirt, she hung on.

He held her tighter. "No, Red. Take a breath. I'll let you go when you calm down." He stroked her back. "That's better." He sighed deeply then took a breath for himself. "I wasn't laughing at you. I was laughing at me."

Her hand relaxed the grip on his T-shirt, and she buried her face in his chest. "You?"

"Hope to die." He rocked her from side to side and ran his hand over her back and neck.

"It's not funny, I just want...I want..." She massaged the spot where she'd gripped his shirt, as if to iron out the wrinkles.

"Shhh." Tilting her chin with his finger, he brushed his thumb across her mouth. "Don't talk. Look at me, sweetheart." Her eyes met his and he nearly choked. "I want to kiss you." He dipped his head, hesitated a split second, and then kissed her for all he was worth.

———

Marla's world tilted on its axis. When he'd kissed her this morning, she'd been sure it was the best kiss of her life. Now that wasn't true. This was no mere kiss. The heat of their two bodies formed and melted, churned and flamed. She gripped his broad shoulders and gave herself up to him. He had a fistful of her hair in one hand, gripped her bottom with the other, then slid down, down, onto his back.

Gasping for air, she drew away, then hated herself for the instant of lost contact. Her mouth found his again. She never wanted to stop, never—she wanted to drown in him. The kiss went on, went deeper.

He stilled. She held her breath. "What?"

"I need to see you, Danaher. All of you." His fingers stroked her cheeks, curled behind her ears, and he sucked her bottom lip. "I want to look at you. Please. Let me see you. Don't torture me."

White-hot heat filled her, molten metal flowed into every tiny, empty crevice. Without analyzing, she pushed away from him and pulled off her sweater, then her tank top.

Dwayne tucked his fingers under the top edge of her plain white bra and tugged it free when her hands flew behind and unhooked it. "Sweet, Jesus."

Marla knew as sure as the earth was round that Dwayne found her beautiful and desirable. His groan, the grateful watery shimmer in his blue eyes a clear declaration. He couldn't be faking it. She leaned in to give him access to her breasts when he reached for her, arched her back with ecstasy at his touch. "Oh, I want..."

His smile had the power to melt granite. "What do you want, beautiful. Tell me."

Never having been so sure of anything else in her life, she spoke the words freely and honestly. "You, Dempsey, I want you." The depth of her passion overwhelmed her. More alive than she'd ever been, she said, "Do what you said this morning, say you want to make love to me."

He crushed her against his chest with a satisfied chuckle. "What do you think, Danaher?"

She melted against him. "I think...I can't think. I've forgotten how to think. I don't want to think, I just want to feel." She slid her hand under the hem of his shirt. "Why did you put this on?"

"Your orders."

"Since when do you do what I tell you?"

He shifted her away. Got to his feet, pulled the shirt over his head, and threw it on the floor. His arms went around her back and under her knees when he lifted her. "I'm going to do exactly what you tell me to do for the rest of the night."

Her heart bounced into her throat at the feel of his hard, bare chest pressing against her breast. She gasped, "Oh, be careful, your..." She bit her tongue.

"My...?"

"I'm too heavy."

"Like hell you are."

And without being cognizant of exactly how it happened, they were in his bedroom, on his bed, and he lay on top of her devouring her lips, her throat, her shoulders, while he held her hands captive, fingers laced together above her head.

She squeezed his hands and said, "Undress me. Touch me everywhere. Be slow." Tremors slithered upward from her thighs.

"Yes, ma'am, I'll take as long as you want. I'll do whatever you want." On his knees, eyes burning into hers, his hands whisked ever so lightly across her breasts and abdomen. The intensity of his gaze stole her breath away when he tugged her stretchy yoga pants below her hips and smiled.

A warm, delicious fog descended on her brain. Desire and deep need burned in every cell of her body. His lips and hands were everywhere. His warm breath brushed across her skin from her neck to her knees and had her writhing, begging for more. His name: Dempsey, Dempsey, Dempsey rolled off her lips time and again.

Dismantling her piece by piece, he smoothed every sharp edge, sealed every cold hollow place, then put her back together again, whole, complete, better, safe.

Stroking a rough hand down the side of her face, he rasped, "Do you want me, Danaher? Do you want me now?"

She smiled with her lips and her eyes. "Yes, please."

———

Nestled together with her like two spoons in the silver drawer brought home to Dwayne the emptiness of the past six years of aloneness. He ran his fingers down her side, then snaked his arm between her breasts and kissed her ear. He could stay like this forever with her against him, warm, soft, yielding.

"Are you asleep?" He nipped her neck and buried his nose in her hair.

"No. I may never sleep again."

She shifted, but he dragged her back tighter against his belly. "Don't move. This is where you belong, here next to me. The only thing wrong with this picture is the varmint snoring with his nose in my neck." If he moved a fraction he'd squash the miniscule creature.

"Skip's not a varmint. He's a critter."

At the sound of his name, Skipper scrambled to his feet and whined. Dwayne rolled his shoulders with relief.

Marla patted his arm. "I have to take him out."

"Let him pee on the floor."

"He won't. He'll just keep nagging until I get up." She lifted his arm and pulled away from his warmth. "Do you have a bathrobe or something I can put on?"

Dwayne rolled to his edge of the bed, switched on the light, and sat up. There she stood in all her glory, naked as the day she was born. "I like seeing you this way, Danaher. Don't cover up for my sake."

Her hands flew to cover her breasts then shifted to cover the curls between her legs. "Where is it?"

He sighed with defeat. "Back of the bathroom door."

While she ran across the room to grab his robe, he put his manmade foot on and stood. "I'll go with you."

"Like that?"

"Like what?" He knew what she meant but enjoyed her moment of discomfort. Naked wasn't a problem for him. He'd welcome the chance to parade naked around her forever and enjoy every moment of it.

She pointed at him. "Like...that. You can't go outside like that."

"Look, Red, you're wearing my robe, and it's the middle of the night. Who's going to see me?"

Marla sniffed, pressed her lips together, and flounced out of the room. "Come on, Skip. Let's go pee-pee."

Dwayne sauntered behind her to the door off the kitchen. When she stopped, he switched on the light over the small porch and stepped aside so she could follow the mutt outside without taking a header down the steps. "Hurry it up you mongrel. This woman belongs in my bed."

"Shush. Do you want the whole neighborhood to hear you?"

"Yes." He followed her out the door, threw his arms wide, and shouted, "This woman belongs in my bed!"

She whirled on him and slapped her hand over his mouth, but not before she spotted his erection standing at stiff attention like a full-dress Marine, waiting to be awarded a medal by his commanding officer. Her neck and cheeks went red, and her hands flew to her face. "Dwayne. Stop that."

He smirked and touched himself. "Stop this? Only you can stop this, you bad girl." He pulled her into his arms and tugged open the robe, giving him access to her soft, silky thighs. Pushing between her legs seemed the most natural thing to do because she was the perfect height. Made for him.

Instead of resisting as he'd expected, she yielded. He slid the robe off her shoulders and let it drop on the grass as the mutt trotted back inside. He snapped off the porch light. "My god, woman, where have you been all my life?"

"Don't you dare use that creaky old line on me, Dempsey." Her hips pressed closer. "Now are we going to do something about your... problem, or stand here the rest of the night exchanging barbs?" She pressed her lips against his throat and nearly brought him to his knees.

"Either one works for me." He gripped her bottom and walked her backward to the kitchen counter where he lifted her to a sitting position, pushed her legs apart, and ran his hands between her thighs, around her hips, up her ribs then across her stomach and breasts. "You feel as beautiful as you look. I knew you would. I never doubted it for a minute." Finding her lips with his, he gripped her head in his hands and gave her a bruising kiss.

Her lips parted when he forced his tongue in her mouth, and her nails dug into his bare back as she groaned with pleasure.

What little piece of his brain survived intact warned him he might not survive the best night of his life.

Chapter Fifteen

HE COOKED BREAKFAST FOR MARLA WHILE SHE SHOWERED IN HIS bathroom. The bathroom where he wanted her to shower from here on out. But enough of schoolboy dreams, he told himself. Slow down and do a thorough recon of the battlefield before you go charging into the unknown.

"Hey, Dempsey." She'd drifted into the kitchen without him realizing it.

"Hey, Danaher. I hope you like spicy sausage links because that's what you're getting with your eggs this morning."

"Sounds great, but don't give them to Skip. Pork gives him gas." She grinned and sat in the same chair where everything had started last night.

"Too late. The little fart already talked me out of a couple."

She scratched the mouse's chin. "You know what? I really did come here last night to talk to you about something important." She fussed with her damp curls. "Do you have a rubber band? My hair is going all over the place."

"I do, but you can't have one. I like it that way."

"I'm on my way to the jobsite. I can't show up there looking like a floozy."

"As long as you look like you're my floozy it's cool." He sat. "Eat, we're late as it is."

"No, it's not cool, Dempsey. What happened last night is between us. I'm not Charlene, flaunting it to the whole world." The twist of her lips and blush on her cheeks belied her harsh words.

"Don't be so hard on your sister. She's a good lady with a healthy appetite for what comes natural, that's all." He opened his mouth and shoved in a forkful of eggs, chewed, and then winked when she stuck her tongue out at him. "Is that an invitation?"

"No. Clear your mind. I need to talk to you. It's important."

He shrugged and forked up a hunk of sausage. "Shoot."

"I've been invited to join a private consortium to purchase a prime piece of real estate. In order to do that I'd have to put the condo project up for sale."

This had come out of nowhere. He put down his fork and stared. "Sell it?"

"Don't look at me like that. I haven't made up my mind, but I do have to let them know by tonight. I wanted to ask what you thought of the idea, if it would be a problem for you."

"It's no problem for me. What about the renters who moved out and are waiting for me to finish so they can get back home?" He took a swallow of coffee. "What of Miss Emmaline? Are you planning on selling her unit right out from under her?"

"No!" She crumpled her napkin. "I'm trying to find a way to make good on what I promised and still get in on the real estate deal."

Eyes boring into hers, he asked, "What do you want me to say, Marla? My interest in your building is to finish it, collect my money, then move on to my next contract."

"You can say that to me after last night?"

He warned himself to consider his words with caution. Last night was important to him. She was important to him, but he couldn't make, wouldn't make, decisions for her, especially where a great deal of money was concerned. He reached for her hand. "Let's not mix business with pleasure, honey. Last night was great, you're more than great, but right now I'm not sure what you want from me."

"I should have known." Marla snatched her hand away, grabbed her dog, and stalked from the room. Two seconds later his front door slammed, then her car door slammed, followed by the sound of her engine firing up.

Nice going, Dempsey, you did it again.

"Dammit." He carried the dishes to the sink, then found his jacket and car keys.

———

Instead of heading for the condos, Marla drove through a maddening mist of tears to her house. Skip sat in the passenger seat, still as a lawn ornament, and stared at her with his oversized black eyes when she pulled into her driveway and stopped. She sat in the car and stared, unseeing, at her house. He watched her and his ears twitched as if to ask, what now?

"Skippy, you're looking at the sorriest doggy mama in the world." She choked on a sob and lifted him to her chest. "What am I going to do?"

Skipper whined and licked at her chin. His warm little tongue had the power to turn on the tear faucet. She hadn't known she could feel so low, so broken-hearted, so confused. The one time in memory she'd willingly handed over control to somebody else—and look what happened. What a moron. She hated herself. She hated Dwayne Dempsey.

Who was she kidding? If she hated him, she wouldn't feel so rotten. Maybe she'd call Char? No. Dadley?

She pressed a thumb to her father's picture on her phone. He was probably still at home. He didn't usually go to his office until after nine. "Come on, Dad, be home, please. I need you."

He picked up on the first ring. "Good morning, sweetheart."

"Dad?" she replied in a tear-clogged voice. "I...uh..."

Dadley's voice boomed an octave higher than usual. "What's the matter?"

Of course he'd be alarmed to hear her crying. She never cried. It was out of character for her. "I'm okay, Dad, but I need your advice. Can I talk to you before you go to your office?"

"No, honey, I'm on my way to an early meeting. If it's an emergency I'll cancel, but if it can wait until ten-thirty, I'll be free for the rest of the morning. Are you sure you're okay?"

"Um..." She cleared her throat and sucked in a shaky breath. "No emergency, it can wait. Shall I come to your office at ten-thirty then?" That would be better anyway, a couple of hours and she'd have time to get her head together and do some quick number crunching for the consortium deal.

"Yes. Nobody else is in the office today. We'll have privacy. Are you sure you're okay, sweetheart?"

"Yes, thanks, Dad. I'll be there. You're a life saver." She sighed. "Don't worry, I'm fixable."

———

In a black temper, Dwayne stormed through the building looking for the smallest flaw to criticize. "Get that shit out of here. I don't want to see it lying around tomorrow." His crew gave him wide berth once they recognized the Gunnery Sergeant glare on his face. Good, he wasn't in a mood for excuses or backtalk.

He pushed through the door of the trailer and sat at his desk to tally the final material costs and early finish bonuses. The sooner he cleared out of here the better. It would be worth paying out extra money. He got on the phone and set up a meeting with the owner of the property where Big D had been hired to build a large storage facility.

"That's great news, Mr. Dempsey. I'm glad you'll be available a couple of weeks earlier than I expected."

"I'll drop in on you Monday afternoon."

Cluny entered the trailer and went straight to the coffee pot. Dwayne concluded the phone call and ignored him, but the way he flexed his hands and shifted his feet, he knew his old buddy had something on his mind. After a minute he said, "Spit it out, McPherson!"

Arms straight at his sides, Cluny stood at stiff attention. "Yes, sir, Sergeant, sir."

"Kiss my ass."

Cluny saluted. "Yes, sir, Sergeant, sir. Drop your pants and bend over. Way over, and I'll tickle your balls while I'm at it."

Teeth clenched, lips pressed together, Dwayne fought to hang on to his mad, but lost the battle when they burst into laughter.

"Jeez, I'm such an asshole today."

"No argument from me there, Gunny." He sat in the chair across the desk and stretched his long legs. "For a man who just got laid, you look like shit."

"What the hell are you talking about?"

"Hey, I saw the look on the boss-lady's face when you walked out of here yesterday. It was only a matter of time. So, spill." He leered past the rim of his coffee cup.

"I'd rather talk about the Store n'Lock job. I called the guy to tell him I could get on it earlier than expected." No way was he going to talk about Marla. Not even to his best friend.

"Okay by me. Talk. Is there anything in it for my guys?"

"Not much, except for a utility bathroom and a public restroom in the office and a sprinkler system in the main building. You want it?"

"Sure. I got nothin' on tap except maintenance and small remodels for the next couple of months. You got the blueprints and specs?"

Dwayne reached under the drafting table next to the desk and selected a thick roll of blueprints covered with fine dust. He blew on the bundle, and Cluny joined him at the tall table. They spent about forty-five minutes poring over the plumbing details then grabbed another cup of coffee and returned to sit at the desk.

"Get your cost estimate to me by next Monday morning. I've got a meeting with the main man that afternoon."

Cluny stood. "You got it." He rinsed out his cup and set it on the shelf behind the sink. "Fifty bucks says she was beyond hot, Gunny."

"You win. Now get the hell out of here. I gotta think."

Marla stood in front of her dad's office and ran her fingers over his nameplate. *Bradley Danaher.* She turned the knob and peeked inside.

"There's my girl." He stood, rounded his desk, and embraced Marla. Arm around her shoulders, he led her to a large, brown leather sofa. "Have a seat, honey. Tell old Dad all about it."

The love she had for her father was deep enough to drown in. She trembled a watery smile. "You're not old, Dad. You aren't even eligible for Senior Citizen discounts until next year." She grabbed his hand.

"Old in experience, if not years." He rubbed her knuckles. "What's on your mind?"

"Two things but promise you won't laugh or say I told you so." She wondered if there were many women out there who had such a close, comfortable relationship with their father as she. Talking to him about anything came naturally to her.

He chuckled. "I'd be falling down on my father-of-the-year job if I made that promise. Let me venture a guess." Playing the wise man, he rolled his eyes, puckered his lips, and tapped a finger on his chin. "You're in love and you're broke."

"Dad," she groaned and rocked back, "how do you do it?" Face buried in her hands she mumbled through her fingers, "I made a schoolgirl mistake." Her cheeks grew hot. "I spent the night at Dwayne Dempsey's house. I don't know what came over me. I never should have gone there so late. I swear I had business to discuss with him, but I could have done it over the phone." She rocked back and forth. "I'm so stupid."

He rubbed her back. "I've had the misfortune to be acquainted with many stupid people in this life, and you, my dear girl, cannot be counted in their number." He paused. "Now tell me why it was stupid."

She gasped and stared. "Because we…because we…ended up in his bed, that's why!"

"And it's a mistake because you slept with him?"

"Dad!"

"Was he abusive? Did he force you? Was the sex disgusting?" He raised his eyebrows and waved his hands. "What? Why are you in such a tizzy? Do I need to call the County Sheriff?"

"No!" Marla jumped to her feet and paced the length of his private office twice. She opened her mouth to speak and closed it, more than once. Finally, she stopped in front of her dad, slammed her hands on her hips, and blurted, "It wasn't bad. It was good. It was excellent." Her neck blazed with a blush she knew he couldn't miss. "I don't know what to do!" Grabbing handfuls of her hair, she paced some more.

Dad fell against the back of the sofa and laughed. He shook his head and laughed some more.

"Dadley, you promised!"

"No, I most certainly did *not* promise. I *specifically* did *not* promise." He patted the space next to him. "Sit down. I need to explain the birds and bees to you even though it's very late in the game."

Scalp burning, palms sweating, Marla slumped next to him. He patted her knee, then put his arm around her shoulders and hugged her to his side.

"My beautiful daughter, tell me why you guard your feelings with such vigilance? What is it about this big bad world that has you so skittish? Sexual desire is normal and healthy. You and Dwayne are unattached, normal, and healthy. Why run away from it?"

"I'm not Charlene, Dad."

"No, you're not, but you must admit she enjoys life and has a sound attitude about love, sex, and men."

Instead of answering him, she moaned and closed her eyes.

Brad squeezed her shoulders. "Dwayne Dempsey is a respected, hard-working man. A good father. I've never heard a bad word about his character or his values. As long as he treats you with respect, I don't see why you'd make a federal case out of an enjoyable fling."

"This morning I asked him to help me with a big business decision and he flatly refused."

Brad sat straight and stared into her eyes. "Why wouldn't he? You always have an air of complete control about you, and you seldom welcome advice or meddling. He's too smart to walk into that mine field."

"I thought he'd…I was afraid he'd be disappointed in me if I made the wrong decision. I cared about his opinion, and all he wanted to do… Go on as if nothing had happened between us."

"You were expecting an apology or a marriage proposal?"

"No. I don't know what I expected." Her dad had posed a very good question. She was old enough to know expectations were too often the doorway to disaster.

Brad uncrossed his legs. "Okay, let's back up. Tell me about the problem you asked him to help you with, how you got your wires crossed and ended up in his bed." He rose from the couch and went to his desk, opened the bottom drawer, and removed a bottle of Jameson's. Without bothering to ask her if she wanted some, he poured a dollop into two glasses and handed one to her.

She told him, to his chuckles, how she and Dwayne had been talking on two different subjects during the first several minutes of their conversation. "Go ahead, laugh. I was mortified, but in retrospect it's funny." She rolled her eyes. "Once we got on the same page though, things moved fast."

Dadley grinned. "No intimate details please. I get the gist. So, this morning you asked for his opinion on the real estate deal and he took a hands-off attitude. A wise man, in my opinion."

Marla sighed and shook her head. "You're right. I know it. But I'm still in a quandary about this deal."

Brad moved to his desk. "Come over here. Let's run some numbers. It shouldn't be that complicated."

"I figured you'd ask." She took some folded papers out of her purse, sat across from him, and slid the papers to the middle of his blotter. "I did this after I called you this morning."

Brad spent several minutes studying the numbers then sat back and removed his reading glasses. "Risk taking is often the road to success, but in today's real estate market it's wise to be cautious. I can see you've been vigilant with your finances, and I commend you on what you've accomplished."

"But?"

"But." He leaned back in his chair. "I imagine you already know this deal would leave you with very little to fall back on if it went south."

"That's what's nagging me. It seems like a great opportunity, almost too good to pass up, but it's taken me years to finally reach the comfortable position I'm in. The thought of going back to square one scares the bejabbers out of me."

"It wouldn't be the end of the world. You're young. You have many earning years left to replace any possible losses. The question is: How much risk are you willing to take, and more important, what is your ultimate goal?"

Marla stood and paced some more. "The problem for me is that this deal came out of the blue. I usually plan and think about decisions for a while before taking a leap. I only have until this evening to decide."

"I think you've already decided."

"I have. Thanks, Dad. You know me so well."

Chapter Sixteen

MARLA'S PHONE RANG AS SHE STEPPED THROUGH HER FRONT door that evening, and she almost stepped on Skipper hopping around her legs. "Wait a minute, baby. Mama has to answer the phone."

She scooped him up and grabbed the handset on her coffee table. "Hello?"

"Hey, Red."

"Hey." Her heart pounded at the warm male sound of Dwayne's voice. Skipper barked. "Skip says, 'hey.'"

"Look, I've been thinking about that real estate deal you asked me about. I shouldn't have brushed you off like that."

She plopped in the middle of the sofa and petted Skipper. Dwayne's words soothed her like a warm, slow massage. "It's okay. I decided to pass on it. I just got home from meeting with the other investors. It's more risk than I'm willing to take right now."

"That's what I thought, but it wasn't my place to say anything. It could turn out to be very lucrative, but you never know. Undeveloped land can be a bottomless money pit."

She sighed, so gratified he agreed with her. "Not only that...the development costs are always way more than projected. It'll be years before they see a return on their investment." She hugged Skippy and let him lick her cheek. "Where are you?"

"I'm just pulling up in front of your house."

She stood so abruptly Skipper did a back flip on her couch. "What?"

"Turning off the engine, Danaher."

Marla ran to the front door, opened it, and watched him step out of the truck. Her heart and lungs floated to her throat when he grinned and waved. His testosterone-oozing stroll melted her resistance. Not that there was much to begin with.

He opened his arms. "I missed you today, beautiful."

A lump the size of a Ping Pong ball formed in her throat, choking off words. She met him halfway and fell into his embrace. An unexpected surge of desire for him warmed her in all the right spots.

His broad chest bounced when he laughed. "Wow. This is a better reception than I expected." He kissed her. "I've wanted to do that all day."

Heart tripping, Marla kissed him back. "Me too."

Skipper barked and clawed at his jeans. Marla lifted him up and pressed him to her cheek. "Skip missed you too." She took his arm. "Come inside."

Dwayne closed the door with his elbow. "Put down the mouse. I want to touch you." He brushed his hand over her bottom when she bent to set Skip on the floor.

Marla rolled into his arms and kissed him. He pushed her back against the door, pressed his body hard against her, stealing her breath. She pushed his jacket off his shoulders without letting up on the kiss. On fire, she yanked his T-shirt over his head and pressed her lips to his neck then grazed his collarbone with her teeth.

Dwayne's head dropped back. "My God, I want to take you here and now, but I need a shower. I've been riding my crew for ten solid hours."

She stroked his chest. "My shower is big enough for both of us. I have a teakwood sitting bench in there, but I don't want to wait, Dempsey. Can we shower…after?" Where was this mindless need for him coming from? What did it matter? Nothing mattered more than making love with him again.

"Don't want to wait? That's my favorite song, Danaher." His hands went to her breasts, her sides. "Get out of these clothes."

Marla reached for the light switch.

"No, leave it on. I need to see you. All of you."

Her clothes hit the floor, the blouse landing on the dog. Skipper yelped and skittered out of the way. Dwayne shoved his jeans below his hips and urged her shoulders and back against the door.

"Wrap those sexy legs around me, Red. We're going for a wild ride."

———

Hot water sluiced over his back in the steam-fogged shower stall. Dwayne sat on the teak bench and reveled in the feel of her hands shampooing his hair, massaging his scalp and shoulders. Arms around her hips, he pulled her against him and buried his face in her breasts. If struck dead this moment, he'd die a happy man.

She was very quiet, too quiet.

"Where are you, Marla?"

She jerked. "What?"

"You're too quiet. Having second thoughts?" God, he hoped not. He wanted this relationship to last a long time.

She squirmed away from him and grinned. "Yes, I'm having second thoughts. I think we should do that a second time." She kissed him and reached for the sprayer to rinse shampoo from his head.

His breath couldn't get past the catch in his throat, but he didn't need to say anything, he hummed his pleasure. When she turned off the water, he caught her around the waist and pulled her back against his chest, her luscious bottom to his lap. Hands slick with water, he stroked her belly and legs. "You're the best surprise since I got my first pony."

"Is that a compliment?" She twisted her hips.

"Coming from a Wyoming cowboy? You bet." He shifted her to her feet. "Be my crutch. I don't know where I left my foot. I had other things on my mind at the time."

Marla eased under his shoulder. "It's next to the bed. I remember because when it hit the floor, poor Skipper just about had a heart attack."

Dwayne laughed then sucked in a breath when her hand drifted to caress his bottom. He pulled her into him and kissed her. "I don't know if I can handle you, Danaher."

"Yes, you can, Dempsey. Not only that you have. And you will." She led him to the bed.

He flopped on his back and threw out his arms. "You're gonna kill me."

"I am?" Her eyebrows went up, and she grinned wickedly. "Why?"

He chuckled and patted the bed beside him. "I'm so tired I'm seeing double. I need sleep, then food. Then…we'll improvise."

"Are we calling in sick in the morning?"

"Oh, yeah."

"Good. I'm feeling under the weather already."

The woman of his dreams crawled in beside him and wrapped her soft arm and silky leg across his well-used body.

———

Marla stroked his chest then his cheek. How wonderful it would be to wake up beside him like this every morning. "Dwayne?"

"I'm awake, honey." His eyes opened and he cracked a small grin.

His smile could melt the polar icecap, and she sighed at the delicious tingling between her legs then poked his belly. "I'm getting up to fix breakfast."

He rose on his elbows. "I can do that."

She threw the sheet over his face. "It's my turn. I'll call you when it's ready. Come on, Skippy. Time to visit the outdoor comfort station."

On her way to the back door she grabbed Dwayne's T-shirt from the hall floor and pulled it over her head. She inhaled his scent and groaned. It barely covered her bottom but was wide and roomy otherwise. She unlocked the doggy door, and Skipper scampered out to complete his mission.

What to fix? Marla settled on a western omelet and set about chopping onion, tomato, and green pepper. Bacon bits would have to fill in for ham. When Skip nosed her ankle and whined, she filled his water bowl and put a handful of kibble in his dish.

Eight eggs should probably do it. She cracked them into a large bowl with a handle. Whipping them to a frothy liquid, she poured them in the hot pan then lifted the edges with a rubber spatula.

"The toast!" She quit daydreaming about Dempsey's sexual prowess and dropped four slices on the rack of the toaster oven. Then she thought about that prowess again.

"Dwayne! Come and get it!" she hollered.

"That's my intention."

She jumped, startled by his voice so close behind her. "Darn it! How long have you been standing there?"

"Long enough to soak up the best view in Spring Grove."

A hot flush rose from her neck at the sight of his bare chest. Dwayne had a manly chest. Not ripped like he worked out with weights, but a solid, working man's chest. "I...um...I put on your shirt."

"I see." His blue eyes burned with desire.

"Breakfast is ready."

"I see that too."

Heart pounding, she pointed to a chair. "Sit. I'll dish it up." She gingerly pulled the hot toast from the rack and dropped two pieces on each plate next to the eggs.

"I could get used to this."

So could she. "I'm not a very good cook."

"I wasn't referring to your cooking, Danaher." He ran a callused hand across her bare bottom when she bent to put the plate in front of him. "Yum, yum."

Would she ever breathe normally when she looked at him, felt his hands on her skin? Determined not to play the part of a needy, clinging vine—although *needy* described her perfectly this morning—she sat across from him and poured orange juice into his glass. "I...um...forgot to make coffee."

The back screen door squeaked open. "Hello-oo, Mar-laa."

"Oh, no, it's Charlene." She cast a desperate look at Dwayne. "What should we do?"

He shrugged.

Char charged into the kitchen. "Hi, sis, I..." Her eyes darted from Dwayne's bare back to Marla's face then his back again. "I do hope I'm interrupting something."

She closed the distance to the round table and sat between them. "Good morning." She took a piece of toast from Marla's plate, spread a generous amount of marmalade on it, and took a bite. "Any more of that omelet? I'm starving."

Dwayne pushed his plate toward her. "Good morning. You're welcome to some of mine. Marla was generous with me."

"Don't mind if I do." Charlene got up, opened the cupboard, and took a plate for herself then she opened the utensil drawer and removed a fork.

Marla's chest constricted and her ears rang. Unable to move or speak, she stared at her sister and Dwayne chatting as if nothing was out of order. It was perfectly normal for him to be found half-naked at her breakfast table, right?

Char gave her a brief glance and turned to Dwayne. "No tattoos? I was sure you'd have at least one, being in the Marines and all. Donnie's got a big one right here." She touched Dwayne's pectorals and took a bite of the omelet. "Mmm, good."

He smiled at her sister and took a swallow of orange juice. "No tattoos. I didn't want to mar my magnificent bod."

Charlene waggled her brows. "I see. Where's the coffee? Marla, did you make coffee?" Her head swiveled as she looked to the counter where the coffeemaker sat cold and unused. "No? Okay, I'll make some."

Marla sat in mute mortification while Charlene busied herself making coffee. Of all the mornings for her twin sister to show up unannounced. She made the mistake of glancing at Dwayne.

He winked and chewed on his toast as if he were here every morning, half dressed, having breakfast with her.

Charlene poured water in the well, added coffee grounds to the basket.

"You okay?" Char asked, her big eyes shining.

"Char, what you are doing here at this hour?"

"The question, dear sister," she said as she pointed at Dwayne, "is what're you doing here at this hour?"

"I take a little cream with my coffee," Dwayne said with a grin. He gazed at Marla. "Right, honey?"

Marla gave up. She moaned and dropped her head in her hands. "Please, lightning strike now."

Charlene poured a cup of coffee for Dwayne, opened the refrigerator for the half-and-half then put it on the table. "You take yours black, right, sis?"

Hands still covering her mouth, Marla nodded and uttered a muffled, "Yes." She knew Charlene would absolutely, positively, never, ever let her live this down.

Dwayne poured cream in his coffee and stirred it with his fork. "Smells great, Charlene. Thanks."

"You're welcome, I'm sure you earned it." She winked at Marla. "Did he? Earn it?"

"Yes, Char." Marla glared. "He earned it. Every last drop. Anything else you'd like to know?" She'd get even with her sister for this embarrassing moment if it was the last thing she ever did.

Charlene gave Dwayne a sassy grin, accompanied by fluttering lashes. "I'm sure he did, and yes, I'd like every lurid detail, but I doubt you're in a mood to share."

Marla's lips twitched a small smile. "I have to hand it to you, Char. You're so perceptive." She poked her arm. "Why are you here?"

"Ow." Charlene bounced in her chair. "Oh, oh, I'm so excited. Donovan called to see if the three of us could come to Camp Pendleton Friday night. He got a weekend pass." Her gaze bobbed between them. "Want to go? He reserved two rooms at the Hotel Del Coronado. I've always wanted to go there. It's so historical, so romantic." She sighed and crossed her hands over her heart.

"Two rooms?" Marla asked, her brow furrowed.

"Donnie said we'd only need two rooms because Dwayne would have gotten you in bed by now, and obviously he did, so you can stay together. Sound like a plan?" She gazed at Dwayne.

"Sounds like a plan to me," he said. "Want to go, honey?"

"But what about Skipper? Do they allow pets?" What did it matter? She had no intention of spending the weekend with Donovan, Charlene, and Dwayne, in a hotel, in San Diego.

"No," Char said. "I already asked Sil to watch him for the weekend. Any other reason you can't go?"

Apparently she had no say in the matter. Coronado Island for the weekend sounded romantic, now that she had a few moments to consider it. "Um, no, I can't think of any."

"Oh, goody. Let's take the train. It'll be fun. Donnie will meet us at the San Diego station. We'll go in his car from there. Coffee refills, anyone?"

Chapter Seventeen

Friday morning, Marla and Charlene shivered in the cool morning fog at Simi Valley Amtrak Station. Dwayne set the bags down and put his arms around them and hugged them for warmth.

"Brrr, I hope it's warmer when we get to Coronado Island." Marla snuggled closer.

Dwayne kissed Marla's forehead. "I talked to Donovan last night. He said balmy, and more of the same expected for the weekend."

Char pointed. "Look, the signal lights are flashing. The train will be here in a couple of minutes. I haven't been on the choo-choo for years. This is fun." She lifted her bag from the platform and leaned to peer down the track.

Dwayne grabbed his and Marla's bags as the engine's headlight appeared from the north. "Here she comes."

The sleek Pacific Surfliner rolled to a stop at the platform, and Marla checked their tickets again to see if she could tell which car to board.

Char bounced on her toes. "Over there, Marla, Business Class car. See?"

Dwayne grinned. "Your sister is like a kid. I'm not sure if she's more excited about seeing my brother again or taking a ride on the train."

Marla enjoyed Charlene's excitement and felt a twinge of her own.

She and Dwayne had crawled out of her bed at five that morning with the benefit of little sleep. "I hope I don't look as ragged as I feel this morning."

"You look well-loved, Red." He nodded to the car where Charlene spoke to the conductor. "Takes four hours to get there. You can have a nap."

"Fat chance of that. I need more coffee. I'm hungry."

"I had no idea you were so high maintenance."

"Welcome to Marla's World." She followed her sister inside the car, and they selected a row with facing seats near the center of the car.

"This looks comfy, sis. You sit across from me and we can play cards."

"Dwayne can play cards with you. I plan to snooze."

"Party poop." Char smiled at Dwayne. "Sit across from me. Marla doesn't like cards." She removed a deck from her purse. "Poker, Twenty-one, Gin, name your poison, Sergeant Dempsey."

"I like strip-poker, but Amtrak probably doesn't allow it."

"I don't know if I can stand the two of you for four straight hours."

"What a grouch. That woman needs coffee."

"So she said." Dwayne hefted their bags onto the overhead luggage rack.

The train rolled away from the station in less than five minutes. Marla sighed with contentment when Dwayne sat next to her.

He took her hand in his. "Okay, Danaher?"

"More than Okay, Dempsey."

Charlene propped open the small table and set the cards on top. "I'm not sure what kind of magic you weave, Mr. Dempsey, but you've definitely mellowed my little sister's uptight personality."

Marla stuck her tongue out at Charlene, and they exchanged identical sour faces.

Dwayne reached for the cards and opened the box. "Am I going to have to referee you two all the way to the end of the line?"

The Surfliner crawled into the long tunnel in the Santa Susanna Mountains separating Ventura County from Los Angeles County. Marla yawned when lights winked on in the car.

The conductor made her way through the coach checking tickets and chatting with passengers. Dwayne handed over their tickets. "Any chance of getting a cup of coffee?"

"Absolutely. Self-serve coffee and juice are at the end of the coach, and the snack bar is two cars back."

He stood. "Shall I bring you two hot babes a cup of coffee?"

"Oh, yes, please," Marla said.

"No coffee for me. I'll have juice," Char answered.

"You got it." He walked to the back of the slightly swaying car.

"How can you keep your hands off that hunk of man? He makes my heart go pitter-pat."

Marla pointed at her twin and smiled. "He's off limits to you, Charlene."

"Oh pish, I have my own Dempsey. He's all yours. That doesn't mean I can't appreciate him for the next few hours, does it?" Charlene crossed her slender legs and bobbed a sandaled foot.

Marla leaned forward and whispered in a conspiratorial hiss, "Have you ever wondered what it is with Danaher women and Dempsey men? I mean, even our mother had the...whatever it is."

"You always have to analyze everything, don't you? Me—I'm just going to sit back and enjoy it." She reached up with her hand as Dwayne returned with the drinks. "Thank you, Dwayne. What is it, cranberry?"

"That's what it says on the bottle." He handed the other cup to Marla. "Here's your coffee, honey. You want a doughnut or something from the snack bar?"

"Thank you, yes, whatever looks good." She tilted her head back for his kiss.

"*You* look good." He kissed her soundly.

Char put her hand on her chest when Dwayne walked away. "Oh lordy, I could have an orgasm just looking at that man."

"Charlene!"

"What?"

"You and your mouth."

"Tell me you don't feel the same way, Miss Starchy Pants."

Marla rolled her eyes. Would she ever get used to her sister's every thought rolling off her tongue for the entire world to hear?

Her cheeks caught fire when she noticed the man across the aisle grin and then quickly hide behind his newspaper. Mortified, that's what she was, mortified. "I love you Char, but sometimes I want to slap duct tape over your mouth."

Dwayne soon appeared carrying a tray loaded with a variety of snacks. He set it on the small table. "Did you finish your coffee already? I'll get another cup for you."

"No, sit, I'm fine for now. What did you bring us?"

"Good stuff, doughnuts and three breakfast sandwiches. Take your pick." He sat next to her and winked lasciviously at Charlene.

Char pointed her finger at him. "Careful. Your brother has a jealous streak."

Dwayne said, "I can take him down in under a minute."

"Hmmm?" She lifted a sandwich off the tray and removed the paper wrapper. "Have one of these, Marla. Packed with nutrition, loaded with the three essential food groups. Fat, salt, and carbs."

Marla helped herself to one of the sandwiches. "Smells good and I'm famished. Thanks, Dempsey."

"Any time, Danaher."

Dwayne stretched out his legs and pulled the bill of his baseball cap over his eyes. "I'm gonna grab a few Z's, ladies." And just like that, he was out.

Marla's eyes grew heavy and she leaned into Dwayne's shoulder. "I can't stay awake another minute, Char."

She woke to find herself on her side with her head in Dwayne's lap. He joked with the man across the aisle, who was in the middle of a card game with Charlene. "Better quit while you're ahead, buddy. That woman takes no prisoners."

Marla moaned and sat up. "How long did I sleep?" She smoothed down her hair and rubbed her eyes. "Gosh, I went right out."

Dwayne grinned and stretched his back. "We noticed. You slept about two hours."

Charlene leaned forward. "I didn't know you snored, sis."

Marla jerked back. "I do *not* snore! Do I, Dwayne?"

He kissed her. "I'm taking the fifth on that one, honey."

She snored? They had to be teasing her. She couldn't imagine anything more embarrassing than being caught snoring on a crowded train. She tossed back her hair and stood. "I'm going to the ladies room." She stepped over Dwayne's legs. "Excuse me."

He let his hand brush her hip and bottom as she stepped across him, and chuckled at her offended glare. "Hurry back."

———

Dwayne leaned into the window and searched the arrivals platform as the train glided into the Spanish Colonial style San Diego Union Station. "There's Donovan."

The three of them stepped off the train. "Donovan!" Charlene called and waved. She ran to meet him and jumped into his arms, legs around his waist and arms around his neck.

Dwayne shook his head at the look of adoration on his little brother's face. Donovan was a goner, for sure. "Looks like he's glad to see her. What do you think?"

"I'm going to kill Char if she breaks your brother's heart."

What about his heart? Had Marla given any thought to that? "Hey, baby bro!" The two men bumped fists and slammed into each other like hockey players who'd just scored a goal. "How's it going?"

Donovan took Charlene's bag. "Come on, I'm parked in a pick-up zone. Don't want to get ticketed." He put his arm around Charlene's shoulder and hugged her to his side.

Dwayne followed suit and urged Marla after them. "Yeah, I'm itching to get my toes in that swimming pool."

Donovan grinned over his shoulder. "You mean the five you've still got left?"

"Watch it, kid. I can still whip your ass."

Laughing, the four of them piled into Donovan's none-too-new Range Rover and fastened their seat belts as he pulled away from the curb and waved to the traffic enforcement officer.

"That was close." Charlene said, and gave the uniformed woman a big smile.

Donovan drove a couple of blocks, pulled to the curb, and snapped off his seat belt. He grabbed Charlene and planted a kiss on her lips. Then another.

Dwayne punched his shoulder. "Hey, get a room."

"That's what I intend to do." Donovan shifted back to the driver's seat and moved into traffic. "I couldn't wait to kiss my woman. You know how it is."

Yeah, Dwayne knew how it was. He instinctively took Marla's hand and leaned in for a kiss.

She whispered in his ear. "Can't wait to get in the pool? I had something else in mind." Didn't take any more than those few words and he went hard.

Time to take a breath and do some recon, soldier.

Were they moving too fast? Heading for a flameout? He sure as hell hoped not.

He leaned close to Donovan's seat. "How long till we get there?"

Donovan's shoulders bounced. "What is this? An are-we-there-yet-daddy moment? Relax. Enjoy the scenery."

Charlene stared adoringly at his brother. "I'm enjoying the scenery, Donnie."

He smiled back. "Me too, sweet thing."

Dwayne faced Marla and waggled his eyebrows. "Think we'll be seeing much of them this weekend?"

"Nope. Could get lonely all by ourselves."

The heat of her gaze went right through him. Front to back. Head to toe. He could be in very deep shit in no time.

Chapter Eighteen

Saturday morning the four of them lounged around the pool after breakfast and took advantage of the warm sun and clear blue sky. A soft breeze ruffled the palm fronds over Marla's head, and two gulls danced in the air above them.

She pointed to the birds. "Look. I wonder what it would feel like to be a bird. Do you think birds have fun?"

Dwayne's gaze followed her hand. "Never doubted it for a minute." He sat up and threw his legs over the side of the lounge. "Think I'll go for a swim. You game?"

She stood to follow and the thought of him swimming with his prosthetic foot puzzled her. The mystery was solved when he sat at the edge of the pool and removed it.

A small boy wearing inflatable water wings paddled to them. "What happened, mister? Are you a soldier?"

Without a hint of embarrassment, Dwayne leaned forward on his hands. "I used to be a soldier. Got it blown clean off in the war."

The child's eyes widened. "Did it hurt?"

"Not when it happened, but it was pretty sore while the doctors were patching me up."

"Can I touch it?" The boy's innocence touched Marla's heart.

Dwayne's relaxed attitude with the child was wonderful to behold.

The little boy's mother ran to them just as he reached tentatively for Dwayne's stump. "Logan! What are you doing? Get out of the pool and leave this man alone." She turned her red face toward Dwayne. "I'm so embarrassed."

Dwayne lifted the boy from the pool and set him on his lap. "Don't be. He's curious. A normal kid." He ruffled the child's hair. "My daughter touches it all the time, Logan. She even helps me put my wooden leg on once in a while." He winked at the kid's mother.

Marla touched the woman's arm. "It's okay, really."

Donovan strolled to the pool's edge. He smiled at the woman and went down on his haunches. "My big brother is showing off for the kids again, I see." He picked up the boy and handed him to his mom then shoved Dwayne into the pool. "I'll see if I can drown him for you." He jumped in.

When Dwayne's head surfaced, he shook the water out of his eyes and pounced on Donovan. Marla was afraid they'd have to call the lifeguard to save both of them at this rate. She scooched back from the edge. The last thing she wanted was to be in the middle of their splashing and horsing around. Let them drown each other. Men! Did they ever grow up?

Charlene stood next to her. "Is your Dempsey trying to kill my Dempsey?"

"Can't tell who's ahead yet. Let's go to the bar and get a Bloody Mary. We'll come back and claim the bodies later." She picked up the hat from the lounge and wrapped her sarong around her hips.

Char lowered her sunglasses and made squinty-eyes. "Starting early aren't we? Who are you and where is my sister?"

Half an hour later, the two dripping men joined them at the pool-side bar. Once they got the shoving out of the way, they squeezed onto barstools between her and Char.

Charlene made goo-goo eyes at Donovan. "Did big bad Dwayne hurt you, sweetie?"

Donovan laid a kiss on her. "Nah." He signaled the bartender. "A Corona and a Dr. Pepper over here when you get a chance." He kissed her again. "You already on the hard stuff?"

Marla giggled when Charlene replied, "Don't worry, we won't drink enough for you two cavemen to take advantage of us."

She leaned into Dwayne's wet shoulder. "Speak for yourself, Char." She wrinkled her nose when he poured the Dr. Pepper into his ice-filled glass. "Did you hold your own in the pool?"

"Donovan can beat me in a foot race, but he's no match for me in a swimming competition." He reached across Charlene and smacked him on the head. "Right?"

Donovan picked up his beer bottle and raised it in a salute. "Right."

And that's the way the weekend went.

Marla wondered about all the fun she'd been missing over the years. She peered at her sister through different eyes. Maybe Char was on to something.

———

Dwayne and Marla stepped off the train mid-day on Monday. Charlene stayed in San Diego for a couple of more days.

On the drive from Simi to Spring Grove Marla asked him, "Do you think your brother will deploy to the Middle East again?"

"I doubt it. If he re-ups, he'll probably go to K-Bay on Oahu. He'd like to be a drill sergeant. He'd be good at it."

"How long would he be there?"

"Until they send him somewhere else. When you're a Marine you go where they tell you." He'd probably still be in if it wasn't for the RPG that nearly killed him and Cluny. "He has a few months to decide."

Marla was quiet for a few moments then said, "Do you miss the military? Do you ever wish you were still on active duty?"

"Sometimes, but I've got different responsibilities now. Life has a funny way of playing dirty tricks. Sometimes the dirty tricks have a silver lining."

Marla nodded. "Amber."

"Exactly."

That one word told her all she needed to know about his priorities.

They drove to the condos. "I've got to grab the paperwork and get to my appointment with the storage facility owner. I'll be back in a couple of hours to take you home."

"I'll ask Cluny or one of the other men to drop me off."

"See if Cluny has time. My guys are on the clock. We're heading down the home stretch and they can see bonuses on the horizon."

"Oh, I forgot about that. Silly me. I've had this persistent distraction for the past three days."

"Hmm, wonder what that's all about." He gave her a quick kiss.

"Stop that! Somebody might see you."

"I checked. Nobody's around."

They stepped down from his truck and entered the trailer. Cluny had the phone to his ear but nodded his acknowledgement.

Dwayne took the storage facility blueprints and file and immediately headed for the door. He leaned to whisper in her ear, "I'll cook tonight. Come over about seven."

"I can't. I promised Rosie we'd go to dinner and a movie tonight. Can I come over after?"

"You have to ask?" He winked and, with a nod to Cluny, left.

She got a cup of water, sat across from Cluny, and waited for him to get off the phone.

He smiled and hung up. "Hey, looks like you got some sun. How was Coronado?"

She returned his smile. "Beautiful. We had a good time. The hotel is fantastic. Charlene and Donovan still have today and tomorrow to enjoy it. I need a ride home. Do you have time to take me?"

He pressed his lips together and took a breath through his nose. "No, sorry. I'm on my way to put out a small fire for a customer in the opposite direction. That's who I was on the phone with. I can ask one of Gunny's guys to take you, or if you can wait for an hour, I'm happy to do it."

"I can wait. No problem. I'll answer the phone and do some paperwork while I'm here."

"You sure?"

"Yes. Go on." She rose to let him pass then sat in the chair he'd just vacated.

"Okay, thanks. My cell number is programmed into the phone if you need to call me."

"Take your time. I've got enough to keep me busy." She waved as he went out the door then picked up the phone to call Rosie and confirm their girlfriend date.

———

"That movie was hilarious," Rosie said. "Pete and I'll enjoy getting out more often. There's no such thing as a sixteen screen stadium cinema in Buffalo. We have one small movie house that shows two movies a week."

"How did you like the Mexican restaurant?"

"I loved it. We do have a couple in Buffalo, but when I told you coming here was like the big city for us, I wasn't kidding."

"It's interesting to see my home town through your eyes. I'd love to see where you came from."

"We'll have to make it happen then."

"I don't see how."

"Really? Your family and the Dempseys go back a long way. I'm surprised you haven't visited that part of Wyoming before now."

"The Danahers and Dempseys do have history, but it's complicated. In any case, I hardly remember Dwayne's mother. She went home to her family's ranch when I was about twelve. I doubt she remembers me. My mother was very jealous of her."

"What was that all about?"

Should she tell her? "Um, okay, I'll tell you, but I'm invoking the girlfriend ground rules."

Rosie waved her hand. "Goes without saying."

Marla proceeded to tell Rosie the tale of her parents and John Dempsey. "Our dads, known as the Double D's, have been friends since the Stone Age, even when they were both in love with my mother, Silvia."

"That is complicated."

"Yes, well when John fell for Kathleen Burwell and dumped Mom, Dad jumped in to pick up the pieces and she married him."

Rosie's mystified expression told her she needed further explanation. "It's not like Silvia didn't love my dad. It's just that she thought she was 'in love' with Uncle Johnny."

"Uncle Johnny?"

"That's what the four of us kids have always called him. Sounds incestuous, doesn't it?"

Rosie chuckled. "Well, if John were your uncle, I'd have to look askance at your relationship with Dwayne. What? Don't look at me like that. Dylan told me."

Was it front-page news? Marla groaned and came to a standstill. "I need ice cream."

"Great. I'm in."

They sat at a table outside the ice cream store. It was cool but still nice enough to enjoy the outdoors. Marla decided to admit what Rosie and everyone else seemed to know.

"Dwayne and I, we're…seeing each other."

"Mm hm." Rosie picked a big chunk of Butterfinger out of her ice cream cup but said nothing else.

"Say something!"

"You having fun?" When Marla just stared, Rosie added, "You want out of it?"

"Yes to the first question, no to the second, but I doubt it will last long." At the thought of breaking up with Dwayne, her heart squeezed painfully.

"Won't last long? Why? You and Dwayne should be good for each other."

"He has other priorities."

"And those would be?"

"Amber is his number one priority, and she should be. He has a business to run, a payroll to meet, and responsibilities to his mother and the ranch. I'm way down on his list."

"Oh, for heaven's sake. Do you think Dwayne can only sing in one key? We all balance dozens of balls in the air. Sometimes one thing takes precedence over another, but we manage, don't we? Having a partner is high on the scale of what's important."

Yes, Rosie was right, but she wasn't sure it was high on Dwayne's list.

Chapter Nineteen

MARLA ROLLED OVER AND WATCHED DWAYNE AS HE SLEPT. SHE felt as relaxed and contented as he looked. Stealthily, she lifted the sheet and rose on her elbow. She stared at his naked body, appreciating every muscle definition, every hair, the rise and fall of his chest, the way he smelled.

He threw off the sheet. "Do I pass inspection?"

Startled, she screeched and fell back on her pillow. "One of these days you're going to give me a heart attack!" Pounding his shoulder she said, "I thought you were asleep."

"You can look anytime you want to, Danaher. You don't have to peek at me when I'm sleeping." He crawled on top of her and kissed her neck, ear, and lips. "I like looking at you too."

Marla wrapped her legs around him. His quick arousal excited her every time. "Get off me then and have a look."

"I'm busy right now." He raised himself on his elbows, stared into her eyes and rocked against her. "How about you?"

By way of an answer, she tugged his head down for another kiss and pushed her hips into his. "You're insatiable."

"Me?" He chuckled, slipped inside her, and drove her passion several degrees higher. "It's not me, honey, it's us."

Marveling at how she'd lived to the ripe old age of twenty-seven and was just now discovering her deep needs and desires, she lost herself in him. Lighter than a cloud, her climax took flight and left her breathless. She clung to him, not wanting him to stop.

It's us.

———

Dwayne gasped, heart pounding against her breast. "You good?" He brushed his lips against her cheek and tasted tears.

Startled, he raised his head. "Did I hurt you?"

Marla rolled her head on the pillow and touched his cheek. "You moved me, Dempsey." Another tear trickled down her face. She tightened her grip around his waist. "Don't go yet."

What was happening between him and this woman? He'd never thought it possible to be so in sync with someone. So consumed to the point he was unable to think of anything beyond making love to her. Now. Today. Tonight. Tomorrow. The next day. Forever.

He'd thought Donovan was a goner? He'd been so driven with his desire to get Marla into bed he hadn't noticed he was nearly drowning in her. *You moved me,* she'd said. No, it was definitely the other way around.

He pressed his forehead against hers. "I'm falling for you, Danaher." To his shock, she went still and let her arms drop on the bed. He waited a second then looked into her eyes. Her flat expression staggered him like a slap in the face.

She moved beneath him. "I have to go. Let me up."

What a fool. They weren't anywhere near on the same page. Why hadn't he kept his big mouth shut?

He rolled to his side and pulled the sheet up to his shoulders. "No problem."

"Dwayne."

He shrugged off her hand. "I said no problem. You have to go. So go."

In less than five minutes, she was gone. A cold, sick feeling gripped his gut when he heard the sound of her car engine recede down the street. Paralysis took root in his body and mind.

What went wrong?

———

Marla drove to her parent's home, realized it was too early to pick up Skipper, and kept going. Without realizing how she'd got there, she found herself in Charlene's parking spot at the building where they'd briefly shared an apartment years before. She still had a key.

The empty apartment was eerily quiet, dark, and cold with the drapes drawn. She moved to the first window, pulled the wand, and let the morning sun streak across the living room. Without letting go, she pulled them closed again, and lay on her side on Char's new chintz upholstered couch. Her knees drawn to her waist, she choked on a sob.

She should have been flying high with happiness, but instead she wallowed in grief and let the tears fall. She'd known going in, she was opening herself to a shattered heart. Like a self-fulfilling prophesy, she'd brought it to a head by walking out on him when he'd said, in the heat of their passion, *I'm falling for you.*

What was she to do? She couldn't possibly face him again. The building project was nearly finished, but she'd have to do a final inspection and pay him.

Shocked when the door opened, she leaped up from the sofa and faced the door, knees wobbling, heart pounding.

Her mother's voice called, "Marla? Are you here? I saw your car downstairs."

"Mom?" She ran to Silvia and threw her arms around her. The floodgates opened.

"Marla, sweetheart, what is it?" Silvia clung to her and patted her back. "Talk to me. What's happened?" She edged them to the sofa and pulled her down beside her.

Marla sobbed, inconsolable, unable to speak. She'd never been so glad to see her mother in her whole life. She leaned into her and dropped her head in Silvia's lap.

Her mom rubbed her arm and stroked her hair. "Take your time. I'm not going anywhere."

Marla placed her hand on top of her mother's. "I love you, Mom."

"I know, honey. I love you too, with all my heart." Her words started the waterworks flowing again. "Shh, all will be well."

After a while, Silvia murmured, "It's Dwayne Dempsey, isn't it?"

"How did you know?" Marla rubbed tears and snot off her face with the sleeve of her blouse, not caring how gross it must look.

"Your father told me you were interested in him and wary of getting involved." She sighed. "I'm sorry the Dempsey curse has roped in both my daughters. They're heartbreakers, every one of those magnificent bastards! What did he do to you? I'll kill him."

Marla shook her head and giggled. "Thanks, Mom. I needed that. I'm a mess."

"Did he make love to you then walk out like a total shit heel?"

Was this her mother? The woman she so condescendingly called Silly Silvia? Shame descended on her with a sickening thud.

"No. I walked out on him like a total shit heel."

Silvia stood and went to the window. "Let's get some light in this dungeon." She swept back the drapes and Marla covered her eyes in the glaring light, squinting at her mother.

"Oh, my darling. You look like you've been to hell and back. I'm sure he deserved it. What did that Dempsey devil say to you?"

"He said he was falling for me."

"He...my word, that was a nasty thing to say, wasn't it?" She took Marla's shoulders and turned her so they were face to face. "Oh my, you're in love with him."

Marla sucked in a sob and nodded. "Mom?" She took a breath. "Mom, were you in love with Uncle Johnny?"

With an abject sigh, Silvia nodded. "Completely."

"But...what about..."

"...your father? Bradley Danaher is the most wonderful man in the world. When John walked out on me, he was there to mend my broken heart. I can't explain to you how much I love Brad. He has never once thrown John up to me. I don't deserve him."

"Oh, Mom, you do. Dad's crazy for you. He said the day John eloped with Kathleen was the luckiest day of his life."

"Did he? Such a dear man. He tells me I'm his pot of gold at the end of the rainbow, but I had no idea he shared his feelings with you. I can't imagine living without Brad. He never complains about the money I spend, some of the silly things I do and say, but he did lay down the law about John's wife. Told me it was time to snap out of it. He was right, you know. She's a lovely person."

"Even though she married Uncle Johnny?"

"You know something, honey? Not once did John Dempsey ever tell me that he loved me or that he was 'falling' for me. It was wishful thinking on my part. We were together, but in his mind we were merely pals with benefits. Very hot benefits." She pointed her finger in Marla's face. "That is *not* for publication."

Marla smiled and pretended to lock her lips and throw away the key.

They took a few moments of exchanging loving looks and Marla hugged her mother with new appreciation. "What should I do, Mom?"

"What do you want to do?"

"Why do people always say that when you ask for advice?"

"Because it's the right thing to say. You must do what you think is best for yourself, not what someone else thinks is best. What do you want to do?"

Marla put her hands on her cheeks. "I want to get in my car, drive straight back to his house, get down on my knees, and beg him to forgive me and forget what I said."

"That's a bit drastic but can easily be modified." She sat back against the cushions, crossed her legs, and bounced her foot just the way Charlene often did. She tapped a finger on her chin.

"How about this? Go home, shower, change clothes, then find him and suggest you go out for coffee and talk it over."

"Finally, some advice I can use." She kissed her mother, grabbed her purse, and headed for the door.

"Marla!"

She stopped and turned, hand on the doorknob.

Silvia smiled. "I dropped Skipper off at your house on my way here to water Char's plants. He'll be happy to see you even if Dwayne isn't."

Marla chuckled. "I'll always have Skip's loyalty. Bye, Mom."

———

Cluny met Dwayne's eyes when he thundered into the construction trailer, took in his black expression, and said, "Oh, shit."

Dwayne glared. "Don't say another goddamned word or you'll be picking yourself up off the floor." He pulled off his leather jacket and flung it in the direction of the coat hook, kicked a wastebasket out of his way, and poured a cup of coffee that looked and smelled like yesterday's sludge into his unwashed mug. Just what he needed.

The door snapped shut when Cluny departed. There was a man who knew when to keep his mouth shut. He'd be around when Dwayne needed him and wouldn't expect an apology.

He removed files from desk drawers and the filing cabinet. It was time to wrap up this damn job and get out of here. He'd tally the final expenses, give Danaher a bill, collect his money, pay his crew, and disappear from her life.

First though, he had to line up materials for the storage facility job scheduled to start next week. He spent an hour on the phone lining everything up for the first phase of the project.

The door opened. Slim stepped inside. "We're done, Gunny. Do you want to walk through the building one last time before the Boss Lady does her final inspection?"

Dwayne stood and stretched. "Yeah, tell the painting contractor to hang around until I have a look."

Slim tipped his head. "I'll make sure he doesn't leave before you're ready." He backed out and closed the door.

"Wait, Slim. Tell Jack I want him to start packing and securing the trailer this afternoon so we can haul it to the new site."

"He's just heading out to his kid's Little League game. I'll catch him."

"No. Forget it." He waved Slim off. "He can get to it tomorrow."

He carried his mug to the sink. The door opened again. "Now what, for chrissakes!"

"Hey, Dempsey."

His head whipped around. Marla stood in the doorway, her backlit hair floating red-golden around her shoulders. "What do you want, Danaher?" He turned his back on her.

"You."

Unable to breathe under the enormity of the weight on his heart, he stood still and stiff.

"I want you." Her footsteps approached, and then her hand rested on his back.

A moment of hurt and anger almost prevented him from doing what he most wanted to do. He turned around and drew her into his arms. With her chest crushed against his, their heartbeats spoke through the silence.

"God, I want you too."

"I love you, Dwayne."

He crushed his mouth on hers. This time he wouldn't let her walk because he needed this woman in his life. He held her beautiful face in her hands, sighed deeply, and then smiled.

"Come with me. Let's take a final walk through the building, let the painting contractor take off then we'll go home."

Chapter Twenty

"We need to go shopping. You're out of milk and there's not a single fresh fruit or vegetable in this place. By the end of summer you'll have a good case of the rickets. I swear I don't know how men survive." Marla loaded dishes in the dishwasher and glanced over her shoulder to see if Dwayne had been listening.

He looked up from the paper. "Yes, honey, I heard you. You'll have to go without me. We're hauling the trailer off your lot today so the paving and landscaping contractors can get in there."

He put down the paper and went across the kitchen. Standing behind her with his body pressed against her, he reached around and fondled her breasts. "You are one bossy woman, Danaher."

"You're one horny man, Dempsey." She pushed back with her butt. "Go then. I'll stop at the store on my way home from the office."

He took a small step back, but not before running a hand down her torso and resting it on her magic triangle. He gave her a squeeze. "Let's go back to bed."

Chuckling, she grabbed his wrist and pushed his hand away. "We're both late. Beat it."

"Hey, I'm the man of the house. I'll make the decisions."

She turned and crossed her arms. "And when, exactly, do you plan to begin?"

He pulled her into his embrace and kissed her soundly. "One of these days." Another kiss. "Maybe."

Marla draped her arms around his neck and smiled. "Really? We'll see about that. Now, I really do have to get to work. I'll see you later."

"Your place or mine?"

"Mine." She pointed to Skipper sitting on his haunches, studying their every move. "He's homesick."

Dwayne scooped Skip up and pushed his nose against the mutt's. "You homesick, soldier? I didn't think so." He set him on the floor and pecked her on the cheek. "He's not homesick, he likes it here."

"Yes, and so do I, but we need to go home once in a while. What do you want for dinner?"

"I'll get takeout. There's a great Chinese place half a block from the new jobsite." He took his heavy work shirt from the back of his chair and his keys off the hook by the door. "I'll try and get there before eight."

Marla waved at his retreating back then finished cleaning the sink and loading the dishwasher. Her heart tripped a happy beat, and just because she had to, she lifted Skipper to her face and kissed him right on the mouth. "You're my real boyfriend, Skipper. Our secret."

She dropped Skipper off at home, retrieved her briefcase, and checked to make sure she had her listings file. On the run till mid-afternoon, she cleared off her desk and peeked into her boss's office. "Ted, I took a deposit on the Seymour property. Won't it be great to finally get that turkey sold?"

He laughed and nodded. "Let's keep our fingers crossed. We've been down this road before. You taking off?"

"Yes, I've got company for dinner and I still have to get to the grocery store. I'll see you tomorrow."

She had one foot out the door when the receptionist called her name. "Marla, your sister's on the phone."

"Oh boy, what now?" She returned to her desk and lifted the handset. "Hey, sis, what's up? I'm on my way out the door."

"I know. That's what she said. I'm glad I caught you. Want to have dinner tonight? I thought we'd go out. I'm too pooped to cook."

"You cook? I didn't know that."

"Ha ha, smarty pants. Where should we go?"

"Dwayne's coming over tonight. He's bringing Chinese takeout."

"Can I come?"

Marla picked up a note of distress in Char's voice.

"Sure. If I know him, he'll bring more than enough for three. He probably won't be there much before eight though. I'm on my way to the store, but I'll be home in about an hour. Come over whenever you want."

"Thanks, sis. I'll bring a bottle of Shiraz and we can get plastered while we're waiting for Mr. Wonderful. See you later." She clicked off before Marla had a chance to answer.

She wondered what Char's problem was.

Charlene's car sat in front of her house when Marla returned home with a trunk full of groceries. The kitchen door opened when she raised the garage door and drove inside.

"Do you need me?" Char called.

"Yes, help me carry this in and separate Dempsey's stuff from mine."

Charlene helped her haul in the bags then proceeded to rag her about doing Dwayne's shopping. Marla ignored her jabs.

Char pushed her toward the table. "I'll pour the wine. Sit down and relax. Point to what goes where, and I'll put it away. I got off early today, and all I can do is feel sorry for myself because I won't see Donovan for a whole month."

"Ah, so that's what's bothering you. I thought you sounded frazzled about something."

"I can't stand it. I'm madly in love with that man. At least tonight I get to drool over his brother for a couple of hours."

"Here, give me the bottle and the corkscrew. I'll open the wine while you get a couple of glasses. Grab a small bowl for Skippy's dinner."

"I let him out in the backyard when I got here. He squirted pee in about ten places."

"The raccoons have been around again. He's letting them know it's his territory. Not that they give a hoot." She twisted the corkscrew into the odd-shaped blue bottle.

Charlene set the glasses and bowl on the table then sorted out the cold groceries and squeezed them in the fridge. "The rest can wait till I have a glass of wine. This is good stuff. Trader Joe's started carrying it recently. Have you tried it?"

"Nope. I'm a virgin." She poured two glasses. "This'll be my very first time. I hope it's good."

"Like I said a while back: What did you do with my sister?"

Marla kicked off her shoes and put her feet on one of the empty chairs. "I sold a piece of property today that we've been trying to get rid of for two years. Keep your fingers crossed until escrow closes."

Char held her glass up and admired the color. "The Seymour parcel?"

"The very same."

"Tell me again why it's so difficult to unload?" Char put her nose in the glass and sniffed. "Oh, do I need this."

"It's that darn easement the State obtained over forty years ago for a future freeway extension they'll never build. All the development went in the other direction. The buyer and his wife plan to breed exotic rabbits, and the zoning and location are perfect for them."

"Exotic rabbits? I never heard of such a thing. What do they do, teach them to belly dance?"

Marla laughed. "I don't know Char, but if they close the deal I'll suggest it."

They polished off the first of the wine then set about unpacking the bags and separating out what Dwayne would take home.

The front door opened, and Skip yapped with excitement.

"Honey, I'm home." Dwayne carried two large white bags with Chinese writing on the sides. One was stained with grease spots, and Marla nearly swooned at the delicious aroma.

His eyebrows went up at the sight of her sister. "Hey, Charlene." He leaned in for Marla's kiss. "I don't know if I can stand all this pulchritude. We having a threesome?"

"For dinner, yes." Marla tapped him on the chest. "Behave yourself. Charlene's missing Donovan and she's in a fragile state."

Charlene puckered her lips in a pout. "Yes, poor me. I'll have another glass of wine."

Dwayne kissed Char on the forehead. "Let me know if I can be of help." He grinned at Marla. "Mind if I take a quick shower, honey?"

"No, go ahead. We'll set out dinner. There's a clean T-shirt of yours on top of the dryer."

"I brought a change of clothes." He held aloft a brown grocery sack. "I'll make it quick." He rushed down the hall and the bedroom door closed.

Char twisted her mouth and nodded. "Um hum, and now you're doing his laundry."

Heat burned Marla's cheeks. "No, I am not! It's a shirt I borrowed to wear over my swimsuit in Coronado. I forgot to pack my cover-up." She put hands on her hips and gave Charlene a stern look. "What?"

"Nothing." A knowing smile danced across her lips. "I'll set the table."

———

Well, hell. His plans to spend the night alone with Marla got shot square in the ass when he saw Charlene. Maybe she'd take off early. Nah, he suspected she planned to stay all evening.

He scowled at the bottles of Marla's shampoo and conditioner lining the shower shelf. He lifted one after the other, pushing them aside until he found one that looked promising. He screwed the cap off and sniffed. Coconut. Not exactly manly, but not too girly either. He squirted some on his head and scrubbed.

Five minutes after he stepped inside the shower, he was toweling off. Ten minutes after he'd kissed Marla hello he was walking back to the kitchen. He did a male-model turn. "I know I'm irresistible but see if you ladies can keep your hands off me until I've had something to eat."

Marla shook her head. "See what I have to put up with? Sit down, Dempsey, before we put our hands on you in ways you won't welcome. The last thing you want is for my sister and me to gang up on you."

Dwayne sat and raised his hands. "I'll be good."

Charlene winked. "I don't doubt it."

"Oh, please you two. Can we just eat?"

Charlene's mood lifted considerably during dinner and lively banter. She glanced at her watch. "It's after ten. Mind if I skedaddle without helping with the dishes? I have to be at work by seven."

"No, go ahead." Marla carried dishes to the sink. "The mess looks worse than it is."

Skipper ran to the front door and yapped with alarm.

"What's with your mutt?" He stood and walked into the hallway. "What's the matter, boy?"

Marla followed him. "He probably thought he heard something."

Dwayne picked up an envelope. "What's this?"

"Did somebody put that under my door?"

He opened the door and stepped out on the small porch. "I don't see anybody." Back inside he turned the large brown envelope over. "I'll be damned. It's addressed to me." He held it so she could see the name.

Charlene joined them. "What's going on?"

"Somebody left this for Dwayne." She pointed to the envelope. "It wasn't here when you came in, was it?"

"No."

He ran a finger under the flap. "Not when I got here either." He pulled a small sheaf of papers and a photo from the packet. "What the...?"

Marla switched on the ceiling light. "What is it?"

He held a picture of Amber in her school uniform then continued to the living room, switched on the lamp next to the sofa, and sat. "What the hell is she up to?"

Marla and Charlene watched him silently while he shuffled through the papers.

"Who?"

"Francine. That witch! I've got to call my lawyer." The Chinese food sat like lead in his stomach. He raked a hand through his hair.

"At this hour?" Marla tipped her head at the crystal Waterford clock on her mantel. "It's too late, isn't it?"

"Lordy, Dwayne. What does she say?"

He set a typed paper on his knee and smoothed out the crease. He looked it over once more, and then read it to them.

So now I know what my kid looks like you sneak. And it proves you aren't her biological father for sure. Bring her to my lawyer's office in the next two days or I'm having you arrested for kidnapping. I demand a DNA test, you bastard. I mean it. Francine Henry

He gazed at the shocked expressions on Marla and Charlene's faces. Most likely they reflected his own. He paged through the other papers then dropped the packet on the table next to the sofa.

Marla came to sit beside him. "That woman is crazy. You know you're Amber's dad. What is she after? I don't believe she really wants custody, do you?"

He dropped his head back and reached for her hand. "I wish the hell I knew."

Charlene reached for the photo of Amber. "Where do you suppose she got this?" She turned the photo over. "It's an official school picture, see the stamp?" She held it out for Marla.

154

She took it. "That's the same photographer who's been taking school photos in Spring Grove since we were kids. It probably wouldn't be too hard to get one from his studio. All she'd have to do is say she's Amber's mother and needed another copy." She squeezed Dwayne's hand.

"Shit, shit, shit! Why did she have to surface after all these years?"

Charlene stood and gathered her jacket and purse. "I better go, it's really late. Marla, please call me tomorrow after Dwayne talks to his lawyer."

He pulled himself up. "You're not going anywhere until I check the street. If she and the jailbird are hanging around, you stay here tonight. They don't need to know where you live." He turned to Marla. "Got a flashlight?"

"Yes, several. I'll get one for you." She went to the kitchen, opened the utility closet, and removed a large flashlight from a holder on the wall next to her vacuum cleaner.

"Sheesh, this thing's a weapon."

"I hope you don't have to use it. Be careful. Should I call the sheriff?"

"No, She's long gone by now. But I need to make sure. Sit tight. Both of you."

Chapter Twenty-One

I SUSPECT MRS. HENRY IS ATTEMPTING TO INTIMIDATE YOU. HER lawyer is a shyster, and he's probably giving her ideas on how to get access to your daughter by going around the law. As I said before, she has no standing. If this ever got as far as a judge, she'd be thrown out of court."

Dwayne fidgeted with his keys. "How do I get rid of her?"

"As long as she doesn't break the law, I'm afraid all you can do is wait for her to tire of the game."

Dwayne shifted in the hard chair. "Amber's safely out of the state with my mother in Wyoming. Francine's from there. That's where we met and married. If she's sneaking around here trying to find my daughter, she may figure out that Mom's ranch is the most likely place I'd send her."

Anger burned in his chest at the audacity of Francine showing up after all these years, demanding access to the child she never wanted and couldn't desert fast enough. What in hell did she want from him? He didn't believe for a New York minute that she cared a damn about Amber.

The lawyer's voice interrupted his thoughts. "I'll send a strong letter to her attorney today, telling him to advise her to desist, or you'll file charges against her for stalking and harassment. If there are any other incidents, tell me immediately."

"You think that'll work?"

"One never knows, but the courts take very seriously any misbehavior affecting minors. Let's give it a few days and see what happens." He stood and extended his arm across the desk.

Dwayne shook his hand and left the office. He returned to Marla's jobsite to help Jack secure the trailer so it could be hauled off the lot this afternoon. He'd keep it at his facility until the new site had a fence constructed around it. An empty trailer on a vacant lot was an invitation for mischief.

He checked the screen of his phone when the Marine Hymn sounded off. "Hello, woman of mine." Nearly sunset, he'd just pulled into his driveway. "You miss me as much as I miss you?"

"More, Dempsey."

"Not possible, Danaher."

"How did it go with your attorney today?"

"I was about to call you to see if we could go for dinner, and I'd fill you in." He dug in his pocket for the house key and unlocked his front door.

"Um, my parents just called. They'd like us to come over to their place for dinner tonight. Is that okay with you? I'm afraid my dad is going to give you the 'What are your intentions with my daughter' speech. So embarrassing."

He laughed. "He must have given it a dozen times with Charlene's lovers."

"I doubt it. Char would laugh her head off if Dad ever attempted it."

"I've got to shower and change. What time do they want us there?"

"Why don't you bring a change of clothes and shower here? I want you to come home with me after dinner tonight." She paused. "Do I really sound that needy?"

"As long as it's me you need, no problem, Red. I'm on my way. Do we have time for a quickie?"

"No, but we'll have all night to make up for it. I bought a copy of the Kama Sutra at Books-A-Million today. It's full of very intriguing pictures. Things I never imagined possible. I've got some wicked ideas I'm itching to try."

"You're killing me." He pressed down on his raging hard-on and grabbed his gym bag from the closet. "We may never make it to your parent's house at this rate."

"I'll sic Skipper on you if you try anything."

"That's a terrifying thought. I'm on my way."

He'd barely scratched the surface with this woman. Every day she said or did something that caught him off guard. Wow, maybe he'd have to take up drinking after all.

He knocked on her front door. She opened it a crack and peeked out. "Yes?"

"Is the lady of the house home? I have some free samples she requested." He winked.

"Oh, please come in." She stepped behind the door and pulled it open. He couldn't see her until she closed it.

"Sweet Jesus, Marla."

She wore panties and bra, thigh-high nylons and high heels. "You can leave the samples in the bedroom. The lady of the house will be out this evening. I'm sure she'll want to try them as soon as she returns."

He stood with his mouth hanging open as she walked down the hallway, hips swaying, Skipper trotting alongside.

He caught her and threw his arms around her waist. "Oh, no you don't. Come back here and kiss me. You must think I'm a man of steel."

"Oh, I think you are." She pressed her breasts against his chest and ran her hands up the sides of his face and dug her fingers into his hair. "Oh, yes. You are. See?"

He wiped the wicked smile off her face with a bruising kiss. Then another. "What time to we have to be there, because late or not, we *are* having a quickie." He walked her backward to the bedroom, fell onto the bed, and pulled her on top.

She unsnapped her bra. "Oh, if you insist." With her knees on either side of his hips, she put her face close to his. "You do realize you've turned me into a wild sex-crazed harlot, don't you?" She unzipped his work pants.

He arched his back and dug his head into the pillow. "Get out of those panties quick, Danaher, or you'll have to call the paramedics."

She swung a leg over him and made quick work of the lingerie. When he went to nudge her over she said, "No. Stay right there. I memorized a couple of the pictures in my new book. I want to try something to see if it's possible."

Oh, it was possible, and then some. They lay panting like a couple of tri-athletes at the end of an endurance trial. Marla was comfortably spread across him like hot fudge. All he could manage was a silent prayer for his unbelievable good fortune.

"I'll tell you something," he gasped. "At this point, I'm so vulnerable I'll agree with anything Brad asks. I'm at your mercy. I'm your slave. I'm…" He chuckled. "…exhausted." He smacked her bottom. "I've still got my work boots on, Danaher."

She stretched languidly and grinned. "You're a pig, Dempsey."

He nipped her silky shoulder. "Oink."

———

Silvia opened the door. "There you are, right on time. Brad just dropped the steaks on the grill. Come out back. We've got the gas heater going on the patio." She put her arm under Dwayne's elbow and led him across the living room to the sliding doors.

He looked over his shoulder at Marla and grinned. "We thought we might be late." He tugged the slider and waited for Marla's mom to step outside ahead of them.

"Welcome!" Bradley Danaher waved a pair of long-handled tongs. "What's your poison? There's guacamole and chips on the table. Silvia whipped up a batch of her frozen margaritas."

"Got anything soft, Dad? Dwayne doesn't drink."

"It's all soft tonight, sweetheart, nothing but O'Doul's and virgin margaritas. We're off to Catalina Island early tomorrow morning."

"Mom! You've talked about going over there for years."

"I know. We watched a TV special on the island and wondered what we were waiting for, so Brad called and booked tickets for us on the boat and two nights at the best hotel."

Dwayne enjoyed the mother-daughter chatter for a minute then took an O'Doul's and strolled to join Brad at the grill. "Those steaks smell terrific. What's in the foil pan?" He twisted the cap off the bottle and dropped it on the table.

"Grilled peppers and asparagus. Marla's favorite."

Dwayne waggled the bottle of alcohol-free beer. "Can I get you one of these?"

"I'm halfway through my margarita." Brad leaned in for a close look at the steaks. "How do you like yours?"

"Medium rare." The sizzling aroma went right to his stomach and it growled with hunger. "But I'm easy to please when it comes to food."

"Good man, that's what we're all having. Saves a lot of shuffling on the grill." He peeked under the foil on the pan. "Perfecto." He called, "Sil, bring the salad. These'll be ready to come off any minute."

She fluttered her hand and went inside. "Marla, carry the garlic bread for me."

———

Dwayne put down his fork and sucked in a contented breath. "Brad and Sil, that was fantastic. You could open your own steak house." He glanced around the table. Memories of past barbeques and picnics at the Danaher house when they were kids were many and varied. Brad and his dad had maintained their friendship since they were students at Royal High School, back in the 70's.

Except for several months during his dad's marriage-divorce blips, the Dempsey boys had considered the Danaher place a second home. The pool they'd tried to drown one another in every summer sat sparkling with reflected moonlight.

"You use the pool much anymore?"

"Oh, yes," Silvia answered. "Especially the spa. Now that Brad installed the solar panels on the pool house roof, it's warm year round. We couldn't afford to heat it except in summer when all of you were children."

Brad nodded. "That pool was what sold us on this house. We knew our kids and their friends would get a lot of use out of it."

"I certainly recall the good times. Charlene would jump right in with the boys, but Marla sat in the shade scowling and reading all summer."

"I did not!"

"You'd chase the twins and make sure they had their water wings on, but I don't remember ever seeing you in a bathing suit. I can't imagine why not, either." He directed his next words to Silvia. "In Coronado she looked sensational in that red number she wore at the hotel."

Silvia brightened. "Oh, I bought her that suit." She smiled at her daughter. "See, I told you it was perfect on you."

Dwayne smiled at the memory of rubbing sunscreen on her back and legs. "You've got great taste, Silvia. Every man at the hotel had their tongues hanging out ogling her."

Marla poked him. "They did not!"

"Oh, yes they did. And I was loving it because you were all mine." He pecked a quick kiss on her cheek and enjoyed her furious blush.

She stood abruptly. "I'll help you clear the table, Mom. It's late." She stacked dishes and carried them inside. Silvia did the same and followed her.

Brad put his hand on Dwayne's shoulder. "Could we have a word while I wipe down the grill?"

Here it comes. Marla wasn't kidding. How…quaint.

"Sure, Brad. What can I do to help?"

"Just pick up the disposables and put them in the bin over there. Put the lid on tight. Raccoons have been menacing the neighborhood lately."

Dwayne cleared up the napkins, plastic glasses, and bottles. He bundled them in the heavy paper tablecloth and carried them to the side of the house, speculating on how Brad was planning to broach the subject of his daughter's honor.

"Look, Brad, let's cut to the chase. I'm very fond of Marla and we're having a great time together. I'd never do anything to deliberately hurt her. I consider myself a fortunate man that she's even interested in me. So don't…"

Brad put up a hand. "Understood. That's not what I wanted to talk about."

"It isn't?"

"No, I wanted an update on what your ex-wife's been up to and ask if there's anything I could do. My partners and I have used the services of a very good private investigator for some insurance fraud claims. I'd be happy to put you in touch with her."

He clapped Brad on the shoulder and laughed.

———

They were halfway to Marla's house when she asked, "So was it terribly embarrassing when Dadley laid down the law about his daughter?"

He glanced at her and grinned. "No. I hate to break it to you, but he's not the least bit interested in your chastity. He wanted to offer me the services of a private dick that does investigations for his firm."

161

"You mean all the agonizing I did this afternoon was for nothing?"

The fact she wanted to spare him embarrassment warmed his heart. He laid his hand on her knee. "He as good as turned on the green light, Danaher."

"He did?"

"We're good to go."

Chapter Twenty-Two

FRIDAY AFTERNOON, MARLA WAVED TO DWAYNE AND JACK WHEN they pulled the big trailer off her lot. They got out of the way just before the pavers arrived to begin work to resurface the parking lot. She breathed a sigh of relief that her project would be fully completed in less than a week.

"Buenos días, señora." A burly Hispanic man approached her carrying a clipboard. "We ready for begin." He reached over and petted Skipper on the head. "Yo quiero Taco Bell?" He winked and guffawed at his own joke then wiped his eyes with a large red bandanna.

She giggled and hugged Skip then walked through the job with the man and pointed out the areas she was particularly concerned with. "The landscape contractor is scheduled to begin next Tuesday. Will there be any problem with him parking here? Will that be long enough for the surface to...um, be ready?"

His face broke into a dazzling grin. "No problema, we gone tomorrow sundown. Plenty time, okay?"

She returned his smile. "Okay." Nodding, she went inside the building to do a final check of Miss Emmaline's apartment. It had to look perfect for the old woman she'd come to love.

Before entering the elevator, she checked to make sure all the shiny new mailboxes in the lobby had keys in the locks. As soon as the elevator doors opened on the second floor, Skipper trotted down the hall and stood waiting for her at Emmaline's door. "You're a smart doggie, Skippy."

She took her time. Adjusted a picture frame here, moved a lamp there. Kneeling, she ran her hand over the new, short-pile carpeting. "Look, Skip, isn't this nice?" She was amazed at what a good job Dwayne had done putting the place back together just the way Emmaline had it. "She'll love her new home."

Lifting Skipper, she slid her purse over her shoulder and opened the front door. She jumped back and gasped at the man standing in the hall blocking her exit. Skip barked and bared his teeth in a low, menacing growl.

"Who are you? What do you want?" Momentarily paralyzed with indecision, she held her keychain with the apartment key gripped firmly between her fingers in case she needed to use it as a stabbing weapon.

"Mean little bastard, ain't he?" The wiry, unshaven man with dead black eyes stared back. A faded rattlesnake tattoo wound around his ropy neck.

She had no idea who he was. "Get out of here, whoever you are. You have no business in this building." She prayed the pulse pounding in her throat wasn't betraying her fear.

"I came to tell you to keep your nose outta my wife's business. You're asking for trouble."

What in the name of all that's holy was this thug talking about? "I don't know you, and I'm sure I don't know your wife. Now, please leave."

"You're the bitch fuckin' Dempsey, aren't ya?"

A blow to her stomach wouldn't have robbed her of her breath as much as this evil man's evil words. Unable to breathe or speak, a cold wave of nausea built in her throat, sweat bloomed on her forehead.

He sneered with satisfaction. "I see we understand each other." He turned on his heel, his retreating steps snapping loudly on the hard surface under battered, black cowboy boots.

Tears of raw shock flooded Marla's eyes. She sucked in a ragged breath, backed into the apartment, and flipped the lock. Leaning her back against the door, she slid down and landed on the carpet with a thump, dislodging Skipper from her arms.

He whimpered and stared into her eyes, silently imploring her. "It's okay, baby, it's okay." But was it?

She rose and crept to the window overlooking the parking lot. No sign of him, but he wouldn't have parked where the paving crew was working. She moved to the corner window with a view of the street and spotted an old, battered blue car disappearing down the road.

Hadn't Dwayne or one of his brothers said something about a blue car the night Francine showed up on her dad's birthday? The man must be her husband, Luke Henry, the convict. A cold chill raced down her back and she hugged herself for warmth.

Should she call Dwayne? Marla paced and nuzzled her dog for comfort. "What should I do, Skippy? I feel like a coward for allowing that bad guy to scare me. You were ready to defend me, weren't you, baby? And him a Goliath compared to you."

On a sudden inspiration, she took her cell phone and called Rosie. She answered on the first ring.

"Hi, girlfriend. What's up?"

"Rosie?" Her voice broke and she cleared her throat. "Rosie, is Dylan in the factory?"

"He just walked in. Do you want me to find him?"

"Yes, please."

"Hang on." Rosie said something to someone. Marla couldn't make out the words, but she got the sense Rosie was walking through the showroom into the factory. "Dylan! Marla Danaher wants to talk to you. He'll be right here."

"Hey, babe. What can I do for you?"

To her shock and embarrassment, she was unable to answer.

"Marla? Hello? I think I lost the call."

"No! Um, Dylan." She swallowed. "Did I overhear you say Francine was in a blue car the night of my dad's party?"

"Yeah, what's wrong? I can tell from your voice that something is wrong."

She cleared her throat again. "Um, give me a minute." After a calming breath she said, "I'm at my building, Dwayne left almost an hour ago. I think...I'm not sure, but I think Luke Henry was just here."

"What did that bastard want?" His voice took on an angry quality that reminded her of Dwayne.

She closed her eyes and took a breath. "I'm not sure it was him, but he threatened me. He told me to stay out of his wife's business. And something else I won't repeat."

"Did he touch you? Are you hurt?"

In the background, Marla heard Rosie say, "What happened, Dyl. Is she okay?"

"He didn't hurt me! He scared me."

"She's not hurt. Where are you, Marla? Are you in a safe place?"

"I locked myself inside Emmaline's apartment. It's probably okay for me to leave. I saw a blue car drive away toward Simi."

"No! You stay right where you are. I'm coming over there. Give me half an hour." He clicked off.

The phone rang before she had a chance to put it back in her purse. "Hello?"

"Marla, it's me, Rosie. What happened?"

She dragged herself across the room and slumped into Emmaline's recliner. Skip jumped to her lap. "I got a scare, but I'm okay. Here's what happened..."

She told Rosie the whole story including the part she wouldn't say to Dylan. Rosie insisted on staying on the phone with her until he got there. Talking to her friend calmed her to the point where her breathing went back to normal and tears no longer threatened.

The doorbell buzzed. "Rosie, there's somebody at the door."

"Don't open it until you know who's there. I'll stay on the line."

"Marla, open up, it's Dwayne and Dylan."

"Rosie, it's..."

"I heard. I'll talk to you later, okay?"

"Okay, thanks. It was a big help talking to you."

"Marla!"

"Coming!" She opened the door and in an instant Dwayne had his arms around her.

"Are you okay, honey?"

"I am now." She rested her forehead against his neck where the pulse in his throat tapped rapidly.

"I'm going to find that sonuvabitch and strangle him with my bare hands."

A nervous giggle escaped her. "My hero." She hugged him hard and said, "I don't want you to kill anybody for me, but I wouldn't mind if you scared the pee out of him."

The brothers laughed.

———

When Dylan's van pulled into Big D Construction and his brother hailed him, Dwayne knew something was wrong. Heart pounding, he met his brother at the front of the building and prayed that nothing had happened to Amber or their mother.

After Dyl related Marla's phone call, his vision was blurred by a haze of red rage. The thought of anything bad happening to her was more than he was prepared to consider. "Let's find them. Enough is enough. I'd like to kick the shit out of both of them."

He laid a hand on Dwayne's shoulder. "Me too, but that's not gonna happen. Marla wasn't hurt. We'll take her home, then see if we can find Francine and Luke. Like your lawyer said, your next step is to file a complaint."

Jaws clenched so tight his teeth ached, Dwayne hadn't felt this level of tension since his last combat mission in Iraq. "I know, I know. I don't want to do anything stupid. I'm glad she called you instead of me. God knows what I would have done."

"She's a very smart lady."

"I'm in love with her." He paced in a circle and clutched the back of his neck. "Francine created this shit storm. I want to be rid of her." He hadn't realized his fist was clenched so hard. He deliberately relaxed his hands and flexed his fingers.

"I'll go inside and tell Slim and Jack that I'll be out for the rest of the day. Let's take your van. I haven't had time to unload my truck."

"I'll wait for you out here. I want to call Grace and let her know what's going on before we go looking for them."

"I'll be back in five." He rushed inside, found his two main guys, and quickly related what he knew. "Jack, call Cluny and give him a head's up. I want everybody to keep their eyes peeled for Francine and Luke, and let me know the minute they learn anything."

"We're on it, Gunny."

He headed for the door and stopped. "Oh, Slim, would you finish unloading my truck?"

"Yep. Beat it, we've got it covered here."

———

Now his woman was safely in his arms. She'd never felt so precious to him. "I love you, Danaher."

"I love you back, Dempsey." He held her tighter, never wanted to let her go. "I'm taking you and your mutt home."

"My *mutt* was eager to attack that snake tattoo on Luke's neck. I had to hold him back. He's my brave little protector."

Dwayne looked Skip in the eye. "That right? Okay then, Private Danaher, I'm giving you a battlefield promotion. You're now Corporal Danaher. Let's go."

Dylan sat behind the wheel, Marla and Skipper in the middle, and Dwayne on the passenger side of the front seat of the furniture factory van.

"Which way was the car going when you saw it, honey?"

Marla leaned forward and pointed straight ahead. "Simi Valley."

"Before we take Marla home, let's take a run down that way. We might get lucky and spot the car."

Dylan's van was already facing the direction he wanted him to go, so he eased back onto the road. They drove through the hilly, mostly undeveloped land between Simi and Spring Grove. "I doubt we'll find them, but it's worth a try. If we don't see anything by the time we hit the east end of Simi, we'll turn around and take you home."

"You don't need to take me home. I'm fine. I'd rather help you look."

Dwayne leaned over and kissed her on the cheek. "Whatever you say, boss." He admired her spunk. She was strong and smart. How did he get so lucky?

She chuckled. "I'm not your boss anymore, remember? I already paid you off so I could be rid of you."

Dylan chimed in, "You may not be his boss, but I doubt you're rid of him." They'd reached a fork in the quiet road. "Which way do you want me to go?"

"There's nothing up there, go left. It's more likely they're staying in one of those fleabags at the edge of town." Not sure what to do if he found them, Dwayne took out his wallet, found his lawyer's card and tapped the number on his cell.

Marla nodded at his phone. "Who are you calling?"

"My lawyer. I want him to know what happened." The man was with a client, so he left his number. The receptionist told him it would probably be at the end of the day before he'd call back because he'd be in court all afternoon.

"Dylan! There's the car! Over there. See?" Marla bounced in the seat and flapped her hand at the pot-holed parking lot of the Nighty Nite Motel. "I'm sure that's the car."

"I'll park by the office."

Dwayne's heart rate increased. He squeezed Marla's knee. "We'll go inside. You stay in the van."

"But…"

"Dammit, just do as I say for once, please!" He didn't miss the offended expression on her face, but he didn't care either. He yanked open the door and stepped out.

He and his brother entered the seedy, deserted office. Dylan nodded to a sign that said Ring Bell for Assistance. He slammed his hand on it a couple of times. They waited.

Finally a potbellied man in his fifties pushed through the swinging door. "Can I help ya?"

Dwayne stepped close to the counter and gave the man a friendly smile. "Yes, we're friends of the Henrys. Luke and Francine. I don't remember the number of the unit they're in."

"Lemme have a look." Dwayne caught a whiff of the man's body odor when he leaned forward and tapped his computer. He squinted at the fingerprinted screen. "They're in 14A, first floor. Down that-a-way."

Dwayne slapped the counter. "Thank you."

They stepped outside. Dylan stuck his hands in his pockets. "Now what?"

"I'm going down there and throw the fear of God into that bastard, Luke. You can come with me or wait in the van with Marla. This isn't your fight."

"Like hell it isn't. Let's go."

Dwayne pounded on the chipped orange painted door. Luke opened it but left the chain in place.

"Well, lookie who's here, Frannie. Your ex-husband, the gimpy war hero."

Dwayne put his shoulder to the door, slammed into it, and the chain snapped, hitting Luke on the cheekbone. He shoved the door open, grabbed him by the neck, and slammed him back against the wall.

Francine screamed, "That's assault! That's assault! I'm calling 911!"

Dylan stepped inside and grabbed the phone from her hand. "I'd keep my mouth shut if I were you, Francine." He hung it up and faced Dwayne. "Take it easy, brother. We're just here to impart information, remember?"

His big brother's words seeped through Dwayne's blinding rage. He eased up on Luke's throat but didn't let go. "Here's some 'information' for you, asshole," he growled through gritted teeth. "If you ever approach me, my family, or any of my employees or my friends again, I will personally tear you apart piece by piece. Do you understand this 'information,' Henry? Because if you don't, I'll gladly repeat it."

For emphasis, he tightened his grip. Luke Henry's murky black eyes bulged, and he tore at his hands, struggling to breathe. The more he fought back, the tighter Dwayne gripped.

Dwayne felt Dylan's hand on his shoulder. "I think he got the message. Let's go."

Francine pointed to the damage on the door. "You're gonna pay for that! I'm still gonna call the cops on your ass."

He whirled around and glared at the harridan wildly waving her arms and wondered what he possibly could have ever been attracted to. "Go right ahead. I'll wait till they get here."

Luke bent over, grasping his throat and gagging. Francine ran to him. "Get out! Get out!"

Dylan gripped his arm. "Let's go. Now."

When they exited the room, he headed back in the direction of the office. Dylan kept pace with him. "What are you doing?"

"I broke his door. I'm going to pay for it." He pushed inside and slammed his hand on the bell.

The man came in. "Need somethin' else?" He took a step back when he got a good look at Dwayne's face.

"No, sorry, I broke the security chain on your door." He took out his wallet and tossed a hundred dollar bill on the counter. "This should cover it."

Chapter Twenty-Three

MARLA AND SKIPPER SAT ON DWAYNE'S SOFA WHILE HE showered. She took her phone from her purse and called Rosie Wyland.

"Wow, Marla. Dylan told me what happened. Are you okay?"

"I'm still a little wobbly, but I have to tell you—this morning was the first time anybody ever threw the F-bomb in my face. It's not like I never heard it before, but it was pretty shocking. Don't mention it. Dwayne already has murder in his eye."

The memory of the black look on his face when he came out of Francine's room still gave her pause. One thing she knew for sure—she hoped she'd never see him that angry again. It was downright unnerving in such a physically powerful man.

"I won't say anything. No need to throw gas on the fire."

"My thoughts, exactly." An idea popped into her head. "Look, Rosie, I was thinking you'd like to meet my sister, Charlene. Can we get together for lunch or dinner before you leave for Wyoming?"

"I'd love that! Just think—two girlfriends in less than a month. That's a record for me. Comes from a lifetime lived in the wide open spaces, I guess." Her laughter tinkled over the phone. "I'll only be here till Tuesday morning. That leaves three nights."

"Great, let's aim for Sunday. I'll call you after I have a chance to talk to Charlene. Dwayne's finished his shower. We're going to dinner then he'll stay at my house tonight. My big, strong bodyguard."

"Aren't you the lucky one?"

"Yes. Got to go. Bye."

She got up and walked down the hall to his bedroom. He was dressed except for a shirt. Her heart tripped when she admired his bare chest.

"T-shirt okay?"

"T-shirt is fine. I thought we'd stop by the burger joint and get carryout. We can relax and eat at home." She looked in the open drawer and lifted out a neatly folded rugby shirt. "I like this one."

"I don't know how I ever dressed myself."

"Oh, shut up. I'm hungry. Skip's hungry. Let's go." She ran her hand across his chest and flashed what she hoped was an irresistible smile.

"Keep your hands off me, Danaher, or we're not going anywhere."

"I'll try, Dempsey." She grinned and went back to the living room to retrieve her jacket and purse. She called, "We're way-aa-ting."

———

Having polished off three hamburgers and a couple of Dr. Peppers, Dwayne groaned and dropped his head on the back of her couch. She waved a French fry under his nose. "Don't you dare go to sleep on me. We need to talk."

"Oh, shit, I just love it when a woman says, 'We need to talk.' It usually means 'You're out the door, buddy.'"

"Not this time." She snuggled next to him. "I want to talk about what you think will happen next with Francine and her husband—what you'll do if they don't back off."

He threw his arm over her shoulder. "We've got an old saying up in Wyoming: Don't borrow trouble." Nuzzling her hair, he whispered, "I'm ready for bed."

She straightened. "Everybody has that saying, and you're always ready for bed." She smiled. "Don't give me that look."

"I don't want you in the middle of my mess, Danaher."

"I am in the middle of it, Dempsey."

He pressed his lips together and sighed. "Yeah, I guess you are."

He rubbed his hand up and down her arm until she relaxed and snuggled next to him again. "I'm in love with you, honey."

"I know, thank you. That makes me very happy. There's nothing sadder than unrequited love, don't you think?"

"God, you turn me on when you use those big words. Kiss me, or I can't be responsible for the consequences."

She tilted her head up for his kiss and was surprised at the tenderness of it. "You have a few big words of your own, don't you?" She caressed his cheek and thanked her lucky stars that this wonderful man hadn't been snatched up by another woman. "I love you, Dwayne Dempsey."

"I know, thank you." He took her hand from his face and pressed it on his lap. "Big words are nice, but I've got something bigger for you."

"You are bad, bad, bad." She pressed down. "Real bad."

He stood and pulled her to her feet. "You haven't seen bad yet."

————

Saturday morning around eight, Dwayne, shirtless, wearing only exercise shorts, answered the knock on Marla's door.

Skipper scrambled to get there ahead of him.

A small man with thick sandy hair, wearing glasses, about his own age, stood on the doorstep and stared back at him with shock on his face and in his eyes. He stood stiffly in pressed khaki pants and a blue button-down shirt. "Is Marla home?"

"Yep." He turned and yelled, "Somebody here to see you, honey."

She called from the bedroom. "Who is it?"

He raised his eyebrows at the man. "You are?"

"Edwin Plimpton. I've obviously come at an inconvenient time."

"Not at all." Dwayne berated himself for deriving so much satisfaction from the man's words and outraged demeanor. This was *the* Edwin he'd heard about. *Marla's boyfriend.* No wonder she thought she was fat. Edwin was not more than an inch taller than her, and he likely weighed ten pounds less. He extended his hand. "Dwayne Dempsey. Come on in."

At first Edwin didn't move. He stared at Dwayne's leg, tore his eyes away, then tentatively stepped inside. Skipper yipped with excitement, happy to see him. He hopped on his hind legs and clawed at the man's pants. Edwin gave him a little push with his foot and ignored him.

Dwayne called again, "It's Edwin Plimpton, honey. Are you decent?" It took all his willpower to suppress an evil chuckle. He was no better than a cur marking his territory, but he didn't give a shit. He was enjoying this. He felt a moment of shame for his behavior. This guy didn't deserve it.

Marla answered with a choked voice. "I'll, um, I'll be right there."

Dwayne gestured toward the sofa. "Have a seat." He went ahead of Edwin and picked up the debris of last night's hamburger feast. "Sorry for the mess. Will you excuse me? She should be here in a minute or so."

Marla entered the living room as he was leaving. Her face so white the usually invisible sprinkle of freckles on her nose glowed like neon. Bewildered, she pressed a hand on her chest. "I..."

He leaned close and pecked her on the cheek. "Gotta go, honey, I'm meeting Cluny at the gym." He left her standing there, grabbed his gym bag and keys, and walked out the door.

———

If it were humanly possible to be more embarrassed, Marla couldn't imagine how. *Caught with your hand in the cookie jar,* took on new meaning. Anger at Dwayne flared in her chest. What a lout, what a dolt, what a Philistine! She slapped a hand over her mouth to stifle a nervous giggle and stared at Edwin's flabbergasted face.

She took a deep breath. "Edwin. I, uh, wasn't expecting you."

"That's the best you can come up with, Marla?" The snap of anger in his words was out of character. He rarely displayed emotion, and it caught her off guard.

"No, I...I mean. When did you get back in town? You've been gone for weeks. I..."

"I got back yesterday. I left more than one message on your home phone and a text message on your cell."

She glanced at the phone on the hall table and immediately saw the flashing red light. "I...um...didn't notice. Sorry."

"Obviously you were far too busy and distracted." He shoved his hands in the pockets of his perfectly pressed pants. "Am I allowed to ask who he is?"

"Um, his name is Dwayne Dempsey. He's John Dempsey's son. You've met John." She swallowed. This wasn't going well. "Uh, Dwayne's the contractor, Big D Construction? I hired him to renovate my apartment building." Was she making any sense? She had to pee. She wasn't sure what to do or say.

Edwin sneered. "And were Big D's after-hours activities part of the contract?" He took a step in her direction. "I find it hard to fathom your unfaithfulness. I'm very disappointed in you, Marla."

"Unfaithfulness? Wait, wait just a minute." She put up her hands and shook herself. "Unfaithful to you? Is that what you mean? Edwin, you never even touch me. Other than a handshake or a brief kiss, what was there for me to be unfaithful to?"

He pressed his lips together and slowly shook his head. A smirk of disgust filled his face. "I was merely following your lead. You've always been reserved, held yourself apart from me. It appears I've misread your true nature."

What could she say to that? It was true, all of it. She *had* held herself apart from him. He was dull, uptight, dignified, and devoid of sexual appeal. Why had she hung on to him for the past two years? It wasn't his fault. The blame lay with her.

"Edwin, I'm sorry. I haven't meant to deliberately mislead you. You're a fine man and have always behaved like a gentleman. I suppose we stayed together because of inertia. I don't believe I ever thought our relationship would go beyond friendship. If you expected more from me, I wasn't aware of it."

He stood straight. "I'll take my leave now. I feel I must warn you —that man, that laborer who just left here is beneath you. He's unsuitable. You're wasting yourself on him. I pray you'll come to your senses." He brushed past her on his way to the door.

"No…he's…"

He pulled open the door and there stood Charlene with her key in her hand. Her eyes got big. "Oh, hello, Edwin. How nice to see you. Should I leave?"

He sniffed. "Not on my account." Then brushed past her and stalked across the lawn.

Char eyed her. "Lordy, you're one surprise after another, little sister. Anybody else in there I need to know about?"

"Bite me, Charlene. Come in and watch me hang myself. After

yesterday and today I've come to the conclusion that real life isn't for me."

She retreated to the kitchen, poured herself a cup of Dwayne's strong coffee, and plopped in a chair.

"Don't mind if I do," Charlene said. She poured herself a cup of coffee, dumped three spoonsful of sugar in it then sat across from Marla and stirred. "Good morning to you too."

Marla smiled. "I did invite you for breakfast, didn't I?"

"Yes, you did. What are we having, besides drama pancakes and break-up sausages?"

There were times, and this was one of them, when Marla realized how much she truly loved her flighty, carefree sister. The sister who'd flitted through life enjoying every minute of it, while she'd had her nose pressed to a self-inflicted grindstone. "I love you, Char."

"I know, me too...you I mean." She took a sip of the coffee, grimaced, got up to add more sugar, and returned to the table. "Ugh. Dwayne made this? I won't sleep for days." She grinned. "So, what's new?"

———

Cluny acted as his spotter while he pumped iron. His pectorals trembled under the massive weight. He grunted, "Eight!"

"You're at the upper limit of what I can lift off you, Gunny."

Dwayne panted. Sweat streamed down his neck. "Yeah, I'm done." He pushed the weight up, dropped it in the cradle, and gasped for air.

Cluny gave him a hand up. "You planning on entering the Mr. Universe competition? Or just showing off?"

Dwayne laughed and scrubbed his face and neck with a towel. "Neither. I was imagining how much stronger I'd need to be to rip Luke Henry's ugly head off. Let's hit the steam room."

"He's stupider than a rock, going after the boss lady like that. I don't know what he thought you'd do."

"You're assuming he's capable of thinking."

"He's tough but a moron. What're you going to do now?"

"My lawyer told me to back off. He said I was playing into their hands by chasing them down. He's right. I shouldn't have touched the skinny weasel."

"Did you hurt him or just scare him?" Cluny pushed open the

locker room door. They got out of their shorts and underwear and wrapped clean towels around their waists.

"Both. I imagine he had Francine take pictures of my fingerprints on his neck to use against me in court, if that's where they're going."

He removed his prosthesis and took crutches from his locker. It was men-only on Saturday mornings, so they'd be able to remove the towels and stretch out in the steam room. They could even fart if they had to without raising eyebrows.

"I wish they'd go back to more men-only days. I hate co-ed gyms."

"Hey, spoilsport! I've picked up a couple of good-lookin' babes in here. You want to kill my love life?" They stepped in the steam room, and Cluny snapped him on the butt with his towel.

"Careful, buddy. Somebody might think you're in love with me."

Cluny chuckled and plopped down on the wooden bench. "Not likely, Gunny, I go for the petite, soft, curvy fem-in-nine type. The he-she muscle girls are a real turnoff."

Dwayne groaned, poured water on his head, and rubbed his belly and knees. "I hear you."

They ate a massive breakfast at Denny's then parted company. He went downtown to shop for a gift for Marla. After an hour, he was ready to give up when he spotted the perfect thing in the window of a jewelry and accessories shop. He had the sales clerk gift wrap it in a large box, and then for good measure he grabbed a bouquet of irises from a street vendor.

He had plans for the evening. Big plans.

Chapter Twenty-Four

MARLA SHOOK THE WEIGHTLESS BOX. "YOU BROUGHT ME AN empty box? What are you up to Dempsey?" She gave him a sly look and puckered her lips.

"Open it, Danaher." He sat back, took Skip from her lap, and grinned. "Come over here, Corporal Danaher. I'll rub your fat belly."

"I don't trust you."

"Good. You shouldn't. I always have some sneaky ulterior motive, don't I?"

She pulled the ribbon. "I can only hope." Digging through mountains of crumpled tissue paper, she was about to concede he was joking when her hand touched a small package. She lifted it from the box. "What is this?"

"I don't remember. You'll have to open it to find out."

Her heart thumped. "Will it explode?" She shook it.

"Nope. I never got trained in explosives. Guaranteed not to explode."

Marla slid off the ribbon, ripped through the paper, and squealed with delight, "I love it! It's perfect!" She threw her arms around his neck and kissed him on the lips.

She sat back and grinned. "Look, Skippy, Dwayne bought you a present." She held the sparkly dog collar in front of his tiny pointy face. "It's covered with diamonds, sapphires, and rubies. You'll be the fanciest dog in Spring Grove."

She grinned at Dwayne. His face was full of pleasure at her reaction. "Put it on him. See if he likes it."

He unbuckled the narrow leather collar and fastened on the bejeweled one. "This is far too fancy for a Corporal."

Marla kissed Dwayne again and giggled. "He needs another advance in rank, wouldn't you say?" A warm swell of love for Dwayne filled her chest. She studied his profile and thought he was the handsomest man she'd ever known. She traced his forehead and nose with her fingertip.

He caught her finger in his mouth and growled. She squeaked and yanked back her hand.

He snapped off a salute to Skipper. "I think Master Sergeant will do for now. Soon as he learns how to man a Bushmaster on an M-3 Bradley, he'll qualify for Gunnery Sergeant."

"Dwayne."

He faced her, a brief flash of alarm in his eyes, then he smiled. "Yeah?"

"I love you."

"Beat it, Sergeant Mutt." He pushed Skipper off his lap and dragged Marla over to replace him. "I love you more. Dig down to the envelope in the bottom of the box."

Her heart soared. "There's more?"

"Oh, yeah." He lifted the box and held it while she reached inside.

Marla found the envelope and he tossed the box on the floor. "What's this?"

"Open it."

The outer envelope was unmarked. Inside she found a theatre ticket envelope for Disney Concert Hall. She lifted the flap, shrieked, "Joshua Bell!" and leaped off Dwayne's lap. "Oh, my gosh, they're for tonight." She hopped with excitement. "I have to change clothes. I have to get ready. You have to wear a suit, do you have a suit? Get up, we only have three hours. It takes an hour or more to drive there. Get up!"

He stood and put his arms around her. "Go change. My suit's in the truck. Charlene is going to baby sit."

"When did you plan all this?" How could he possibly have known that she loved Joshua Bell? She'd longed to go to the hideous Disney hall ever since it had opened.

"Pack an overnight bag. We're staying at a hotel downtown tonight."

"We are?" What next? Heart racing, she ran to her bedroom and grabbed a small rolling bag. She wished she had some filmy, sexy lingerie, but she didn't, so she threw in a change of underwear and slacks and a blouse for tomorrow.

Dwayne entered the bedroom with a suit bag over his shoulder and carried a prosthesis with a dress shoe attached. "Do we have time for a quickie?"

"No!" Was he crazy? Yes, he was. She loved him for it.

He chuckled. "Just checking."

She dressed in her new Vera Wang outfit that Sil and Char had picked out for her. Short of attending a snobby wedding, she hadn't known when she'd have the opportunity to wear it. Tonight—it was perfect for tonight.

He caressed her bottom and headed for the bathroom. "I gotta shave before I change."

"No. Not tonight. I kinda like that dangerous look."

She hadn't known he could possibly look more masculine and delicious that he already did, but when he put on his dark blue pinstripe suit with a snowy white shirt and blue-green tie that matched his eyes, her heart did a little tap dance.

He did a three-sixty and grinned. "Whadaya think?"

Hand on her heart, she sighed. "I can't say it. You already think you're God's gift."

"So now you want to argue with God?" He kissed her on the ear. "You look sensational, Danaher."

"You look sensational-er, Dempsey."

"You ready? Let's go out and get Charlene's opinion." He picked up the bags and stepped into the hall.

Charlene stood wide-eyed as they entered the living room. "Lordy lord, you better get out of here, mister. If Donovan Dempsey shows up you're toast. He's a jealous man. And, who is that supermodel with you?" She ran to her purse and grabbed her phone.

"Stand over there. I have to get a picture. Marla, pick up Skipper. He's all dressed up too."

Marla gazed at the man she loved. He kissed her as Charlene took picture after picture. She'd spend a lot of time mooning over them later.

"Okay, Charlene," Dwayne said. "We gotta get going. I expect we'll be back late tomorrow afternoon."

Marla put the strap of her Carlo Fellini evening bag over her shoulder and kissed Skipper good-bye. "What car are we taking?"

"She doesn't know?"

"She's about to find out. Come on, honey. One more surprise." He led her out the front door and pointed to the emerald green Lincoln MKZ parked in front of the house.

"Is that yours?" Realizing she was gawking, she closed her mouth and stared.

"Nope, I borrowed my daddy's new car for the weekend." He extended his arm. "Shall we?"

"Uncle Johnny loaned you his new car? How did you talk him into that? Dad said he won't even let Irene drive it."

"Blackmail." Dwayne laughed. "I'll tell you on the way."

She waved. "Bye, Char. Bye, Skipper. See you tomorrow."

Charlene returned her wave. "I left something for you in the trunk. Have fun!"

"What did she leave?"

"No clue." He carried their bags to the back of the car after Marla was seated and grinned from ear to ear when he sat behind the wheel.

"What are you so happy about?"

"Must be that Victoria's Secret bag in the trunk."

Her breath caught and an unexpected blush warmed her neck and cheeks. "Charlene's a troublemaker."

"My favorite brand of trouble." He reached for her hand, brought it to his lips, and brushed a kiss on her palm.

Her breath caught and her eyes shimmered. She was in deep, deep trouble if this relationship ended.

———

He held her hand and pressed it to his cheek. He hadn't known it was possible to fall this hard and fast. He glanced across the seat. Her lips were pressed together, and she'd closed her eyes. He hoped she was feeling the same. He would ask her to marry him, but not yet. They needed more time.

"Did I say you look beautiful, beautiful?" He laid her hand on his knee and covered it with his.

In answer to his question, she choked on a slight sob and nodded but didn't say anything.

"God, Danaher, I am so in love with you."

She gazed at him with a wobbly smile. "Is this a dream?"

"Let's make it one."

———

During the concert, he spent more time looking at her than the performance. She caught him at it and pushed his chin with a finger so he faced the stage. He immediately turned and gazed at her again. A woman behind them snickered. Marla lowered her forehead into her hand and shook her head. He loved teasing her.

After the valet brought the car, they drove less than a mile to Hilton Checkers hotel. When the bellman removed their luggage from the trunk, Dwayne took the Victoria's Secret bag and insisted on carrying it through the lobby to the check-in desk where he set it on the counter. He grinned at Marla's embarrassment and the obvious amusement of the young man who checked them in.

"You have a supper reservation in our restaurant, Mr. Dempsey. Shall I have the bellman take the bags to your room while you dine?"

"Yes, thanks." He took the key card. "Shall we go, honey?"

She leaned close to his ear and whispered, "If you carry that shopping bag into the restaurant I'll kill you."

He chuckled and gave her a quick kiss. "Have the bellman take this with the bags, please."

"Very good, sir."

He put his arm around her waist as they walked away. When his big hand drifted low on her hip she said, "You have a death wish, Dempsey."

Marla's breath caught when they entered the restaurant. "Oh, this is lovely." She looked around the room. "I'm surprised to see so many diners this late in the evening."

The maitre d' seated them at a candlelit table in a quiet corner. A chilling bottle of champagne waited for them in an ice bucket that stood guard next to the table. She cocked her head in confusion. "Are you drinking alcohol tonight?"

"I have a confession. It's sparkling fruit juice. I hope you don't mind. I wanted the festive look." He laid his hand over hers.

Uh oh. She wasn't sure she wanted to hear his answer, but she asked anyway, "Why don't you drink? Are you a recovering alcoholic?"

"Nope, nothing like that. It's a long story, and I'll tell you another time."

The wine steward approached their table and asked Dwayne's permission to open the bottle and pour for them. He lifted it from the bucket and studied the label. With a perfectly straight face, he said, "An excellent vintage, sir."

Dwayne winked and nodded toward Marla. "Yes, I need my wits about me tonight."

Blushing hotly at the man's knowing smile, she held her breath until he filled their glasses, bowed, and left.

"You certainly enjoy mortifying me. First the Victoria's Secret bag and then that comment." She shook her head, sighed deeply, and fanned herself with the leather-bound menu.

"So, what's wrong with me telling the world I love you and I'm going to make love to you?"

What could she say? He was incorrigible. A part of his character, and she wouldn't deny she found it attractive and erotic. "I don't know. I'm just not used to it."

"Get used to it. I'd like to shout it from the rooftops." He picked up his menu. "What looks good?"

She opened hers and perused it for a moment. "Hmm. You look good."

He leaned forward and whispered, "Yeah, besides that."

"You pick. My brain isn't functioning at top speed right now." In fact, her brain hadn't been functioning at top speed since the first time they'd made love, two weeks ago. Only two weeks? How had this man become the most important person in her life in two weeks?

He signaled the waiter. "We'll have the Seared Maine Sea Scallops to start, Roasted Jidori Chicken for the main course, and then decaf Cappuccino after dinner, and please, have the Vanilla Bean Crème Brulee sent to our room, ten-seventeen."

"Excellent choices, you won't be disappointed, ma'am, sir," he assured them. Before he left the table, he topped off their *Champagne*.

"I had no idea you were such a sophisticated gourmet, Dempsey."

"You mean because I like Cheerios? There's a lot you don't know about me yet, Danaher."

———

Groaning with satisfaction, Marla leaned back in her chair. "That was one of the best meals I've ever had. Or maybe it's the ambience, or the concert afterglow."

He laid his hand, palm up, on the table. She leaned forward and put her hand in his. "Could the company have had anything to do with it? Hmm?" If he ever got tired of teasing her it would be because he was dead.

"Quite possibly. Thank you for this lovely day and evening. I don't know when I've enjoyed myself so much." She sighed. "But you might want to cancel the crème Brulee. I couldn't eat another bite."

"That's for later. I predict you'll be hungry during the night and need something to restore your strength." The flash in her brown eyes and the slow nod sent heat soaring through him.

"You may have a point." An eyebrow went up, and she squeezed his hand. "I might not want to know where you learned to plan ahead so well."

"Blame it on the USMC. Plan ahead or be dead. But even then something can go wrong. In that case we learn how to improvise."

"Yes, I've noticed you do that quite well."

He stood. "Shall we?" He drew her to her feet. "It's time to see what's in that pink bag Charlene left in the car."

When they got to the room, Marla snatched up the bag. "I'll look at it first by myself, in the bathroom. You stay out here."

He stuck his hands in his pockets and rocked back on his heels. "Where's the fun in that?"

"Just stay out here!" She turned when she had her hand on the bathroom door. "I mean it."

He raised his hands. "Got it." He chuckled and went to the table to examine the service tray, lifted a lid, and sniffed at one of the rich sugar-encrusted custards. He took a crispy, rolled-up cookie he didn't know the name of and popped it in his mouth in one bite.

"Oh, I'm not wearing this thing! Char might wear it, but she's out of her mind if she thinks I would. She knows me better than that." He heard paper rattling. "Oh, wait a minute, there's something else in here. Okay, this is better. Not much, but better."

"Can I see?"

"No! I'll be out in a minute."

Her sister had bought something that had her in a total tizzy, but he'd find a way to talk her in to wearing it later.

"Shake a leg, Danaher. I'm in a fragile state out here."

The minute was more like five minutes and seemed like an eternity to him. The water went on and off. The toilet flushed. A hangar scraped the back of the door. What the hell was taking her so long? The doorknob turned.

"Close your eyes."

"Why?"

"Because I asked you to!"

"I've seen you naked, honey."

"Just close your eyes and stop arguing, please."

He crossed his arms and sighed. "Okay, Miss Sunday School Teacher. They're closed. Come out here." The door hinges barely made a whisper.

"Okay, open them."

He opened his eyes, clutched at his heart, and gasped dramatically. "Your sister wants to kill me. Call a corpsman."

"Oh, stop it! Is it too, um, daring? I feel like I should be putting out my hand and asking you for money in this getup."

Instead of answering, he twirled his finger in a circle. She turned slowly, the hem of the satin, leopard-print slip, trimmed with lace, barely covered her mouthwatering ass. "Look what you did to me, Danaher." He ran a hand over the bulge in the front of his suit pants, moaned, and reached for his wallet. "How much?"

A bright pink blush on her chest, she sauntered to him using exaggerated hip movements, her breasts swinging, and extended her hand. "Five hundred dollars. In advance."

He grinned. "Can I have credit for what I've already spent?" He pulled some bills out. "Otherwise, I'll have to owe you."

"People in my profession don't extend credit, Marine. But because you're obviously so new at this, I'll make an exception." She draped her arms around his neck and tilted her head for his kiss. "Just so you know, we don't usually kiss our customers either."

"Where does this vast knowledge of the oldest profession come from? Is there something you should tell me?"

Marla pressed her pelvis against his erection. "I read a lot."

He grabbed her bottom and kissed her until she was breathless. "I'm going to make love to you until you beg for mercy, Danaher."

"That'll cost extra, Dempsey."

"Stay right there."

"Where are you going?"

"I want to see what else is in that bag. I may have to run out and find an ATM."

"You can look, but I'm not wearing that thing."

He grabbed the bag and brought it to the bed. His hand closed on filmy black and white silk, lace and ruffles. When he lifted it out of the bag, he dropped his head back and hooted with glee.

"Oh, I have plans for this, my little French Maid." He held up a white lace cap and twirled it on his finger. "Oh, yeah. You will wear it before morning." He took her hand. "Come here, for five hundred dollars I'm entitled to a favor." Pulling her close, he ran his hands over her sides, back, and front, then lifted the slip over her head and dropped it on the floor.

Eyes big, she choked out a whisper. "What?"

"Undress me."

"That's the favor?"

"Use your imagination."

Chapter Twenty-Five

IN THE MIDDLE OF THE NIGHT, DWAYNE ROLLED OVER AND LAID his left arm across her stomach. For some reason she seldom noticed his two missing fingers. Sighing under his touch, she covered his hand. "How do you do it? I'm exhausted. I'm hungry." Never having imagined what it would be like for a man to so completely overwhelm her, Marla felt like a babe in the woods.

"Time for my next favor." He kissed her shoulder.

Melting with the heat of passion he'd stoked in her, she let her mental images run wild. "The price just went up, soldier." She shifted to face him and stroked his cheek.

"This favor's pretty wild. Think you can do it?"

"I doubt it but tell me. Leave nothing out." Her heart pounded so hard she was afraid she'd choke.

"You're going to get up. Put on that filmy little French Maid's getup, and serve me crème Brulee, and you're going to do it like the dirtiest little hooker on Sunset Boulevard."

She grinned, barely able to see his face in the faint city lights through the sheer curtain on the window. "I had no idea you'd spent so much time on Sunset Boulevard."

"I read a lot."

When she woke in the morning she heard the shower running. She dragged herself out of bed and took off what was left of the French Maid costume and wondered how much Char had paid for it. At least she got her sister's money's worth and wondered if she'd be able to crank up the courage to tell her how.

Steam billowed from the bathroom when she opened the door. It felt wonderful on her face and body. She definitely needed a day at the spa to recover. What a good idea. She'd treat Char to the works.

"Hand me a towel, honey. I forgot to bring one over here."

A huge fluffy white towel in her hand, she opened the glass shower door. He swiped water off his face and smiled. When she didn't hand him the towel, he raised his eyebrows and held out his hand.

"In a minute. I want to enjoy the view first."

In answer, he stood balanced on one leg and held out his arms. Water droplets slid down his shoulders, chest, and legs. Beautiful, every inch of him, even his ruined left leg.

Marla handed over the towel. "All right, enough for now. My turn." She stepped aside.

Dwayne took the towel, rubbed his head and wrapped it around his waist then with a series of hops and scoots, made it to the adjacent marble tub where he sat. "You'll love that great shower, and best of all, I can watch."

He watched her for a few minutes then pulled on the thick sock that protected his stump, attached his prosthesis, and stood. "I'll order breakfast. Don't take too long, we have to be out of here by eleven."

She threw him a kiss. "Order French toast in honor of the saucy maid who gave her all." She flashed a wicked grin then examined the shampoo bottle.

He was on the phone when she came back to the room wrapped in a fluffy terry robe. Fully refreshed, she reveled in the afterglow of the previous night. Everything tingled and in all the right places.

"Okay, squirt, I'll ask her. Give Grammakat a kiss and hug from me. Love you. Bye."

"Amber?"

"Yep. I call her every Sunday morning. She's having a great time with Mom, the dogs, and horses. I'll bet she has the wranglers eating out of her hands by now."

"What did she want you to ask me?"

They were interrupted by a knock on the door. A man's voice called, "Room service."

Dwayne, fully dressed, opened the door. The waiter entered, cleared the remains of their middle-of-the-night snack, ignored the satin slip on the floor, and set up their breakfast. He handed the check to Dwayne, tilted his head, and wheeled last night's dishes to the door.

Just before he stepped out, he smiled at Marla and winked.

She drew in a breath. "Did you see that?"

"Should I call the manager and have him fired?" He embraced her and kissed her on the forehead. "At least I hid the maid outfit in the shopping bag. No need to torture an innocent man."

"Pish, you enjoyed every minute of it, strutting around here like an Arab sheik."

"Yes, I did, Red. Let's eat." He lifted the silver cover of one of the plates. "This one's yours." He sat and removed the dome from the other plate to reveal a gigantic plate of roast beef hash and eggs with a mountain of country fried potatoes. A smaller dish was piled with toasted English muffins.

Marla leaned forward to sniff the spicy golden French toast. Half a dozen strips of crisp bacon lay alongside it. A pot of warm syrup and a small dish of sliced almonds completed the presentation. "I want to live here."

Halfway through breakfast she said, "Oh, you never told me how you convinced Uncle Johnny to loan you his Lincoln."

Dwayne's shoulders bounced with mirth. He held up a finger, swallowed, then took a sip of coffee. "I told him I knew what he was up to and would spill it to Irene if he didn't let me take the car."

"What is he up to?"

"Damned if I know, but there must be something, because he handed over the keys without another word."

"I hope you take after your mother's side of the family."

"And I hope you take after your father's side of the family."

She grinned. "I leave Mom's side to Charlene. They're two peas in a pod."

"And a lovely pod, at that."

On the way back to Ventura County they passed the Getty, gleaming white on the hill above the freeway. "Have you ever been there?"

His eyes followed her gesture. "No. Let's do it this afternoon."

"We could just visit the gardens. They're very unique and beautiful."

"Let's do it. I'll get off and circle back. If they have a restaurant we'll get lunch."

"Oh, they do. One is a nice terrace café with beautiful views of the gardens and the city."

"How many times have you been there?"

"Dozens, and it's still not enough."

They strolled through the gardens hand in hand, stopping frequently to examine a certain plant or just enjoy a particularly nice spot. She noticed his limp was more pronounced than usual.

"Is your leg hurting? Let's sit over there in the shade and take a breather. We don't have to do it all in one day."

He leaned forward and rubbed his knee. "Once in a while this thing stings like a sonuvabitch. Feels good to sit for a while."

"What did Amber want you ask me?"

The stress lines on his forehead relaxed as he flexed his leg. "Oh, yeah. I'm going to the ranch when I finish the storage facility job, around the first of August. I'll stay for about three weeks, then bring her back home before school starts. She wants you to come with me."

"I can't possibly be gone for that long. I need to hustle up some real estate sales. This is the time when people with kids make plans to move. There's not much money coming in for me until I get my building fully rented."

He put his arm around her and pulled her close. "Have you considered a new profession? I think you have the hooker thing down pat."

"Shut up!" She glanced around to see if any strollers had heard. "Like I said, you have a death wish, Dempsey." She scooted away from him.

"Sorry, honey, I just love teasing you." He hugged her again and kissed her cheek. "I know you can't be away for a month, but how about a week? You could drive up with me and fly home from Sheridan. You'd love the ranch. My mom remembers you and Charlene."

"I'll think about it. There's a lot on my plate right now, a lot happening at the real estate office." Marla's emotions bounced like a trampoline. She loved him and wanted to be with him as much as possible, but she had a life before they became a couple. She didn't want to lose her identity or independence.

His sharp perception surprised her again. "Are you feeling smothered by me?"

"No!" She shook her head and knew her response had been suspiciously over the top. "Well, maybe a little. I've never been in love and I had no idea it could be so wonderful and so scary. Please don't read more into it. I love you. I'm just…"

He stood and took her hand. "Let's get lunch and head home. We won't talk about it now. Take all the time you need."

They made their way to the Terrace dining area and discovered it had just closed.

"Let's go on home, Dwayne. I can wait until we get back to Spring Grove. I'm tired."

———

Her admission hit him like a fist in the gut. Had he gone too far, too fast? He didn't want to lose her, but maybe she needed some space.

He'd driven several miles when she said, "You're very quiet. Are you mad at me?"

"Jesus, no, honey." He put his hand on her head and ran his fingers through her hair. He took his eyes off the road for a second and saw a tear slipping down her cheek. "Did you think I was mad at you? Please don't cry. I have no idea what to do or say when a female cries. I love you."

Marla lowered her face in her hands and sobbed.

"Oh, shit, honey, please don't do that." He quickly took the Sherman Way off-ramp and pulled into a Taco Bell parking lot. His stomach in knots, he turned off the ignition and gathered her into his arms. He kept his mouth shut and let her cry.

Racked with sobs, she gasped raggedly, "I don't know what's wr… wrong with me. I never cry. I'm a grownup."

Still, he remained quiet because he was sure to say the wrong thing if he tried to comfort her. He held her as best he could with the damn console digging into his hip bone and stroked her back.

After an eternity of him getting sicker by the minute, she wiped her face with her fingers and dropped her head against his neck. A wave of relief went through his chest when he felt her relax. "Better?"

She nodded.

Not sure how long they'd sat there, all he could do was wait for her to compose herself. Finally she pulled away and said, "I have to blow my nose. I need a tissue."

He chuckled and handed her the tail of his shirt. "This is the best I can do, honey. I can go inside and grab some napkins if you want."

She reached for the latch on the glove box. "Maybe John has some in here." She shrieked and slammed back against the seat like she'd encountered a rattlesnake.

His heart stopped for a split second. "What?"

"There's a gun in there."

"Dad has a CCP. I should have looked before I took the car."

"A CCP?"

"Concealed carry permit. Don't worry, it has a safety, you can't fire it accidentally. Takes a lot of strength to release it."

She leaned into him and wiped her face on his shirttail. "Sorry. You offered."

"I guess I can't complain. What say we go inside and have a cup of coffee?"

"How do I look? And don't say beautiful!" She wiped her fingertips under her eyes and smoothed down her wild hair.

"Like you got smacked in the kisser with a two by four. Come on, who cares?" He opened his door and stepped out. Leading with his left leg wasn't ideal, but unless he moved to Britain, where the steering wheels were on the right side, he was stuck with the situation. He leaned in. "You coming?"

She pushed her door open. "Yes."

He met her at the back of the car, took her hand, and they walked into the fast food place together.

She smiled when he carried a tray to the table with two cups of coffee, two soft drinks, and several greasy paper bags containing tacos and burritos. "Looks like this is dinner."

"Looks like." He slid onto the bench across from her and set the tray on the table.

She leaned forward on her elbows, cupped her hands around her mouth and whispered, "Don't let it get around, but I love their tacos."

He winked. "Something else we have in common. The Mexican guy who owns the Gaggin' Wagon comes in a pretty close second."

"Yummy."

His heart bounced when she ran her left foot up the inside of his right leg. "Don't start something you can't finish, Red."

"Oh, I can finish it, you common lowlife laborer."

———

When they got to her house, he asked if it was okay if he dropped her off and didn't come inside. "I promised Dad I'd have his car back before six."

"That's fine. Charlene and I need some time to catch up before she leaves. I'll carry my bag."

"Don't you sisters talk about me."

"No promises."

"Where shall we have dinner tomorrow? My house or yours?"

"Char and I are taking Rosie out tomorrow evening. It'll have to be later in the week. You're starting your new project on Tuesday, aren't you?"

"Yep. I'll call you during the day Tuesday if I can find the time. First few days are pretty hectic." He prayed she wasn't giving him the brush-off.

She smiled in a way that set his mind at ease. "No problem. You know where to find me, Dempsey."

"That I do, Danaher." When she made a move to open her door, he grabbed her arm. "Don't even think about leaving me without a kiss to hold me over."

"Never, lover man. Never."

Chapter Twenty-Six

CHARLENE'S CAR WASN'T PARKED IN HER DRIVEWAY. SHE CARRIED her bag to the porch, set it down, and unlocked her front door. The house was dark and quiet and the message light on the phone flashed. She closed the door, turned on the lights, and pressed the play button.

"Hey, sis, Skipper and I are at my house. Somebody kept calling your phone and hanging up when I answered. I tried to call your cell, but you must have turned it off. There was a blue car that kept driving past the house this morning. It was creepy, so I decided to leave, call me when—"

The message cut off. She needed to change the recording time allowed. Fifteen seconds wasn't long enough for Charlene's messages. Tapping *69, she waited while her phone redialed her sister's number.

"Charlene's superior doggy sitting service."

"Hi, Char. I'm back. I'm on my way to your place. Are you going anywhere tonight?"

"Nope. The love of my life is in San Diego, and I'm true blue. Want to have a pajama party?"

"I'm on my way."

Marla changed clothes, replaced the things in her overnight bag, and turned out the lights. It was full dark outside now, no moon. An icy feeling in the pit of her stomach sent chills down her legs as she was about to turn the doorknob. She put her eye next to the peephole, screamed and reared back when a shadow passed in front of it.

"Marla?" A man's voice. "Marla, are you there?"

She yanked open the door. "Edwin, are you trying to scare me to death!"

His back stiffened, his expression indignant. "Certainly not. Why would I engage in such a schoolboy prank?"

Was this really the man she'd thought would be her forever after? She sighed and switched on the porch light. "I'm just leaving. What do you want, Edwin?"

"I can only assume you're rushing back to your unsuitable lover. Is it too much to ask for a minute of conversation?"

She sighed and stepped back. "I'm on my way to Charlene's for your information, but do come in, we might as well get it over with."

"Indeed." He brushed past her.

"Turn on the light in the living room. I need to let Charlene know I'll be delayed." She lifted the receiver and redialed Charlene's number. After a brief conversation, she joined Edwin.

"What do you have to say to me, Edwin?" She sat across from him, hands clasped tightly in her lap.

"I've reconsidered my initial reaction to your indiscretion, and I think we can repair the breach."

"My indes—?"

"I accept the premise that I've been absent for long periods of time and may have been somewhat aloof and unaware of your physical needs."

"My phys—?"

"I assure you, I'm fully capable of satisfying your needs. I'm willing to accept a position with my employer that will not require excessive travels. We need to spend more time together."

"Toge—?"

"I'm quite aware that for a liaison to flourish, for your physical and emotional needs to be satisfied, I shouldn't travel so much at this stage of our relationship."

"Our relation—?"

"I'm fully prepared to accept your impropriety and my part in it."

"Your part?"

"I do believe however, that it is incumbent upon you to fully explain your peccadillo with the construction individual. Who is unfortunately, handicapped."

"Handicapped!"

"Your mother explained to me that the man was wounded in the lamentable war pursued by our politicians. I know you have a deep love for the country, and no doubt that's what brought about your untoward lapse in judgment."

"My lapse in…?"

"So, to summarize, Marla, all is forgiven."

"Forgiven?"

"I would like to resume our relationship as if nothing happened. I am in a far better financial position than the carpenter could hope to aspire, to support you in the future. I'll give you time to think over my proposition, and I expect you'll come to the realization that we are a good match." He stood. "I'll take my leave."

He did just that. Marla sat in stunned silence.

———

Charlene did a double take. "He said what?" She slapped a hand over mouth and fell back on the sofa laughing through her fingers and kicking her feet in the air.

"Don't laugh, Char. I'm ashamed of myself."

Charlene rolled on her side and propped her head in her hand. "Shame is such a colossal waste of time, sis. You are not perfect and all wise. Everybody makes mistakes."

"But I did disrespect him. The least I could have done is phone him or e-mail him when I started seeing Dwayne. Not let him find out by practically walking in on us."

"Marla." Char sat up. "He never respected you. He's one of those…I don't know how to label them, but I sometimes have to have an accountant who works under me go over tax returns with clients like him."

"What do you mean?"

"Men who think because I'm an attractive woman, I couldn't possibly have a brain in my head. It's insulting, but it's their problem, not mine. All I have to do is look at the way they do business to know I'm smarter than them." She patted the couch. "Come here you little sweetie."

Skip jumped up and wallowed in her baby talk and ear-scratching. "I'm keeping your dog."

"No, you are not." How lucky she was. Her sister loved her little guy and was always available to babysit. "Get your own."

"Never mind, I'll just borrow him once in a while."

"Char, did you leave my house because you thought it might be Dwayne's wife calling and driving past?" She wondered whether or not to tell Dwayne about it.

"I don't know, but you said they had a blue car. I'm more comfortable in my own place anyway."

"Dwayne asked me to go to his mother's Wyoming ranch in August. He's planning to spend a few weeks there when he finishes his new job, and then bring Amber home."

Char's eyes widened. "Weeks? Are you going?"

"I told him I couldn't possibly be gone that long. He suggested I drive up with him and fly home after a week. He's got a lot of work to do up there, repairing fences and the barn roof. But it would be nice to spend some time with Amber and Kathleen. Did you know Miss Emmaline is there?"

"Yes, Donovan told me. He'll visit his mom when he gets liberty later this summer. He wants me to come with him. I'll go and stay as long as he wants me to."

"What about your job?"

"I'll tell you something, but you have to promise not to tell anyone, including Dwayne. Do you swear?"

"Have I ever told one of your secrets?" She put a mock expression of insult on her face and stared at Charlene.

"No, but this the biggest secret I've ever told you. Do you swear?"

She pinched her lips, rolled her eyes, and crossed her heart. "I swear."

"Donovan and I are engaged."

Marla sucked in a startled breath. "When did that happen? When are you getting married? Why is it a secret?"

Charlene hugged herself, sheer joy on her face. "He proposed when we were in Coronado. We decided not to say anything until he makes up his mind about reenlisting, whether to make the Marines his career. We'll set a date after that decision."

"Oh, Char. That's wonderful, but it's awful. He'll be gone so much and in danger. How will you stand it?" The thought of Dwayne being sent to some foreign land where he might get killed made her sick to her stomach.

"He's applying for a stateside job. If he can get the drill instructor assignment he wants, we'll move to Oahu. He'll be stationed at the Marine Corps base at Kaneohe."

A sudden sense of loss engulfed Marla. She and her sister had never lived more than ten miles apart all their lives. Tears sprang into her eyes.

"Sorry." She waved her hands. "I want to be happy for you, and I am, but Hawaii is so far away. I never thought we'd live so far from each other. Mom and Dad will be devastated."

"Oh, they will not. They still have you and the boys, and that's what life is all about isn't it? Leaving home, moving on?"

"Yes, but…"

"We plan to have lots of kids. Sil and Dadley will love being grandparents. Donovan wants a big family, like Dylan and Grace." She stared at Marla. "Say something."

Instead of a verbal reply, Marla went to the couch, sat next to her sister, and hugged her. "All I want is for you to be happy, no matter where you live." She leaned back and smiled. "You're my favorite sister after all."

They changed into their pajamas and sat at the kitchen table to eat ice cream, just like they used to after their parents went to bed.

Charlene said, "You haven't told me whether or not you liked my thoughtful role-playing gifts."

"Dwayne did." Warmth at the memory of last night's hotel stay spread through her body.

"Yes, and?"

She blushed. "At first I wouldn't put on the maid's uniform, but before the night was over, Dwayne forced me to."

Charlene's spoon stopped halfway to her mouth. "He forced you?"

"What could I do? He was my employer. I was a lowly maid who couldn't afford to lose her job."

"I can't wait to hear the details." She leaned forward, elbows on the table and goggled. "Tell me, tell me."

"I'm not telling you any details, Char, but I will say you got your money's worth. For both outfits. However, the only one that survived the night was the leopard print silk slip."

Charlene shrieked, put her hands over her mouth, and rocked back in her chair. "I knew it. I knew it."

"You knew what?"

"I knew there was a part of you, you didn't even know about. I'm unashamedly proud of myself."

Marla laughed. "And how did you know that?"

"I was there when you were born, remember?"

"What? You were only ten minutes old."

"I've always had super instincts. Don't question me. Was I right or not?"

She flipped a spoonful of ice cream at Charlene. It hit her on the forehead.

"Oh, you want to play that game?"

"Uh, no, I don't know what came over me." Her response was too late. Charlene plopped a handful of peanut butter and chocolate on top of her head. And rubbed it in.

Things went downhill from there.

Except for Skipper. He had a great time running between and around the table legs licking up what landed on the floor.

"Stop!" Marla covered her head with her sticky chocolaty hands. "Look at us! I have to take a shower, and Skip needs a bath. I don't have any other pajamas. Mercy, Char!"

"Not before you admit I'm just as smart as you are."

Marla peeked between her fingers. Charlene was poised to smack her with another dripping gob of ice cream.

"All right. You're just as smart as me. You're smarter. Please stop."

"You started it."

"I did, didn't I?" She pulled her pajama top away from her chest. "Ick." Grinning at Charlene, she added, "It was fun though, wasn't it?"

They screamed with laughter and made ugly menacing faces at each other.

"Oh, lordy, who's going to clean up this mess?"

Marla lifted Skipper off the floor and stood him on the table. "He can do some of it. Have at it, Skippy."

"If he pukes, you're going to clean it up."

"So, what else is new? Grab the paper towels. We can get the worst of it, then do a better job after we shower."

Ten minutes later, Marla stood under the shower, Skip hugged to her chest. There wasn't a hair on his little body that had escaped the ice cream fight. She'd never seen him so excited, and that probably wasn't a good sign. She sighed and washed him from head to toe, not a huge task.

Wearing Charlene's robe, she returned to the kitchen and had most of the mess cleaned up by the time her sister came in. She tossed Char a wet towel. "Rinse this out and hand me that clean one. I'm almost done."

The doorbell rang. They stared at each other. Charlene shrugged and went to the door, Marla following close behind. She peeked through the peephole and jumped back, hand on her chest.

"Is that Francine?" Char whispered.

"Let me see. Yes, and that's her husband behind her. I'm calling Dwayne."

"No, don't do that. I'll call the police. Those people are nuts. They scare me."

Chapter Twenty-Seven

MONDAY, DWAYNE MADE PHONE CALLS, LINING UP FUTURE JOBS, and then called on some previous customers to make sure there were no problems or complaints he needed to be aware of. He depended on referrals for future business. One disgruntled customer could be very bad news.

At the end of the day, he stopped by Cluny's location to see if he'd like company for dinner. He hadn't spent much time with Cluny for the last several weeks while he'd been obsessed with Marla. They usually made it a habit for at least one guy's-night-out every week.

Cluny looked up from his desk. "Hey, Gunny, what's up?"

"How about a few beers and some pizza tonight?"

"Yeah, right." Cluny laughed. "We know the beer ain't gonna happen, but pizza, I'm all yours." He gestured to a chair. "I have a couple of phone calls to make. Should take less than ten minutes. You want to wait? Or you wanna meet at Angelo's?"

"I'll wait." Dwayne sat and picked up a tattered and greasy copy of Sports Illustrated. The magazine was published the previous year. He snorted with disgust and tossed it back on the table. Cluny gave him the finger.

He'd been tempted to call Marla all day, but hadn't. They both needed a little breathing room. She had business to take care of and so did he. She'd hesitated when he asked her about going to the ranch. It had rankled, but what did he expect? He sprang it on her out of the blue.

"Where are you?"

Dwayne's gaze shot to Cluny who stood before him dangling his keys. He huffed his response, "Not here, that's for sure. Ready?"

They were halfway through their first pizza and pitcher of lemonade when Cluny asked, "So how's it going with you and the boss lady?"

Dwayne pressed his lips together and shook his head. "I'm in deep shit. I'm in love with her."

"What's wrong with that? I wish I was in love with somebody."

"Are you kidding me? You get more women than any guy I've ever known. I don't know how you keep them straight."

"Not the same. I was in love once, it was great." He grinned. "The sex is a shitload better when you're in love."

"When were you ever in love? And how come I didn't know about it?"

"Remember Esther Grossman?" Cluny gave him a sly smile and waggled his eyebrows.

"You played hide the salami with Esther Grossman?" Cluny was a wellspring of surprises. How had he not known this? They'd hung out together since tenth grade. Esther Grossman was the hottest girl in senior class. Every guy in school wanted to get in her pants, including him.

"Oh, yeah." Cluny's expression was priceless.

"What happened?"

"Her papa married her off to a nice Jewish boy when we were doing our first tour of Iraq. The next time I saw her," he held his hand out in front of his stomach, "she was out to here. Broke my heart, Esther did."

"I'll be damned. How come you never told me?"

"I'll give you the low down on Esther if you share the dirty details about you and the boss lady."

"No way, pal. Esther is ancient history, Marla is now."

"Hell." He grinned and threw down his napkin. "I'll tell you anyway."

For the next hour Cluny regaled Dwayne with colorful details of his sexual exploits with the sultry Esther Grossman.

Every now and then Dwayne would rear back and say, "No!"

Cluny grinned, nodded, and added another sensational detail.

———

Rosie gasped. "Oh, my gosh! How long did it take the police to get there?"

"A sheriff's patrol car was making nightly rounds a couple of blocks away," Charlene said. "Those nitwits were still pounding on my door when they pulled up with their lights flashing." She shook her head and snickered.

"Wow. What did they say when they were caught red-handed?"

Marla sighed. "They weren't actually doing anything illegal. Luke told some lie about looking for a guy named Homer Wilson, said he wrote down the wrong address."

"The deputies weren't buying that," Charlene said. "Especially after Marla spoke up and told them Homer Wilson didn't live at her house either."

"It was obvious to the deputies they knew Char and me. And the fact they look like your average mug shot didn't help their case."

"Were they arrested?"

"No, they were warned to leave the area, unless they had a permanent local address. Otherwise, they'd take them in and run a check on the Wyoming license plate and Luke's parole status. From the look on his face it was pretty clear he knew he could end up back in jail."

"Yes," Charlene added, "they left fast after that."

"Does Dwayne know?"

Marla shook her head. "No. I was afraid of what he might do." The thought of those two people ever having access to Amber was too terrible to imagine. What must Dwayne be going through?

"Lordy, sis, he might find out. Isn't it better if you tell him? You can't keep something like this to yourself."

"I know. I'll tell him. I will, but I don't want him to go after them. What good would that do him or Amber? I'll tell him. I promise."

Rosie patted her arm. "I'm sure you'll know when the timing is right."

"First I need to talk to him about going to the ranch. I saw hurt in his eyes when I hesitated. It's…he surprised me when he asked. Instead of saying I had to think about it and make a plan, I said I couldn't possibly be gone that long."

Charlene shook her head. "Just call him. Men aren't like us. They get over things faster. He probably shrugged it off."

"I would like to go. I just wasn't prepared to answer when he sprang it on me."

"She's right," Rosie said, nodding in Charlene's direction. "Tell him you're looking forward to going, and then mention the incident with Francine and her husband like it was no big deal. If he thinks they scared you, he'll have blood in his eyes."

———

About eleven that night, Marla picked up the phone and called Dwayne.

He answered on the second ring. "Hey, Danaher."

"Hey, Dempsey." When she didn't answer him immediately, he said, "What's wrong?"

"Nothing, except my willpower failed. That's why I called."

He chuckled. "I'm glad you did. My willpower lasted about three minutes longer than yours, honey."

How she loved the sound of his voice. "Heck. You mean if I'd lasted another three minutes I could have saved my dignity?"

"That's about the size of it. But I won't hold it against you or take advantage. I promise."

"Since my dignity's already shot…do you want to come over?"

"I'm on my way." The line went dead.

———

When he got to her place, she stood on the porch waiting for him. His woman. The swelling sensation in his chest gave him a sense of lightness.

Marla met him halfway down the walk. They stopped a few feet apart and stared at each other for a split second. She opened her arms and sighed deeply. "Hello, my love."

Body and mind on fire, he gathered her in his arms. "Hello, my love."

She tilted her head for his kiss. He was eager for her to feel all the emotion he experienced every time their lips met. The kiss consumed them. He crushed her against him then eased up, afraid he might hurt her. "I want you every minute of every day."

"That's good." She stepped back. "Can we take a walk?"

"Something on your mind?"

"Always, but it's such a balmy evening, and the only sound is the whippoorwill across the road, I thought we could enjoy it a while before we go inside."

His arm around her shoulders and hers around his waist, they strolled down the quiet street. Having her beside him filled him with a quiet comfort he hadn't known was missing. He made a small, involuntary sound.

"Is your leg hurting?" She stopped and studied his face in the moonlight.

"Yeah, it's been giving me fits all day."

"Why didn't you say something?" She tugged his hand. "Let's go back." When he resisted, she smiled. "Come on, big guy. Don't be a hero on my account."

Grinning, he pulled her into his arms. "I want to be your hero."

"You are."

Back inside the house, she led him to the bedroom. "Sit on the bed. I'll help you undress. It's my current favorite thing."

"Happy to oblige." He groaned with relief from the pressure of the prosthesis. "I gotta get this damn thing adjusted. It's been bothering me lately."

Marla knelt and removed his shoe. He lifted his leg clear of his jeans. Grinning, she pulled off his sock and bit his big toe. He yanked back. "Hey, that's my good one."

She stood and pulled his T-shirt over his head. "Get that contraption off and I'll find something to rub on it. I'm not your regular nurse, but I can improvise."

"Plain old Vaseline will do the trick when all else fails."

He removed the equipment and reclined against the pillows. "Got any Tylenol or Advil, honey?"

"Coming right up." She returned to the bed with a glass of water and two green capsules. "Hope this helps."

"If you took off your clothes it'd be a great distraction." He winked and swallowed the pills then set the empty glass on the nightstand. She lowered the zipper on her only item of clothing, a long robe. He'd never get enough of the sight of her standing before him without a stitch.

He nodded at his growing tumescence. "See, it's working already." He crooked his finger. "Come here."

She held up the tube of petroleum jelly. "Let me take care of your owie first. You'll be more useful to me if you're not thinking about it."

He reached for the tube. "I'll do it."

Pulling it out of his reach, she shook her head and said, "I want to." She sat on the side of the bed and lifted his blown-up leg to her lap and gently massaged his inflamed stump.

Dwayne sighed and lay back. "That feels good, honey."

"Let me know when you've had enough. I just got an idea of another place where I might apply this stuff to make you feel even better."

He sat up and dragged her across his body. "I've had enough." For a woman who'd apparently come late to the game, she made up for lost time, surprising and thrilling him with the depths of her abandonment. "How'd I get so lucky, Danaher?"

She rolled over in his arms and pushed herself to a sitting position, straddling him. "Funny, Dempsey, I was just wondering the same thing." She picked up the tube and put a devilish twist on her lips.

————

At the breakfast table, Marla told him she wanted to go to the ranch for a week or so in August and how much she was looking forward to seeing Amber again.

"The little squirt asks about you every time I call her."

"Is Kathleen keeping her busy?"

"Mom said she falls into exhausted sleep every night. Poor old Jarhead too. He hasn't run so much in years." He dug into the thick Belgian waffle she'd put in front of him.

"Jarhead?"

"Dylan's old dog. He brought him to the ranch and gave him to me when he went in the Marines."

"Holy hail, how old is he?"

"Fifteen. Amber gave him a new lease on life. Mom said his coat is shiny and he's put on a couple of pounds." He shook his head. "I often wonder how many more times I'll see him. He's already outlived the profile for the breed."

She reached down and scratched Skipper's ear. "Teacup Chihuahuas can live to be twenty. Skipper's two. Even with knowing how long he may live, it kills me to think of losing him."

Dwayne snapped his fingers. "Come over here, Sergeant Danaher." Skip scurried to him.

"Little turncoat," Marla grumbled.

While he was making a fuss over her dog, she thought it would be a good time to tell him about her latest encounter with Francine and Luke. "Oh, I almost forgot. Sunday night Francine and Luke showed up on Charlene's doorstep while I was there."

"What!" His voice was so loud Skipper cowered and Marla jerked. "When were you planning to tell me this?" He dropped his fork on the table with a clunk.

Realizing that there probably wasn't a good time to tell him, she soldiered on. "I didn't think it was important. Char called the sheriff and they got there in a couple of minutes. Nothing happened. The deputy told them to get out of town, and they left." The look on Dwayne's face terrified her. "They didn't do anything."

He stood so fast he knocked over his chair. "Goddammit! I'm going to kick that sonuvabitch's ass all the way back to Montana. Hers too!"

"No, Dwayne! They've already left."

"I'm gonna make sure."

"No. Don't go, Dwayne. I mean it."

He whirled on her. "You mean it? Let's get something straight, Marla. Stop giving me orders—and stop now!" His jaw muscles twitched, his fists clenched. "Is that clear?"

She shrank from his glare. Like a chameleon, he'd changed in an instant. Her umbrage built at the tone of his voice. "I'm not ordering you. I'm asking you."

"It sounded a helluva lot like an order to me." He threw his napkin on the table and headed for the door.

"Dwayne, wait. I didn't tell you until now because I was afraid you'd fly off the handle. I was afraid you'd do something that might jeopardize your standing in court, if this business with your ex-wife and Amber ever gets that far. You need to calm down."

"Another order?" He snatched his leather jacket off the back of a chair and kept right on going.

"If you leave like this, Dwayne Dempsey, then don't come back!"

The door slammed so hard it rattled the dishes in the kitchen cupboards.

Chapter Twenty-Eight

The impossible woman! She kept that information from him then ordered him not to do anything about it? He was mad as hell.

Dwayne drove straight to the motel where that scum had been staying. He scanned the parking lot for their car. It wasn't there, but that didn't prove anything. He parked in front of the office and slammed inside.

The same clerk came to the front desk and stopped. He shook his head. "Did you break something else?" His attempt at a joke shriveled when Dwayne glared. "Something I can do for you, sir?"

Dwayne put his hands on the counter. "Are those assholes still here?"

"No sir, they left on Sunday night. Stiffed me on the bill too."

He slapped the counter. "Figures." He turned to leave then changed his mind. "Sorry. I didn't mean to be so…"

"No offense taken, sir." He backed up. "Have a nice day."

Back in his truck, Dwayne fumed with indecision. He pulled out of the lot and drove up and down streets and roads at random looking for Luke's car until he was satisfied they had gone.

He phoned his attorney to give him a heads-up. "She didn't tell me until this morning, otherwise I might have been able to catch them."

"And what would you have done then, Mr. Dempsey?"

The question caught him off guard.

"I don't know. I'm just so damn pissed that she didn't tell me." He dragged a hand through his hair and pounded his fist on the steering wheel.

"I think the lady did you a favor." He paused. "No disrespect, Mr. Dempsey, but I warned you about acting against your own interests in this matter. By this latest incident, they've established a police record here showing a pattern of harassment. It may be used to your advantage at some point if necessary, but not if you ruin it by harassing or threatening them back. In the meantime, I suggest you back off and let me do what you're paying me to do."

Dwayne didn't miss the frustrated tone in the man's voice. He'd behaved like a fool and he knew it.

"I'm sorry. I see your point. Ms. Danaher and my daughter are important to me. It makes me nuts something could happen to them while I stand by and do nothing. It was a knee-jerk reaction. I'll cool it."

"Good. I'm presently waiting for a response from Ms. Henry's attorney regarding her claim of standing. I'll keep you in the loop."

"Thanks." Dwayne pressed the off button and laid the phone on the passenger seat. He picked it up again with the intention of calling Marla to apologize. He'd call her later and make it up to her somehow. His watch told him he was late on the jobsite.

Jack and Slim were conferring with the concrete contractor when he arrived. Jack waved him over. "They're ready to start with the foundation but didn't want to go ahead without your final sign-off, Gunny."

He greeted the concrete boss with a wave. "Come to the trailer. We'll take one last look at the foundation plans, then you can get started."

After the man was satisfied they were on the same page, Dwayne went outside and got his crew to work. They'd lay all the framing this morning, and the concrete trucks would come to pour the foundation as soon as Cluny and his men placed all the underground pipes.

The job ticked along right on schedule. He looked at his phone but decided to have a cup of coffee before he called Marla. If he gave her more time to cool off it was less likely they'd have *words*.

Jack entered the trailer. "There's nothing to keep me and Slim here today, boss. We're going to the construction yard to double check the wall framing materials and make sure those guys we hired will be able to start when we call them."

"Okay, I'll check with you later." He'd finished his coffee, nobody needed to talk to him. He'd run out of excuses, so he picked up the phone and tapped Marla's icon.

It went straight to voicemail. "Crap! Marla, honey? It's me. I'm sorry about this morning. Call me back."

She didn't call back. He didn't hear from her all day, and he wasn't about to leave a bunch of groveling voicemails. He said he was sorry. That should be good enough.

———

Marla splashed water in her face. Enough crying over the big jerk! Her frazzled reflection in the mirror startled her. She was so angry and hurt she was tempted to swear. That's how mad she was. "Damn him!" Great, now she felt worse. Hissing with frustration, she dressed for work.

She'd spend the day trolling for new listings and follow up the inquiries she'd recently handled. If she put the right customer together with the right property it usually resulted in a sale. A couple more good commission checks would be welcome in her ever-skinnier bank account.

After lunch she went to the condos to check the progress of the landscape and paving. The parking lot was finished and the spaces clearly striped. She noted with satisfaction the amount of shade her tenants would have under the canopies Dwayne had cleverly designed.

The landscape supervisor grinned when she parked. "Hola, señora." He made a sweeping gesture. "She looks good, yes?"

"It looks fabulous! Nobody would guess this was bare ground a few days ago."

"Si, I tole you."

"Yes, you did, Jesus. You're a miracle worker. When did you do all this?" Her gaze swept the landscaped areas with wonder.

"We bring plants last night. Plant today."

"You did all this today? I can't believe it. When did you start?"

"This morning, still dark. You like?" His face beamed with pride. "Last of sod going now."

"Oh yes."

She smiled, remembering how he'd virtually bullied her into giving him the job. As soon as Big D's trailer pulled into her lot, he'd driven his old truck in and asked to see the owner. When Dwayne told him she wasn't ready to talk about the landscaping yet, he left, but stopped by at least once a week to sell himself.

Finally, he browbeat Marla into getting in his truck so he could take her to see some of his other projects. He did creative work. She finally gave in and hired him, even though he'd argued vociferously about her choice of some shrubs and trees.

He pointed to the flowering red myrtle trees lining the front walkway. "I put your mortal trees over there and my borch trees in front of building."

She'd had to fight for those myrtles. Jesus loved birch trees and had fought tooth and nail to put them everywhere. "I think we're both pleased with the results. It looks just like I pictured it." She gasped. "Oh, the hydrangeas under the windows are beautiful and they're in full bloom." She pressed a hand to her heart and sighed. She'd wanted color and she'd gotten color. "If I'd known you'd be finished so quick I'd have brought you a check."

"Is good." He grinned. "I come back tomorrow to office inside." He pointed to the building entrance. "I so hoppy you like."

Marla unlocked the building and entered a small room off the lobby that served as an office. She hadn't decided which of the long-time tenants she'd offer the onsite manager job. It would pay little and be mostly symbolic because all the residents would have phone access to her when needed.

She sat at the utility desk and began calling her tenants to let them know their units were ready, and they could begin moving back whenever they wanted. Then she placed her laptop on the desk and created an ad for the local paper for the condos that were still available to rent.

Dwayne was never far from her mind. Her hurt feelings warred with her anger over his ultimatum. She wasn't giving him orders. She'd merely offered a suggestion that was in his best interests, hadn't she? He's the one who made a federal case out of it. Well, he could just cool his heels for all she cared. How could she possibly cope with a man with such a hair-trigger temper? She'd had his best interests at heart and he'd shown no appreciation, just anger. They'd be butting heads forever, and she didn't want all that emotional turmoil in her life.

Better to break it off now, before she got in too deep.

"Who am I kidding?"

———

Why hadn't she returned his call? He'd left the message hours ago. Should he call again? Leave another message? Maybe she didn't get the first one. No. She could stew in her own juices for a while.

He hit his knee with his fist. "Dempsey, you are a total shithead."

What did he expect when he'd hollered at her like a drill sergeant? So she was bossy and controlling, so what? He wasn't exactly Mr. Rogers in her neighborhood.

There was the problem. They were both bossy and controlling. How was that going to work? Would they be battling over every minor thing? What she did wasn't minor by a long shot, but his attorney was right—she'd done him a favor. She knew him pretty well. *God, what an ass I am.*

He picked up the phone and got her damned voicemail again. He checked his watch. To hell with it, time to take charge of the mission. Keys in hand, he locked the trailer door, waved good-bye to the framing crew who were nearly finished and climbed in his truck.

He drove to her house and pulled in the driveway. She usually parked there, so she wasn't home yet. He waited. About a half hour later, Marla's car slowed down at her driveway, but instead of pulling in alongside him, she swerved and kept going.

"Shit!" Dwayne backed out and followed her. She wouldn't drive around trying to avoid him for long because she'd eventually worry about her mutt and head home. All he had to do was follow her until she gave up the chase. What a soap opera!

Several minutes later, he pulled up alongside her at a stop sign and angled the truck so she couldn't move forward. He hopped out and stalked to her car and twirled an unwind gesture with his finger.

When she sat there stubbornly ignoring him he shouted, "Lower the window, Marla."

She stared straight ahead, her knuckles white on the steering wheel.

"Lower the goddamned window!" His angry voice raised the eyebrows of a man sitting on his front porch. He rose and went inside the house.

"Do you want to get me arrested? That guy is probably calling the cops right now." He straightened. Arms akimbo, he looked skyward and rolled his eyes.

He heard purr of the window sliding down. He leaned forward and saw a tear slide from the corner of her eye. "Oh, honey, I'm so sorry. Please get out of the car."

Mute, she shook her head.

"Please, sweetheart. Don't make me beg." He would if he had to, but he sure as hell would rather avoid it.

"You should be begging me, you colossal jerk!" She reached for the door and unlocked it.

He pulled it open. "Get out, honey, please."

The second her feet hit the pavement he crushed her in his arms. How had he lived so many years without the sensation of her body against his, the brush of his lips on her hair?

She held herself stiff for a few seconds then slowly melted into him and placed her arms around his waist. Tears pooled in his eyes. What a fool he was to come so close to losing her.

A black and white Sheriff's vehicle with lights flashing pulled up behind them. The deputy spoke into his radio, set it on the dash next to the Dash-Cam, and stepped out.

"What seems to be the problem, folks?" He approached slowly, his hand resting lightly on his holster.

Dwayne cleared his throat and swiped the heel of his hand across his eyes. "We uh, everything's fine, officer." He patted Marla's back. "Isn't it, honey?"

"Ma'am?"

Marla turned her head to face the officer then rested it on Dwayne's chest. "Um...we..."

"Ma'am, I won't leave until I'm sure you're all right. Is there anyone else in your car?"

"No." She took a shuddering breath. "We, uh, we argued. I'm okay."

The deputy stepped forward. "I'll need to see your I.D. please, both of you."

Dwayne reached in his back pocket for his wallet. Marla leaned through her open car door and retrieved her purse from the passenger seat. They found their licenses and handed them over.

He scanned Marla's license into a hand-held device and held it out to her. Holding Dwayne's in his hand he squinted. His forehead wrinkled.

Dwayne wondered what was so puzzling. "Is there something wrong, officer? Is it expired?"

"No, sir, but I think you were in my sophomore class. Are you related to Dylan Dempsey?"

Dwayne smiled with relief. "He's my big brother."

"How come you didn't come back in junior year?"

"I moved to Wyoming to live with my mother until I joined the Marines."

The deputy grinned, held out his arm and pointed to a USMC fouled-anchor tattoo above the inside of his right wrist. "Semper Fi."

Chuckling, the two men bumped fists.

The officer introduced himself, "Bob Wallace."

"Yeah, Bob, you were on the tennis team, right?"

"Right."

Marla interrupted them. "We're blocking traffic and attracting attention. Can we...uh?"

Her cheeks flamed bright pink. She'd never looked more beautiful to him.

Bob grinned and tilted his head at Dwayne's truck. "Big D Construction. I'll see you around, and it would probably be a good idea to take your lover's spat home." He touched the bill of his cap. "Ma'am."

Marla glared at Dwayne. "I'm so embarrassed. You make me crazy, Dempsey."

"I know the feeling, Danaher." He pulled her close and kissed her. "Go straight home. I'll follow you."

"Look who's giving orders now."

Chapter Twenty-Nine

WERE THEY CLOSING IN ON THE END OF JULY ALREADY? ONE DAY with Dwayne led to a night with Dwayne then led to another day. How had she spent all her time before?

Edwin Plimpton called her while they were having dinner. She looked at the screen and groaned. "Hello, Edwin."

Dwayne rolled his eyes and took bite of his steak.

"May I call you later? I'm in the middle of dinner. How do you know I'm not home? You're there? Edwin, please don't come to my house without calling first." She paused. "Because it's rude, that's why." She sighed. "Yes, I'm at a restaurant. Yes, I'm with the same man. Call me tomorrow around noon. Yes, we do need to talk. Good-bye."

"Persistent little pipsqueak, isn't he?"

She jabbed a finger at him. "That's not nice. He's a decent man. I never thought we had a real relationship, but apparently he did. It's sad, really."

"Sorry. I shouldn't gloat, but it feels so good."

She smiled reluctantly. "What am I going to do with you?"

"I can come up with a couple of suggestions."

Sawing away at her chicken, she said, "You have a one-track mind." And wasn't it wonderful?

"I like to call it keeping the successful completion of the mission as my primary focus."

"You're not a Marine anymore, remember?"

"Once a Marine, always a Marine, honey. It is what it is."

"I wonder if Charlene and Grace have to listen to that stuff day and night."

He stood. "Stand up."

"What?"

"Stand up."

"Why?"

"Just do it, Danaher."

She stood, and he leaned across the table and kissed her. In public, as if it was the most natural thing to do…he kissed her. She remained standing in a blissful fog. "Now, sit down and finish your dinner. Soon as we leave here I want to call Amber. Wyoming's on Mountain Time. Mom will be bundling her off to bed soon."

"I thought you called her on Sundays."

"I call her whenever I can, but always on Sunday."

"You're a good daddy." He had to be missing her. He'd said they'd never been apart for more than two days since she'd been born. "I bet she misses you."

He grinned. "She's too busy with horses, cattle and dogs to miss me, but I miss her like crazy. We're a team."

A team of two. Where did that leave her? Marla hoped there was room on that team for one more member. And if there was, where would she end up in the pecking order? She loved both of them, but wasn't at all sure if Amber was willing to welcome a woman into their tight little team. She'd always been number one with Dwayne, always had him to herself.

Sitting in her car in the coffee shop lot Marla listened to Dwayne's half of the happy daddy-daughter conversation. Every now and then he'd look at her and smile or put his hand on her as if to reassure her. She suspected he'd given thought to the three of them.

He said and showed that he loved her, but he'd never suggested marriage. It was far too soon to go that extra step anyway, in her mind. She wished she could just relax and enjoy him…them. She'd never felt so whole, so completed. Why did she have to over-think every gesture and word? Charlene had the right attitude. Jump in with both feet and enjoy getting wet.

"You want to talk to Marla? Yes, she's right here." He held out his phone. "Amber wants to say hello."

"Hi, Amber. Are you having fun?"

"I'm learning to be a cowgirl. It's a rill lot of work, but it's fun."

"Tell me some of the things you do."

"I feed the chickens before breakfast, then after breakfast Grammakat and I go for a long ride to check the fences. The cows are always escaping. I don't get it. They should stay close to their babies and take care of them."

Marla heard a muffled voice in the background then Amber said, "Grammakat told me they're calfs, not babies. Only humans have babies."

Marla chuckled. "If you're going to be a real cowgirl I suppose it's important to know the proper name for all the animals on the ranch."

"Oh, guess what? I saw a coyote rill close. He stared at the chicken pen, and I stomped my feet and hollered. Jarhead barked at him."

"Did he leave?"

"Yes, but they're always hanging around the chickens. They must be rill starved if they want to eat a chicken that's not cooked and still has all its feathers on. Yucky."

"I wonder if Skipper would chase the chickens."

"Probly, but they're bigger than him."

Marla laughed. "I think you should tell your daddy the coyote story." She handed Dwayne the phone.

"What happened, squirt?" He nodded. "Oh, yeah? Did you tell Gramma? Uh huh. Then, you listen to her, she knows all about the wildlife. You have to go to bed? Okay then, put Gramma on the phone. Love you more than anything. Good night, nurse." He made some silly kissing noises.

He chuckled. "Hi, Mom. Everything good? Yep. Marla's coming with me. Not sure. Soon as I wrap up this job. Is that right? I'll tell her. Love you too. Bye."

"Tell me what?"

"Donovan called her today to say that he and Charlene will be there about the same time as us. Did you know that?"

"No. I wonder why she didn't tell me." She took her cell phone from her purse. "Oh, there's a text message from her. I didn't notice it earlier."

"What does it say?"

"Call me. I have news." She nodded. "What do you want to bet that's why she called?"

"Call her. It's early yet."

Marla tapped Charlene's picture. "Char? What's the news?"

"Donovan got his liberty and his assignment in Hawaii. We're going to get married in Wyoming while everybody's there visiting the ranch."

"Oh, sis, that's great news…I guess, but…"

Charlene chattered on, not waiting for her answer. "We want to have a big pre-wedding reception here at Mom and Dad's, before we leave for Wyoming. I need you to help me plan it."

Charlene getting married and moving to Oahu? A sense of loss overcame her, and she couldn't answer. Her eyes swam with unshed tears. "Um." Dwayne kissed her hand and that made it worse.

Charlene said, "Marla?"

She cleared her throat. "I'm already crying because you're leaving. Of course, I'll help you with your party. Let's make it the best party we've ever had. We'll invite everybody."

"Oh, good. We only have a week. Can you come over to Sil and Dadly's tonight? We need to get started yesterday."

"Can Dwayne come?"

"You mean my soon-to-be brother-in-law? Sure! The more the merrier."

"Good, I'll fill in the details for him then we'll be on our way. Bye."

"Hey, honey, what's wrong?"

"They're getting married," she bawled.

Dwayne laughed and hugged her. "That's happy news, isn't it?"

Marla nodded. "Yes, but they're moving to Hawaii," she bawled again.

He brushed a tear from her cheek with his thumb. "I can't think of better people for us to sponge off for a nice vacation, can you?"

She shook her head and nodded through her tears. "We're supposed to go to my parent's house tonight to help plan their big party. Do you want to go?"

"Sure, let's get Skipper and head over there."

How could she love this man any more? He was going to get her dog. She didn't even have to ask him. All she could think to do was rub her fingers along his arm and attempt a wobbly smile.

———

Amused at the flurry of activity over the next few days, Dwayne helped where he could and stayed out of the way whenever possible. When Brad suggested they rent a portable dance floor, Dwayne leaped at the chance. "I can knock out one of those in a few hours. No need to rent one." He grabbed his keys and waved. "I'll go to my equipment yard and get to work on it. Call if you think of anything else you want me to do."

Brad smiled and waved him off. Silvia, Charlene, and Marla, frantically finishing up the last-minute details, took no notice of his departure.

His lawyer called as he was pulling in to his construction yard. "Dempsey here." He'd been wondering when he'd get an update.

"Mr. Dempsey. It looks like your ex-wife and her husband are scrambling to come up with any delaying tactic they can. The latest demand is that you and Amber submit to a DNA test."

"What! To hell with that." His stomach churned. "I don't have to do that do I?"

"You're under no legal obligation to do so. As I said, they're grasping at straws. I have a source who tells me their attorney is fed up with them and has advised they drop the suit. The original divorce and child custody ruling was reached after due process and was uncontested by them. He can find no loophole in the original judge's ruling, and he wants to be paid."

"Does that mean I'm off the hook?"

"There's nothing to prevent the Henrys from attempting further legal maneuvering in the future, but my take on it is they thought by harassing you they might be able to force some kind of shared custody arrangement."

"They can go f…to hell. I'm not intimidated by their antics. I did everything by the book. Amber is my daughter. As far as I'm concerned, Francine has screwed herself out of ever getting access to her. Especially after putting me and my family through this."

"I understand. I'll tell them you refuse the test and are prepared countersue if they don't back off."

"I can't help wondering if Francine had some idea of extorting money from me. Maybe she got wind of my future inheritance of the land in Wyoming, but that's not likely to happen for years."

"I wasn't aware you had any real estate holdings, other than your home and business here."

"I didn't think to mention it to you because my grandfather's will stipulates the ranch as my mom's as long as she's alive, and she's only fifty-four. I'll be an old man before it ever comes into my hands."

"What provision was made for your siblings?"

"My two brothers stayed in Spring Grove with Dad when our parents divorced. I went to live with Mom on the ranch. Grandpa had no hard feelings about their choice and when his lawyer drew up the will he asked them about their interest in the land."

"Is there any chance they'll contest the will later?"

"That's unlikely. They had little interest in the land, and my mom has all the correspondence between her dad and my brothers. Dylan has a family and business here and Donovan is career military. All they cared about was having access to the family ranch for vacations and holidays. My mom's door is open whenever they want to visit. She's always asking them to come."

"I see. Well, being a lawyer, I'm cautious. It would be good if you make sure your mother preserves those letters and any other documentation concerning their choice. I'm sure you don't want to hear it, but inheritances have a way of bringing out the worst in families."

He was right. Dwayne didn't like hearing it, but he was no babe-in-the-woods. He'd make sure the papers were in a safe place and he'd discuss it with his mom and brothers when they were together next month in Wyoming.

"I'll take your advice. But if it came right down to it, I'd be happy to split it three ways when the time comes. As far as I'm concerned, it's Mom's ranch."

"Good. I'll let you go. I have to be in court this afternoon. As for the Henry's, I'll let you know if I hear from their attorney again."

"I'll do the same. Thanks for calling." He chuckled. "I'm sure I don't need to say 'send me your bill.'"

The man chuckled. "No, Mr. Dempsey. Barring the unexpected, you'll have it in a couple of weeks. Nice doing business with you."

"Likewise." Dwayne disconnected and went inside the lumber storage area to find material suitable for constructing a portable dance floor.

God, I'm getting paranoid. Was that Francine's car that just drove past? He shook himself and pulled down on the bill of his baseball cap. *Get to work!*

———

"You're a lousy dancer, Dempsey," Marla teased as the reception wound down on Friday night. Most of the guests had departed, and they were the only two left on the dance floor. "All you do is stand in one spot with your arms around me swaying from side to side."

"Are you complaining?" He held her tighter and leaned in for a quick kiss. "Hmm?"

"In case you hadn't noticed, the DJ packed up and left five minutes ago."

"He did?"

"Yes." She tilted her head toward the tables. "They're laughing at us."

He looked where she indicated and grinned at her parents and his dad and stepmother. "They're just jealous."

"More like they're pooped. We should help by folding up those chairs and stacking them at the side of the house." She pulled back.

He held tight. "No you don't. Brad hired a crew to cleanup. You stay right here with me. I can still hear the music." To prove it, he took a few dance steps and turned her in the other direction.

Donovan came up behind her. "We're leaving. Charlene's driving back to the base with me. We're going to clean out my billet and head up to the ranch."

"This soon?" She turned in Dwayne's arms and faced him. "What about her job?"

He grinned. "She quit yesterday. She's all mine now, twenty-four-seven."

"It only takes a couple of days to drive there." A pang of separation stabbed Marla's heart. Charlene. Leaving.

"I've got thirty days before I have to report, so we're going to make a honeymoon of it. She wants to see Bryce Canyon and Zion Park." He took Marla's arm. "Come here, my future sister-in-law. Give us a kiss and a hug good-bye."

She hugged Donovan and kissed him. "I hardly know you, Donovan. Charlene has kept you all to herself. She never did like to share."

Dwayne said, "I don't like to share either. Enough with the lovey dovey, little brother."

She smacked his shoulder. "Dempsey, you're not jealous of your brother?"

"I'm jealous of everything on two legs, Danaher." He took her hand. "We'll walk you to the car. Where's Charlene?"

"Saying good-bye to her co-workers. We're packed and ready to roll." He waved to their respective parents and led the way through the house to find Char.

Marla put on a happy face when they said their good-byes. She and Dwayne stood arm-in-arm and waved as their car disappeared down the quiet street, but her heart ached.

Chapter Thirty

AMBER GALLOPED HER HORSE ON THE DIRT ROAD TO MEET THEM when Dwayne's truck crested the last hill on the ranch road. He couldn't hear her, but it was apparent she was yelling, "Daddy!"

"My god, will you look at her ride that little mare."

"Your mom turned her into a cowgirl all right. She looks like she's grown a foot and she's as brown as a beach bum."

He lowered his window.

"Daddy! Marla! I saw the dirt cloud on the road, and I knew it must be you." Her broad grin gleamed in a rosy, freckled face. "Everybody else is already here."

His heart swelled with pride. She sat a horse like she was born in the saddle. "We got here as soon as we could, squirt. Did you miss me?"

"You're rilly silly, Daddy, a'course I did." She leaned close to Dwayne's window. "Hi, Marla. Skipper! Oh, he's so cute. I can't wait to hold him."

Dwayne rubbed the mare's nose. "Turn this lady around and head to the house. We'll follow you."

Amber turned the horse and galloped away, leaving a trail of dust floating on the road.

"Dwayne, she's so grown up. I can't believe how much she's changed since June."

He raised the windows and moved slowly down the rutted track. "Yeah, next thing I know I'll be walking her down the aisle."

Marla laughed. "Why don't we get her through middle school, high school, and college first?" She placed her hand on his arm and gave him a comforting squeeze.

Her use of the word "we" resonated in his brain. "You're right. There's a lot of time yet but being away from her for more than two months makes me realize how precious my time with her is." Her hand loosened. Had he said something wrong? He stopped the truck.

"What's the matter?"

"Nothing, Danaher, I felt like kissing you." He put his hand behind her head and pulled her close. "I love you. Don't forget that."

She relaxed into the kiss and he felt her lips smiling beneath his. "I love you too, Dempsey." She pulled back and met his gaze. "It scares me how much."

"I know the feeling." He put the truck back in gear and proceeded on the road. "Look at that mob. She wasn't kidding, everybody is here."

"Where did your mom put everybody? How many bedrooms are in the house?"

"Six. Don't worry. There're plenty of beds. We might have to get in line for the bathroom though." He laughed at the wide-eyed look she gave him. "In emergencies we can use the outhouse behind the barn."

"We?" She crossed her arms. "I'm really good at holding it, Dempsey. I can hold it for hours."

He pulled to a stop, and they were surrounded by his extended family and some of the ranch employees. This could turn out to be the best ranch vacation ever for the Dempsey tribe.

Charlene was first to reach the car. "Sis! You've got to see my wedding dress." She reached through the open window. "Give Skippy to me. Hi Dwayne, come on you slowpokes. We've got so much to do by day after tomorrow."

He feigned ignorance. "Why? What's happening?"

Char gave him the evil eye. She smiled at Marla. "How can you stand him?"

Dwayne climbed down from the driver's seat and embraced his mother first. "Mom, thank you for taking good care of my baby."

Amber pushed herself between them. "Make a Amber samich."

She put her arms around his and Kathleen's waist and they squeezed together until she squeaked.

He picked her up. "Whoa! I can barely lift you. What has my mom been feeding you?"

"Cookie feeds me. She told me your favorite things to eat, and I like all of them."

He hugged her tight. "I missed you so much."

"Put me down, Daddy. I want to give Marla and Skip a hug."

Reluctantly, he set her on her feet and watched every step she took to the porch where Marla was surrounded by his family. Dylan introduced her to Cookie and Arturo, the couple who'd been living at the ranch as long as he could remember.

Kathleen leaned against his arm. "How are things going between you and Marla?"

He sighed and put his arm around her shoulders. "I'm in love with her, Mom. I want to marry her, but there's so much going on with Charlene and Donovan, and my worry over when Francine might meddle again, I've decided to wait a while before I pop the question."

"She's certainly attached to that little dog."

He grinned. "Charlene told me if the mutt and I were both drowning, Marla would jump in to save Skipper."

Kathleen chuckled. "She was joking."

"Sometimes I'm not so sure."

"If we get a few moments alone later today or tomorrow, there's something I'd like to talk to you about."

Whenever a woman suggested a conversation it always hinted of something wrong that would take hours of talk to sort out. He sighed. "What is it?"

She could often read his mind and that's what she did. "It's absolutely nothing to worry about, and it can wait. Let's join the others." She called to her granddaughter, "Amber. Take Lulu to the barn and take care of her before supper."

Amber made a disappointed scowl, but hung her head and said, "Okay." She took the mare's reins. "Come on, Lulu."

Kathleen whispered to Dwayne, "She likes riding and enjoying the fun part of horses, but like every other kid I know, doesn't want to do the work that goes along with it."

"Can she unsaddle Lulu by herself?" He knew the weight of a Western saddle and the tightness of the cinches.

"Bart's in the barn. He'll help her, but he makes her do most of it. He'll put a crate on the floor for her to stand on while she brushes Lulu." She squeezed his arm. "She'll be a while, let's go inside."

Dylan's three kids ran after Amber to the barn. "Amber, wait up!"

Kathleen laughed. "That'll speed things up. Lulu will have four kids brushing and fussing over her."

———

Marla and Charlene trudged up the polished pine stairway to the second floor. Skipper hopped up the steep stairs one at a time. Marla lifted him in her arms. "Come here, baby. Are these stairs too high for my Skippy baby?"

"Lordy, you and that dog."

"Char, this house is amazing. All this beautiful wood and antique western light fixtures. I had no idea. Dwayne always said it was a plain old ranch house."

Her sister sniffed. "Men. They're oblivious. I said the same thing to Donnie when we got here. He just stood there like a kid, mouth open, stared around, then said, 'Oh, yeah, it's nice, isn't it?' Wait till you see the bedrooms."

Char opened a door near the end of the hall and stepped inside. Marla followed her and took a breath and put a hand on her chest. "This looks like something out of Sunset Magazine. Those quilts, the furniture, everything looks handmade."

"It is. All the furniture in this house was crafted here on the ranch by Kathleen's grandfather and father. They cut the wood from the surrounding area and built all these beautiful pine pieces right out there in the barn. Isn't it wonderful?"

Marla nodded with appreciation. "I can't imagine how long it took." She stroked the bedposts and the handmade quilt on the bed. "Is this your room?"

"No, it's for you and Dwayne. We're right next door so keep the passionate groans to a minimum, please. Donnie and I need our beauty sleep for the wedding."

"Hah!" Marla snorted. "Where did Kathleen put everybody else?"

"Dylan and Grace are on the other side of you. Kathleen's bedroom is on the first floor behind the office. Miss Emmaline is staying in the small adjoining sitting room, and the kids are on the third floor. They have two big bedrooms up there that look like bunkhouses. Beds everywhere and a connecting pocket door. It's where the three brothers stayed whenever they visited their grandparents."

"What's in here?" She walked toward a partially open door.

"Every bedroom has a private bathroom. Do you believe it?"

Marla smirked and crossed her arms realizing Dwayne had been teasing her about the outhouse. "Dwayne told me we might have to get in line for the bathroom, and if I couldn't wait, there was an outhouse out in back of the barn. Wait till I get him alone!"

Char giggled. "Part of it's true. There *is* an outhouse behind the barn."

Charlene boosted herself up on the edge of the bed. "This was Dwayne's room when he lived here." She nodded to the large gun rack on the wall. "Kathleen keeps it just like it was when he was a teenager."

Marla sat beside her. "This place must be bulging at the seams with wonderful memories."

Charlene nodded. "It's easy to understand why those boys never wanted to go anywhere else during summer, isn't it?"

"Isn't what?" Dwayne thumped into the room, lugging their baggage. He set it on the large pine chest at the foot of the bed. "Beat it, Charlene. I want some alone time with my woman."

Char hopped off the high mattress and took Marla's hand. "No way, cowboy. My sister and I have serious business to take care of."

Marla grinned at his look of comical dismay, thrust Skip into his arms, and followed Char. She leaned close for a quick peck as they passed him. "I'll make up for it later." She dodged his attempt to grab her and followed Charlene to the room next to theirs.

In the center of Char's room stood an old-fashioned dressmaker's form outfitted in a ruffled white blouse, long, faded denim skirt with wildflowers embroidered around the flared hem, and a pair of red cowboy boots on the floor beneath it.

"Oh, Char, is that your wedding outfit? I hope so, because I love it!"

Squealing with barely contained glee, her sister took her hands and hopped them in a circle. "I'm so happy, sis. I didn't know it was possible to love somebody so much. Donovan Dempsey's the most wonderful man ever born. I'm so lucky."

Marla dropped her hands and put her arms around her sister's shoulders. "He's the lucky one, you know. I'd be willing to bet everything I have, and will ever have, that your marriage will be very happy." She gave her an extra hard squeeze. "But I don't like it one bit to have you halfway across the Pacific Ocean."

————

Dinner was a festive affair and lasted until after seven. The eight adults were seated in the dining room, and the kids ate in the kitchen with Arturo and Cookie. Peals of childish laughter poured through the door when Dwayne peeked in to check on them.

"Daddy! Cookie's telling stories on you."

He grinned at her singsong snitching and pointed an accusing finger at the woman who'd been like a second mother to him. "Be careful, Cookie. I have a few of my own stories."

Amber stood and rushed toward him. Cookie stopped her. "You know better than to leave the table without permission, miss."

Amber groaned, rolled her eyes, and went back to the table. "May I be 'scused please?"

"Yes, you may. Take your dish to the sink then visit with your Daddy for a while. It's almost bedtime. Those chickens get hungry early."

Dwayne swung her up into his arms when she was done and carried her from the room. He got her squealing by growling and chewing at her neck.

"Daddy, stop!" She placed her hands on his cheeks, stared into his eyes, and solemnly said, "I'm too big for that."

He bounced her in his arms. "Who says?"

"Me. I growed up this summer."

"Well, that does it. I'm taking you home tomorrow to slow you down. I don't want you to grow up."

"You're silly." She hugged his neck. "I love you, Daddy. Is Marla going to be my new mama?"

"Whoa. Where did that come from?"

"Is she? Because I want her to be my mama. She told me Skipper can sleep in my bunk tonight."

Ah, that was it. She was in love with the mouse. "What's the hurry? Day after tomorrow the whole gang of us is driving over to

Buffalo to watch Charlene and Donovan get hitched. One wedding at a time, my too-big girl."

She gave an excited bounce. "We're going on a rill wagon train ride after and have a rill cowboy cookout. I can't wait. Is Marla going to sleep in your bed tonight?"

He stumbled on the doorjamb and caught himself before he dumped both of them on their butts. What should he say? The truth might be best. "Uh, yeah, we're sharing my old bedroom. Why?"

"Is she cuddly? I like sitting on her lap, Marla's rill nice and soft, and she smells good. That's why I want her for my mama. She's rill bossy, but if she's cuddly you probly want to keep her."

"Keep who?" Marla asked as she strolled in.

"You!" Amber struggled. "Put me down, Daddy." She ran and embraced Marla. "I want him to keep you."

Marla's gaze caught his. He detected a flash of panic in her eyes and a rosy glow burned her cheeks. "Um."

He swatted Amber on the butt. "Bedtime. Go check in with Cookie and Grammakat then off you go. That old rooster will be crowing before you know it."

"Night, Marla. Night, Daddy. Come, Skipper." She ran off, Skip bouncing along beside her, and left them standing staring at each other.

"She wants you to keep me?" Her lips made a wry little twist. He couldn't look at her mouth without getting that deep-down buzz.

"Get a sweater. Let's go out on the porch." When she turned to leave, he grabbed her hand. "Wait." He put his arms around her and planted a kiss on her lips. "For the record—I'm keeping you."

———

Marla found Dwayne standing in the empty living room in front of the wide, riverbed rock fireplace. He was peering at photos lining the roughhewn pine mantel. She put her arms around his waist and propped her chin on his shoulder. "Who are all these handsome men in uniform?"

He pulled her to his side. "This is my mom's grandfather, Hector Burwell, in his World War I Marine uniform."

She rested her head against his shoulder. "So handsome. He reminds me of a 1930's movie star. What was he, in his twenties?"

"He enlisted at nineteen and was assigned to the 6th Marine Regiment. He later named this ranch Belleau Wood after the battle that won him the Navy Cross.

"Mom changed it to Big D after she married Dad and had three sons whose names all started with D. If you look at the brand for the ranch, it's a big D with a small BW inside."

He took a step to his left. "This is Grandpa Douglas Burwell in his World War II Marine uniform. He won the Silver Star at the battle of Iwo Jima. Then he went to Korea and fought at Chosin. Gramps was a Bird Colonel when he retired."

Her heart warmed at the pride in his voice. She gave him the once-over. "You look like him."

He grinned. "Yeah, I do." He took another step to his left. "You know the rest, Dylan, Afghanistan, me, Iraq, and Donovan, Afghanistan and Iraq. As you can see from the photo, Donovan has a chest full of medals. Dylan and I got a few minor ones and Purple Hearts."

"Dylan was wounded?"

Dwayne chuckled and leaned close to her ear. "Don't tell him I said so, but he got shot in the ass diving for cover during a firefight."

She gave him a big grin. "It's our secret. What about Uncle Johnny? Was he in the military?"

"No. Like your dad, the timing was off for that age group. This rogue's gallery represents the Burwell side of the family."

"I see where you and your brothers get your physical characteristics. It always puzzled me that you didn't much resemble John."

He turned her in his arms. "Come take a walk with me, there's something I want to tell you."

Heart pounding, she stood on tiptoe and kissed him. "I can't wait to hear it."

Chapter Thirty-One

THEY LEANED AGAINST THE PORCH RAILING. CLOUDS OVERHEAD obscured the sky. No stars were visible, but the moon glowed bravely, shining light through the cloud cover, and gave the night an ethereal glow. A cool breeze ruffled Marla's hair.

She leaned into Dwayne's side, his arm draped around her shoulders. "It's so quiet here. It's almost too quiet to sleep. I never thought of Spring Grove as a big city but compared to here, it is."

What was it he wanted to tell her? He'd told her many times over the past two months that he loved her, so it couldn't be that. Not that she'd mind hearing it again. Was he about to propose marriage? No. It was far too soon for that, and it would need to be something he talked over with Amber before saying anything to her. He and Amber hadn't been alone since they got here. Maybe he talked to her on the phone? Why not just ask him what he wanted to talk about?

She tilted her head to look at his strong, chiseled profile. She loved him so much. "What did you want to tell me?" Her heart thumped.

"Mom told me this afternoon that she'd had a DNA test done on herself and Amber." He looked into her eyes, but she couldn't interpret his expression.

"Did you know about it, um, before she went ahead with it?"

"No. She knew I'd refused Francine's demand for the test. I had no intention of ever doing it, because it didn't matter to me."

"I'm afraid to ask, but what were the results?" She held her breath.

"Amber has Mom's mitochondrial DNA."

"But…that means you're her biological father."

"Yeah."

"What would you have done if the test had shown otherwise?"

"I'd never have known because Mom had no intention of telling me unless it proved I was her father."

"It's good news, but are you angry with Kathleen?"

"I was pissed when she told me she'd done it without asking me, but I understood why she didn't. She doesn't care a whit whether or not the test proved paternity, but she wanted to know for my sake. Amber is her granddaughter, period, no matter how the test came out."

"Weren't you always sure you were her father?" She couldn't imagine the mental agonizing he'd been through lately.

"I never thought seriously about it until Francine said I wasn't then I started questioning my instincts. I'm still not sure why she climbed out from under her rock after all these years."

"Does she know you're heir to this property?"

"How could she? Grampa died and left it to me two years after Francine ran out on us. I don't know who would have told her. Why?"

"Don't be dense. It's a matter of public record. She probably thought she could extort money out of you."

"I don't have any money lying around. Everything I have is invested in my business and my home."

"This ranch is worth millions. Like I said, don't be dense."

He took her hand, stepped off the porch, and led her to the fence surrounding the corral. Leaning back against it, he wrapped her in his arms. "It'll be decades before any of this comes to me, but just in case, would you be willing to marry me for my money?"

Had he proposed? He had to be joking. That was it. "I might consider it, but it's your big strong alpha male body I'm interested in." She put her arms around his waist and pulled herself tight against him. "Very interested in, Big D."

He planted one of his magnificent knee wobblers on her mouth then deepened it, taking his time with her. The feel of his hands in her hair and on her neck turned her insides into molten gold, beautiful and so painful. How could she ever get enough of his lips on hers?

She came up for air. "Dempsey," she gasped. "I love you."

"I know." He grinned in the faint moonlight. "What say we go upstairs, and I work on keeping your interest keen?"

———

Breakfast was a raucous affair. Elbows bumped at the long pine table in the kitchen, and Donovan and Charlene were the target of endless ribbing about their wedding later today. Cookie placed mountains of bacon and pancakes on the table next to a huge platter of eggs fried sunny-side up.

Arturo cuffed one of Dylan's boys on the back of the head when he pulled his sister's ponytail. When the boy gave him a sour look of protest, Dylan pointed his finger at him with an unmistakable look of *you had that coming, son.* "Apologize to your sister."

Before he could get the words out, the girl punched him in the shoulder and got rewarded with a small smack from Arturo. "You city dudes finish breakfast and get to work in the barn. Them cows don't milk themselves. And we got a weddin' to go to later."

Another warning glare from Dylan was all it took to quiet them down and concentrate on eating. Amber wore a smug smile, having been left out of the ruckus.

Dwayne leaned close to Marla's ear and whispered, "When we kids are on the ranch, Arturo is our foreman. We do as he says."

"Your mom's good with that?"

"Believe me, no hand who works on this ranch would do anything without Mom's prior approval. Yes, we do what Arturo says." He chuckled and picked up his coffee mug. "You've been warned, Danaher." He winked and took a sip of strong ranch coffee.

Marla studied the faces of Kathleen, Cookie, and Arturo. The affection they had for the extended Dempsey family was unmistakable. She thought the lessons the boys and their children learned on this ranch went a long way to molding them into such a close family.

"Do you realize how lucky you are, Dempsey?"

"Every day, Danaher."

———

Charlene, Marla, Kathleen, and Grace fussed with the small amount of packing needed for the wedding in Buffalo. Miss Emmaline sat in a rocking chair in Charlene's room, stroking Princess Elizabeth, and wearing a benign smile. A lifelong spinster, she'd never married, but it was obvious to Marla that she'd caught the romantic spirit of the day.

"Lordy, it's only an hour drive. I'm wearing my wedding outfit when we leave here. Donovan's carrying his dress uniform because he doesn't want a single crease in it. He'll change in the men's room at the courthouse."

Marla had packed extra shoes for herself and Amber, along with jackets and sweaters. "Is he planning to wear it all day?"

"No, just for the ceremony. He packed jeans and boots for the barbecue and wagon ride. He's my Marine for the wedding, but my cowboy for the rest of the day." She winked. "And night."

Miss Emmaline hooted with laughter. "You girls these days. I was born sixty years too soon for all the fun."

Kathleen shook her head and grinned. "I happen to know you didn't miss *all* the fun, Emma."

Miss Emmaline wagged her finger. "Don't you go telling secrets on me, miss. I have the goods on you."

Grace's eyes rounded. "Oh, please, tell a couple of them to me. I'd love to know some of my mother-in-law's deep, dark secrets. Might come in handy one day."

Kathleen smiled at her daughter-in-law, Grace, her soon to be daughter-in-law, Charlene. "I love both my son's wives," she said. "And I hope," she tipped her head at Marla, "future wife."

Heat rushed from Marla's neck to her cheeks. She probably looked like a pickled beet. What had Dwayne said to his mother? She ducked her head and fussed with the gym bag carrying her and Amber's shoes and sweaters. "Um...I..."

Grace came to her side and placed her hand on Marla's shoulder. "That's what we all want, Marla. You're perfect for him, and Amber is crazy about you."

Boots sounded along the hall. "You gals got your stuff ready?" Arturo called. "Me and the boys are ready to start loading up."

Charlene squeaked with excitement and happiness. "We're ready. Come in." She hugged Marla. "Come on Maid, ha-ha, of Honor. You have to help me do this. I'm getting nervous."

Marla smoothed her hands over Charlene's lovely blond hair. "You will be the most beautiful bride in Wyoming today, sis." Just when she'd begun to fully appreciate her sister, Char was about to be married and move to Hawaii. A sad lump settled in her chest. "I love you." *I didn't know how much until now.*

Tears sparkled in Charlene's rusty brown eyes, identical to her own. "I know. I love you too. I wish Sil and Dadley and the twins were here."

Marla knew that their parents and Harry and Barry, and John and Irene Dempsey were already in Buffalo waiting for the wedding party to arrive. They'd planned a wonderful surprise for the bride and groom. Charlene, who loved surprises, would have one today to remember all her life.

"They'll be here in spirit, and we'll take tons of pictures on our phones to send to them." She kissed Charlene on the lips. "Ready?" She grinned and held the secret close to her heart. "Okay, then let's get hitched!"

———

"Daddy, Auntie Charlene looks like a rill princess, doesn't she?"

Dwayne smiled at his daughter and laughed at himself for being startled to hear her say, "Auntie Charlene." Marla's sister was her aunt now. Part of the Dempsey family. His sister-in-law. Did that fact complicate things further between the two families? He and his brothers knew Silvia Danaher and their father, John, had long ago been lovers, before he met their mother, Kathleen Burwell. Now here they were, all together, celebrating the marriage of the youngest Dempsey son to the eldest Danaher daughter.

"Yes, she does look like a real princess. And Uncle Donovan is a warrior prince. He's the best looking of us three brothers."

"Nuh uh, Daddy, not rilly."

His chest warmed at her innocence. His little sweetheart thought her daddy was the best-looking. "Well, if it's not Donovan, who is it?"

"Uncle Dylan." That knocked him down a peg.

"Who told you that?"

"Uncle Dylan did." She sighed. "It's a fairytale, Daddy." She pointed to Marla, dancing with one of her twin brothers. "Marla's brothers are handsome princes. Barry is going to dance with me when the cowboy line dance music comes on."

"How do you know it's Barry? Those boys are identical. Maybe it's Harry."

"Nope." She grinned a secret smile. "Marla told me how to know them apart. But she said it was our secret, so I can't tell you it."

He pulled her onto his lap and growled into her neck. "Is that so? We'll see about that, squirt." She giggled and struggled.

"Stop, Daddy. Stop, I'll tell you, but you have to promise to keep the secret, okay?"

"What secret?"

Dwayne and Amber hadn't seen Marla leave the dance floor. Amber's eyes got huge and she put her hands over her mouth.

"Hey, Danaher. Enjoying the party?" He tilted his chin. "Kiss me, beautiful."

She kissed him and sat in the chair vacated by Amber. "Wow!" Eyes wide she wagged her chin at the far tables. "Do you believe that?" John Dempsey had just taken Kathleen Burwell's hand and escorted her to the dance floor.

"Shit no."

"Daddy!"

"Sorry, squirt. You can wash out my mouth with soap later. I really want to eat another piece of that wedding cake." He gave her a quick squeeze.

"Then you better watch it, soldier!" She smacked his arm, and he and Marla exchanged eye smiles.

His gaze returned to his parents, and he found it hard to come to grips with the expressions on their faces. They smiled and talked like long-lost friends. "I worried how Mom would react when she learned Dad and Irene would be here today."

"Looks like you worried for nothing. They have children and grandchildren together. Perhaps they felt it was time to bury old grudges. I think it's great." The sparkle in Marla's eyes had the usual effect on him. He brushed his hand on her neck and imagined them climbing into his old bed together tonight.

Amber sang, "Here comes the bride."

Charlene and Donovan joined them. Char kissed Dwayne on the cheek. "I know you don't like to dance, shiny new brother-in-law, but there's no rule that says you can't hold me and sway to the music."

He set Amber on her feet and stood. "What red-blooded Marine could pass up that offer?" He took her hand and led her away. When he embraced Charlene, he noticed Donovan offer his hand to Marla.

Donovan leaned close to him, his forked fingers pointing to his eyes. "I'll be watching you, bro." He winked and pulled Marla into a tight embrace.

"Goes both ways, baby brother. I still outrank you, don't forget."

Charlene whispered in his ear. "Let's have some fun with this, Middle Dempsey." She sighed and rested her head on his shoulder, lips close to his neck. "Isn't this nice?" She reached to slide his hand lower on her back.

He nuzzled her cheek, one eye on Donovan. "You trying to get me killed, gorgeous?"

Char laughed and placed both her hands on his neck. He obliged and circled both arms around her waist. "Ride 'em cowboy," she whispered.

"Yippee-ki-yay."

Yeah, it was nice. A hot, gorgeous blond melting into him. Why wouldn't it be nice? He drew her a little closer and splayed a big hand just above her ass.

"I was broken hearted Marla saw you first, Dwaynie."

He chuckled. "Yeah, sure, until my brother appeared on the scene. Don't kid a kidder, sis. Marla was the only woman on my radar from day one, you bad girl." He hugged her against his chest and kissed her ear. "My brother is one lucky man to have all this in his arms every night."

"And that's why I love you, Dwayne. You're true blue. I know you'll be good to my baby sister."

He moved his head back, grinned into her big brown eyes then grazed her neck with his teeth.

"Okay, okay, break it up!" Donovan bumped them with his shoulder. "Time to switch partners." He took Charlene's hand and pulled her away, leaving Dwayne and Marla standing, staring at each other.

She put a wry twist on her lips. "That was quite a show, Dempsey."

"Your big sister's a very bad girl, Danaher. My little brother has his hands full." He embraced her. "Want to sway for a while?"

"Um hm." Her arms went around his neck.

God, she felt perfect in his embrace. Aroused immediately, he whispered. "Step back a couple of inches, honey, or I'll have to dance you to the front desk and get a room."

"You sure know how to charm a lady." She grinned and took a half step away from him. "Your brother doesn't have a thing to worry about. Char is disgustingly, sickeningly, madly over the top in love with him."

"I know. He's one lucky Dempsey, and so am I." The next wedding for their two families would be his and Marla's. He crooked his finger at Amber. She skipped across the floor to him, and he lifted her in his arm, tucked her between them, and swayed with his two best girls.

———

Amber fell asleep on Marla's lap on the drive back to the ranch. Miss Emmaline nodded off in the backseat with Dylan's girl lying across her knees. Every now and then Dwayne would reach across the seat and brush his knuckles on Marla's cheek.

The next time he did it, she turned and kissed his fingers. "This was very special day, Dempsey."

He nodded and smiled. She'd never get enough of his smile. Every time he touched her, she got the familiar warm, melting sensation in her bones and all her special places. She studied Amber's face and stroked her silky hair, ashamed of the twinge of jealousy she felt for the innocent child who worshiped her daddy. Amber's child-woman relationship with him didn't leave much room for Marla.

She didn't doubt Dwayne loved her, he'd told her many times in the past few months. Did he love her enough to marry her? Her chest squeezed painfully. She mentally shoved away the doubt.

Stop it, Marla. Just love them and don't worry about tomorrow.

Chapter Thirty-Two

Dwayne snuggled against Marla's bare back and kissed her ear. "I gotta get up, honey. Dylan, Donovan, and I are riding out to repair a break in the fence line and round up some feisty heifers that decided to take a walk in the park." He stroked her bottom with his big, rough hand. "God, I love your sweet ass."

She caught his hand and laid it on her breast. "Stay." She cracked open an eye. "It's still dark." It seemed to her they'd only been asleep a couple of hours. "What time is it?"

"Five. Gotta go." He nipped her shoulder. "Cookie's already in the kitchen. I smell coffee and bacon." He rolled away from her and hop-slid to the bathroom, holding onto the bed and furniture.

She groaned and rolled onto her back. "Five! Just shoot me." He chuckled and began to close the door. "Wait!" She jumped up and raced past him, her bare feet slapping on the cold wood floor. "I have to go first. Close your eyes."

"Like I haven't had my eyes, hands, and mouth on every inch of your body by now, Red?"

"Close them! This is different." She made it quick and artfully dodged his hand when he grabbed for her on her way out of the bathroom. She jumped back in bed. Warm with a predictable glow from his casual sensuality, she pulled up the quilts and snuggled into the low spot in the mattress he'd just left nice and warm for her.

Water splashed in the sink as he washed and shaved. There wouldn't be a drop anywhere on the counter, sink, or floor, and the bathroom would seem like it had never been used when he left.

By the time he came back to the bedroom she was wide-awake and treated herself by watching him dress. Clad in jeans, two T-shirts and a heavy flannel shirt, he attached the prosthesis with his work boot on it. He took a quick glance in the mirror and finger-combed his thick black hair.

He caught her smile in the mirror. "What are you looking at, Danaher?"

"I'm admiring my man, Dempsey. Come over here and kiss me before you go."

"Nope. No way. If I do, I'll never make it out the door. If Donovan can show up the morning after his wedding night, what would it look like if I didn't? I have an image to maintain."

"If you don't kiss me good-bye, I'll get up and follow you down the hall in my birthday suit."

He grabbed his heavy barn jacket and winked. "I dare ya." He threw her a kiss and closed the door. She heard male voices in the hallway. Dwayne and his brothers trooped down the stairs.

Marla fell back with a sigh. Holding the quilt tight against her chin she sighed again and counted the knots in the pine ceiling, wishing she could go back to sleep.

She groaned, crawled out of bed, and lifted her pajamas off the floor and pulled them on. She went to the bathroom and took Dwayne's heavy flannel robe off the hook and wrapped it around herself and cinched the belt. It was so big on her she felt positively dainty.

She slipped her feet into slippers and headed to the kitchen to join the men. Might as well drink in some eye candy while she had breakfast. Skipper bounced downstairs from the kid's rooms and skittered happily around her feet.

"How's my teeny weeny widdle Skippy Wippy cuddle bunny-poo?" She scooped him up and nuzzled his warm wriggling body.

"You and that dog."

She turned at the sound of Char's voice.

"Do you think I love him too much?" She gazed into his big, buggy eyes and grinned. "Do I love you too much, Skip?"

Charlene scratched his chin. "How would I know how much is too much where a dog's concerned?" She grinned. "He is a little sugar pie."

Char didn't have a trace of makeup, her thick blond hair tumbled around her shoulders, and the belted robe she wore did little to disguise her fabulous curves.

"You look like a woman in love, Char."

"That's because I am." She took her arm. "Let's go down and enjoy looking at my brand new husband before he leaves for the day."

"Just what I had in mind."

Greeted by loud wolf whistles when they entered the kitchen, the twin sisters bowed slightly, fluffed their hair and tossed it over their shoulders as if they'd rehearsed it before coming downstairs.

Char swayed her hips as she vamped her way around the table. "Howdy, boys, mind if we join you?"

Donovan threw an arm around her hips and pulled her close. "We'd mind if you didn't, sweet thing."

Dwayne scooted over on the bench to make room for Marla. He puckered his lips for her kiss and slid his hand down her back when she took her seat. "Good morning, my love."

"And good morning to you, my handsome hero."

Cookie's shoulders bounced with silent laughter. She flipped a pancake, her back to the room. "It's gettin' mighty thick in my kitchen."

She carried a heaping platter to the table. "You boys eat up, then skedaddle. You got work to do, and I got a lot more folks to feed this morning. You hear?"

Dylan smiled at the woman who'd been cooking for the Burwell-Dempsey family beyond memory. "Thanks for this great breakfast, Cookie. We love you."

"Go on now, I know you boys think you can butter me up, you jest git and use your charm on them cows you're lookin' for today."

Marla had asked Dwayne about Cookie shortly after they'd arrived, but he'd told her he couldn't remember a time when the woman wasn't there, creating her special magic at the big kitchen stove. Another reason Dwayne and her brothers loved the ranch so much. Kathleen had maintained a wonderful home-away-from-home for her sons and their families.

Despite the early hour, the big house stirred with laughter and voices from upstairs. One-by-one the kids made their way to the kitchen. Grace came in, fully dressed, and kissed Dylan. "See you this evening, honey." She grinned when he smacked her on the butt before heading out the door behind Dwayne and Donovan.

Charlene stood. "Cookie, Marla and I'll finish our coffee and make room for the kids. Will there still be some breakfast left after we shower and dress?"

"You gals go right on, sugar. I'll be cookin' for another hour yet. I got all them men in the barn to feed. Don't you never worry about gettin' enough to eat in this house." She tossed warm bacon to Jarhead and Skipper.

Marla shook her head. "Skip's been completely spoiled by you, Cookie. How will I ever convince him to eat his dog food again?"

Cookie chortled at the dogs anticipating their next treat with enthusiastic tail wagging.

The sisters left the kitchen, but before going upstairs Char opened the front door in time to see the brothers and Arturo ride off in the distance, the sun barely up. They clutched their robes tight against the cold morning air.

———

The Dempsey boys had covered many acres of land before they found the break in the fence. They dismounted and removed tools and wire from their saddlebags.

Arturo inspected a couple of broken posts. "I can fix this if y'all want to see where the heifers run off to."

Dylan unloaded the rest of his tools. "Go on. I'll help Arturo. Keep an eye out for anybody who looks like he doesn't belong. Len told me he saw a light in the old trapper's cabin on Wolf Creek the other night. It was too late to investigate, but we'll ride over there tomorrow and have a look."

Dwayne and Donovan touched the brim of their hats and rode through the fence break to search for the cows.

It took a few hours to round up the escape artists, but they found all of them. They drove them slowly back to the fence line and urged them through the small break Dylan and Arturo had left open. "Looks like you're about done with it," Dwayne remarked.

Dylan straightened his back and wiped his face with a bandanna. "Yep, just waiting for you and the cows."

Arturo and Dwayne piled up the debris and packed the tools while Donovan and Dylan secured the last of the wire to the posts, then they mounted and headed at a leisurely pace back to the ranch house, their heavy jackets tied to the saddles.

Dwayne rolled his shoulders in the warm sun. He loved this ranch with every fiber of his body and soul, but he couldn't see himself living here full time. He thought perhaps he'd change his mind years down the road when their mother could no longer handle it alone.

They dismounted at the barn and unsaddled the horses. Bart led their mounts inside where he'd finish taking care of them after the long day on the range. "I got 'em. Go ahead to the house and drink some of Cookie's lemonade."

Jarhead lay sprawled in the sunlight on the porch steps, snoring in the last of the afternoon warmth. Dwayne bypassed the kitchen and headed up the stairs to use his bathroom and wash up. He hadn't seen Marla or Amber in or around the house. He entered the empty bedroom, shrugged at not finding either of them there, and then removed clean jeans and a shirt from the closet.

He finished quickly and went downstairs, entered the kitchen, and gave his mom a hug when she poured him a big glass of lemonade. "Where're my two girls?"

"They took Skipper for a hike in the south meadow. Amber wanted to show Marla the last of the summer's Indian Paintbrush blooming out there."

"How long have they been gone?"

"About two hours."

"My God, we'll be picking ticks out of that mouse's hide all evening." He finished his lemonade, set the glass down, and stood. "I'll walk down the road and meet them."

"Help!" Marla's frantic screams alerted everyone within hearing range. "Help me! Somebody, help!"

Dwayne and his mother charged out the door as men ran from the barn and corral.

Marla collapsed on her knees at the bottom of the steps, sobbing, hugging Skipper to her chest. "They…they…took…" she gasped.

Dwayne bellowed, "Where's Amber? Is she hurt? Where is she?" A horrible feeling of dread filled his chest, paralyzing him. *His daughter, his little girl.*

Kathleen rushed to the bottom of the steps and helped Marla to her feet. "Sit here, honey. Tell us what happened." Marla slumped down on the top step, still hugging her baby. He hadn't moved.

Dwayne grabbed her shoulders and shook her. "Where's Amber! Was she hurt?"

She looked at him with stricken, devastated eyes. He'd seen this look on soldiers in battle when someone got killed. His gut twisted and he gulped air, afraid to hear her answer.

"Francine...on horseback...they took her."

He screamed in her face. "You let them take her?"

Charlene rushed to Marla's side and shoved Dwayne out of the way then sat next to her. "Are you okay, sis? What happened? Are you hurt?" She touched the knees of Marla's torn and bloody jeans.

Dwayne grabbed fistfuls of his hair and paced in a circle. He stooped to look at Marla's face and said, "You let them take her?"

She shook her head. "No, I, I couldn't stop them. I tried. Skip chased after them. One of the horses kicked him. He...he...won't wake up." Her body wracked with sobs. "I'm sorry, Dwayne, I couldn't—"

Charlene brushed her hand on Marla's hair. "It's all right, sis. You didn't do anything wrong. It's not your fault."

"Like hell it's not her fault! She let them take my daughter, and now she's crying over a goddamned dog? Where in hell are your priorities, Charlene?"

Before he saw it coming, Donovan's open hand slammed into his chest and shoved him against the rail post. "Listen up, bro, because I'm only going to say this one time. You ever speak to my wife or her sister in that tone of voice again, so help me God, I'll..."

He threw Donovan's hand away and leaned into him. "You'll do what?"

Dylan shoved between them. "Enough, you assholes! Get to the barn and saddle up. We're going to get Amber back. What the hell's wrong with you two?" He glared, daring either of his younger brothers to defy him.

Kathleen stood next to Dylan. "He's right. You shut your mouth, Dwayne Dempsey. Now, let's go!"

He turned to his mother. "You're not going."

"You and who else is going to stop me?" She scoffed and turned her back on him. "Bart you and Len saddle up too. Cookie, call the sheriff and tell him we're heading out to the abandoned trapper's cabin on Wolf Krik."

She shoved Dwayne who continued to glare at his brothers. "Get moving. Francine will not hurt her daughter." She shouted loud enough for everyone to hear her, "No guns!"

"To hell with that!" Donovan shouted.

"No, she's right." Dwayne grabbed Donovan's sleeve and pulled him toward the barn. "I don't want any gunplay endangering my daughter."

———

Miss Emmaline put her hand on Marla's shoulder. "Let me take a look at your doggie."

Marla shook her head. More wracking sobs choked from her throat. "No, he's…he's…" She buried her face in his lifeless, still-warm body and cried like it was the end of the world.

Charlene held her and rocked her. "Oh, sis, I'm so sorry. The poor little guy." She squeezed her shoulder. "Dwayne didn't mean those awful things he said. He was terrified for his little girl, that's all."

Marla sobbed against Skipper's side. "You were so brave. I love you so much." She leaned against Charlene, raised her head, and smeared her eyes with the heel of her hand. "He meant what he said. He…he didn't even ask if I was hurt." The ice pick stabbing her heart, shattering it piece by piece, wouldn't stop. She'd never felt such pain and devastation.

Miss Emmaline gently lifted Skipper's body from her lap. "Let me take him, dear. I'll take good care of him." A huge, bottomless black pit opened in her chest when Emmaline took Skipper away.

Charlene pulled Marla to her feet. "Let's go upstairs and lie down. You need to rest."

Marla clenched her jaw. "I need to go home. I'm leaving. I can't bear to face him again." "I need to go home. I'll write down everything that happened for the sheriff's report, then I'm leaving. I can't bear to face him again."

"But, sis, how——?"

Miss Emmaline said, "She's right. I know Dwayne. There's no reasoning with him when he's like this. He's apt to say something even more unforgivable before the night is out."

246

She held Skipper to her chest and nodded to Charlene. "You drive us to the airport in Sheridan. I'll pack my things and get Princess Elizabeth. I'll go home with her."

Marla's eyes streamed tears. "Oh, Miss Emmaline, you don't need—"

"Hush, child. It's settled. Go upstairs and pack your things. Charlene will drive us in Donovan's car. If we can't get a flight out tonight, we'll check into a motel and leave in the morning. I'll leave a note for Kathleen, telling her we'll call when we get there to make sure Amber's home okay. Those men will bring her back no worse for wear. You can be sure of that." She cast a sad and loving gaze at both sisters and kissed Marla's cheek. "Off with you."

Chapter Thirty-Three

THE SIX MEN AND KATHLEEN STOOD QUIET AT THE EDGE OF THE woods, their horses tied behind the trees. Dwayne stepped out. Kathleen grabbed his arm and hissed, "Listen to me! You need to get your head straight. What are you planning to do? Charge in there like Special Forces?" She put her hand on his chest. "Let Dylan finish."

His stomach knotted and his ears rang. His mother was right. They had to give Dyl time to do a thorough recon of the cabin and surrounding woods with his binoculars before proceeding. He knew better, but he'd never been so worried and frantic in his life. This was worse than any firefight he'd ever been in. His baby, he had to find his baby, and bring her home.

Dylan spoke softly. "It's quiet. The three of them are eating supper, looks like. Amber appears unhurt; she's talking to Francine."

Dwayne gasped with relief. "Thank God."

Dylan and Donovan stood in front of him. Donovan said, "We're going to run this operation. If you can't follow orders then stay here with Mom. Are we clear?"

Tears of relief filled Dwayne's eyes. He nodded and choked out the word, "Clear."

"Good." Dylan pointed. "Spread out to the right with Donovan, and Bart, Len, Arturo, and I will go to the left. Keep your eyes on me. Don't make a move until you see my signal to advance on the cabin.

Ready?" The men nodded. "Mom, you keep those horses ready. This shouldn't take long."

Kathleen nodded and stepped back as the men began to creep forward. "I'll watch you with the binoculars."

Dwayne joined Bart and Donovan moving to the right, several paces apart, they followed his little brother's lead. Donovan glanced frequently in Dylan's direction, watching for his hand signals. One of them stepped on a dry branch. It cracked loud underfoot. They stood dead still and waited.

Dwayne was close enough now to see through the dirty window. An old Coleman lantern hung from a hook over the table. Amber spooned food into her mouth and nodded at something Francine said. She was okay, his baby girl was okay.

Dylan made the signal to go in through the doors on both sides of the dilapidated log cabin. They'd enter simultaneously, assuming they weren't barred or locked. Dyl raised his hand. They stopped while he whispered something to Len, and then Len ran, crouched, to Donovan.

Donovan nodded and Len returned to his position. He whispered to Dwayne and Bart, "Dylan is going to wait at the door on his side until we knock on this door, then he'll enter as soon as we're in."

"Assuming they open it," Dwayne said in a hoarse whisper.

They crept to the door and waited half a minute. Donovan nodded for Dwayne to knock. He raised his arm and pounded twice with his fist. Loud scrambling and excited voices emanated from inside. "Who's there?" Luke yelled.

"Dwayne Dempsey. I'm here to get my daughter."

Amber screamed, "It's my Daddy."

When the door didn't open immediately, Donovan kicked it down at the same time Dylan and his men busted in from the other side.

Dwayne shouted, "Amber, get under the table," just as Dylan grabbed Francine from behind and dragged her, arms flailing, foul language spewing from her mouth.

Donovan slammed Luke face down on the floor, his heavy-booted foot planted hard on his neck. "You're on your way back to the slammer, moron. If I shoved your brain up a gnat's ass it would rattle around like a BB in a boxcar."

Dwayne barely heard him. His knee screaming with pain, he reached the rustic table and dragged Amber into his arms. "You're fine,

Daddy's here." He hugged her to his chest, heart threatening to explode through his ribs.

"I told them you'd save me, Daddy." She clung to his neck. Her sweet little-girl scent a gift from heaven.

Tears slipped from his eyes as he rocked her side to side. "Did they hurt you?" he whispered.

"No, but they hurt Marla." Her breath stuttered against his neck.

Marla! Oh, Jesus, the filthy accusations he'd thrown at her—the woman he loved. What had he done? He shifted Amber back and looked into her eyes. "What did they do to her?" His stomach clenched as an icy blast of guilt froze his chest.

Amber pointed at Luke. "That bad man hit her and dragged her in the dirt. He told her he was my rill dad. He's mean." She turned her head in Francine's direction. "The lady who talks bad told him he better not hurt *me*, but I still don't like her."

"Nobody move!" Sheriff's deputies rushed in both doors, Kathleen behind them. Dwayne saw her eyes sweep the room to make sure her sons were not hurt, then she went to Dwayne's side and hugged Amber. "Are you okay, baby girl?"

"I'm okay. I wasn't a'scared of them because I knew Daddy would come and get me."

Dwayne suppressed a smile when Amber scowled furiously at Francine. "Go away! I don't like you! I want Marla for my mother." She pulled away from her father and stood, hands on her hips, chin thrust forward. "I told you my rill Daddy would come and get me away from you."

Francine struggled in Dylan's hard arm around her waist. She began to yell, and he slapped a big hand over her mouth. "Shut up, Francine, before you pound a few more nails in your coffin." He released her when a deputy approached, handcuffs at the ready.

The sheriff approached Kathleen. "You folks go on home now. I'll come to the ranch and get your statements tonight." Dwayne didn't miss the man's hand brush across his mother's shoulder and the softness of his expression when he gazed at her.

"Thanks, Harmon," Kathleen said. She smiled at the six men who'd rescued her granddaughter. "Let's head home, boys."

The slow ride home took two hours. The house lights burned bright and could be seen from a mile away. Dwayne hugged Amber

250

close during the long trek and brushed his lips on her hair countless times. "You good, squirt?"

"Daddy, I heard Skipper crying when we rode away. Did he get hurt when he chased the horses?"

He swallowed at the memory of Marla's sobs for her tiny dog. What a bastard he was to yell at her when she was afraid for Amber and devastated over the little guy. He prayed she'd forgive him. He had a lot of apologizing to do for what he'd said. His heart squeezed into a hard, cold knot.

God, Marla, honey, I'm so sorry. Please forgive me.

"Did you hear me, Daddy?"

He cleared his throat. "Yes, sweetheart, the brave little soldier got hurt when he tried to save you."

"Will he be all right?" Her trembling voice asked, full of worry and hope.

"I don't think so. He was hurt pretty bad."

Her little body jerked with a monster, choking sob. She fell forward against his arm and cried, breaking his heart. She loved the wee mutt. What would she do when they got home and learned he was dead? He dreaded every step his horse took closer to the ranch house.

Grace waited on the porch, a sweater clutched tightly around her shoulders. Cookie whistled and a couple of wranglers stepped out of the barn when the men reined in the horses.

Grace stepped to Dwayne and Amber and extended her arms. "Come to Auntie Gracie, baby." She held her and hugged her, relief painting her face. "Let's go in the kitchen and get warm. Cookie has cornbread and a big pot of hot cocoa on the stove."

Dwayne dismounted, wincing when a sharp pain shot fire through his stump. He limped to the porch and immediately headed up the stairs to find Marla.

"Dwayne," Grace called and handed Amber off to Cookie. She pressed her lips together and shook her head.

"I have to talk to her." He couldn't put off making amends. He loved her and she needed to hear his apology. He needed to offer it.

Dylan and Donovan walked in.

"She's not here," Grace said.

"Where is she? Is she hurt? I have to see her."

"Charlene drove her and Miss Emmaline to Sheridan to get a flight back to L.A."

Donovan sucked in a loud breath. "Charlene left?" He faced Dwayne and glared. "What in hell have you done? I should kick the shit out of you."

Grace put her hand on Donovan's arm. "Your wife will be back tomorrow. Marla and Emma couldn't get a flight out tonight. They're staying overnight at the Day's Inn near the airport." She linked her hand in his arm and steered him toward the phone. "Call her and let her know everybody is home safe then let's get you something to eat."

The scene had played out in sickening slow motion for Dwayne. He turned and sat on the stairs with a thump and dropped his head in his hands. "Jesus, God, what have I done?" He rolled his head in his hands.

Dyl sat next to him and rested a hand on his shoulder. He didn't speak for several seconds then said, "Everything will look better in the morning. Come to the kitchen and sit down to eat with your daughter. Don't let her see you like this." He clapped him on the shoulder. "Suck it up, brother."

Numb, Dwayne followed his big brother to the kitchen. He arrived in time to hear Amber's blow-by-blow of her afternoon for the others at the table while Cookie bustled in front of the stove. For the moment, at least, she seemed to have forgotten about Skipper. He slid onto the bench next to her and kissed her head.

A few minutes into her recitation, Kathleen entered the kitchen and lifted the big, stainless steel coffeepot off the stove. "I'll take this out to the men in the barn, Cookie."

Cookie nodded and said, "I'll get the other one going pronto. You come right back and eat some supper. Those cowboys can look after themselves." She turned and set a big plate of steaming cornbread on the table next to a crock of home-churned butter.

Dwayne's stomach rebelled at the thought of food. He shifted and rubbed his knee. His vision blurred with unshed tears. Marla had left him. His fault. There was no excuse for the way he'd treated her. His mind flooded with self-hatred.

All he wanted to do was drag his tired bones and aching leg up the stairs and fall in bed, but he wouldn't leave somebody else break the news to Amber about Skipper. No. He wasn't that much of a coward. He stroked Amber's hair and listened to her chatter away.

As much as he loved his daughter, and it was immeasurable, he knew to the depths of his soul how desperately he needed Marla in his life. He spoke in Amber's ear, "When you finish eating let's go sit in Grandpa's chair by the fireplace."

She yawned. "I'm done, Daddy."

He stepped over the bench and lifted her into his arms. The rest of the family stayed put. He was grateful to them for that. In the living room, he sat in his grandpa's big old recliner and rested Amber's back against his chest. "Do you know how much I love you?"

"Uh huh. Me too." She tilted her head and met his eyes. "Was that skinny, mean lady rilly my mom?"

He sighed and ran his hand up and down her fragile arm. "Yes, baby. Francine is your birth mother, but she couldn't be a mom for you. She's had a lot of problems in her life. Don't hate her. I'm sure she loved you when you were born, but then things happened, and she ran away. I don't know why she came back now."

"You're my rill dad, aren't you?"

A pain pierced his chest.

"Absolutely, positively." He hugged her tight and kissed her cheek. "I'm your real dad."

"That's good, because I didn't want to go with those people and leave you."

"Nobody will ever take you away from me, baby." Her innocence cracked his heart.

"Skipper died, didn't he, Daddy?"

"Yes."

Her beautiful amber eyes filled with tears. "Poor Marla. I bet she'll cry forever and ever." She twisted in his lap to sit sideways. "Can I hug her before I go to bed?"

He took a shaky breath. "Marla went home. Miss Emmaline went with her to keep her company."

She sat back and stared at him goggle-eyed. "Why? What did you do, Daddy?"

Her childlike perception took his breath away. He dropped his head back on the chair. "I yelled at her. I was angry she let them take you. I'd cut off my other leg if I could take it back."

"Don't you love her anymore?"

How did this child know he was in love with Marla?

"I love her very much, but I don't know if she can forgive me for the things I said."

"She has to, Daddy. I want her to be with us."

What could he say? He shook his head slowly and closed his eyes.

Amber slid from his lap. "I'm rill tired. I'm going to bed. Tomorrow we'll make a plan. I'll help you fix everything. G'night, Daddy."

Dwayne kept his eyes closed and reclined the chair. "See you in the morning, sweetheart." He couldn't face going in that empty bedroom and climbing in that cold bed without Marla. No, he'd sleep in the chair tonight. In front of the fireplace. Alone.

———

Marla's eyes opened before dawn. She rolled on her side, careful not to wake Charlene, and watched Miss Emmaline asleep in the other bed, Princess Elizabeth curled up close to her. After a few minutes, she slipped from the bed and quietly made her way to the bathroom to use the toilet without turning on the light with the loud, grinding fan. She'd flush in the morning.

She'd slept, but she'd had troubling, disjointed dreams. During the night she sprang to a sitting position when she heard Skipper bark. Tears poured from her eyes. She stared through the darkness at the shoe box on the table where his little body rested inside, wrapped in a tea towel.

Wrenching pain consumed her. She clasped her hands over her mouth and lay back, pulling the lumpy motel pillow over her head to muffle her sobs. Not just for her precious dog, but for those brutal accusations Dwayne had thrown at her. She hadn't known the man at all. Charlene snuggled close and put an arm around her.

When their flight arrived at LAX the next afternoon, Miss Emmaline touched her arm as they reached the baggage claim area. "Look, dear. Those precious brothers of yours are waiting for us. Charlene must have called them."

Wearing identical sober faces, Harry and Barry met them and silently embraced Marla then Emmaline. A new round of tears poured from her eyes. She hadn't known there were so many tears in the world to be shed.

"Let's go home, BS."

The boys took their luggage from the carousel and led them to the short-term parking lot. Barry drove and Marla took the passenger seat. Harry sat in back with Miss Emmaline, Elizabeth's carrier on the seat between them.

Her brothers' silence comforted her. She knew how much they cared. Words were unnecessary.

They went to the condos first and the boys escorted Miss Emmaline and her bags to her new apartment. Marla waited in the car until they returned. Other apartments were occupied with returned tenants. Lights winked from several windows.

When they reached her house, the boys carried her luggage inside. She clutched the shoe box, holding her baby to her chest, unwilling to let anybody touch it. "You don't need to stay, sweeties. Thank you for meeting us. I'd really like to be alone, if you don't mind."

"Dadley and Sil wanted us to call when you got here so they could come over."

"No. Please, I don't want them to do that. Tell them I'm fine by myself. I'll go to their house tomorrow."

"Okay." They hugged her and left.

Marla locked the door behind them then closed her eyes and leaned her forehead against the cool, smooth wood. Swallowing back tears, she headed for her bedroom. Skipper's dishes sat on the floor next to the kitchen sink. A stab of pain pierced her stomach when she averted her eyes and kept walking, switching lights on in every room as she passed them on her way.

For some reason, as exhausted as she was, she needed light. Every light. Every room. She sat on the edge of her bed with the box in her lap and stroked it lovingly. Anguished cries escaped her throat so fast she didn't recognize her own voice. How long would it take for the pain to ease?

Hand under her bed pillow, she dragged out Dwayne's T-shirt, the one she loved to sleep in, clutched it to her face and curled on her side. Please, she wanted to stop loving him, stop loving Amber.

Some time later, she rose from the bed and went to the garage to find a shovel. Stopping at one of Skippy's favorite spots at the edge of the flower bed, she dug a deep hole. The monotonous action of stomping on the back edge of the shovel and lifting the heavy, wet soil out of the ever-larger gash increased her breathing and eased the ache in her heart. She slumped on the grass to rest.

On her knees, Marla untied the knotted string then lifted the lid on the shoebox to stare at the wrapped bundle that a day ago had been her lively pet. She lowered the box in the little grave and sat back on her heels.

A sad smile cracked her face. Remembering Charlene's words, "You and that dog," she used her hands to scoop and push the dirt back in place. "Sweet dreams, baby. Mama loves you."

Instead of returning to the house, she lay on her back on the damp lawn and stared at the cloudless Southern California sky. So many fewer stars were visible here than in Wyoming. Were Dwayne and Amber looking at the stars tonight? She raised her hand in a silly, futile wave. Tears leaked from the corners of her eyes.

Get up, Marla.

She carried the shovel back to the garage, removed her muddy jeans and shoes, and dropped them on the floor in front of her car. After a long, hot shower, she pulled Dwayne's shirt over her head and went to bed. The phone rang as she reached for the switch on her lamp.

"Hello, Char," she answered.

"Hi, hon, how are you?"

She fell back against her pillow and sighed. "I'm all right. I was about to turn out the light. Please tell me Amber was unhurt."

"Yes. Kids can be so resilient. She's fine, but very sad that you weren't here, and Skip was…"

"Killed. It's okay to say it. Don't worry about me. I know you and Donovan are scheduled to leave on your honeymoon in the morning. Go, have fun."

"We want you to fly over there, sis. You can help me move in. I'll have to buy tons of stuff for the house. We can have fun shopping in Honolulu and lounging on the beach."

"That sounds wonderful, Char. Please give Amber a hug for me and thank Kathleen and Cookie and the rest of the ranch people for their hospitality."

"I'll see you when we get back to Spring Grove. We'll be staying a couple of days at Mom and Dad's before we fly to the islands. Good night, sis. I love you."

"Love you too." She turned the phone off and turned out the light. She dreamed she was in Dwayne's strong arms, felt his hands and lips on her face and body, Skip snoring between them.

Chapter Thirty-Four

Dwayne called Marla several times during the last two weeks he and Amber remained at the ranch. She had to be screening his calls. He could never get past voicemail. He had no intention of leaving a long, incoherent apology on her phone. He needed to speak to her in person. When they returned to California, he'd find her and get down on his knees if he had to.

"She still not answering?" his mother asked.

"She doesn't want to talk to me."

"I don't blame her, do you?"

"No. I'm the worst kind of jackass." He raked a hand through his hair.

Kathleen stood behind his chair and put her arms around his neck. "Not quite, I was married to the worst kind of jackass—your father."

"Yeah, guess who I got it from." He leaned back against her and smiled, loving the soothing sensation of her hands on his cheeks. "Do you hate him?"

She chuckled and sat across the table. "Heavens, no, I wish I did. I'll always have a soft spot for John Dempsey. He's impossible to hate, but I was very angry at him for a long time."

Dwayne leaned on his forearms and re-arranged the condiments on the table. "How come you never re-married, Mom?"

He thought of the look of longing in the sheriff's eyes the night they arrested Francine and Luke. Kathleen was a good-looking woman, still barely into her mid-fifties.

"Oh...I'm not really sure. Living way out here, I got lost in the work of running the ranch, helping Daddy. Don't forget, you came with me and lived here for almost five years, and your brothers stayed most summers."

"Yeah, well, I was mad at Dad too." He pushed himself to a standing position. His leg still tender, he winced.

"Is your leg still bothering you? Let me take a look at it."

He shook his head and grinned. "Nah, Nurse Amber takes good care of me. It's not red now."

"Dwayne, your care is not Amber's responsibility." She raised a hand. "Don't glare at me like that. I'm not telling you how to raise your own child. But it strikes me she's a bit more sober than a six-year-old should be. You're responsible for her, not the other way around."

"I know, Mom, but it's been just the two of us since the day she was born. It's all she knows. She thinks of herself as the woman of the house."

"Have you ever given any thought to how your tight, exclusive relationship with your daughter appears to others? Marla's place in your hierarchy of values was quite obvious to her, and the rest of us, the day Amber went missing."

"I'm still coming to grips with why I went off like that, behaved like such a jerk that day. I love her. Amber loves her. I want her to marry me."

"You mean *marry us*. Amber will be smack in the middle of any relationship you have with any woman—regardless of how often she declares she wants Marla in your lives. Power struggles and vying for your affection and attention are inevitable."

"I fully intended to avoid any thought of marriage or a serious relationship with a woman until after Amber went off to college." He huffed and clawed at his hair again. "I wanted to sleep with Marla, not to fall in love with her."

He paced the kitchen. Stopped and stared out the window. "I want her back, Mom. I can't see living without her." He raised his arms and gritted his teeth. "God! She's so...I can't explain...what...she means to me."

Kathleen joined him in front of the window and put her arm around his waist. "There's a phrase in the wedding vows about 'forsaking all others.' That means if you truly want to marry Marla, she must come first in your heart. I don't think you're ready for that reality. You certainly gave your true feelings away the day her dog got killed."

He swallowed and took a deep breath. "I don't know what to do. How can I choose between them?"

"That's the thing, son. You don't have to choose between them. You choose *them*. It's a package deal." She reached up and smacked him affectionately in the cheek. "Now get on out to the barn and start shoveling horse shit!"

He kissed her forehead. "Yes, ma'am."

On the three-day drive back home he and Amber visited Zion Park and stayed overnight in Salt Lake City to take in a performance of the Mormon Tabernacle Choir. They dressed in the outfits they'd worn at Donovan's wedding, and after the music, he took her on a *date* to Franck's where she sipped lemon soda from a champagne glass like a proper lady and tasted her first escargot. She loved it until he confessed it was snails. Her glare of disgust could have stopped a runaway train.

On the last day of the road trip, she watched the monotonous scenery flying by the truck windows. "Daddy, when we get home can we go see Marla?"

"She doesn't want to see me."

"You have to do something."

"I'm working on it."

"You better."

"You know something, squirt? If I ever get Marla back, you're likely to end up low man on the totem pole."

She squinched her eyes and forehead. "I don't know what that means."

"It means that if Marla decided to forgive, even God help me, marry us, I'd be giving her permission to discipline you, set rules, and be lady of the house."

She mulled over the information for several seconds. "She's rill bossy."

"Oh, yeah? Well, I've got news for you. You're *rill* bossy too."

She glared, her chin trust forward. "I am not!"

"You just proved my point."

259

She harrumphed and crossed her arms. He bit the inside of his cheek and they drove several miles before she spoke again.

"Am I, rilly?"

"Really." He squeezed her knee. "But guess what? I think you're perfect, and I love you this much." He took his hands off the wheel and threw his arms wide.

"Daddy! Pay attention to the road!"

A deep laugh rumbled from his chest. "Yes, ma'am, Sergeant Bossy, ma'am."

———

Late that night, he carried her in the house, removed her sneakers, and tucked her in bed in her traveling clothes. He checked his bulletin board in the kitchen for any important messages from Cluny, who'd been keeping an eye on his house and business for the past month. The only thing on it was a handmade Father's Day card from two years ago.

He punched Marla's number into his phone and waited for the inevitable toneless, machine-recorded voice. "Shit!" He tossed it on the coffee table and reclined for a quick rest. When he woke it was broad daylight, and Amber was poking his chest.

"What?" He scrubbed a hand over his face and blinked.

"I'm fixing breakfast. Get up."

"Sheesh, the last thing I need is a boss this morning."

She grinned and shuffled to the kitchen in her bunny slippers. "Too bad for you."

Did he really want to live in a house with *two* strong-willed, stubborn, single-minded, bossy females?

———

"I've had enough sun for one day, Char. Let's go." Marla inspected the fresh crop of freckles on her arms, wrapped a beach towel around her hips, and folded the sand chair.

Charlene followed her lead. "Donovan will be coming home for dinner soon, so yes, I need to get a move on."

"We still have half that roasted chicken in the fridge. Let's make a man-sized salad and eat out on the lanai. The weather is perfect."

"Can you whip up a batch of those great cheese biscuits he loves so much?"

"Anything for the best-looking brother-in-law on Oahu."

The Marine base housing wasn't far from the beach at Kaneohe, so it only took a few minutes to get to Char's house.

Charlene asked, "So what are you going to do?"

"Make biscuits."

"You know what I mean."

"If you're referring to Dwayne, I won't discuss the matter." A bolt of pain went from her ribs to her spine whenever she mentioned his name or even thought of him. Which, face it, was a zillion times a day.

"He's my brother-in-law, sis. He's family. You know you're going to have to face him sooner or later, and probably often. Amber is my niece now."

"You think I don't know that?" She sucked in a shaky breath. "Those things he said to me and the way he said them? It still hurts." She pressed a hand on her stomach. Protection against more hurt?

"I was there, remember? In fact, Marla, he said them to me, not you." She parked in her driveway and popped the trunk.

Marla exited the car. She had no intention of discussing Dwayne Dempsey further.

"You know he must be beating himself up over his outburst."

"I don't know any such thing." So much for not discussing him.

"He loves you. He was wrong. He knew it. We all knew it, but his little girl had been taken, and he just blew. He didn't mean it, sis."

"He did mean it when he said it. He might be sorry now, but there was no mistaking where I stood with him. He's got no room for me in his life with Amber. What he said, in front of everybody, was a horrible way for me to realize it."

Charlene unlocked the front door. "Aren't you at least willing to give him the chance to apologize?"

"Why? So we can start sleeping together again, as if it never happened?" She shook her head and carried the cooler to the kitchen. "No, Char, that's not enough for me, but apparently it was enough for him. Do you have any idea how that makes me feel?"

"No, I..."

The front door slammed. "Are there any beautiful women in my house?"

"In the kitchen, Donnie." The smile of joy on Charlene's face said everything about her feelings for Donovan.

"Good. There're only two places for a woman to be. The kitchen or the bedroom."

Charlene and Marla grinned and said, "Shut up!"

Donovan strolled into the room looking dangerous and sexy in his camos and Marine haircut. He lifted Charlene off her feet and swung her in a circle. "Gimme some sugar."

She answered in a giggle, "All you want, honey pot."

He kissed her then winked at Marla. "Mind if I take my bride to help me out of these boots, sis?"

She returned his grin. "Not at all, but I thought basic training covered that." She smacked his arm. "Keep the noise down, please. I've got to concentrate on my cheese biscuits."

"Cheese biscuits? Awesome! Now I don't know which sister I love the most." He pecked a kiss on her cheek and turned to leave, Char's legs and arms wrapped tight around him.

Marla feigned insult. "That decision didn't take long."

He bounced Charlene in his arms and went straight into their bedroom and kicked the door closed. Marla grabbed a bottle of Arizona Iced Tea, opened the slider off the kitchen to the lanai, stepped outside, and closed it.

It was time to go home.

———

Dwayne knocked on the front door of Marla's parent's house. A few seconds later, Silvia opened it. "Oh dear, you look awful. Come in, hon."

He entered and walked past her into the hallway.

"We're enjoying the patio." She pointed in the direction she wanted him to take. "Come join us."

"I should have called ahead. Is anybody else here?"

"No, just us." She took his arm. "Come, you're family. You don't need to call ahead, Dwayne. Our door is always open." She stepped outside. "Dwayne's here, Brad."

He looked up, raised his glass, and smiled. "I'd offer you a tot of Jameson's, but I know you don't drink. Have a seat, son."

Dwayne sagged into a chair. "I may start drinking."

Silvia sat next to him. "Where's Amber?"

"She's spending the evening with Miss Emmaline and Princess Elizabeth. She can stay up late tonight, no school tomorrow." He reached for the can of soda she offered. "Thanks."

Brad leaned forward, elbows on knees, heavy crystal glass dangling from his fingers. "What was the outcome of Francine's arrest and her custody demand?" He took a sip of Irish whiskey. "You don't have to answer. It's really not my business."

"I disagree. Now that my brother married your daughter, it's family business. I don't mind talking about it." He gazed in the direction of the treetops on the perimeter of their large backyard and considered what he'd say.

"Her husband is back in jail for resisting arrest and violation of parole. He was Francine's accomplice, he didn't actually snatch Amber, she did. I wasn't interested in pressing charges of kidnapping. What would that accomplish? She's Amber's biological mother. I'm not out for revenge. Francine stupidly thought she could extort money from me using Amber as leverage. I didn't want my daughter's mother, as much as I despise her, to end up a convict. What good would that do Amber? I just want her gone from our lives."

Silvia rested her hand on his arm. "Do you think she understands how much trouble she could have been in? Will she stay away?"

"For the present. At some point I may allow her to meet with Amber again, but not till she's older. She didn't like Francine and says she never wants to see her again, but as time goes on she might change her mind."

Brad sat straight. "No doubt you're right. She's just turned seven, far too young to make such a big decision."

Dwayne emitted a rueful chuckle. "Seven going on twenty-seven. She's mad at me for allowing her to nurture fantasies about Francine all her life."

Silvia nodded. "That's understandable, but in time she'll come to understand why you did it. Children are very resilient."

Dwayne clasped his hands in his lap. "I came to talk about Marla."

Brad shook his head. "We only know what Charlene and Donovan told us. It goes without saying...however, I will say it...you bungled your relationship with her badly. She's deeply wounded."

Dwayne heaved a bottomless sigh. "Yeah."

"That's because she's in love with you," Silvia added. "I always felt when, and if, she ever fell in love it would be complete surrender. There are no half measures for Marla. She's paying a heavy emotional price for your behavior."

He deserved every single word her parents spoke. In fact, the pain of hearing them somehow provided balm to his wounded heart. "Me too," he whispered. "Me too."

Chapter Thirty-Five

MARLA TUGGED HER WHEELED SUITCASE TO THE CURB OUTSIDE the baggage claim area at LAX. She didn't have a plan to get home yet and hadn't told anyone her flight arrival time, but she knew Charlene would have called Dadley the minute she stepped through the boarding gate at Honolulu.

Sure enough, there he was. "Hi, Dad!" She smiled and waved her orchid lei in the air to catch his eye.

He snaked through the crowd to reach her side and encompassed her in a mighty hug. "Welcome home, beautiful girl. Your mother and I haven't seen much of you this summer. Are you home for a while?"

The warmth of her father's arms never failed to comfort her to the depths of her soul. She clung to him for a few seconds longer than she normally would have then put the lei around his neck. "I'm home for the foreseeable future. Got to get back to work so I don't end up moving back home to live with my parents into my old age."

Brad chuckled and led her to the baggage carousel. "No danger of that happening."

She pointed to the exit. "I didn't check a bag. We can go straight out. Char's shipping the rest of my stuff in return for my help settling her in. Where's Mom?"

He gave her an indecipherable look.

"Is something wrong?"

"Depends on how you interpret it." He pressed the remote key to unlock his car. "Silvia is out to dinner and a movie with Amber Dempsey."

That stopped her dead in her tracks.

"She's...what...how...? I don't believe this. How could she?"

"It's complicated. Dwayne had an emergency on a construction job, and Miss Emmaline is visiting a niece in Covina. He couldn't find John and Irene or a babysitter. He didn't know who else to call."

"He asked *my* mother to babysit!" She didn't move.

"You're standing in the middle of the road, Marla. Let me take your bag. Get in the car."

When he opened his door and sat in the driver's seat she whirled on him. "I don't believe this! I'm so...so... Grrrr... I'm so mad! He could have found somebody else. Why *my* mother?"

"Like it or not, Dwayne's family. Amber is our niece-by-marriage. We were glad to help in an emergency."

Her anger at the nerve of Dempsey, trying to worm his way back into her life by asking her parents to take care of his daughter was just too much. "Emergency, my ass!"

Brad chuckled and backed out of the parking space and aimed his car for the exit. "I don't believe I've ever heard you utter a curse word."

"Well, you damn well better get used to it, because I'm royally pissed!" She slapped her palms on her knees hard enough to sting. "Damn that devious bastard."

By this time Brad was roaring with laughter. He almost cut off a car entering from a side aisle when he reached the lift gate. "Careful, you'll get us killed."

"I don't give a sh...a sh... I can't have that word in my mouth, dammit." She looked at her dad from the corner of her eye and suppressed a smile. "It's not funny."

He brushed tears from his eyes and made no attempt to answer. His chest bounced with suppressed laughter and he patted the hand gripping her knee.

"What am I going to do, Dad? How am I going to avoid him?" She heaved a deep sigh and closed her eyes. "Maybe I'll move to San Francisco. I've always wanted to live there." She cracked an eye open to see his reaction. He was still grinning.

Brad checked his side mirror and merged with traffic on Sepulveda Boulevard. "You could always marry Edwin Plimpton. That would knock Dwayne Dempsey out of the running."

"He's not in the running!" She crossed her arms. "I don't believe we're having this conversation. Whose side are you on?"

"My rotten, arrogant, high-and-mighty, egotistic, swaggering ex-lover dumps his child in Mom's lap and you think he's still 'in the running'?"

"After that diatribe, I'm sure he is."

"Dad, you're not helping. What am I going to do? Fall back into his arms and wait for his next insulting outburst? I don't think so." She raised her hands to her face and dropped her head on the neck rest. "I hate him."

"Is that so?"

"Yes. He's an ass, a blustering bully. He's... How could he have screamed at me like that with Skipper lying dead in my arms? I was in pain. He didn't even ask if I'd been hurt." She sighed. Her next words were spoken softly. "I love him."

"Which is it? You love him, or you hate him?"

"I don't know. Right now, I'm so angry I could explode." She clenched a fist and held it up. "I'd like to let him have it."

"That's good. That's progress."

She turned her head and stared at him. "What are you talking about?"

"You're working your way through the various stages of grief. Very healthy. Anger is good. Use it."

"Use it? How?"

"Confront him. Tell him how you feel. Let him know how angry you are. Don't waste all those epithets and pejoratives on me. Give him a piece of your mind. Get it out of here." He touched her head. "And here." He tapped her chest. "It will do wonders for you."

She scoffed. "Pish-tosh! As if you've ever exploded at Mom."

He smiled. "You have no idea."

She had no idea. His words buzzed in her brain. How much did she know about her parent's private life? Did she know them as well as she'd always assumed?

She shook her head and sighed. "Boy, oh, boy. Am I stupid or what?"

"I believe we had that conversation before."

Their talk during the rest of the trip home was all Charlene and Donovan. Their new home, his new assignment, and her stay with them on Oahu. "She's very happy, Dad."

"I could see it in their eyes at the wedding and during the two days they stayed with us before they left California. She made an excellent choice. Donovan adores her."

"I guess you know how that feels."

"Indeed I do." He turned off the freeway at the first Simi Valley exit in the direction of Spring Grove. "I'll drop you at your place so you won't risk bumping into Dwayne tonight."

"Thanks. I need to work on my mad for a while before I see him again."

"Make him pay."

"Right."

"Make him suffer."

"Right again."

"That's my girl."

Dadley carried her bag inside, checked the house, then kissed her goodnight at her front door. "Call your mother tomorrow. She'll want every detail of Char's new life in the tropics."

"I love you, Dad." She hugged and kissed him. "You're the best."

"I try." He grinned, put the lei around her neck and left her at her front door, calling, "Sweet dreams," over his shoulder. Then she laughed when he turned, put up his dukes, scowled fiercely, and did some fancy boxing footwork.

Somebody, probably her mom, had removed any sign of Skipper. She wandered from room to room then finally to her garage, where she found his bed, toys, leashes, and dishes. Marla ran his leash through her fingers. Tears threatened. "I miss you Skippy, but you'll be happy to know that I intend to give that big bad Marine a piece of my mind. He'll be sorry he ever crossed Marla Danaher."

———

Dwayne arrived at the Danaher home to fetch Amber, but she and Silvia hadn't returned. The house was dark. He was about to leave when Brad's car pulled into the driveway.

Brad called, "Dwayne, come in. The girls should be back any

time." He stepped from his car, opened the front door, and turned on the hall light.

Dwayne met him on the porch, shook Brad's hand, and went inside. "I got done sooner than expected. Where did they go?"

"They went to get pizza and then a movie."

Dwayne grinned. "Oh, boy. If they went to the Disney festival at the Regal, Silvia will be treated to Cinderella."

Brad gestured in the direction of the living room. "That was the plan."

Dwayne sat in a wingback chair next to the unlit fireplace. "I know that damn movie by heart. She can't get enough of it. She ran out of Cinderella books so she wrote her own version for a class project."

"Comes with the territory." Brad switched on another lamp and sat across from him. "I had the pleasure of memorizing E.T. when Harry and Barry were her age."

"That movie was made before they were born."

"I think you're right, but we had a video of it. Marla and Charlene used to hold the twins on their laps and watch it over and over. I doubt the boys would admit it, but they probably have a DVD of it to this day."

"Would you care for a soft drink?"

"No thanks, Brad."

They sat in silence for a while. Then, no longer able to put off the question, Dwayne asked, "When are you expecting Marla to return?"

"I picked her up at LAX this afternoon and dropped her at home."

Heart pounding, blood rushing in his ears, Dwayne took a breath. "Do you think she'd...?"

Brad raised a hand and shook his head. "Not if you value your life. She's in the anger and fury stage. She actually hurled some curse words on the drive home. I've never seen her in such a state." He nodded and twisted his lips into an ironic smile. "She'll be fine. Give her time. But I doubt she'll give you another chance if you mess up again."

Brad thought she *might* give him another chance? Hope warmed his chest. Now what? How long should he wait before attempting to talk to her? Then sadness and guilt made an unexpected appearance, and he was full of doubt. He'd relived his outburst so many times, remembered the words he'd hurled at Charlene, but meant for Marla.

Why would she even think of forgiving him, let alone allow him to touch her?

The front door opened. Brad rose. "Sounds like the girls are back."

They met Silvia and Amber in the hallway. Amber wore yet another Cinderella T-shirt. Dwayne shook his head and grinned. "Hey, squirt. Looks like Mrs. Dahaner took you shopping at the Disney store. Did you have fun?"

Silvia nodded. "We both had fun. I forgot what it was like pretending to be a kid again." She kissed Brad on the cheek. "How was your afternoon and evening? Did everything go as planned?"

"As planned." He hugged her to his side. "Dwayne knows."

"Knows what, Daddy?"

"I know lots of things. Now, it's time to thank Silvia for your fun time and get home to bed. School starts day after tomorrow."

They said their goodbyes, picked up the shopping bag Amber had set by the front door, and went into the warm September evening. All during the drive home his mind raced. He envisioned a hundred different scenarios in his head. How to approach Marla, what to do first, and when to do it.

Amber squirmed in her seat. "This isn't the way home, Daddy. Where are we going?"

He snapped to attention and realized he'd turned into the development where Marla lived. "Whoa, I must have been on auto-pilot." He chuckled and made a U-turn.

"This is where Marla lives."

"Yeah, I was thinking about her. That's why I took a wrong turn."

"When is she coming home?"

"She got back today."

Excitement in her voice she said, "Let's go see her then."

He shook his head and sighed. "Not yet, she's still mad at me. We have to make a plan."

"I know what to do."

"What's that, smarty pants?"

"Tell her you're sorry and you'll never yell at her again."

He put his big hand on top of her head. Kids. Everything so simple to them. "How did you get to be such an old soul?"

"I don't know what that is, but Grammakat told me I take after her."

"As usual, she's right." Thank God she didn't have his hair-trigger temperament. It hadn't done him any favors.

For an active duty Marine, a hair-trigger temper could be put to good use in a combat situation. A soldier forgot his fear and focused on what needed to be done, no matter how perilous.

"She told me grammas know everything. Maybe you should ask her to help us make a plan."

Chapter Thirty-Six

Dwayne picked up the phone in his warehouse office. He dialed the local florist. "I want a dozen American Beauty roses delivered to Marla Danaher at Spring Grove Real Estate." It was safer at this point than delivering them in person. The most he could lose was eighty bucks, not his front teeth. He'd read somewhere that women loved to show off flowers delivered to their place of work.

This afternoon he had to take Amber school shopping. As usual he'd put it off until the day before school started. She'd made a list of the supplies she needed, and her legs had grown too long for last year's uniforms. "Thank goodness for school uniforms." At least he didn't have to try to figure out what trendy clothes to buy for a girl going into second grade.

Cluny dropped by with his final receipts and invoices for the storage facility job they'd finished over a month ago.

"Must be nice to have so much dough lying around that you don't have to bill me for weeks." He smiled at Cluny's dog Queen, a magnificent Belgian Malinois. "Come here, Queenie, you beauty." He grinned at Cluny. "How's she doing?"

Queen wore her service vest today. Cluny had acquired the retired Navy SEAL dog for help with his infrequent bouts of PTS.

"She's doing great. We completed her training a few days ago. I've never known a dog as smart as her. She's sensitive to the least change in my mood."

"How does she react?"

"She leans on me or nudges me. Sometimes she whines. Mostly she stares into my eyes with a get-a-grip expression on her muzzle."

"I hope you're sleeping better." Dwayne was well aware of his buddy's on and off struggles ever since they'd been hit by the RPG, the same one that blew off his left foot. Very few people ever noticed anything out of order with Cluny. He managed to maintain a cheerful, upbeat attitude nearly a hundred percent of the time. When he couldn't get enough restful sleep, Dwayne and those closest to him saw how it affected him during the day.

"Who wouldn't sleep better with a beautiful female in his bed every night?" He grinned and patted Queen's hindquarters. "Who's my best girl?" The dog turned to face him, and Dwayne would have sworn she grinned at her master.

Cluny scratched her chin. "She's a beauty queen. Her pop was Cairo. Royalty in my book."

"Cairo. How do I know that name?" Dwayne tilted his head, and his eyebrows drew together.

"Her pop, Cairo, accompanied SEAL Team Six on the bin Laden operation. That old dog could do anything, including parachuting out of an aircraft."

Dwayne nodded. "Of course." He couldn't help comparing Queen, who looked like a smaller version of a German Shepherd, with Marla's mouse, Skipper. Pound for pound, that tiny mutt was as brave as they came.

As if he'd read his thoughts, Cluny asked, "So, what have you heard from our former boss lady?"

Almost everyone who knew either him or Marla knew about the incident in Wyoming. "I just sent flowers to her office. I didn't know what else to do at this point."

"Her office? Mistake. You should have had them delivered to her house."

"Why? I thought women liked to receive flowers publicly." He wondered if it was too late to call the florist back.

"Don't believe everything you see on TV. By delivering them to her office, you put her on the spot. Now she's going to be bombarded with questions from her co-workers. Questions she might not want to answer."

Dwayne grabbed the phone. "Shit!" He hit redial and fidgeted the few brief seconds it took them to answer. "This is Dwayne Dempsey, yeah, the American Beauty roses. No, no, I was just hoping you could deliver them to her house instead." He smacked his forehead and raked a hand through his hair. "No, don't worry about it. Thanks."

"Already delivered?"

"Yep."

Cluny chuckled. "Sorry, it's not funny, but I have a vision of her showing up here and hurling them through your window." He rose, picked up Queen's leash and prepared to leave. "Good luck, Gunny. Hope I don't see your obit in the paper tomorrow."

"Go to hell, McPherson. Have I ever mentioned how great it is to have friends who take so much pleasure in my misery?"

"Anytime, pal."

———

The florist delivery man set the huge bouquet of roses on the receptionist's counter and held up an invoice. The girl turned and pointed at Marla. He lifted the dark green vase and headed right for her.

Oh no. Please no.

"I believe these are for you, miss." He grinned as if he knew a salacious secret and set them in front of her. "Have a great night."

The little twerp winked. He actually winked.

She wanted to scream and demand he take them back. She didn't want them. She didn't want to look at them, and she was furious they smelled so good. Florist flowers weren't supposed to have such a strong, romantic scent.

Two grinning realtors descended on her, squealing with excitement. "Who are they from?" "They smell heavenly." "Look how beautiful they are." "Have you ever seen such a sexy shade of red?" "Somebody has the hots for you, Marla Danaher." "Is it your birthday?"

One of them snatched the card and handed it to her. "Who sent them?"

Glaring, Marla took the envelope. The handwriting didn't look like

Dwayne's bold slash. Maybe they weren't from him after all. "I don't know who they're from, but probably a happy customer."

"Open it!"

"I, um, I have to make an important follow-up call right now. I'll look at it later." She waved a dismissal and picked up her phone.

The two women wore identical expressions of astonishment at her incuriosity and returned to their desks, but not before exchanging a *look*.

She didn't care what they thought. Her fingers touched the edge of the envelope, and she slid it to her lap then proceeded with her non-call call.

After a few minutes, most of the others in the office were either on the phone or counseling clients. She quickly lifted the point of the envelope and slid the card out.

Please forgive me. I love you Marla.

She got up, crossed the room, and tapped on Ted's office door. He'd asked to speak with her when she had time.

"Come in." He pointed to the door. "Close it and have a seat." He stood and reached into the top drawer of the filing cabinet behind his desk, removed a thick file, and placed it on his desk blotter.

"You had news about the Cartwright deal?" She hoped it hadn't gone sour. Ted knew she wasn't prepared to risk such a large investment, so he couldn't be planning to ask her about that again.

Ted grinned and slapped the file. "The old man has agreed to sell to us."

"That's great news, Ted! That means your group of investors raised enough money for the deal. Congratulations." She smiled at the look of satisfaction on his face. "I'm really happy for you."

"Thanks. That's the good news, now for the better news. Our consortium has decided to add a few smaller investors to help expedite the first phase of the development. Spread the wealth."

Marla cocked her head. "Spread the wealth or spread the risk?"

He chuckled. "A little of both, but it's not much of a risk."

"How much? Investment and percentage?"

"Now you're talking like a wise business partner." He opened the folder and turned it to face her. "This is the core group. We've decided to add two more levels. One for the residential part of the plan and the other the hotel and golf course part of the plan. The percentage of profit is proportional to the investments shown here."

Marla studied the detail and the graph. "So, I'm assuming new investors can select either or both."

"Right. Personally, I think the residential part is lower risk, even though home prices are still depressed. The first phase is two years down the road. We feel it will be on the upswing by then. What do you think?"

"I think thirty thousand is a lot more realistic figure for me to consider than the hundred thousand it would have cost me to get in, in July." She ran her finger down the list of core investor names. "Has everyone here already ponied up?"

Ted grinned. "Every mother's son of them. And daughter. Impressive, right? What do you think?"

She nodded. It looked like a sound business plan. Every name she recognized was a solid citizen. She wrinkled her nose when she read the name John Dempsey, Dwayne's dad. That helped her make a decision. She didn't want to have any more dealings with a Dempsey, even on a limited partnership basis.

Marla squinched her face. "You know what? I'm going to pass again, Ted. I really appreciate the fact you wanted to include me, but I've got other priorities in my life right now. I'm not sure what I plan to take on next."

Ted smiled graciously and nodded. "I'm sorry to hear that, but I hope your future plans don't include leaving the office. You're a valuable asset."

"No! I'm staying, and I look forward to drinking champagne at the grand opening of the project when that time comes."

A huge flower arrangement sat in the shade on her front porch, when she pulled into her driveway. She opened the garage door, drove in, closed the door, and ignored it.

For days, flowers accumulated on her porch. Her house looked like a funeral home. Neighbors gave her strange looks, but she merely waved and smiled as she came and went.

Chapter Thirty-Seven

AMBER WAVED AND RAN TO THE CONSTRUCTION TRUCK. DWAYNE pushed open the door and she bounced in. "Hi, Daddy."

"Hi, squirt. How's my big second grader doing?"

"I got a A on my math test today."

He ruffled her hair. "Sweet! That calls for ice cream."

"Yay!"

He exited the school parking lot and turned toward the edge of town where a new ice cream parlor had opened a few days ago. "Let's check out the new place, shall we?"

"Uh huh. I hope they have bubble gum flavor. That's my favorite."

"No kidding? I didn't know that."

She wrinkled her nose. "Yes, you did. You rilly like to tease me."

"My favorite pastime." He stopped at a four-way corner.

"Daddy! That's Marla. That's her car."

Amber waved frantically to catch Marla's attention.

Breath caught in his throat, he willed her to look in their direction as she drove through the intersection, eyes staring straight ahead. But he hadn't missed the brief glance in their direction. It was a small town. This was bound to happen.

"She didn't see us." Amber huffed a frustrated breath and bounced her shoulders against the back of her seat. "I guess the flowers aren't working then."

"Don't seem to be."

"What's Plan B?"

"What say we work on it while we stoke up on ice cream?"

Amber crossed her arms and gave him a skeptical look.

He dropped his chin and scowled. "What?"

She pursed her lips like a spinster librarian. "We can work on it at the ice cream store, but you're wasting time and money."

"Whoa, look who's my newest financial advisor. What do you know about money?" She was maturing far too fast for him. How was he going to stay a step ahead of her? He grimaced as a streak of terror hit him. How would he cope with her teen years?

She gave him her best *you're clueless* expression. "I can do math. I can read. Flowers cost big money."

For a moment he sucked air, then slowly shook his head and expressed a small sigh. He turned into the mini-mall where the new ice cream store had opened. The Grand Opening sign fluttered in the early autumn breeze and bunches of balloons tied to weights bounced around the outdoor tables and chairs.

He found a parking space in front of his barbershop two doors down. "Here we are."

She let herself out of the truck and waited for him at the door. When they went inside and looked at the menu on the wall, he began to read the choices out loud.

"I can read, Daddy."

He put a big hand on her shoulder. "I know, sorry, but do me a favor. Get some of the snark out of your voice and show some respect for your father, please?"

Amber leaned into his side and nodded. He noticed how tall she was. On the tall side for a seven-year-old. At the beginning of summer she came just past his elbow, now she was almost to the middle of his chest. "I love you, squirt."

"I know, Daddy, me too."

"How about you reading the menu to me? I can't decide which flavor to try, so many to choose from. I'll close my mouth and listen." He tugged her tighter to his side.

Amber turned her face up, elbowed him on the hip, then began to recite the long list of flavors which included, of course, Double Delicious Double Bubble. They settled on their choices, carried the cups outside, and sat at one of the wire bistro tables to enjoy their ice cream and the cooling evening.

"You know what we could do, Daddy?" She had a devilish sparkle in her big golden eyes.

"From the look on your face, I'm afraid to ask." He scooped a big spoonful of Moose Tracks into his mouth and winked.

"Let's be bad. After we finish this we could pick another flavor, and ice cream will be our dinner tonight. Then if we're not full we could buy another flavor and take it home for dessert."

He put on a serious face and enjoyed the flash of disappointment in her gaze. "I think that's one of the…best ideas you've had in a long time."

Her face lit up. "Rilly?"

"Really, but let's hope child welfare never finds out or they'll put you in foster care, and I'll have to take parenting classes before I can get you back."

She grinned and wiped a drippy pink smear off her chin, her little butt bouncing on the wire chair seat.

Now for Plan B.

———

Oh, she'd seen them all right. Dwayne caught her quick sidewise glance as she drove past. Thoroughly disgusted with herself, Marla drove on home, parked, dragged her waste barrel to the front porch, and dumped all the dead and dying flowers. What was she, sixteen? *Do I intend to forgive him or not?*

She wanted to forgive him. It was taking more and more energy to hang on to her insult and anger. What was the point? She dragged the barrel to the side of the house, muttering all the way. "He's sorry. What more do I expect him to do? He's a man. Men are clueless about patching up a relationship. So, does that mean it's up to me?" She kicked the barrel for good measure. "Dang it!"

———

The next day at her office Marla froze when she saw Dwayne walk in the door carrying another bouquet of roses. She heard him say,

"Delivery for Ms. Danaher," and then stroll right past the receptionist, straight for her.

He set the vase on her desk and leaned forward. "I'm coming to your house later, Danaher."

"No!"

"Yes! I'm prepared to sit on your doorstep until you open the door."

"What are you up to?"

"Plan B."

Marla wracked her brain. "I'm...uh...I'm not going to be home tonight. I...um...have a date."

"No problem. I'll wait until you get home." He turned on his heel, proceeded across the office and out the door.

Her mouth hung open. She snapped it shut and stared at the top of her desk, hoping nobody had noticed. Silly her.

"Oh, my, gawd! Who was the big hunk of eye candy? You've been keeping him all for yourself? Shame on you, Marla Danaher." The bouncy receptionist hovered over her desk, fluttering like a flag in a stiff breeze. "My, gawd! I can't breathe. Call 911."

"For the love of goats, Jessie, stuff it."

"Who is he? Does he live around here? I've never seen him in town. His shiny black pickup looked familiar, but I couldn't read what it said. He doesn't work for the florist—that I do know. Give. Give." She picked up a file folder and fanned herself.

Marla snatched it back. "For somebody who can't breathe, you seem able to talk endlessly." She snapped a shoo gesture with her wrist. "Go away. I have work to do."

"Not till you tell me who he is. Spit it out. I'm not moving."

Marla rolled her eyes. "Okay, okay, his name is Dwayne Dempsey. He owns Big D Construction. I hired him to do the renovation on my condo project. Happy now?"

Jessie's face morphed in to a sly, slit-eyed smile. "And why is he bringing you flowers, huh?"

"Because the project was successful?"

"There are different ways to define success. Whatever 'success' you had on the project must have been spectacular. He sent those other flowers here too, didn't he?"

Marla grabbed her purse. "I give up." She shoved her desk chair in and stormed past her co-worker, spun around, went back and snatched the flowers, then flounced to the door. "I'll be back when I get back."

She felt her face go hot when laughter and applause followed her out the door.

———

At seven-thirty, her doorbell rang. She'd been pacing for an hour and was surprised there was any hair left on her head the way she'd been tugging and twisting it. Okay, this was it. Now's your chance to have it out with the big lout, Marla. Take a breath. Tell him exactly what you think of his unforgivable behavior. Let him have the full force of your anger and frustration. Teeth gritting hard enough to make her jaw ache, she tromped to the door and flung it open. "What!"

Edwin Plimpton gasped and stumbled back. "I..."

Mouth slack, Marla grabbed her throat. "Edwin, what are you doing here?" Color drained from his face. He looked as if she'd induced a heart attack. "Edwin?"

He waved a hand. "Let me get my breath. You startled me." He sucked in some air and let it whoosh out.

"I'm sorry. I didn't mean to scare you like that. Are you all right? You don't look so good. Maybe you'd better sit down." Great, she'd almost killed Edwin. The poor guy's complexion went from death white to mottled purple. She extended a tentative hand. "Breathe, please, Edwin. You're scaring me."

He shook his head and waved his hands. "I'm fine, good. Let me catch my breath. I thought we could talk, Marla."

"No, I, um, Edwin I'm..." Her eyes scanned the street for signs of Dwayne's truck. "Tonight isn't a good time for me."

"Are you expecting someone?" The pathetic look on his face nearly evoked affection for him.

Without either of them having noticed his arrival, Dwayne strode to the porch. "She's expecting me, aren't you, honey?" He glared at Edwin, who actually shrank under Dwayne's steely gaze. That had to be his Gunnery Sergeant glare. "You have business with my woman, Plimpton?"

Edwin's mouth opened, his lips moved, but no words came out.

Dwayne slammed his hands on Edwin's bony shoulders. "No? Good. Then I suggest you beat it."

Marla sputtered, "What do you—?" She cleared her throat. "Edwin, I'm sorry, this man, he..." She wished she kept a baseball bat by her front door because Dwayne could use a couple of good whacks about now.

By way of answering, Edwin raised his hands, took a step back then another, and stepped off the porch. He scurried down her walk like a mouse outrunning a snake. She whirled on Dwayne.

"You! You!" She felt her eyes grow big and hair prickle on the top of her head. About to explode, she stamped her foot, clenched her fists. Dwayne grinned. "Damn you, Dempsey!"

He didn't answer. Just stood there grinning.

She crossed her arms, daring him to move. "This is your Plan B? Threatening my friends? Showing up on my doorstep uninvited? You are the most arrogant, the most infuriating, obnoxious, maddening... stop grinning! What is there to grin about?"

The grin grew so wide it seemed to her his face might crack. Was he crazy? Why didn't he say something?

"Are you drunk? Say something, Dempsey, or I'll turn the hose on you. I mean it!" She extended her arm and shoved him back, away from her door. "If you think you're coming in here, you're smoking funny stuff."

"God, you are magnificent, Danaher. I love you. Marry me." And before she had a chance to react, he grabbed her upper arms and pulled her into a hard kiss.

Marla shoved him. Sputtering again, she was unable to utter a clear response. The man was insane. Did he actually think he could walk right up to her front door, toss poor Edwin out, then ask her to marry him? As if nothing had happened between them in Wyoming? She had her pride. Dwayne was nuts if that's what he thought.

He released her and she immediately missed the warmth of his big hands, his lips. Her insides got all gooey and soft. Watery knees threatened to give way. She actually considered dragging him inside, pulling off his clothes, her clothes, and falling on the floor arms outstretched to reach for him. She got so warm in her girly place she feared for an instant she'd wet her panties.

Dwayne brushed his finger down her cheek, took a step back, then another. "I'll see you around, Red."

He left. He actually left her standing there all melty and wide-eyed, staring at his butt as he walked away from her. She heard his truck fire up and continued to watch when he drove past the house.

Down the street.

Around the corner.

Away.

———

Three weeks later, he hadn't called, hadn't sent flowers. She'd been tempted to cruise past his house to see if he was in town. What game was he playing with her?

Marla spent a lot of time reading books, working on her rose bushes, hustling for listings, puttering around the condo office, calling on her tenants to make sure they were happy with their new homes, ready to sign new leases, had no problems.

The afternoon before Halloween she visited Miss Emmaline, her new building manager. Where the old woman got all her energy was a mystery. She'd been thrilled when Marla had asked her if she'd be interested in handling tenant inquiries and concerns and collecting rents. "You got yourself a manager, young lady," she'd said. "I've got no interest in sitting around waiting for the Grim Reaper."

Marla knocked on Emmaline's door. Amber opened it, shrieked, and threw herself at Marla nearly knocking her over. "Marla! Miss Emmaline, it's Marla."

Surprised at how much Amber had grown over the summer, Marla released her and held her at arm's length. "You're so tall. When did you get so tall?"

"That's what Daddy said. He told me to slow down. I'm seven. You missed my birthday. Auntie Silvia bought me Cinderella pajamas and sparkly Scrunchies for my hair." She turned and pointed to her ponytail.

To hear her mother referred to as Auntie Silvia startled her, but of course, when Char married Donovan, Amber's uncle, she became her aunt, and Silvia her great-aunt. She blinked. She was Amber's aunt too. Why hadn't her mom said anything about the child's birthday? Didn't she know how much Marla loved her—Dwayne or no Dwayne?

She let Amber drag her inside Emmaline's apartment. "I just realized something. I'm your Auntie Marla."

"I know." She wrinkled her freckled nose. "I'd rather have you for my mom, though."

Leave it to kids to say exactly what they were thinking. Racking her brain for an answer, she was saved by the arrival of Emmaline. "Come in, dear. We were just sitting down for afternoon tea. Please join us."

"I'd love to."

Still holding her hand, Amber led her to the kitchen. The table was set with a Cinderella tea set and a plate of sugar cookies in the center of the table. "This looks great, Amber. Is this your tea set?"

"Daddy bought it for my birthday. Miss Emmaline and I have a tea party whenever she babysits me. Daddy said tea parties are rilly not for grown men. So I leave my dishes here."

Bursting with curiosity about why Dwayne had left Amber with Emmaline this afternoon, and where he was, it was all she could do not to ask. They sat at the table. Marla admired Miss Emmaline's hand-crocheted table cover. Amber poured tea as pale as water. She set down the pot and passed the cookies to her.

"We made these cookies when I got here from school today. They're still warm. Miss Emmaline has a rill old recipe for sugar cookies. It has sour cream in it. Taste one."

Marla took a bite of the big soft cookie, moaned with pleasure and rolled her eyes. "Mmm, so good." She definitely had to have the recipe.

The three of them sipped tea and nibbled cookies like proper ladies. Uneasiness began to nag Marla. Dwayne might show up any minute. Tomorrow was a school day. Surely he wouldn't leave Amber here too late.

"Um, I think I better go. I, uh, I have a couple of errands."

"Don't you want to wait till Daddy gets here? He went to get something special for Halloween."

"Um, no, I can't." She stood. "Thank you for the tea and cookies. I really have to go. I, um, I can let myself out."

Eyes downcast, Amber said, "Okay, but I know Daddy wants to see you."

Oh yeah? Well, he hadn't made any attempt to see her for the past three weeks. She didn't know what she'd do if she bumped into him now. She made a quick exit.

Chapter Thirty-Eight

"Trick or Treat!"

Marla opened her door for the umpteenth time holding a large bowl of wrapped candy for the neighborhood goblins. She'd barely had a chance to sit since she arrived home at five. Nobody was there. "Hello?" She stepped onto her porch and checked the walk in both directions. "If you want candy you have to show me how scary you are."

It was full dark now and she didn't see any children near her neighbor's doors. She'd definitely heard a child's voice. "Are you playing tricks on me?"

Silence.

Shrugging, she turned to go inside and kicked a picnic basket with a note taped on top. Not at all sure she wanted to check the contents she stood still then turned her head to check both sides of her porch. "What the—?"

She reached for the note and snatched her hand back when the basket shifted. Sidling past it, she stood in the relative safety of her doorway. She took a breath and yanked the paper off the handle. The note was written in childish cursive.

Hello, Marla Danaher. I don't have a mama. Will you be my mama? My name is Dandy, but you can call me DD.

A barely audible whine sounded from the basket and it wobbled again. Marla's heart pounded. A dog? Had someone left a dog on her porch? She knelt down, and with a trembling, tentative hand, lifted the hinged lid. A Yorkie puppy stared at her with imploring eyes far too large for its bitty head. It stood on its hind legs and pawed the air with a tiny foot.

Marla's hands flew to her face but couldn't stifle her sob. She blinked back tears, lifted the pup from the basket, and hugged it to her chest. "Oh, you sweet thing, you sweet, adorable baby."

Eyes damp, she hugged the tiny creature whose little heart tapped rapidly against her collarbone. "Oh, you precious baby." A miniscule tongue lapped her chin and the small body nearly wriggled from her grasp.

Holding the pup in both hands, she lifted it level with her face. "Hello, Dandy DD. Would you like to live in my house?"

Marla stood and kissed DD's nose. "You can come out now, Dempsey."

Rustling of the large bush at the corner of her house gave away his hiding spot. Amber, dressed as Cinderella, blond wig and all, stepped into the light first, followed by her dad.

Amber bounced on her toes. "Do you like her, Marla? She's rilly cute, isn't she? Will you keep her?"

Marla nodded and met Dwayne's gaze. Neither of them spoke. One corner of his mouth twitched a brief smile, and he stuffed his hands into the pockets of his heavy work pants. He mouthed, *I love you.*

A Ping Pong ball-sized lump formed in her throat. She pressed her lips together and told herself to breathe.

Amber reached for the dog. "Can I hold her?"

By way of answer, Marla put the pup in her outstretched hands. Amber sat on the top step and cradled DD in her lap.

Dwayne took a step, removed his hands from his pockets, and held them open. The motion was a question. Marla answered by stepping into the circle of his embrace. He nearly crushed her. No words were exchanged. She merely rested her forehead against his neck and breathed his wonderful scent of soap, sweat, and newly sawn wood. The scent no longer detectable on her pillows.

He took a deep breath. "I'm so lousy at this, Red."

She smiled against his neck. "I know."

"Damn, I want you so much. Please find a way to forgive me, before I hang myself."

She tilted her face to him. "I'm working on it, Dempsey."

"That's all I ask, Danaher."

"Trick or treat!" A couple of stragglers came down her walk. Amber slid the bowl of candy to the step, reached in and took a handful for each kid, and dropped the treats in sagging pillowcases. They happily accepted the mini-Milky Ways, grinned, then patted DD's head.

Dwayne whispered close to her ear. "I have to get Amber home. Tomorrow's a school day. Please say I can come over tomorrow night. Rosie and Pete offered to keep her for the weekend." He tightened his arms and ran a hand into the back of her hair. "Please, honey. I'm begging you. I'll get down on my knees if I have to."

She stroked his cheek. "Kiss me, and make it a good one, Dempsey."

"My pleasure, Danaher."

His kiss was a good one. In fact it was a great one. She didn't want it to end. Light as a feather, she was ready to float away.

Amber muttered, "Everybody in the whole world can see you. You're rilly embarrassing me."

Dwayne dropped his arms but didn't take his eyes off Marla's. "Give DD to her mama, squirt. It's almost your bedtime. We're outta here."

Amber got to her feet and held the puppy up. With trembling hands, Marla took it and pressed it to her cheek. She directed a pointed look at Dwayne's eyes. "Um, DD?"

"Danaher and Dempsey?"

He pecked a quick kiss on her forehead then on DD's head while sliding a surreptitious hand across her derriere. "See you tomorrow, Red."

———

Every cell in Dwayne's body vibrated at the thought of winning Marla back, of having her in his bed again, but not just that, having her in his life. In their life. He wanted a wife, and he wanted more kids. At least one kid with Marla. She'd be a great mom, a dream-come-true wife and partner. How could he have screamed at her like that? Why should she forgive him?

He glanced across the cab of the truck. Amber carefully sorted through her plastic pumpkin filled with candy. She chose some of her favorites, opened the console and dropped them inside. "These are special for you, Daddy."

He grinned and rubbed her neck. "Thank you. Is that my reward?"

"Yes. Marla rilly likes DD, and she said you could come to her house tomorrow night. I think Plan B is working."

"I hope you're right."

"Are you going to have a sleepover over with Marla tomorrow?"

Holy shit, did his kid miss anything? He sucked in air between his clenched teeth, patted her head and answered, "If she'll let me."

"Don't mess up, Daddy. We might not get another chance."

A cough of laughter erupted from his throat. He pulled into their driveway and switched of his engine. "I'll do my best, squirt. We need a woman in our family. And Marla is the only woman I want."

She nodded slow and deliberate. "You know what, Daddy?"

"What, sweetpea?"

"I think I'm getting too old for Cinderella." She brushed her hands across her sparkly costume. "I want to go shopping for clothes at Justice."

He rolled his eyes. "We had this discussion before. I'm not paying forty-five dollars for a skirt or thirty-five dollars for a T-shirt for a seven-year-old child."

"I'm the only one in my class who doesn't get to buy clothes at Justice." Her bottom lip stuck out far enough for a bird to sit on it.

"How would you know that? Every girl in school wears the same school uniform every single day."

"They told me!"

"It's out of the question. End of discussion."

"You're mean!" She crossed arms over her flat chest and kicked her feet under the dashboard.

All of a sudden he longed for the endless evenings watching Cinderella DVDs and reading every Cinderella book ever published. He was deep in Shit Lake and had a huge hole in his boat.

Patience, all he needed was patience.

"Who are you, little girl, and what did you do with sweet Amber Dempsey?"

"Very funny." She rooted around in the console and removed all the candy she'd given him and threw it piece by piece in the pumpkin.

She scowled, yanked the car door open, jumped down, and stomped to the front door.

He whooshed out a sigh. "Whatever."

———

Marla set DD back in the basket and carried it to the kitchen. Dwayne had put a small bag of puppy chow and a chew toy in with her. Maybe she was hungry? She lifted her out and set her on the kitchen floor, where she peed a puddle the size of a small lake.

Oh joy.

"Okay then, DD. We start potty training." A handful of paper towels and a spritz of Nature's Miracle took care of the immediate problem. Marla gingerly held the sopping paper towels then shoved them through the doggy door and pushed DD through after them.

She waited a few seconds, opened the door, and stepped outside. "This is the doggy potty, DD." Strolling across the yard, the Yorkie prancing behind, Marla gave her plenty of time to sniff and explore. DD got a big whiff of the wet towels once they made the entire circuit. Marla nudged them off the stoop with her foot, held DD next to them and said, "DD's a gooood girl. Good girls pee out here, got it?"

No more accidents happened in the kitchen while Marla ate ice cream and DD nibbled on puppy chow. DD hadn't had time to pee in the house again because Marla pushed her through the doggie door three times in the next hour, carried her to sniff the wet towels, and told her she was a good doggie. She'd forgotten what a pain in the neck it was to train a puppy.

———

The next day she took DD to work with her for the short time she planned to spend in the office. Staff members ooohed and aaahed over the tiny mutt, taking turns holding and hugging her. Even Ted.

Marla's lack of sleep the night before descended quick and hard. The puppy had whined all night long, she'd had to take her outside half a dozen times. It was time to get DD out of there and catch a nap before Dwayne got to her place. A flutter in her chest at the thought of him unsettled her. "I'm not expecting any calls today, Jessie, but you know how to reach me."

"Uh huh, I guess since the flowers didn't work, Mr. Hunk switched to dogs? Can't throw that little sweetie pie in the wastebasket, can you? I do hope the dark circles under your eyes were the result of a hot—"

"Bite me, Jessie."

She didn't expect him to show up before six thirty, and he hadn't mentioned dinner, so just in case, she stopped at the store, bought a frozen pizza and a six-pack of Diet Dr. Pepper. DD didn't make a peep, in fact, she fell asleep in the clever cloth dog carrier while Marla zipped through the grocery aisles. "I'm dead on my feet, and *now* you sleep, you little stinker."

———

No nap. No luck. Marla resorted to putting DD in the padded picnic basket, carrying it to the hall bathroom then closing both the bathroom door and her bedroom door, and plopping a pillow over her head.

She kicked, groaned, and tossed the pillow across the room. How could a puppy who weighed less than three pounds make such a pitiful, ungodly racket?

DD quieted the second Marla opened the bathroom door. She lifted the lid and stared at the tiny, sweet, furry face and sighed. "Okay, baby girl, what am I going to do with you, huh? Sooner or later I have to sleep. I'm open for suggestions."

At six on the dot, her doorbell rang. She dragged herself to the door, threw it open, and stared. Yes, it was Dwayne, whoopee-do.

"Whoa, honey, Marla, what happened?"

She turned, shuffled in the direction of the living room, and pointed at the fur ball dogging her bare feet. "That happened." Doubling in pain when she slammed her big toe into the coffee table leg, she shrieked, "Ow!" and fell on the couch.

"Stay right there. I'll get some ice."

She heard him open the freezer door and root around in the ice cubes, open and close drawers then return to sit next to her. Her expression dared him to say anything when he spotted DD sitting on her chest gazing into her face.

"Put your feet in my lap, honey. Let me look at that toe." He held her foot in his big hand, made a humming sound while he checked it out then applied the dishtowel-wrapped ice to her toe.

Yanking her foot back, she sucked in a breath. "That's cold!"

"It's ice." He grabbed her ankle and pushed her foot back to his lap. "Hold still."

She rolled her head from side to side on the arm of the sofa and whimpered, "I haven't had more than five minutes sleep since you gave this monster spawn of the devil to me."

"Uh oh." He grimaced and rubbed her leg. "She looks so sweet and innocent. What'd she do?"

"She never sleeps, cries all night, pees on the floor and in the yard a hundred times a day. I'm exhausted. If you're expecting dinner, you'll have to fix it yourself. There's a frozen pizza in the freezer. I'm useless." Through narrow slits in her eyes she spoke to DD, "Stop staring, you microscopic demon."

"I'm taking you to bed." He lifted her leg off his lap, stood, and tugged her hand. "Come on."

"Are you nuts?" Was that his solution to everything? "No! We have to talk, Dempsey. I'm too tired. You're out of your mind if you think I'm in the mood for—"

"Beds are often used for sleeping, Danaher of the Dirty Mind." Using both arms, he lifted her to her feet. "You need sleep. I'm putting you to bed."

Marla pointed to DD, watching their every move. "But, she won't...she..."

"Don't worry about her. Come on. No more arguing or I might have to spank you."

He looked like he meant it. "You arrogant jack..." His mouth closed over hers. Her knees gave way as he caught her waist and held her against him. Oh, the man knew how to kiss. She loved the way he kissed. He picked her up by the bottom and carried her to the bedroom, laid her on the bed and covered her with a fleece blanket she kept at the foot of the bed.

He kissed her cheek. "Go to sleep, that's an order." Snaring DD off the floor, he walked from the room and shut the door.

It took her less than ten seconds to nod off. When she stirred, she had no idea what time it was, Dwayne lay beside her, his arm across her waist, and DD twitched, dreaming on the pillow at the top of her head. Smiling smugly, she scooched back into his warmth, his arms, where she belonged and where she would stay.

———

Awake the instant she'd snuggled against him, Dwayne whispered, "You awake, honey?"

"Um hmm." She shifted her hips against him again.

"You want to talk?"

"Yes." She turned and faced him. "You start."

Looking deep in her burnt caramel eyes, he went hard. Running a finger from her forehead, down her nose, to her chin, he dropped his leg over her hip. "I've already said it dozens of times."

"Not that." Her fingers feathered across his lips.

"I love you?"

"Is that a question?" A sassy grin blossomed on her face. "Try again."

"Will you marry me…us…me and Amber?"

She ran her thumb over his lips, trailed her fingers across his neck and back to his mouth. "It's a package deal, isn't it?"

"Yeah. All or nothing." He couldn't take much more of this.

"Hmm. That's a lot to think about. You. Me. Amber." She sighed and picked up the pup and set her between them. "And DD."

He grinned and tucked hair behind her ear. "Mustn't forget DD." He let his fingers trail down her arm. He wanted her so bad he ached, torture, delicious torture. *Bring it on.*

"While I'm thinking it over, you want to fool around?"

"In front of the baby?" He reared back and put a look of shock and horror on his face. "You dirty girl."

She pushed herself to a sitting position and pulled her T-shirt off, then like a porno queen she teased him, running her hands over her breasts, dropping her head back, moaning. He reached for her and she pushed his hand away, shaking her head slowly, smiling wickedly. "Don't touch."

"Are you trying to corrupt me, Danaher?" He hoped to God that's exactly what she was doing, because it sure as hell felt good.

She tucked her finger beneath the top edge of her bra and slid it across and back, across and back. "Is it working, Dempsey?"

"God, yes. More. Corrupt me more." A bead of sweat tickled its way down his neck. He closed his eyes and pictured every place he'd touch her, kiss her.

Marla pushed his leg off her and rolled to straddle him, undid her bra and slowly, slowly let it slip then lifted his hands and pressed them to her breasts. "Want some of this?"

"You're killing me, Red." He ran a finger under the waistband of her Capri pants. "Get out of these quick or I'll have to rip them to shreds."

"Oh, is big bad Dwayne going to play rough? Should I be scared? Hmm?"

"That's it." He grabbed her shoulders and pulled her into a wild kiss. He bit her lip and pulled her head forward with both hands. This woman was almost more than he could handle. Almost. "You tempt me to do something you might not like."

"I can't wait." She ripped open the front of his shirt and bared her teeth against his chest, slid the back of her hand deep inside the front of his pants. "Do it."

Jesus, Mary, and Joseph. He wanted to. "No."

She went still, withdrew her hand, and raised her head. "No?"

He shook his head and his lips formed, *no, no, no.* Hands trailing across her breasts, he sucked in a deep breath at the sensual beauty of her body. "I'm not that kinda guy."

Marla leaned forward, the flat of her hands against his chest. "I've been wrong about you?"

"Yeah, I can no longer do this nasty stuff with a woman who won't agree to marry me. I feel cheap, soiled, used." If he got any harder he'd rip right through his pants. "And our out-of-wedlock baby is giving me the stink eye." He picked DD up in one hand and held her close to Marla's face. "See?"

"I'm so ashamed. Let me correct the situation." She threw her leg off him and scooted from the bed.

He rose to a sitting position and watched her carry the mutt to the bathroom, drop a towel in the tub, and set her on it.

"Night night, baby. Mama loves you, but she loves Daddy more." Marla shimmied out of her pants and panties and slinked her way back to the bed. Her breasts swayed deliciously with each calculated step.

He got out of his clothes as quick as he could and lay back on the mattress. He grinned at his throbbing arousal. "See what I mean? You force me to do bad things against my will." He crooked his finger. "Come to papa."

Crawling slowly back on the bed, she slid her beautiful ,soft hands up the inside of his thighs and caressed him. "Bad? Shall we see?"

She yipped when he grabbed her and threw her on her back, pushed her legs apart, and entered her fast and hard. "Don't say I didn't warn you." Before she had a chance to utter a word he clamped his mouth hard on hers and slammed deeper. Again. Again. All thought of slowing down or prolonging their pleasure flew from his mind.

He was inside his woman, and he would have her like *this*, at least this one time. Ears ringing, blood pounding in his head, he gasped at her shuddering words when she said, "Harder, don't stop, please don't stop."

Stop? There was no way he could stop. He raised his head so he could watch her face. With her eyes, she pleaded for more. He gave her more, and more. He shouted at his sudden, explosive release. Breath left his lungs, he slumped on her unable to move, gasping to breathe. Crushing her beneath his weight, he couldn't summon the strength to move.

She wrapped her legs around him and stroked his back and bottom. "Oh, my, Dempsey. If I agree to marry you, will you do that again?"

"I'll try my damndest, Danaher." He went to push himself off her, but she held on. "Don't you dare move, I want you right here for a while. I love to feel you, on me, in me." She tightened around him, inside and out.

He groaned. "Am I dead?"

Marla dug her nails into his butt. "Feel that?"

He flinched. "Uh huh."

"You're not dead."

He rolled over, clasping her on top of him, careful not to disengage. "That was close though." He felt like falling to his knees, worshiping her, finding new ways to love her endlessly, thanking God she was born, and he'd found her. Tingling grew stronger down below, he grinned and growled.

They were finally forced to get up and take their baby out for a sniff and a pee, and then bring her back in bed with them to keep her from crying all night. They lay spooned, his arm and leg holding her prisoner, his hand resting on DD snuggled against Marla's stomach. Maybe he wasn't dead, but heaven couldn't compete with this.

She whispered, "I have to ask you something."

"Yeah?" A tiny jolt of alarm clogged his throat.

"Would you be mad if I didn't change my name to Dempsey?"

"Will you be mad if I don't change my name to Danaher?"

She elbowed him. "Go to sleep, you impossible man."

"Ooh rah."

Don't miss out on your next favorite book!

Join the Satin Romance mailing list
www.satinromance.com/mail.html

THANK YOU FOR READING

Did you enjoy this book?

We invite you to leave a review at the website of your choice, such as Goodreads, Amazon, Barnes & Noble, etc.

———

DID YOU KNOW THAT LEAVING A REVIEW…

- Helps other readers find books they may enjoy.
- Gives you a chance to let your voice be heard.
- Gives authors recognition for their hard work.
- Doesn't have to be long. A sentence or two about why you liked the book will do.

About the Author

Patty Campbell took up writing for publication after her husband's sudden death. It was her salvation. Kids grown and out of the house, she owned her own successful travel business and coffee bar. Life kept her busy but didn't fill the gap left by his absence. A voracious and eclectic reader, she's all about deep love, family and happy endings. And, oh yes—dogs.

www.pattycampbell.com
pattycampbellauthor.blogspot.com

facebook.com/Patty-Campbell-Author-536855299661241

goodreads.com/goodreadscomuser_PattyCampbell

amazon.com/Patty-Campbell/e/B0092FJY7Y

Also by Patty Campbell

WITH SATIN ROMANCE

Wounded Warriors Series
Heart of a Marine

Love of a Marine

Soul of a Marine

Always a Marine

———

Novels
Risky Business

www.ingramcontent.com/pod-product-compliance
Lightning Source LLC
Chambersburg PA
CBHW020228260626
47156CB00002B/596